Praise for

and is all the more riveting for that."
—*New York Times Book Review*

"Sharp, many layered, and, as always for Leckie, deeply intelligent." —*Kirkus* (starred review)

"Leckie has created an enthralling and well-realized fantasy world, full of not only magic and gods but also characters representing a broad spectrum of gender and sexuality. Highly recommended for...anyone looking for exciting and boundary-pushing fantasy."
—*Booklist* (starred review)

"An enormously compelling novel. It may draw inspiration from *Hamlet*, but...it reweaves the fabric of Shakespeare's play into cloth of a different color entirely....Leckie's worldbuilding is deep and thorough, showing us the edges of a broad, rich, complicated world, and her characters are fascinating." —Tor.com

RAVEN
TOWER

By Ann Leckie

THE

TOWER

ANN LECKIE

orbit

www.orbitbooks.net

Copyright © 2019 by Ann Leckie
Excerpt from *The Throne of the Five Winds* copyright © 2019 by Lilith Saintcrow
Excerpt from *A Crown for Cold Silver* copyright © 2015 by Alex Marshall

Cover design by Lauren Panepinto
Cover photographs by Arcangel
Cover copyright © 2019 by Hachette Book Group, Inc.
Map copyright © 2019 by Tim Paul
Author photograph by MissionPhoto.org

Orbit
Hachette Book Group
1290 Avenue of the Americas
New York, NY 10104
orbitbooks.net

Originally published in hardcover and ebook in Great Britain and the U.S. by Orbit in February 2019
First U.S. Paperback Edition: October 2019

Orbit is an imprint of Hachette Book Group.
The Orbit name and logo are trademarks of Little, Brown Book Group Limited.

The publisher is not responsible for websites (or their content) that are not owned by the publisher.

The Hachette Speakers Bureau provides a wide range of authors for speaking events. To find out more, go to www.hachettespeakersbureau.com or call (866) 376-6591.

Library of Congress has catalogued the hardcover as follows:
Names: Leckie, Ann, author.
Title: The Raven tower / Ann Leckie.
Description: First edition. | New York, NY: Orbit, an imprint of Hachette Book Group, 2019.
Identifiers LCCN 2018040311 | ISBN 9780316388696 (hardcover) | ISBN 9780316388702 (trade paperback) | ISBN 9781549115790 (audiobook (downloadable)) | ISBN 9780316388719 (ebook (open))
Subjects: GSAFD: Fantasy fiction.
Classification: LCC PS3612.E3353 R38 2019 | DDC 813/.6—dc23
LC record available at https://lccn.loc.gov/2018040311

ISBNs: 978-0-316-38870-2 (trade paperback), 978-0-316-38871-9 (ebook)

Printed in the United States of America

LSC-C

10 9 8 7 6 5 4 3 2 1

RAVEN TOWER

The Silent Forest

I first saw you when you rode out of the forest, past the cluster of tall, bulge-eyed offering stakes that mark the edges of the forest, your horse at a walk. You rode beside Mawat, himself a familiar sight to me: tall, broad-shouldered, long hair in dozens of braids pulled back in a broad ring, feathers worked in repoussé on gold, his dark gray cloak lined with blue silk. More gold weighted his forearms. He was smiling vaguely, saying something to you, but his eyes were on the fortress of Vastai on its small peninsula, still some twelve miles off: some two- and three-story buildings surrounded by a pale yellow limestone wall, the ends of which met at a round tower at the edge of the sea. On the landward side of the wall sat a town's worth of buildings interrupted by a bank and ditch. Gulls coasted over the few bare-masted ships in the harbor beside the fortress, and over the gray water beyond, flecked white with the wind, and here and there a sail. The white stone buildings and more numerous ships of the city of Ard Vusktia were just visible on the far side of the strait.

Mawat—and Vastai—I knew, but I had not seen you before, and so I looked closely. Slight, and shorter than Mawat—it would be a wonder if you were not, the residents of the fortress in Vastai eat so much better, and so much more regularly than the peasant farmers who were your likely origins. You had cut your hair close to your scalp, a single arm ring and the haft of the knife at your side the only gold on you, your trousers, shirt, boots, and cloak solid and sturdy, all dull greens and browns. The hilt of your sword was wood wrapped with leather, undecorated. You sat stiff in the saddle, even at a walk. Possibly because you'd woken early to a summons and then ridden for three days with only what rest the horses required, and likely before you became a soldier you'd had very little experience riding.

Mawat said, "We've made good time, it seems, and the Instrument is still with us, or there'd be black flags on the tower, and lots of movement in the tower yard. And even if there were, we don't have to rush now. It would be easier for you—and the horses for that matter—if we went the rest of the way at a walk, I think." And then, at the expression on your face, "What is it?"

"It's just…" You took a breath. It's clear that you trust him, more than you trust a lot of other people in the world, or I suspect you wouldn't have been there, riding beside him. And you must have concluded that he trusts you.

servants.

"I haven't said anything secret," said Mawat, "or anything I'm not allowed to say."

Was it strange to hear him talk of his father's impending death so blithely? For the death of the Raven's Lease of Iraden would be the necessary consequence of the Instrument's death. And as heir, Mawat would step into his father's place, commit himself to dying when the next Raven's Instrument died.

Mawat's father's rule as Raven's Lease had fallen less harshly on the common people of Iraden than it might have. Which wasn't to say he'd been particularly generous, or the peasantry noticeably happy during his tenure, but he could have been worse, and a new Lease was an unknown quantity. Accordingly, the people of Iraden generally spoke of Mawat's father only to wish him long life. You're young enough for that to have been as long as you've been alive.

You both rode for a while in silence, sheep-dotted fields to either side of the road, two ravens high above, swooping and soaring, black shapes in the blue of the sky. Mawat frowning as you rode, until finally he said, "Eolo."

You looked at him, your expression wary. "My lord."

"I know I promised I wouldn't pry. But when I'm Lease, I'll be able to ask for things. I mean, anyone can, but there's always a question of whether or not the Raven will listen, and there's always a price. The Raven will at least hear me out, and my price is already paid. Or it will be. I can ask for some extra favors. The Raven is a powerful god. He could...he could make it so you could..." He gestured vaguely. "So you could be who you are."

"I already am who I am," you snapped. "My lord." And after a few moments of silence, "That's not why I'm here."

"No, it's not," replied Mawat, affronted, and then recollecting himself. "You're here because that's not why you're here." He gave an apologetic smile. "And also because I ordered you out of your bed and into the saddle. And you've ridden three days without complaining, even though you're not much of a rider and I know you must be sore by now."

After a while you said, "I don't know if that's something I want."

"No?" asked Mawat, with surprise. "But why wouldn't you? It would be more convenient for you, if nothing else. You wouldn't have to trouble yourself with bindings, or hiding anything." And when you didn't answer, "Ah, now I *am* prying."

Vastai is small compared to cities like Kybal, source of the silk in Mawat's cloak. Or far-off Therete, that possibly no one in Iraden has even heard of. Or Xulah for that matter, that wide-conquering city in the warm and arid south. Compared to these cities—compared, even, to Ard Vusktia across the strait—Vastai is no more than a town.

You rode behind Mawat through the narrow, stone-paved streets of Vastai. People in homespun dull greens and browns, and even one or two in brighter, finer clothing cleared out of your way, pressed themselves against the yellow limestone walls without a word, looking down at their feet. You would have no cause to realize this, but the streets of the town were far more empty than they ought to have been, given the unseasonably warm, sunny day, given boats in the harbor.

Mawat didn't seem to notice. I think he had been tense and uneasy since before you both rode out of the forest, though he concealed it. Now I thought his mood sharpened, his thoughts bent inexorably to his double-edged purpose in coming here: to see his father die, to step into his father's place. He did not stop or slow, or turn to see if you followed him, but rode, still at a walk, down the main, widest street of the town, through the broad, stone-paved square before the broad fortress gates, and, unchallenged, through those gates and into the tower yard. It was paved with the same yellow stone used throughout Vastai. Several buildings—the hall, long and low, with its kitchen behind it; stables and storerooms; two-story buildings that held offices and apartments. In the middle of the yard was a wide stone basin with a ledge around it—the fortress's well. And, of course, the round, high mass of the tower. All in that yellow limestone.

You started as a raven swooped down to land on the pommel of your saddle.

"Don't worry," said Mawat. "It's not him."

The raven made a churring sound. "Hello," it said. "Hello."

As you stared at the bird, Mawat dismounted. Servants ran forward to take his horse. He looked up at you and gestured you down, so that other servants could take yours. "Glad to be out of the saddle?" he asked as you dismounted,

carded wool on her head, the gold and glass beads braided into her hair swinging and clicking against each other, shining against the brown of her skin.

"Oho," said Mawat, watching you watch her go by, her skirts swirling with the briskness of her walk. "Someone caught your eye?"

"Who is the lady?" you asked. And then, perhaps covering your discomfiture, "She seems very…" You failed to complete the sentence.

"She *is* very," Mawat replied. "That's Tikaz. She's Radihaw's daughter."

You knew that name, likely it had been in Mawat's mouth more than once since you'd met him and besides, it's likely nearly everyone in Iraden has heard of the lord Radihaw, the senior member of the Council of the Directions, the highest-ranking of all the advisers to the Raven's Lease. One of the most powerful men in all of Iraden. "Oh," you replied.

Mawat made a short, amused noise. "We've been

friends more or less since we were children. Her father has never given up hope that I might marry her, or at least get her pregnant so he can have a chance at a grandson on the Lease's bench. I'll be honest, I wouldn't mind. But Tikaz…" He gestured, perhaps waving away some thought. "Tikaz will do as she pleases. Let's go to the hall and see if we can…"

He was brought up short by a servant in the loose black overshirt of a tower attendant. "Lord Mawat, if you please," said the servant, bowing. "The Lease desires your presence."

"Of course," Mawat replied, with slightly forced geniality. You frowned, and then, likely realizing that here in Vastai you would need to watch every word, every twitch of expression, you put on a look of bland inoffensiveness. "Come with me," Mawat said to you, shortly. Not a question, not a request. He did not wait for your response but turned and strode across the pale yellow stones of the tower yard. And of course you followed him.

The Raven Tower is a tower only in comparison with any other nearby building. It stands on the farthest point of the tiny peninsula on which the fortress of Vastai is built, three broad, circular stories of yellowish stone, its roof surrounded

curving wall to the next floor. He raised a hand to halt you both, but Mawat ignored him and strode up the stairs, face forward, shoulders square, stepping determinedly but not hurriedly. You trailed behind, glancing back at the hapless guard, with some fellow feeling perhaps for his dilemma, but you turned to face Mawat again after only a moment. As you ascended, your frown occasionally showed through your carefully blank expression. You didn't grow up surrounded by the sort of maneuvering that's so common in Vastai, you clearly hadn't had much practice at it, though I'd say you were doing a creditable job, all things considered.

There is a sound in the tower, a constant, low, barely audible vibration. Not everyone hears it. I thought maybe you did—you looked down at your worn boots, then toward the wall to your right, tilted your head just the slightest bit as though trying to catch some faint noise. Then the stairs reached a landing, and you came up into the wide, round chamber on the next level, and Mawat took three steps into the room and then abruptly stopped.

Here was a dais. A wooden bench carved with a jumble of figures, stylized reliefs of leaves and wings. Beside the bench knelt a man in a gray silk tunic embroidered with red. On the other side of the bench stood a woman in dark blue robes, her thick, gray hair cut short. A man sat on the bench between them, wearing all white—white shirt, white leggings, white cloak, the sort and amount of perfect, unstained white that can be achieved only by a god's intervention, or else the labor of dozens of servants with no other work than bleaching and laundering.

No doubt you assumed that the man on the bench was the Raven's Lease himself, Mawat's father. No one else would have dared sit in that seat, not and survived the attempt. Every Iradeni knows that sitting on that bench—and living—is the last, final proof of the Raven's acceptance of a new Lease. You had never seen it before, but you surely recognized it the moment you set eyes on it.

Likely you knew who the kneeling man was by the angular lines of his face, having seen his daughter just minutes before, but even if that didn't tell you, I'm sure you realized that this was the lord Radihaw of the Council of the Directions. Who else would be so close to the Lease? And the woman, then, would be Zezume, of the Silent. Away from Vastai, meetings of the Silent are little more than an occasion for gossip and feasting by the old women of the area, but it began as a secret religious association. Those village sessions of the Silent still include rites meant to feed and propitiate gods long absent from Iraden. In Vastai, though, the Silent have an essential role to play in

three Xulahns and their servants, who have come from the far south on their way to the north."

"That is a long journey," observed the lord Radihaw. "And there is nothing in the north but ice and stone."

"They wish to see places they have never seen," said the person in jacket and trousers. "When they have seen enough, if they do not die first, they will return home and write down an account of their travels, for which they expect to receive the esteem of their fellow Xulahns."

You were watching this, staring by turns at the white-clad Lease and at the party of half-dressed Xulahns. You'd surely already heard of Xulah. Every now and then goods from Xulah will make their way over the mountains into the hands of the Tel, one of the peoples who live south of Iradeni territory. Or those goods find their way onto a ship. Any sizable ship sailing between the Shoulder Sea and the Northern Ocean must pass through the strait, and must perforce pay a fee to the rulers of Iraden and Ard Vusktia. So the Lease, and the Council of the Directions, and the prominent members of the Silent, wear silk, drink wine, and even, on occasion, eat figs preserved in jars of honey.

Mawat also stared. Not at the Xulahns, but fixedly at the Lease himself, and then blinking, disbelieving, at Radihaw and, frowning, at Zezume, and back again to the Lease.

"Mawat," said the Raven's Lease. "Welcome home." Mawat did not move or speak.

Finally you noticed Mawat's state, his stunned stare, as though, having thought himself safe in secure and familiar territory, he had suddenly taken a blade between his ribs. He seemed paralyzed, unable even to breathe.

"This is my heir," said the white-clad man on the bench, into Mawat's silence, the gaze of the Xulahns, variously appraising or mildly interested. "Come, Mawat, stand with me." He gestured behind him. Radihaw and Zezume were still as statues on either side of him.

Mawat did not move. After a moment, the Lease turned his attention to the Xulahn visitors again and said, "I will consider your request. Come back tomorrow."

This seemed to discomfit one of the Xulahns, and then the others when it was translated. Two of them frowned at their interpreter, then at each other. Looked to the third, who turned to the Lease and said, in strangely accented Iradeni, "We thank you for your consideration, great king." The Lease is not a king, and the word the Xulahn used is from Tel, a language that is familiar in the south of Iraden.

I daresay you speak it yourself. All the Xulahns bowed low, then, and departed.

was forthcoming. "And what are you doing in that seat?"

Ah, that surprised you! You had assumed that the person before you was none other than Mawat's father, the man who had been Raven's Lease for all of your life. There would be no way for you to know it was not.

"My lord Mawat," began Radihaw. "In all respect, recall to whom you are speaking."

"I am speaking to my Uncle Hibal," replied Mawat, still in that tight, flat voice. "Who is inexplicably sitting alive in the Lease's seat, when no one should sit there but my father. Unless the Raven has died and the Lease followed him in death, in which case this tower should be hung with black, and everyone in the fortress and the town should be in mourning." He turned his head to stare at blue-robed Zezume. "And this bench should be empty until I step up to fill it."

"There was a complication," said Zezume. "The Instrument died just hours after the messenger left for you. Much sooner than anyone expected."

"I am still at a loss, Mother Zezume," said Mawat.

"A complication, yes," said Radihaw, still kneeling at white-clad Hibal's side. "You could call it a complication, that would be a suitable term."

"Mawat," said Hibal, his voice disconcertingly like Mawat's. "I know this must be distressing. Please understand we would never have done this if we had any other choice. When the Instrument died, the attendant sent immediately for your father, but..." Hibal hesitated. "He couldn't be found."

"Couldn't be found," repeated Mawat.

"My lord Mawat," said Radihaw, "no other conclusion could be reached but that your father had fled rather than pay the lease."

"No," said Mawat. "No, my father never fled."

"He could not be found," said Zezume. "Mawat, I know this is upsetting. None of us could believe it."

"You will take those words back," said Mawat. Voice still tight and even. "My father never fled."

"Your father could not be found," said Radihaw. "Not in the tower, not in the fortress, not in the town. We asked the Raven where your father was—despite the complications involved in talking to the god when it does not have a body to answer with—we asked the Raven what had happened. But the answer was equivocal."

"What was that answer?" Mawat asked.

"The reply was, *This is unacceptable. There will be a reck-oning*," said Radihaw.

⎯⎯⎯⎯⎯⎯⎯⎯⎯⎯⎯⎯⎯⎯⎯⎯⎯⎯⎯

You have been away from Vastai too long, Nephew," said white-clad Hibal. "It is to our advantage to have access to goods from Xulah, to have the good opinion of Xulahn traders. More comes from Xulah than wine or silk. They also have weapons, and disciplined soldiers who might be lent or hired to help us against the Tel who press us from the southwest, as you well know."

"Oh, and mighty Xulah will lend us an army and then go back over the mountains again, because we ask nicely, out of their goodness and generosity," said Mawat.

"Sarcasm does not become the heir to the Lease," said Hibal.

"No pledges are pledged," said Radihaw. "No deals are struck, no terms even suggested. This is merely caution and good sense. It behooves the Lease to look to the future."

"Indeed," acknowledged Hibal. "And given the last few days, I think you should stay here and become acquainted with such matters, rather than return to your frontier post. Clearly you should have a better understanding of the issues we face here in Vastai. We have warriors enough to guard our borders from the ravaging Tel; I have only one heir."

"My father never fled," said Mawat again, flatly. "And you are sitting in my seat. I want to ask the Raven now why you are sitting in my seat. I have that right."

Mawat would not trust you as he does, would not have brought you with him, if you were not shrewd enough to guess what was happening here. Mawat had known one purpose for all of his life: to step up to that bench when his father died, to rule Iraden, and to die in his turn in order to bolster the power of the Raven, for the good of Iraden.

The office of Raven's Lease offered many privileges and a share (along with the Council of the Directions) in the rule of Iraden, as well as the rule of Ard Vusktia across the strait. But there was a price: two days after the death of the Raven's Instrument—the bird embodying the god that called itself the Raven—the person occupying the Lease's office must die, a voluntary sacrifice for the god. Shortly thereafter, while the next Instrument of the Raven lay in its egg, the next Lease would be secured and pledged. This was a process that took several days. A raven's egg, even one inhabited by a god (or at least this god), takes nearly a month to hatch, but matters are nearly always arranged so that there is still plenty of time to be sure things happen as they ought, to be sure the Lease dies as he promised, and to be sure there is a new Lease ready to take his place before the next Instrument hatches.

raised to it—as Mawat was—and despite their privilege and ostensible power, had very few options should they refuse to step up to the bench.

"If it were not my seat," replied Hibal, evenly, "I would not be speaking to you now. I would have died the moment I tried to seat myself here if the Raven did not accept me. I took that risk, for the sake of Iraden. There is no need to question the god again. You've just arrived after a long and tiring journey. And a shock at the end of it. I only wanted to be sure you immediately heard how things stood. Go, nephew and heir of mine, and rest and eat. We'll talk more soon."

"Take a moment and think, Mawat," urged Zezume. "Please understand. We could not have done anything else, and you are still the Lease's Heir. You haven't lost anything by this."

"Except my father," said Mawat. And again, "My father never fled."

Had you seen him like this before? Ordinarily he is all easy smiles. Up till now his path in life had been set, and he had been assured of respect and every luxury Iraden afforded. But sometimes he seizes on a matter, takes it between his teeth, and will not let it go, and when that mood takes him he is grim and implacable. He has been that way since he was small.

If you hadn't seen it before, you saw it then. It startled you, I think, or frightened you, because with your eyes still on Mawat you stepped back, and half turned and put your hand on the wall, out of the need for support, or else the fear that you would lose your balance so close to the top of the stairs. And you turned fully to stare at your hand against the wall, and then down at your feet, feeling that constant, faint, grinding vibration traveling through the yellowish stones.

Could you hear me, Eolo? Can you hear me now?

I'm talking to you.

Stories can be risky for someone like me. What I say must be true, or it will be made true, and if it cannot be made true—if I don't have the power, or if what I have said is an impossibility—then I will pay the price. I might more or less safely say, "Once there was a man who rode home to attend his father's funeral and claim his inheritance, but matters were not as he expected them to be." I do

... safer for me to speak of what I know. Or to speak only in the safest of generalities. Or else to say plainly at the beginning, "Here is a story I have heard," placing the burden of truth or not on the teller whose words I am merely accurately reporting.

But what is the story that I am telling? Here is another story I have heard: Once there were two brothers, and one of them wanted what the other had. Bent all his will to obtain what the other had, no matter the cost.

Here is another story: Once there was a prisoner in a tower.

And another: Once someone risked their life out of duty and loyalty to a friend.

Ah, there's a story that I might tell, and truthfully.

When I look back, the first memory I can find is of water. Water above, water all around, a great weight of it pressing down. The regular alternation of dark and dim wavering light. Feathery creatures, like flowers, anchored to the ocean floor, waving in the current, straining the water for the tiny lives that drifted past. Fish with heavy, bony-armored heads and sucking mouths. Scuttling sea scorpions and trilobites, coil-shelled ammonites. I had no names for these things, did not know that the light, when there was light, came from a sun, or that there was anything above the ever-present, all-surrounding water. I merely experienced, without urgency, without judgment.

There *was* something above the water, of course. Air and land, bare stone except where mosses grew, and tiny, leafless plants. Later there were trees and ferns and a host of scuttling exoskeletoned creatures, scorpions and spiders and centipedes and even, eventually, fish whose ancestors had dragged themselves out of the sea. I felt no similar impulse to move or explore. I had no questions.

I think it likely that I existed a long while before these earliest memories. But I cannot say for certain.

At length the trilobites disappeared—this after an earthquake that stirred the seafloor I rested on and the calm waters around me, and then a long period of cold darkness. The bone-armored fish dwindled to nothing, leaving fish with jaws and scales to rule the waters. And a long time after that—I don't know how long, I never even

in the universe, that other beings something like myself existed.

This new and (for me) drier, land-bound age teemed with crawling beasts: amphibians of all sizes; squat, beaked reptiles that grazed on the many ferns and horsetails; huge, long-snouted, long-toothed predators; smaller two-legged hunters that might have reminded one of birds, if birds existed yet. And smaller, hairy, almost doglike things—but there were no dogs, not yet.

I was not like any of these things, as I had not been like the fish, or the trilobites. And when the first other gods I ever saw came storming across the hills where I lay, I did not recognize them. I felt the earth shake, the air grow dry and cold and then suddenly hot and humid by turns. Trees swayed, heaved, and were cast down. One hillside in my view broke apart and collapsed into the valley. A river miles away burst its banks and surged improbably into the hills, washing away the insects and the small birdlike reptiles that prowled around me. I was too large for the flood to move, but I felt the bedrock crack beneath me.

I had lain watching long enough to know what was ordinary. I had seen storms, even violent ones. I had felt the distant tremors of faraway earthquakes or volcanoes. This was different. For the first time I can remember, I felt fear.

At length the battle—for it was a battle—moved on. But it had been so suddenly different from anything I had ever seen or experienced that I could not but wonder what it had been, or if it would happen again.

This, then, was my first sight of gods—not counting myself of course—though I did not know it. It had been so frightening, so abrupt and surprising, that for the first time I began to look around me with purpose, to try to understand what had just happened.

In later eras there would have been humans to tell me what I was, who might have recognized me as soon as they encountered me, as indeed the first humans I encountered did. But there were no humans yet.

Does that surprise you? I know that among people who think about such things it is commonly assumed that gods could not possibly have existed before humans did. After all, gods live on the prayers and offerings of humans. What god could live without that basic food, that essential source of power?

I cannot tell you what I lived on. I can tell you only that I lived. In fact, I still don't quite understand how those other, battling gods I saw could do what they did—how

are immensely, implacably powerful, and difficult to kill. That even dead they may return.

But I knew nothing of this. I lay and watched and thought, as the beasts around me gave way to yet other sorts of animals, as the plants and trees changed around me. Slowly mosses gave way to grass, and flowers appeared.

And birds, though I did not know then how birds would complicate my life in the future.

I suppose I could have moved. Could have roamed over the earth, as those other gods did. But somehow I never wished to, never felt the impulse to do it. I wished only to sit under the sun—I could see the sun, these days, and I liked it a good deal, enjoyed its warmth, its daily coming and going, its steady arc across the blue sky from month to month. Enjoyed the stars wheeling thick and bright in the night sky, the occasional comet, the sparking trail of meteors. I wanted to know what those other gods were, but I did not want to do what they did.

I was still profoundly alone. And I remained alone, watching the stars—did you know, aside from their regular nightly and yearly cycles there is another, longer movement? So, so much slower, and I was watching this, and admiring it, alone, until someone arrived to break my solitude.

By then ice had overtaken me. Ice had overtaken everything, for as far as I could see, for so long that I began to wonder if the world would only ever be ice henceforth. But eventually the ice had begun to withdraw. My old hillside, and the shattered hill across the valley, had been pressed and ground flat by the immense weight of the ice, but as it retreated it left behind new hills; mounds of gravel, boulders, and silt.

I found myself atop one of these. And I began to wonder why that was. I ought to have been pressed flat as everything else had been, trapped under the glacier or buried under the debris that had accumulated on its surface over so very long. But I had not. I had stayed above the ice, and now I sat on this new, rounded hill surrounded by rolling, treeless, grass-covered plain.

I had not wanted to be buried in ice, and so I had not been. Thinking back, I had not wanted to be buried in the seafloor, covered over with layer after layer of drifting sediment, and so I had not been. I had willed, and I had acted, so very subtly that I myself had not realized I was doing it.

One night, while I pondered this, a ball of fire streaked across the sky, brighter than any star I'd seen in the night, or any comet. It disappeared somewhere to the west, and

did not realize its true significance to me until years later, when I first saw humans.

They wore deerskins sewn with beads of bone and stone and shell. They carried spears of wood and bone, with tiny blades of chert embedded in the points. These they used to hunt reindeer and moose, which they followed across the grasslands. What I thought were wolves ran alongside them, but of course I would later learn that they were not wolves, though their ancestors had been.

They camped at the foot of my hill, built fires, and emptied pouches of mushrooms and berries and other things they'd foraged along the day's walk. They settled down to cook or watch the fire, or set out to see if anything interesting might be found by the swampy banks of the small river that wandered lazily through the plain.

One of them climbed the hill and addressed me. This did not surprise me in the least, because I barely noticed it was happening. Animals wandered over to me all the time and did the sorts of things that animals do. These animals were fairly novel, but not so much that I was paying them any sort of close attention. Until the person poured milk at my foot.

I understand now why I noticed that, why I found myself suddenly intrigued by the milk, and by the actions of this person who continued to address me. At the time, though, I did not. But rather than tiresomely detailing my experience from moment to ignorant moment, I'll just explain.

The person was a priest of her people. She had been taught by her predecessor, and her predecessor by her own predecessor, and so on for generations, to look for the presence of gods. Any unusual animal (an all-white reindeer, a particularly large eagle, a by then rarely spotted mammoth) or particularly striking natural feature might be the sign of a god's presence. Once a priest had noticed or heard tell of such a thing, they would confront the animal or object, if possible, and speak a series of predetermined words paired with specific actions, and make a series of set offerings. They would repeat this over a series of years, or even generations, passing the details of the procedure down to their successor, until eventually the god responded, or the priest's regular travels stopped bringing them into the vicinity of the possible divine presence. This priest knew to be patient. She knew from experience, hers and her predecessors', that it could take a very long time to teach language to a god.

part will eventually understand and speak a language merely from hearing the people around them speak. But I was not a human infant, and even the possibility of language had not yet occurred to me.

You may find the idea of a god without language impossible or ridiculous. After all, if there is anything people know about gods, it's that they exercise their power through speech. A god's words are inescapably true, and gods make things happen by speaking them—so long as a god has sufficient power, of course. To say something beyond one's power to enforce can wound a god badly, can take decades or centuries or even millennia to recover from. To speak an utter impossibility—there are such, I assure you—is to drain one's own power endlessly, to no purpose. But with sufficient power, with carefully chosen words, a god can do anything it is possible to do. How can a god be a god with no language?

And if language is a thing humans had to teach to gods—my experience suggests this was the case—how did those other gods I saw so long ago do anything?

I do not know. I can only assure you that my account of my history is true.

Mawat's temper has always been fierce, as I said, even when he was an infant. So was his father's, come to that, and his father's father's before him. But grow up surrounded by tempers as fierce as yours, wills as strong as yours or stronger, backed with power and authority where yours is not—not yet—and you must either learn to curb that temper or run the risk of breaking disastrously against opponents far stronger than you, far sooner than you can hope to survive it.

And so, thwarted, Mawat sulked. Without any further word, he spun and strode down the stairs and out of the tower, and you followed him. You did not ask any questions, or try to catch up and walk beside him, but stayed three or four feet behind him as he strode across the stone-paved tower yard. I think you noticed the way the servants ducked and darted out of his path. Nearly everyone in the fortress had heard that the I

...g ....y ....g... ...o..o, ...o ... a .... different errands, greeting each other, stopping a moment to trade chatter or gossip, laughing, even singing. Today there was only the churring of ravens and the servants' hushed and hurried whispers, that fell silent as Mawat passed.

You followed him into a dimly lit two-story building across from the tower, all stone, with plain white plastered walls inside. Strode past anxious servants, across an antechamber and up the stairs, and then Mawat passed through a door and closed it hard behind him, leaving you in the darkened corridor.

For a few moments you stared frowning at the heavy oak door, and then you sighed, and sat down cross-legged, and leaned your back against the door frame.

After a while you closed your eyes, and I think you dozed. No sound came from behind the door. You woke with a start when a servant came silently down the corridor, carrying a tray of milk and cheese and bread, and sausages. "You," she said, stopping in front of you. "Are you his servant?" She was gangly in a way that suggested she wasn't quite used to being as tall as she was, and her wool skirts—worn but clean and well mended—hung only to her shins.

You blinked, maybe still half-asleep. "No. Yes. Sort of." You sat up straighter and pulled your cloak around you. "Is that for the lord Mawat?"

"I'm supposed to leave it by the door. In case he'll come out. He won't, not yet. He won't be out for days, Cook said."

You frowned. "I've never known him to be like this longer than a few hours."

"That's not what I heard," said the girl. "Are you a farmer? You sound like a farmer."

"I'm a soldier," you said. "I'm...I'm an aide to Lord Mawat."

The servant seemed dubious about that. "Well, I have to leave this here. In case he comes out." She bent to set the tray beside you, in front of the door. "If he doesn't come out in an hour or two you should just drink the milk, because it will go bad. I don't know why Cook even sent it. We hardly get any fresh milk, and it's wasted on this."

"He likes milk," you said. "He likes it a little sour."

The girl rolled her eyes and made a disbelieving sound, and turned and strode away.

obtained a promise from the God of the Silent Forest that it would protect the inhabitants of Iraden from disease and invasion. Since the Iradeni also knew from experience that the god was capricious, they regularly rode the edges of their territory—particularly on the south side of the forest, where their Tel neighbors would sometimes raid Iradeni farms and villages. All thirteen districts of Iraden—each one represented in the Council of the Directions—sent volunteers to do this.

For long years there was no more than the occasional raid—nearly all stopped handily by the volunteers who patrolled the border, without need for more obvious godly help. But as time went on, the Tel became more ambitious in their attacks. They brought larger forces, planned more carefully, and methodically tested Iraden's defenses.

In response, the council, with the agreement of the Raven's Lease, ordered the construction of permanent camps along the southern border. Or, more accurately, provided resources for the construction of banks and ditches around camps that had already become more or less permanent. After all, though of course the forest and the Raven both would prevent any real trouble coming from the south, gods are, as a rule, more easily able to help those who have already made their own efforts. And the Raven himself had agreed that stronger fortifications would be useful to him.

This was how things stood when Mawat took command of the border force. That force was fractious and sometimes wayward, largely made up as it was of lords' sons, who did not like to acknowledge any authority over themselves, and farmers and villagers, who were liable to run back home at harvest time, or when some family crisis threatened.

I've heard it said that Xulah keeps a standing army of soldiers officially enrolled, who swear each one to obey the orders of their superiors—and that each grade of superior has a name, and a specific official status granted by that city's central authority. In theory any soldier might earn his way into these upper ranks, and those beneath him must follow his orders, no matter what family he is from, no matter that he might be a peasant issuing commands to the sons of nobles. In theory. I suspect few peasants have ever been allowed to rise so far in the ranks. Even so, it sounds very efficient, and one can perhaps understand how it is that Xulah has managed to spread its rule so far.

The soldiers of Iraden don't work this way. While it's true that whoever commands the forces on the border must ~~be the councilment the I...ad ki...d th...~~ ~~when it comes to assuming command of all the soldiers on~~ the border.

Mawat commanded these forces, supported by a half dozen sons of councillors. There could be no more satisfactorily elevated commander in all of Iraden. Still, Mawat occasionally found his authority challenged.

A year and a half before you came to Vastai, a messenger brought urgent news to the camp guarding the road that goes into the forest. The messenger would give his news to no one but Mawat, and Mawat received him alone, in his own quarters. And then, having heard his news, he called for his aide—for you. He also requested the attendance of three lords' sons.

"The Tel," he said, quietly, when the door was shut, "are gathering in force on the other side of the hills." He meant the line of hills that lay just beyond the land protected by the gods of Iraden.

"Ah, wonderful!" exclaimed one of the men, a councillor's

son named Airu. "Get them all in one place and we can take care of them for good. I'll rouse my men." He made as if to leave.

"There's more," said Mawat, before Airu could go far. "They've made an agreement with the god they call Stalker."

One of the other men scoffed. "Stalker doesn't do agreements. Not the useful sort, anyway."

"Stalker," agreed Mawat, "doesn't take offerings with conditions, and doesn't like to commit herself too far into the future. And she's easily distracted. But the Tel have found a way to do a significant deal with her. Or they think they have." Silence, you standing by the door, on the watch for any interruption. Mawat continued, "They've found someone willing to sacrifice themselves."

Most of the gods associated with the Tel are relatively small. They're connected to a few families, or to some particular place. There are none quite like the God of the Silent—except possibly a river or two that may perhaps come close, but neither of those could be convinced to care about moving into Iraden, let alone capturing Vastai and the wealth that flowed through the strait. So the gods that assisted the Tel in battle were for the most part no match for the gods of Iraden. This didn't stop those gods from trying Iraden's borders, of course, but they rarely worked together for long, and few were powerful enough to do much alone without endangering themselves.

But any god might be made more powerful with the right offering. And one of the best offerings—as any Irad-

"They believe they've found a way to get what they want from her," said Mawat. "If they provide this sacrifice, then once they make their request she'll fulfill it so far as she's able at that moment."

"So we ride down on them before they can perform the sacrifice," insisted Airu. "Why are we not away even now?" His voice was challenging. "Why are we wasting time?"

Mawat seemed to ignore the sudden tension in the room. He said, calmly, "Timing is important to their plan. Make the sacrifice a moment too soon and Stalker will like as not use at least some of it for other purposes, leaving *so far as she's able* a poor matter, or at least not enough for the needs of the Tel. So not only will they not have made this sacrifice yet, they'll have brought their volunteer with them, so that they can make the offering and the petition the instant they set their plan in motion."

"What difference does that make?" demanded Airu.

"If we fall upon them," said one of the other, more

thoughtful lords' sons, "they have but to kill the victim, and they'll have all of that power on their side to use against us."

Airu scoffed again. "And what does that matter? It won't be enough to overcome the Raven, let alone the God of the Silent. I ask again, why are we not even now on our way to destroy them, since we have them gathered together for our convenience, and have moreover the advantage of surprise?"

"Move too obviously," said Mawat, sharply now, "and we will lose what advantage we have. This information has come partly from spies of ours among the Tel. Do you imagine they have no spies among us? And even if we were to take them entirely by surprise, do you imagine they would not make their sacrifice at the first sign of our presence? It might not be enough to endanger Iraden—surely it wouldn't be—but it would be enough to kill many of our men in the process. Iraden's safety may be assured. The individual lives of those of us here are not. Let's do this in a way that won't leave so many of us dead."

"I'm not afraid to die!" insisted Airu. "And neither are my men. We none of us have the Raven watching over us the way you do, Lease's Heir. We're not cowards, even if you are." The room was suddenly deathly still.

"My sword," said Mawat calmly, almost conversationally.

You left the room. Returned with Mawat's sheathed, gold-hilted sword, and stood ready beside him.

"We're here to fight the Tel, not each other," said one of

a foolish charge that a bit of thought might have turned to our advantage. Listen—get your men ready, Airu, all of you, as quickly as you can, but also as quietly as you can. As soon as you get the signal that Stalker's sacrifice has been captured, or at least the petition prevented, you can fall on the Tel in whatever way seems best to you."

"How do you propose to do that?" asked a lord's son. "Someone will have to go down into the Tel camp. And they'll surely have their victim well guarded. If it were up to me, I'd have them in the very middle of everyone, so they're surrounded with armed men."

"Indeed, my source tells me that is precisely how things stand," agreed Mawat. "We'll have to send in a few handpicked men to make their way to where the sacrifice is kept, get past whatever guards there are without alerting anyone, and capture the sacrifice without allowing whoever it is to die." He looked at Airu. "Not your sort of thing, of course, but not exactly an assignment for a coward." Airu made an impatient noise.

"Who are you sending?" asked one of the other lords' sons, apprehensively.

"Oh, never fear," replied Mawat. "I'm going myself."

Just before dawn of the next day, you and Mawat walked quietly through the Tel camp. The source that had brought news of the Tel presence and plans had also provided some few passwords, and they had brought you this far. For the rest I have no doubt that Mawat relied on the Raven's future need of him, but he did not as a rule place all his reliance on that single support, no matter how strong he might think it. He had also brought you—to fight when the moment came, but also to speak when needed; Mawat had some Tel, but his accent would have betrayed him as soon as he spoke a single word. Your accent, coming from the south of the forest as you do, would raise fewer suspicions.

The only specifically godly help Mawat carried was one of the very few godspoken objects the Raven had made— a round bronze token made for passing very, very simple messages. When its holder said the right words, a particular lamp would light. Mawat had given the lamp to Airu,

kept, a broad, circular tent, in a cleared space amid the other, smaller tents. A single guard stood at its entrance flap, dozing.

"I thought this would be one of the difficult parts," Mawat murmured. "They must be very sure of themselves. Why?" And after a few moments, "Because the sacrifice is willing, and there is an entire armed camp all around this tent. Still, I'd have this guard's life for sleeping on duty."

After watching a moment more, Mawat merely walked up to the tent's entrance and very quietly slipped under the flap. You followed. The guard did not stir.

Inside was spare luxury. Clean, tightly woven grass mats floored the tent, and here and there around the perimeter, lamps burned atop lamp stands of polished bronze. The sacrifice lay in a nest of blankets on a pallet beside an iron firebox. He seemed very young, barely out of boyhood, and thin in a way that suggested not merely the awkward lankiness of some youths, but privation.

Likely his death would obligate someone—some Tel lord or, less likely, Stalker herself—to provide for his family.

And certainly he was living the last days of his life in some comfort—the pallet he lay on was thick and soft, the blankets of fine wool, and on a low table beside where he lay, a lamp of chased gold burned beside a distinctively shaped round jar and a gold cup.

"Wine from Xulah," whispered Mawat. "I wonder if anything else here came from south of the mountains." He shook his head—there was no time for such questions. He must move to secure the sacrifice before you were both discovered. He gestured to you, and you both moved toward the sleeping boy.

Someone shouted, away somewhere at the edge of the camp. Mawat swore. "Airu! Curse him!" and fell on the boy, covering his mouth with one hand, grabbing a wrist with another. You knelt atop the boy and, as he struggled beneath you and tried to shout through Mawat's hand, you bound both of his wrists together.

More voices shouting, outside the tent, and suddenly the flap was thrust upward and a man entered, sword in hand, the now wakeful—if not entirely alert—guard close behind him.

The man—tall, taller than Mawat—stopped when he saw you all. The guard juddered to a stop behind him, staring in dismay. Then he drew his own sword.

"Hold him," said Mawat to you, sharply, and rose and

drew his sword. The boy, mouth free, gave a piercing yell
and struggled harder against you, but you held him firm.

таking advantage of your momentary distraction, the
victim wrenched himself free and scrambled awkwardly
away. You sprang after him, grabbing him by the waist
and bringing him down. The guard tripped over you both,
stumbling, and overset the small table. Jar, cup, and lamp
tumbled to the ground, oil spilling out onto the grass mat
beneath.

The boy squirmed free again, got to his feet, and dashed
toward the tall man, who was at that moment attacking
Mawat. You moved to pursue, but the guard recovered his
balance and stepped into your path.

He was larger than you, but you were fast—you
had your knife out and ducked under his sword arm to
drive your blade through the armhole of his cuirass. You
yanked your knife out of him as he hit you with his other
hand, sending you staggering back, into smoke—the lamp
had set the dried grass of the floor mats on fire. The guard
fell to his knees, gasping and choking.

The tall man had been crossing blades with Mawat. The

boy jumped into the blade-swept space between them. With a satisfied grunt the tall man swung his sword at the boy. Mawat blocked the blow, but his blade spun out of his hand.

You drew your sword and rushed the tall man, coughing, as Mawat caught hold of the boy and dragged him out of the smoke-filled tent. The tall man knocked you to the ground and turned to pursue Mawat and the boy.

Outside, the boy tried to escape Mawat's grip and return to the burning tent, but Mawat held firm. The tall man opened his mouth to cry out for assistance, but succeeded only in croaking ineffectually.

"Airu, curse you!" yelled Mawat hoarsely.

As if in reply, half a dozen mounted men came riding fast and surrounded Mawat and his captive. "I told you all we had to do was charge them," said Airu, from atop his horse, as another rider dealt with the tall man. There was blood on Airu's bare arms, and on his sword, and he grinned fiercely.

Mawat handed the boy over to another rider, with orders to bind him more securely and keep him safe. He turned then and made as if to go back into the burning tent when you came staggering out. Mawat gestured to one of the riders to take you up, swung himself up behind another, and you were off.

You were halfway home before the boy, despite all your precautions, managed somehow to get hold of an old brass belt buckle, dented and twisted and sharp enough on one side to cut himself with. By the time anyone noticed, he was beyond help. Much to the profit of Stalker, of course—

promise to the god. As it is, we'll give him a decent funeral, and send word one way or another to the Tel, so that his family knows he died with honor."

No one protested. Like as not, everyone there had been thinking the same thing.

Once you were all back inside the bank and ditch of the road camp, Mawat slid down from the horse he'd been riding, strode over to where Airu had just dismounted, and struck him in the face. "Get your sword out so I can kill you," Mawat said coldly, and drew his own.

"What, because I was right?" Airu protested, drawing his.

"The moment the Tel knew you were upon them they sent someone to be sure of the sacrifice," said Mawat, neither raising his voice nor lowering his sword. "Had he succeeded, you'd have faced a vastly more powerful opponent. He nearly did succeed. If you had only waited a few minutes longer—*as I ordered you*—all of this would have been done much more easily."

"You were never in any danger," Airu argued. "The Raven always looks out for you."

"And he'll look out for me now," said Mawat.

Another lord's son came up to Airu, took his arm, whispered urgently in his ear.

"My lord," you said, having come up beside Mawat, your voice still hoarse from the smoke, "if you kill Lord Airu, we'll probably lose most of the men from the northwestern districts. That's if we're lucky and they just leave rather than attacking us."

"Luck will have nothing to do with it," said Mawat coldly.

"My lord Lease's Heir," said Airu stiffly, his companion still holding tight to his arm. "I spoke in error. I ap—" He swallowed and began again, through gritted teeth. "I apologize."

"Your apology does no good," replied Mawat, "if you won't follow orders."

"I mistakenly thought I saw your signal," Airu lied, his jaw still tense. "I will be more careful in the future."

You opened your mouth to say something to Mawat, but reconsidered. After a few moments Mawat lowered his

That had been a year and a half earlier. Now you were in Vastai, still sitting outside Mawat's room in the fortress. By evening he had not emerged, and the milk had indeed gone sour, as the servant had predicted. You drank it anyway, and then, after some consideration and a shrug, you ate the bread and one of the sausages, and leaned back against the door once more.

You were eyeing another of the sausages when the swish of silks in the stairway made you look up. Zezume, her blue robes black in the corridor's twilight, tall, stately, came to the doorway and stopped before you. She gave the tray of food, with its empty milk bowl, a sharp glance. "Has he been out, then? Have you gotten him to eat something?"

"No, Mother," you said, scrambling to your feet. Surreptitiously wiping one sausage-greasy hand on your trousers, under your cloak.

"Ah," said Zezume, "you've been here all day, have you? You're his aide, I hear. Can you ordinarily get him to eat, when he's like this? Do you have any influence over him at all?"

"Not really, Mother." Zezume sighed, and you added, "I've never known him to be like this for this long. He usually comes out of it in a couple of hours."

"Really?" Zezume asked, visibly surprised. "You've had some experience of his temper, then. And you're not afraid to be here when he does come out?"

It was your turn to be surprised. "No, Mother."

Zezume gave you an appraising look. "You're a very pretty young man, even if you do sound like a farmer."

I think it took you a moment to understand what she meant. "Excuse me, Mother, I don't think I'm the sort of man Lord Mawat might be interested in that way."

"Damn," said Zezume, clearly disappointed. "I was hoping maybe you would be able to calm him down." She sighed then. "It's a difficult situation. I understand that he's angry, and I warned the Lease that this would happen. But there was never going to be any good way to break the news. And it's not as though Mawat has lost anything. He's still the heir."

"Unless the Lease names another one," you said. I think you hesitated just a bit before you said *the Lease*, as though you weren't sure if Hibal really was that.

"I hardly think that's likely," replied Zezume crisply. "What arrangements has Mawat made for your lodging?"

"He didn't have a chance to make any, Mother."

if she's not there you'll find her in one of the storerooms. And tell her she's to give you a chit for the kitchens, so that you can come and go, and get breakfast and dinner."

"Yes, Mother. Thank you, Mother."

"Come back in the morning, if you like," said Zezume. "I think he's not coming out for several days, and he won't open the door to take food unless he's sure no one is in the corridor." She frowned, seeing your expression. "That surprises you?"

"It's as I said, Mother, he usually calms down within a few hours. Sooner if there's an alarm. And he's fine when he comes out. Mostly fine."

"An alarm," said Zezume, realizing. "I see. He can hardly command the border defense if he's spending days locked in his room, can he. It seems he's learned to master himself better, at least a bit, which is all to the good. But this—there are no alarms to call him out of his room here, and this is a terrible blow. His father...I would never have believed it. I would never have thought the Lease would..." She seemed unable to say it. "And leave us in a crisis like this." Zezume shook her head. "I understand that Mawat is angry, I understand why, but we couldn't leave things as they were, we had to secure a new Lease immediately." She gave you a shrewd look. "Don't try to convince him of that, when he does come out. It would only end badly for you. I'll talk to him myself. I've known him since he was a baby, and he'll listen to me eventually."

"Yes, Mother," you said.

You found Giset in a small wooden hut built hard up against the back end of the long, high-roofed hall. More a storeroom than anything else, crowded with piles of wood-cased wax tablets and chests carved from tree trunks and circled with strips of iron. Giset was only slightly younger than Mother Zezume, and kept her gray hair in a single thick braid pinned to the top of her head. Keys and styluses hung and jangled behind the rough-woven apron she wore over her dull green skirts. At first she refused to give you any quarters but a pallet in the hall, once the tables had been cleared away for the night, but when she heard

one notched on two edges and a leather cord tied around, looped so that they could be hung on a wrist or a neck. "One to let you pass through the gate into the fortress, and the other for meals. Two meals a day," Giset admonished, frowning. "*Only* two, not two at your lodgings and two here. They send me the accounts, so I'll know."

"Yes, ma'am," you replied, with the air of someone who had met her sort before and knew better than to argue or contradict her.

"I wouldn't give you both, except Mother Zezume said so and I'm not about to argue with *her*. But you can be sure I'll show her the accounts if I need to." She held the chits out by their cords.

"Yes, ma'am," you said again, and took them.

The lady Tikaz came briskly into the room, heedless of your presence, stepping neatly around a stack of tablets that you'd nearly tripped over when you'd come in. "Auntie," she said, "if there are eels tomorrow, my father would like some. I'm saying so now before everyone else gets them all." As soon as she'd entered you ought to have looked down at the floor, or at least politely away, but instead you were staring at her. She turned her sharp-featured face to stare back at you, took in the leather cords of the chits trailing from your hand, your rough-spun clothes, your one gold arm ring, the gold hilt of your knife. "Who are *you*?"

You looked hastily down. "My name is Eolo, lady. I came with the lord Mawat."

"Whatever for?" asked Tikaz.

"He's the lord Mawat's aide," put in Giset, when you didn't answer immediately. "So a servant, but too good to fetch food for his master, or be any use to anyone else otherwise."

Tikaz scoffed. "Is Mawat sleeping with you, then?"

There was an uncomfortable silence. Then you looked up, looked Tikaz directly in the eye, and said, "Would you be jealous if he was?"

Tikaz scoffed again. "Jealous of which one of you?"

"Either one, my lady. As you prefer."

"I've already turned Mawat down a dozen times, and I'll turn him down again if he needs it. And as for *you* . . ."

For some reason you didn't want her to finish that sentence. "I came here to get these," you broke in, and hefted the lodging token and the bits of wood on their cords. "At Mother Zezume's direction. I have been traveling for three days, I am in an unfamiliar place with no one near who I know, except my lord, who is out of sorts. I only want to find supper and a place to sleep for the night. I am sorry my presence offends you, but I did not come here to be insulted."

out of turn. It isn't only Mawat who's out of sorts at the moment."

"Of course, lady," you acknowledged. "We all are right now."

Tikaz spun and strode out of the room in a flurry of red and green silk. Giset said, frowning, "You'll want to watch that mouth of yours, young man, especially around the lady Tikaz."

"I have no quarrel with the lady," you said. Trying not to sound angry, I thought. "If she won't trouble herself with me, there won't be any chance of my offending her."

"Oh, I'm not worried about you *offending* her," said Giset, with a frown. *"Would you be jealous if he was.* I have eyes in my head! That lady is not someone to trifle with on her own account, and her father presides over the Council of the Directions, and has the ear of the Lease. You could get yourself into a world of trouble if you're not careful, and don't think I won't tell that to Mother Zezume if I need to!"

"I'll come tomorrow to check on the lord Mawat," you said. "If he comes out of his room, could someone send for me?"

"Someone will, never fear," said Giset, still frowning. "Did he eat anything?"

"The tray was still outside his door when I left."

"Well." She made an exasperated sound. "Well. Little wonder he's angry. It's a bad business. Who would have thought."

"It's terrible," you agreed. "How could anyone have thought? He's been Lease all my life." There was no need for you to specify who was meant by that *he*, that you were not talking about Hibal. You hesitated. "I don't think my lord quite believes it."

"No." Giset looked suddenly older, and frightened. "None of us can."

Maybe you thought, then, of who might have ordered that bowl of fresh milk sent to Mawat. In a town, milk usually appears as cheese, or butter, or maybe thick, fermented buttermilk. Fresh milk is a relative rarity. Doubtless you recognized that the tablets all around you held accounts and inventories, realized that it was Giset who managed such things, who knew, day to day and hour to hour, what food there was and who needed to be fed by it. With Giset in authority over the kitchens, taking it upon oneself to set fresh milk on a tray everyone knew would sit ignored in a corridor for hours would be foolhardy indeed. "Do *you* believe it, ma'am?" you asked. "Was there some sign of it? Looking back, I mean."

She eyed you skeptically. "Two meals, mind."

"Yes, ma'am," you said again, and gave her a small bow, and left.

The house Giset had assigned you to was on the square outside the fortress gate, a long, two-story building of stone, wood, and plaster, and a thatched roof. Half the ground floor was taken up by a single large room, tables and benches stacked and pushed against the walls at this hour, a dozen pallets laid out in rows. Most of them held people sleeping—or trying to—under cloaks or blankets.

There was room for a thirteenth, but when the landlady

saw your token, her businesslike demeanor took on just a tinge of deference, and she showed you to a small room of your own, clean and bare, with a decent-enough bed and a tiny window from which you could see the pale yellow stones of the fortress wall. You frowned at the sight, and then sat down on the bed and closed your eyes and sighed. And then tugged off your boots, loosened your bindings, and pulled your cloak around you and lay down, though I daresay you didn't sleep for a long while.

The language the priests of the reindeer hunters taught me is a language no human being has spoken in thousands of years, though there are people far, far to the east, across the sea, who speak a tongue that is a distant cousin of it. In addition to teaching me their language, once the priest decided she had my attention, and that I more or less understood her, the people began to make regular offerings to me—fresh reindeer milk; blood; meat; flowers; small, sour, yellow-pink berries—along with petitions. I took the offerings, of course, each one adding to my strength, such as it was, bit by bit. I didn't know what to do with the petitions, not at first. But every time one of the reindeer hunters would make a petition, and then find their wish gratified,

~~tively by their own efforts or by chance so far as I knew~~

~~tude of the reindeer hunters, who would then make more~~ offerings.

Yes, they trained me as though I were a dog, with attention and treats and constant praise. But I trained them as well. They quickly learned that, while I would take blood or milk or even water, what I preferred was fish from the nearby river, or shells from the now-distant sea. Speech was not a simple matter for me, and so over generations between us we devised a set of tokens—bits of wood, cut and polished into silhouettes of fish, inset with shell, each marked with a particular emblem. A person who wished to speak with me needed only address me, and then reach into a box of such tokens. It was a simple matter for me to nudge the right one into a reaching hand, or even a series of them, to be lined up on the ground and my intent interpreted.

I think I was quite fond of them, though I thought more and more about the other gods they visited and spoke of among themselves. Could I move? Could I go about the world the way these people did and see the things they spoke of? If the chatter of the reindeer hunters was accurate, some other gods did move about, sometimes traveling long distances. Why had none of those other gods visited me?

Well, actually, at least one had. But it had taken me a while to notice her.

Hundreds of years before the reindeer-hunting people had come across me, they had found a reddish, strangely pitted stone that was far heavier than it ought to have been for its size. So far as they could tell it was unlike any other stone in the area, though they were both wrong about that (several other similar stones lay buried in various places nearby) and right (those stones were all of them fragments of a single larger one). In any event, the stone was a prodigy, and the people who found it accordingly treated it as a god.

I had seen that god streak across the sky, felt the earth tremble when she hit. Her arrival left a crater in the ground, even below the thickness of ice she landed on. Before she had fallen to earth, she had unceasingly traveled great distances and seen wonders. She had seen the whole earth, from far, far away, all its lands and its seas, round like a bilberry, but green and brown and blue and much, much larger. The earth moved around and around the sun, which is itself round, and immensely huger than it looks to us, because it is so distant. She saw other worlds besides ours circling the sun, satisfyingly around and around, each in its own precise path. She told me that the shining stars

pose it must be the case.

She learned language relatively quickly, and I suppose it was only natural that unlike me she loved to travel, with the reindeer-hunting people or on her own. She learned early to do what I had never thought or desired to do—to take or build a body to use for travel or speech or whatever other purpose she might have—and it was she who had directed the reindeer hunters to my hillside. In Iraden her name is a curse, but among the reindeer hunters— whose name for themselves meant something like *Us People*—it was a blessing. They called her the Myriad. And by arrangement with the Myriad they roamed their land almost entirely free of interference from the clouds of mosquitoes that gathered when the sun went down.

But I knew none of this when I first met the Myriad. When first I realized I had met her. Mosquitoes were just a part of the world around me. I didn't pay much attention to them except to recognize their existence. They didn't trouble me, of course. I had no blood, and I was impervious to their sharp proboscises. So when my friend first visited me, I didn't see anything except maybe a slightly thicker cloud of the usual summer mosquitoes.

The Myriad had traveled a great deal, and knew many fascinating stories, her own and those of others. Or I thought them fascinating. She, in her turn, was fascinated by my tales of bony-headed fish and trilobites, the long, slow retreat of the sea, amphibians and birdlike reptiles, the ice that had still shrouded the land when she'd first arrived.

She would visit me along with the reindeer hunters, once a year or perhaps once every few years, and we would talk for a few weeks, and then the people would move on, and she would move on with them. It was enough. I was used to being alone. Preferred it, really. But the Myriad had met not only many human beings, but many gods. She had acquaintances all over the northlands, and had once or twice even gone as far south as the Shoulder Sea.

Here is a story I have heard: On the northern shore of the Shoulder Sea sat a permanent settlement, a camp larger than I had ever seen. It had grown into a small city, spread along part of a large natural harbor, sheltered by two small headlands. It was, moreover, located on one of the very few navigable straits between the Shoulder Sea and the open ocean. Boats passed there; boats docked there. Not just the small skin boats I'd seen occasionally on the tiny river in my valley, but boats large enough to hold dozens of people, to carry timber and loads of skins and furs or anything else that was plentiful in one place but rare in another.

The gods of that city received offerings on a scale I

petitions it received were almost entirely concerned with the manufacture, trade, or use of such items.

I myself did similar services for the reindeer hunters on occasion, but if that were all I did I would have sadly limited the offerings I received. This god, however, had grown large and powerful almost entirely on this one thing. Quite a lot of people lived on the shores of the sea; nearly every one of those people would depend on some sort of knife or blade at some point.

Another god there had spent years pondering the construction of walls. She had a plan for the city's harbor—to enlarge and extend it, to line it with stone quays and offices and warehouses. This plan would cost the city a good deal of resources, and the god a good deal of effort, but the result would be more and safer space for more and larger ships. The city's (and no doubt the god's) wealth was tied to those ships, and its population had already outstripped the ability of the surrounding land to feed so many. So the god presented her plan to the people and the other gods of the city. It would take years—years of ritual and sacrifice as the gods involved were strengthened for the purpose. Then the god of walls would push back the sea, and hold it, so that the engineers could lay enormous blocks of stone, and build dams and hollow pillars that would let them construct enormous quays.

Just moving all that water, even for a short period, would take a tremendous amount of power. Then to keep those dams and caissons safe, to move all those stones…

"But this is what the engineers are for," the Myriad told me. "I gather that in the course of her usual business, this god has thought a great deal about cutting and hauling stone. And the builders there have devices for moving such things, she will only have to assist those. But even so, yes, it will take a tremendous amount of power. I imagine it will take decades to accumulate so much, if not longer."

The thought of such power reminded me of the gods I had seen so long ago, before I had met the Myriad. Long before humans existed, I was sure. "Those likely will have been Ancient Ones," the Myriad informed me. And told me that the gods of the seacoast were afraid of the few that still lived. And afraid that the ones who had died might return. She had heard stories of a place farther south even than the Shoulder Sea, where whole armies of ancient gods had battled. One of them had uttered a curse just before it died, and now, tens of thousands, perhaps millions of

years later, the still-cursed bones of its opponents lay in the ground. Anyone disturbing those bones would die horri-
~~bly before the day was out.~~

~~There are no doubt several~~ ways to change the world so that anyone who touches a particular object dies within the day. Perhaps the simplest seeming would be to alter the universe itself in such a way that this is always true. But simple as that sounds, changing the nature of things on such a scale would, I am certain, take far more power than any god I know of possesses, and besides that, even small changes to small things have consequences. What would such an instant, profound change mean for everything else in the world?

Instead, in my experience, when a god speaks in this way concerning an object, the god's power is required only when the conditions of the speech are met. And in such cases, if that god dies there is no longer any power to make those previous words true. And the gods concerned in this ancient battle had, I was told, been dead for millennia.

But, the Myriad told me, a god had said it to her, and said it unambiguously: the ancient god was dead who had uttered the curse, and yet that curse was still in effect.

It must have been true, it was not the sort of thing a god could otherwise straightforwardly say with impunity, not unless that god were unimaginably powerful. There are some actions beyond the power of even the most powerful gods, and one of them is to say something happened that did not, or to say something did not happen that did.

"Did that statement come by itself," I asked, after thinking that over for a year or two, "or did it come, like yours, framed with *a god told me straightforwardly?*"

The Myriad gave a buzzing whine of laughter. "You don't move speedily, but you move to the purpose," she said. "The statement was framed with *a god told me*. But ultimately it must be true. If we follow back the chain of *a god told me*s, there will be a god who first told the tale, and told it without injury, since that was part of the telling."

I thought about that for a while, and then I asked how it was that these powerful Ancient Ones could utter anything, since language, so far as we knew, was a human thing.

"I don't know," the Myriad replied. "But it seems to me that the gods of ancient times are quite different in some ways from the gods of this age."

So it seems to me also. I think it must be so, but I do not know for certain.

What I do know is that the harbor town that the Myriad had visited, that was home to so many powerful,

specialized gods and had such ambitious plans for its harbor, was the place that the Iradeni now call Ard Vusktia,
which you can see if you stand atop the Raven Tower in

In the morning you washed your hands and your mouth
with herbed water. Made a face, briefly—was it because
you were used to different herbs south of the forest, or
because you had become used to plain water in the field?—
and then murmured morning prayers to the Raven, the
god of Vastai, Sustainer of Iraden. Then you sat down to
your allotted breakfast—a flat loaf of barley bread, a hunk
of cheese, small beer—at one of the long tables that had
been pulled back out from the wall, now it was day. You sat
with your back as near a corner as you could, watching the
door to the house, watching the landlady and her daughter
come back and forth out of the kitchen. Watching the other
guests at their breakfasts.

They were a varied lot—two officials from across the
strait in Ard Vusktia, in wool and bright-dyed silk, who
had clearly slept upstairs in their own room, attended by

their servant, who had slept downstairs; an assortment of men and women, prosperous farmers to judge by the fine-woven, sober-colored wool they wore, here in Vastai on various errands; a man in loose shirt and trousers of sky-colored linen, who spoke with a strange accent but was clearly at ease. Across from you, very near the fire, in their sleeveless, knee-length tunics, cloaks on their shoulders, sat the Xulahns you had seen in the fortress the day before. You eyed them as they leaned on the table and chattered in a language I'm quite certain you couldn't understand.

An older man who had been sitting with the farmers stood, came over to where you sat. He wore good plain wool, like a wealthy farmer, but over one shoulder was slung a garment of black silk embroidered with oak leaves. "Good morning," he said to you. "My name is Dera, and I am the Direction for Oenda. You are the lord Mawat's aide? Eolo, is it?"

"I am, lord," you replied, setting down your beer. "How may I be of service to you?"

Dera smiled, as though your greeting had been more than just appropriately polite. As though you had seemed glad to see him. "Someone said they thought you seemed as though you might be from Oenda, and to hear you speak, I think they might be right." You didn't reply to this. "One of the things I do, as a Direction, is help the people under my authority find their way around, if they have business in Vastai. I make introductions when I can. Help out with petitions or suits, that sort of thing. If it's needed. Perhaps I know your family?"

"I'm not here on my own business, lord," you said, your

Mawat's business. Though as he's in one of his moods just now, there's not much business for you to do. Is there?" He looked at you intently, waiting for some sort of response, and, apparently seeing what he wanted in your expression, continued, "Not that I blame him for being angry. This was surely not what he expected to find." He did not specify what *this* was. He did not need to.

"Lord Direction," you said, "I don't know anything about what's going on here."

"Have you been to Vastai before?" he asked you genially. And at your gestured *no*, "Then—to judge by your youth—you never met the lord Mawat's father."

"The trees in the forest forfend," you said, making a quick gesture under the table with your left hand. And then observed, "You knew him."

"I knew him," agreed Dera, with an ironic quirk of his mouth. As though he was bitterly amused by your calling on the forest, and knew what gesture you had just made.

"Can he really have fled? Is it even possible?"

Dera frowned and considered a moment. "If you had asked me that last week I would have said it wasn't. The last Lease was…" He hesitated. "I would not say this to the lord Mawat, you understand. But the last Lease had quite a temper, and in the last few years he had ceased to rein that temper in, even with his friends. Of which he had fewer and fewer. In recent years, he did not govern but rather made demands of the Directions according to his whims. Which we did not always bend to, of course. The Lease may rule Iraden, but only with the assistance and agreement of the Council of the Directions." Dera waved away his last few words. "But no Lease is on the bench forever, and the Instrument was aging. Everyone knew it was only a matter of time. Your lord Mawat might have been wise to spend more time in Vastai these past few years, consulting the Directions and making plain his intentions to govern Iraden responsibly."

"The lord Mawat," you replied coldly, "has been somewhat busy keeping the Tel away from our borders."

"He has," agreed Dera. "For which we're all grateful. Particularly those of us from the other side of the forest, as we two are. Who would have been in command of our forces in the south, if Mawat hadn't been there? Who commands those forces now?"

"The lord Airu," you said, managing to keep your voice bland and even.

"The lord Airu. I know him. Know of him. Hardly a great strategist, but unquestionably brave. And ambitious."

"He is those things," you agreed.

"I see you know him too," said Dera, sardonic. "But your lord might safely have left the border in his hands

away from his father."

You frowned at that. "I'm sure I don't know what you mean, lord Direction."

"Do you not? Well. What's done is done. If the lord Mawat has not been here to reassure us, the lord Hibal certainly has been. Whatever my disagreements with him, the lord Hibal is certainly...less erratic than his brother. And if the lord Mawat is angry and disappointed now—as he surely is right to be—this may work out to all of our advantages. Your lord is young, and he is still heir to the Lease. With the lord Hibal on the bench, Mawat has time to learn to moderate his temper and show us that he is not his father. And one needn't be Lease to work for the good of Iraden."

"Are you certain the new Lease won't name a new heir?" you asked. Picked up your beer, slowly and deliberately, and took a drink. Set the cup back down. "Especially given my lord's apparent deficiencies?"

Dera laughed. "Take my advice, Eolo, and don't lose your accent. Everyone here will underestimate you." You blinked, momentarily confused but covering it well. "But to your question—yes, Hibal might name a new heir. But the Directions and the Mother of the Silent also have a say in such things. As does the Raven himself. Hibal can't just name an heir and be done. And some of us only agreed to support his bid for the bench now precisely because he promised that Mawat would step up to the bench after him. Some of us, despite our involvement in placing the lord Hibal on the bench, still have misgivings. And we would like your lord to come out of his room and attend to various matters."

You stared at Dera. And then asked, "Such as?"

"Now that he's on the bench," said Dera, quietly, leaning forward just a bit, as though wary now of being overheard, "the lord Hibal begins to speak of moving the Raven's household to Ard Vusktia."

You blinked, two or three times. "What?"

"That was my reaction," said Dera. "The Directions have very little authority in Ard Vusktia, the Lease rules there. Or his officials rule there for him. They cross the strait to consult with him nearly every day. Of course the Directions have a say in some things, even there, and of course we've all shared in the prosperity that possession of Ard Vusktia brings to us—the Lease takes his share of the cargo of every ship that passes through the strait, and some of that flows to all the rest of Iraden, through trade and gifts. And of course quite a few of us—myself included—have shares

would be centered on Ard Vusktia, where the Directions hold no real political power, and the council would become irrelevant to the bench. Perhaps the Lease would like to make it so. Ensconced in Ard Vusktia, with all he needs and more, how much attention would the Lease—or the Raven himself—have for matters in Iraden?"

"Can the Lease leave Vastai without breaking the Raven's agreement with the God of the Silent?" you asked, astonished.

"The lord Hibal seems to think so. He has not, you understand, announced his intention to move across the strait. He has only said things that suggest such a possibility. But why suggest it if he doesn't mean to attempt it? And if..." Dera shook his head. "If the Raven has found a way to escape his obligations to the forest, and abandon us, well. That move might be very bad for Iraden. I know"—he held up a forestalling hand—"that we would still have the forest. The forest was enough for us before the Raven came. But things were different then."

"Do I understand, lord Direction," you said, calmly and smoothly, "that you wish me to tell my lord that you would continue to support his succession to the bench after Hibal as long as he can assure you that he will keep the Lease in Vastai?"

"Something like that," agreed Dera. "If it hasn't already occurred to him. Besides that, there is the matter of his father's disappearance. Will the Raven not demand payment of his Lease? The lord Hibal has argued that the matter is dealt with, that responsibility for paying the Raven falls entirely on the Lease himself and the Raven will extract any required payment or punishment from the lord Mawat's father, somehow. He seems entirely unworried about what the god might demand when this new egg hatches and the new Instrument is born. I myself"—he shook his head—"am not so sure. But we shall see."

"Lord Dera," you said. "If the Lease didn't flee, what happened to him?"

Dera took his black silk robe from off his lap and stood. "I hardly know. But he was searched for, all through the tower and the fortress, and no one could find him. And in the end it doesn't matter. Hibal was named Lease by the Mother of the Silent, with the agreement of...*most* of the Council of the Directions. And he sat on the bench and lived. So he is the Lease now, and that is the fact we all must deal with." He pulled the robe on, settled it over his shoulders. "I must attend the Lease. But I'm glad to know

When Dera had gone, you finished your breakfast, and then stood and pulled your cloak around yourself, and stepped out of the house into the wide, sunlit square, and took the two chits that Giset had given you out of your shirt, and went into the fortress.

Mawat's door was still closed. The tray you'd seen last night had been taken away and replaced with another one that held a bowl of now-congealed barley gruel with greens in it and a small heap of pickled turnips. It clearly hadn't been touched. You knocked on the door. Waited. Knocked again. "My lord," you said. "My lord, it's me, Eolo." There was no answer. "Giset assigned me a place to sleep outside the fortress," you said. "If you need me, she'll send for me." Still no answer. "I'll check back tomorrow."

You walked the inside of the fortress wall then, or as much of it as you could. You avoided obviously staring, but it was clear to me that you were searching for something. You did look at the ravens, some of whom turned a curious eye on you as you passed, but everyone else seemed to ignore them, and none of the birds evinced any particular interest in you. Nor did anyone else in the fortress, though the guard at the entrance to the tower eyed you intently as you walked around it, and then as you stood, looking up toward its top.

"Move along," the guard called to you, after a few minutes of this. "Unless you have business here."

You did stare then, and asked, "How tall is it?" The guard rolled his eyes, contemptuous of your gawking. "Sneer all you like, I've never been to Vastai before." Defensive, leaning on that accent Dera had advised you to keep.

"That much is obvious," said Tikaz, who had come up behind you. And then, more quietly, "What are you *actually* doing?"

You gestured toward the tower. "I've never seen a building so tall."

Tikaz scoffed. "You can stop the act. Mawat would never have taken you for his aide if you were that sort of fool." You blinked innocently at her. She continued, still quietly, "And I suppose you just happened to accidentally have breakfast with Lord Dera, of the Council of the Directions?"

And when you couldn't conceal your surprise, "I was there. The landlady's daughter is a friend of mine."

You recovered yourself, made your expression apolo-

"And what did he want with Mawat, I wonder?" she asked, folding her arms.

"I hardly know," you told her. "Tell me, lady, is there a secret way out of the fortress? A way to leave with no one knowing?"

"Is *that* what you're up to?" She didn't unfold her arms, just stood there regarding you skeptically. "They searched the tower, and the whole fortress, and he wasn't anywhere."

"Your pardon, lady," you said, "that wasn't what I asked."

"There are no unguarded ways in or out of this fortress," she said. "The wall is regularly patrolled, and even the sea is watched. No one saw him leave. Nonetheless," she continued as you opened your mouth to argue, "he is not here."

"Thank you for your assistance, lady." You bowed your head, just a bit, and turned to go.

"Is this how you're spending your time, then?" Her

voice was disbelieving. But low, so as not to be overheard by the people passing in the tower yard. "Your lord dispossessed of the bench, everyone in Vastai unsure what to think about his uncle taking his place, or what the Raven might have to say when the egg hatches, or how it might affect the Raven's agreement with the forest, let alone what it will mean for Iraden, the Directions all looking for whatever advantage they might get out of this—and you're trying to track down the runaway?"

"Do you believe the Lease fled?" you asked.

"I don't think it matters if he did nor not," Tikaz told you. "What matters is that Hibal is Lease now. Nothing's gone the way anyone expected, and Mawat will have to accept that. You can tell him I said so, when you see him next." And when you said nothing, "What did you tell the lord Dera?"

"Very little, lady." You ducked your head again and left.

In the square outside the fortress, you looked around at the walls of the adjacent buildings—flat, no projections or nooks, no booths or sheds creeping into the empty space, as

they do in the town's other squares and courts. There was
no place to stop or sit, just flat, yellowish brown stone pav-
ing, warm in the late-morning sun. Then you traced your

again into the sea, by the harbor. The wind blew strong off
the water so that despite the sunshine on the warm sand
you were chilled. Away across the strait, ships crowded
the white quays of Ard Vusktia. A little fleet of fishing
boats dotted the waves, and closer in, several masted ships
floated, tied up to pilings, their sails furled. You frowned
at them. I don't think you grew up near the sea, and so you
likely knew very little about boats, or tides.

You found a place on the sand, well back from the
water, and sat and watched the little boats going to and fro,
watched as the tide went slowly down and exposed more
and more of the broad stone ramp that led out toward
where the ships waited. Watched as, one after another, various small sailboats deposited passengers onto the beach—
some of them serious-looking older men and women in
fine black wool, trailed by servants carrying leather satch-
els filled with tablets and styluses. Did you remember
Dera's words to you, earlier, about Ard Vusktian officials

visiting almost daily to consult with the Lease? After a while those sailboats took on a fresh load of passengers and set back out toward Ard Vusktia. You watched until the fishing boats came in and hauled their catch up onto the strand. The various people with rights to the catch converged on the fish—among them a handful of kitchen servants from the fortress, and the daughter of your landlady at the guesthouse.

Your father could not be found, the lord Radihaw had said the day before to Mawat. *Not in the tower, not in the fortress, not in the town.* And yet it seemed that he could not have left the fortress without someone knowing. You were thinking about that, it seemed, instead of how Mawat might turn the situation to his own advantage, or what any of this might mean for you. Or perhaps you *were* thinking of those things—but had for some reason decided to solve this particular puzzle first.

After a while you pushed yourself to your feet and brushed the sand off your legs and returned to the house where you were lodged. The common room was nearly empty at this hour, but the Xulahns were still there, still sitting at their table so near the fire.

One of them recognized you, elbowed one of his companions, and looked pointedly in your direction, said something quiet. The third stood as you drew closer. "Good person. You are on the assistance of the prince Mawat, I consider." You stopped and stared, but said nothing. "I am practice my Iradeni," he said. "I am begging you to sit and drink beer and I practice to you, if you will be so kind."

"Did you speak to the Lease?" you asked. "Do you have

might have. "The king is not send for us today. We stand wait."

You blinked. "We are waiting," you said. "We are waiting for the Lease to send for us."

The Xulahn frowned in return, and then smiled. "We are waiting for the Lease to send for us. I am think not send for us today. Sit, friend, drink with us."

"Are we friends?" you asked, and then thought better of it and moved to sit on a bench across the table from the other two Xulahns. Stopped and leaned back, just a bit, when the dark brown head of a snake slid out of the armhole of the first Xulahn's tunic. Its black tongue flickered out, sampling the air.

"Is only my snake, friend," said the Xulahn. "Good snake. Nice snake. No worry."

"You keep a snake for a pet," you said, making a fairly good effort to conceal your alarm and puzzlement.

"Is a friend." The Xulahn smiled widely. Held his arm

across his chest, and the snake slid farther out. Its body was a lighter brown than its head, and a row of darker brown spots ran down its back. It wasn't even three feet long. It licked the air again. "Is good snake. We are not the trouble with the mouse. Sit!"

You sat on the bench. The Xulahn sat beside you.

"Are you been crossed the water to Ard Vusktia?" he asked. The snake slid back into his tunic.

"No," you replied, as he poured you a cup of beer from the earthenware pitcher on the table. You affected not to notice that the snake was still watching you from under his arm, eyes intent and unblinking. "I've never even been to Vastai before."

"But you are on the assistance of the prince."

"I'm the lord Mawat's aide," you corrected. "He's been in the southwest for a few years. I'm from south of here, from the other side of the forest."

"The forest!" exclaimed the Xulahn, as the other two looked on, apparently unable to understand their companion's conversation with you. "Why are you call the forest quiet?"

Before you could answer, the Xulahns' interpreter came in, and over to where you were sitting with them. "Come, speak," said the Xulahn next to you, speaking Tel. "What news?"

"The king will not see you today," said the interpreter, also in Tel. From his accent, he was likely Tel himself. A risky proposition for him to come here, but perhaps the Xulahns had paid him exceptionally well. The Xulahns

language that was neither Tel nor Iradeni. Then, "Who did you speak to?" asked the Xulahn sitting beside you, speaking Tel again. You looked only at your cup of beer.

The interpreter glanced at you, quickly, then back to the Xulahn beside you. "I spoke to the councillor. He said the king had other priorities, and might send for you tomorrow, or might not."

"This delay is fine for now," said the Xulahn beside you. "But if it goes on too long we'll have to wait till next spring to go much farther north, if what you say about the ice and cold is true."

"I think he wants more gifts," said the interpreter. "The ones you've already given have made him greedy. They're like that here."

The Xulahn beside you turned to you, and said in Iradeni, "The king is not see us today, I am hearing."

"No?" You seemed unperturbed, and only mildly surprised at the news. "That's inconvenient for you. How long have you been here?"

"Four weeks," said your Xulahn companion. "The king before would not see us at all. So is better! But we like to go."

"Why?" you asked.

The Xulahn blinked at you, seeming perplexed.

"I heard what your interpreter said," you told him, "in the tower. That you only want to write about your travels, for the people back home. That doesn't seem like it would be worth all this."

"Ah, friend, you are not a person that is...I am not know the word." He turned to the interpreter and said, in Tel, "What is the word? Someone who travels to see and learn new things?"

The interpreter shrugged. Suggested, in Iradeni, "Traveler? Wanderer? Discoverer?" And then back to Tel. "None of them is exactly right."

"Discoverer," decided the Xulahn. "For a person who is live to discover, is worth the most, the everything, to see a new thing. That we are know more about the world."

You stared at him skeptically. "You brought a god with you, just to walk around away up north and *discover*?"

"Ah," said the Xulahn, as though you had caught him out in some small deception. "But our snake friend is not at all a very large god. And discover is need...How do you say, we are need food and travel and clothing, and gifts for where people are help us. The more we are travel, the more all these things, and we are travel long and far. We are not so rich, friend, that we are have all this ourselves. But it

may be that there is gold in the north—we are hear that
it may be—and so we are discover if it is and bring that
news to someone who will give us all these things for our

this is good for everyone,

are wish. If we are find gold or other things, the person
who is support us discovering has as they are wish. And if
we are bring gold or other things through Vastai, the king
is take his share, yes? Good for everyone."

"Until Xulah decides they don't want to share any of
that gold. Or other things, whatever those may be."

"Oh, friend," said the Xulahn, reprovingly. "Xulah is
very far away. And it may be no gold at all." He gave you
a more carefully considering look. "So Prince Mawat, is
he..." He searched for a word, or a phrase. "Is the people
of Iraden to love him?"

"He's the heir to the Lease," you said, apparently
uncomprehending.

"Yes," agreed the Xulahn, pleasantly. "That is not the
people love him, I am consider. If Prince Mawat is want to
be king, the people will help him? Or the..." He paused
here, evidently searching for a word. "Is a god a friend of
the prince?"

You looked at him with disbelief. "He's the *heir to the Lease.*"

"Yes, yes." The Xulahn waved your protest away. "And here in Vastai one god is ruling, but always gods are."

Still standing beside the table, the interpreter said, in Tel, "And ravens are assholes. But don't say that. You can't say that here without starting trouble."

The Xulahn said, as though the interpreter had not spoken, "A god that is small now is maybe not small forever, with the right friends."

Were you puzzled by this statement? You were born on a farm, south of the Silent Forest. You've likely never knowingly met a small god there, but you'll almost certainly have sprinkled a few drops of milk onto the ground just before leaving it to separate, or perhaps there was a stone by a well that you wetted when you were sent to draw water, or a rhyme that you said while filling your pail. Some animal your family doesn't eat.

"We don't have small gods in Iraden," you said. A shade indignantly. "If you want small gods, visit the Tel, in the south. They have nothing but."

The interpreter frowned, but said nothing in response.

"Small gods everywhere," said the Xulahn. "In Iraden they hide? They might want a king who allows them not to hide. And the prince is not seem happy with the king."

"He's the *Lease,*" you said. "And you don't understand anything about Iraden." You made as if to stand up.

The Xulahn laid his hand on your forearm. "No offense, friend, no offense. I am consider I say a bad thing, although

The Myriad traveled a great deal, as I said. Or at least a great deal compared to me. She ranged far just on her own, but she also accompanied the reindeer hunters on their travels. The band that visited me was one of many that traveled the northern lands, nearly all of them related to each other in some way. The Myriad told me that they would meet up every few years in summer at a campground to the east and a little south of where I sat, where a river flowed out of a lake. They would greet old friends, exchange gifts, maybe when the gathering broke up some would leave the groups they'd traveled with before and join new ones, to be with a friend or a lover, or just for a change.

This was the time and place one would be most likely

to find things that would usually be rare or scarce. At first these would be things like particularly well-wrought stone blades, or ivory or antlers carved into shapes—fish, birds, and humans were all popular, sometimes simply because they were appealing, but sometimes because they were an emblem associated with a god that was a particular favorite, or who might appreciate the flattery. The people who visited me often carried small, flat stones, each with a stylized image etched into it. With a hole drilled into them, or notched on two sides, they could be tied to a strip of leather, hung around the neck or attached to a coat or a shirt. These became quite popular at the large meetings, and the Myriad was quite pleased with how often they were decorated with mosquitoes. She also pointed out the ones that bore a pair of concentric circles—those were meant to indicate me, she told me. Though they were popular mostly with our own regular visitors. I did not travel, as she did.

Over the decades things changed: The people began to cook with carved stone pots instead of tightly woven sedge and heated stones. Their language changed, a slow smattering of new words, the loss of others, sounds picked up or dropped. And eventually words taken from what the Myriad told me were other, entirely different languages from the south.

I had only ever spoken the one language. And I was accustomed to think of that language as something

naturally occurring, something part of the fundamental
nature of the world. Firstly because it was the only language I knew of, and secondly because I could use that

occurred to her that when she reported on the far-flung
peoples she visited and mentioned words she'd learned, I
would take those words only in the context of the language
we were speaking to each other, and not intuit the existence of the languages from which those words had come.
She thought it was funny, when she realized. And because
she had learned of the existence of those other very different languages much earlier than I had, she had never
apparently thought of our first language in the same way
I had. When I asked her if she could make things happen
by speaking in one of those other languages, she flew tight,
puzzled circles around me for five minutes and then said
that yes, of *course* she could. Did I really think that it was
the sound of the words that did the work? She didn't see
how I could think that, because for one thing the pronunciation of the words we used had changed quite a lot since
we'd first learned language, and for another, if it were just
the sound, why, human beings ought to be able to make

things happen just by speaking in the same way that gods did. And for another, I often spoke to the reindeer hunters using the wooden tokens, which did not convey meaning with sound at all.

I admitted that I had never used communication by token to fulfill a petition. I hadn't realized that might be possible. And then I pointed out that in fact there were many things human beings could make happen just by speaking. Granted, I had never seen one say something like *For the next minute I will hover a foot off the ground* with any actual result in that direction, where I myself had done exactly that once, after very careful consideration of whether I had enough power to make that happen without injuring myself. (What can I say, I was curious and also easily amused.) But I hadn't thought my ability to affect the world with speech to be different in kind from what humans could do, only different in scope.

And the changing of pronunciation (and in some cases of grammar) hadn't troubled me. I knew things changed slowly, and so the right way to say words would also change. It was not essential, I thought, to use one particular set of words or way to say them, but rather to use the words that were right in that particular moment, in those particular circumstances.

That struck her as almost, but not quite, right. And we would have discussed longer, and in more detail, except for the fact that gods have to be very careful when speaking about the nature of things. It might be that if you're strong enough, you can perhaps risk saying something like *The world is round like a berry and moves around the sun, which is*

nature of language. So everything we said to each other had to be couched in qualifiers—*it might be, I suppose, it's likely that*—or else in statements that we already knew to be factual. We didn't get very far in our conclusions.

I spent a lot of time thinking about it, though, when I was alone. I thought of what the Myriad had said about those other languages. I wondered what would happen if I were to say a thing in one of those languages that I did not understand—would it make whatever those words meant true? Even if I did not understand what it was I had said? And what about the tokens, which did not make any sound at all (besides perhaps a faint clicking and rattling in their box or bag)? How did words mean things to begin with?

I thought also of those gods I'd seen in the time before humans had existed, who could not have possibly spoken a human language and yet had wielded great power. Could it be that language was not the source of the power, but one possible tool for using that power? Those other, older gods must have known of a different one. I wondered what it was, and how they had learned of it. And why language worked the way it did for me, and the Myriad, but not (as I'd mistakenly thought) for the humans who visited me. Somewhat obviously, the answer to that second question is, "Humans are not gods (unless they are inhabited by a god, which is of course a special case)," but that doesn't get to the deeper question. What is it that makes language a far more powerful—and risky—tool for gods than it is for even humans? What is it that makes gods gods? *What am I?*

I beg your forgiveness—I have long been in the habit of musing to myself in the chilly silence of my northern hillside. It is still easy for me to be distracted by such thoughts. I will resume explaining my history.

As had happened occasionally over the years, the far north grew colder—too cold for the reindeer hunters to visit me, and so I sat alone for some centuries, not visited even by the Myriad. I knew I was not forgotten— occasionally, perhaps every few years, I felt the satisfying small influx of a prayer or offering, usually (though not always) accompanied by the tug of a petition. Sometimes I had a sense of what the petition was, at least in general terms, but mostly it was just a feeling. Along with watching the snow, watching the geese stream overhead spring after spring, watching the stars and their slow, satisfying movement around the sky, I would sometimes ponder whether I could or should grant these indefinite-to-me petitions. Some of the offerings even seemed to come with

...the reindeer hunters had done that occasionally, in

what they ask for. What could —— p——— y

petitioner had asked for my destruction? Or, unknowing, asked for something that would injure themselves, or a great many other people? Was the offering enough to take such a risk? Could any offering be enough for that? I had no way to know, and so I did not fulfill any of the requests that were made during that time.

Here is a story that I have heard: There was once a god who generally used the form of a snow goose, and this god favored a particular human to the point of making her an extravagant gift. Godspoken objects are exceedingly rare in Iraden—I daresay you could count them on the fingers of one hand, if you were made aware of them. They are less rare outside Iraden—I think you have seen the Tel bring them into battle against Iradeni forces—but even so I doubt they are particularly common anywhere in the world. Either few gods are foolhardy enough to make them (or powerful enough to afford the risk), or else most of the gods who have taken the risk have not survived it long.

In this case, the godspoken object was a spearhead of knapped obsidian. Once each day any creature at which this particular person aimed and cast the spearhead would die.

The danger of speaking this way about an object lies in the likelihood of its being used in an unintended way, one that would end up costing far more power than the god possessed. This is one reason gods so often speak very precisely. After all, it seems a simple thing to say, for example, *I will cross the river.* Humans cross rivers, large and small, quite routinely, with little or no godly assistance. How much, then, could it cost a god to fulfill that statement?

But there are so many ways that statement might be made true. Yes, one might simply walk across a bridge, or take a ferry, or wade across a ford. But one might also fly across that river—and if one is not a bird or in some other form that facilitates flying, that flight might well come at great cost. Or one might simply be on one bank and then suddenly gone, to appear on the other. I think this has only succeeded in very particular circumstances—for instance,

I imagine the Myriad might move very quickly among her many mosquito bodies and the stone in which she fell from the sky. But in most other cases, I suspect that such travel

that I heard, must have seemed safe enough for the goose god. After all, the hunter must actually aim and cast the thing, so that the spear would already be moving more or less in its intended direction. To make that flight fatal to its target should be a small-enough thing—a nudge here or there to make it fly true, with sufficient force to kill. And it could be used this way only once a day, and only by a specifically named person. These are all prudent limits on the use of such an object.

The owner of the spear point died, and her heirs left the spear point at her grave. But long years later it was found again by someone who knew only that he had found a good spear point at a time of great need. Returning home, he gave this spear point to his son. Who, whether by chance or by a long and twisting chain of connected circumstance, had the same name as the point's original owner.

Long years might have passed, and the spear point and its owner might have been largely forgotten (apparently along with the knowledge of how graves were marked in former times), but the goose god still thrived. And it was the goose god who first recognized the spear point. And realized the potential danger of the situation. He had assumed that his obligation had passed when the point's first owner had died. He had assumed that the first owner's name was sufficiently distinctive that it would not be held by some other person in the future. Those assumptions had been unfounded. For now the danger was slight, but no doubt the goose god could imagine the potential for future disaster.

This new holder had not yet realized what he had—he thought only that it was a particularly lucky point. It might, then, be best to convince him to hand it over to the goose god and then find some way to hide it so that it would never accidentally come to light again, and in the meantime the goose god would think of some way to safely dispose of it.

Accordingly, the god approached the point's new owner and asked for it as a gift. Now, this man's family was under an obligation to the goose god, and he felt that he could not refuse the god's request, but it seemed particularly hard to give up the best weapon the man owned, the one that seemed always to bring down its target neatly and surely at least once in a day. He was, in fact, about to head out to hunt when the goose god approached him. And so, with ill grace, he tossed the weapon to the god.

they spoke a different language,

by a different name—the Kaluet. The people I had known had eaten primarily reindeer and fish, with the occasional goose, but these people would not harm geese, let alone eat them. It was from these people that I heard the story of the goose god, and his struggle with the power that had condemned him to destruction—his own power.

These new people carried lamps of clay instead of the stone ones I had seen before. And some of them carried metal knives. During the time I'd been alone, the every-few-years camp by the lake had become a small, permanent settlement. People whose travels ordinarily took them to the east, or the south, brought things they'd found or traded for, and sometimes new people. These people were, themselves, related to people farther east, and farther south, until the lake camp became one of several centers in a web of relationships that stretched across the north, east to the mountains, and south to the Shoulder Sea. The flow of new people and things into the camp, and thus to the bands of people traveling the north, was constant, if slow. Pottery had been one of those new things, and eventually fine spun and dyed wool, glass beads, and metalwork made their way north. These things had been familiar to the Kaluet for decades, but it was all still new to me then.

Despite their new language, these people knew the Myriad by her old name—she arrived along with them and flew straight over to greet me—and they knew my name. "They haven't forgotten you," she told me. "I hear that you saved a child from drowning! And I'm told you saved a family from starvation, when they prayed to you and then found a cache of dried fish that had not been there when last they'd looked."

"I didn't," I replied. "I think some people asked me for things, but I didn't grant any of it. I couldn't be sure what it was I'd be saying yes to."

"Probably wise," said the Myriad. "And yet. How much more famous and powerful might you be, if you had actually helped everyone who called on you this long while?"

"I don't need to be famous and powerful," I replied.

"Do you not?" asked the Myriad. "Well. It's troublesome to be frequently called on, it's true. But for the most part I enjoy it."

I believe she did. And I believe she loved to travel, to meet humans and gods, and loved it when everyone she knew was associated, tied together, trading, traveling. It was partly because of this that the Kaluet carried so much wood.

You grew up on the edge of a great forest, and perhaps think nothing of being surrounded by trees, of making and using all sorts of wooden objects. Of picking up a few

shrub than a tree—that one might find by a stream. Still, wood is useful and necessary for so much. The reindeer hunters I had known before had used wood—nearly all of it driftwood: sticks and even whole trees, and boards from broken-up boats. All of it had floated on the sea, sometimes for years, before washing onto some northern shore. This was hardly a steady supply, but wood was so necessary and valuable that even I, well inland, had received the occasional petition to ensure a good haul of high-quality driftwood in the coming year. So far as I knew, no northern god could fulfill such petitions.

But a southern god might. It turned out that the trees that reached us far in the north had grown in southern forests, beside southern rivers. By some chance they had fallen into the water and drifted to the sea, and if the right current took them, they would arrive eventually in the north. How to make this happen regularly, reliably? It took long years of investigation. Where were those trees coming from? What forests, what rivers, which currents? What circumstances brought a tree from Ard Vusktia to the icy northern sea? And once those questions had been answered, negotiation: What humans and gods could affect those circumstances? What would they want in exchange for doing so?

The Myriad was not the only northern god involved in the project, but involved she was. It was she who had first asked those questions and plotted a way to find answers. While I sat thinking for centuries, she spread out to the south, inquiring, suggesting meetings, convincing gods to come together and make joint agreements for the sake of providing a steady flow of wood to the far north. In the end agreements were made between two groups of gods: most of the major northern gods on one hand, and on the other a coalition of gods located in and around the northern shore of the Shoulder Sea. A predetermined number of trees would be felled and deliberately set afloat, and the gods of the south would be sure they made their way to the north. In return, the gods of the north would send south not only a share of the offerings of various northern peoples (including the Kaluet, and their seagoing cousins and neighbors who subsisted on seals and whales) but also loads of sealskins and obsidian.

"I suspect we have more treasures under the ice," the Myriad told me. "I have been thinking about what sorts of rocks are found where, and I wonder what we might find,

if we could only delve deeply enough in the right places."
But she was pleased with the deal she and others had
~~. . . . .~~ "It has been somewhat difficult for me to reach you

~~believe my current circumstances to be at this~~
moment."

"They may be, if all you wish for is to be a large stone
on a hillside," the Myriad said. "Don't you want to travel?
Wouldn't you like to see new things? I believe you like to
think about things, and ask yourself questions and ponder the answers. Moving about, meeting others, is a way
to learn things that might answer those questions and
enrich your pondering. In short, you may find you enjoy
it as much as you do staring at the sky. Perhaps even more
than that."

"Perhaps," I said. "But I'm not eager to make any long-
term commitments. And moving myself does take quite a
lot of power."

"Granted, that stone is heavy and difficult to move,"
agreed the Myriad. "You could always leave it for a more
portable sort of body. And it might even be one that would
make it easier for you to speak in a way that humans can
hear and understand."

"I'm comfortable as I am," I said. "I don't really like the idea of not being a stone, and I'm not sure how I would make it happen if I did want to."

"It's fairly simple," the Myriad told me. "Though I admit it can be disorienting the first time."

"And I don't believe it's much of a hardship to speak to humans as I am. In fact, there are some advantages to doing it the way I do. For instance, these people who are camped in the valley now. Even if I spoke in a voice they could hear"—which I could, with some effort—"they would not understand me. I don't speak their language. But one of them is carrying a full set of tokens, and she seems to know how to interpret them."

"But do you understand her when she speaks?" asked the Myriad.

"When she uses the tokens to communicate with me, yes. When she speaks aloud? A little." These new people had been camped below me for a week or so, at this point in the conversation. "A different body wouldn't necessarily help me with that."

"But travel would," the Myriad pointed out. "Their language is quite familiar to me because I haven't been apart from them all this time."

"There doesn't seem to be any need for hurry," I replied.

"There never does, to you," the Myriad agreed, amiably. "*Hurry* is not a word I associate with you at all."

"In this case, I may listen to them or not, as I wish. I

do quite well on my own. Which brings me to my second point."

The Myriad waited. And then, as she was relatively

been asked but have chosen not to do the thing I'm asked to do. I can do that with no risk, because I have made no commitments, no promises. The story about the spear point and the goose—was that something that actually happened?"

"I don't know," admitted the Myriad. "There are many implausibilities in the story as I heard it. But I knew the god in the story, and I have not seen or heard from him for long centuries. I suspect something like it happened, but I don't think it is likely to be accurate in all its details."

"A complicated promise," I said, "is a risky one. So many parts, so many people involved, and you don't always know who all those people are, or will be. And gods too. And the world does not stay the same. Things change. Slowly, it may be too slowly to perceive at the time, but things change all the same."

"True enough," replied the Myriad. "Well, do you wish to join the coalition of northern gods?"

"I am still thinking about that."

"I have never known you to be hasty," said the Myriad. "I believe all of us know enough of you to realize you won't decide anything without time and thought."

But I never did join. I was glad of the steady flow of wood, certainly, but my joining or not had no effect on that. I believe I missed out on some benefits—I seem to recall that the gods involved in the agreement were entitled to a larger share of the wood, and apportioned it among their favored worshippers. But it was rare for any human in that time and place to worship one god exclusively, and I never knew any of my own worshippers who did not also make offerings to far more prominent and powerful gods, most of whom were part of that coalition.

Still, it was that agreement over driftwood, and that coalition, that drew me into Ard Vusktia's war against the Raven of Iraden.

That evening you returned to Mawat's room and stood a moment, considering. That morning's tray, with the bowl of congealed porridge, was gone, and no other seemed to have taken its place. The corridor was empty but for you.

You knocked. "My lord," you said, in a conversational

The room was low ceilinged and dimly lit—the windows across the far wall were shuttered, only one partly open to shed some light without exposing the room to view. A high-backed chair with embroidered cushions, red and blue and yellow, sat facing the door, and beside it sat a small wooden table inlaid with ivory and gold. Woolen hangings covered the unwindowed walls, white and black and shot with gold thread that shone dully in the low light. A wooden bench alongside one of the hangings held the tray with the now-empty bowl of porridge, along with two or three other trays you hadn't seen before, but I imagine you had suspected their existence, or at any rate you evinced no surprise at seeing them.

"Where have you been?" Mawat asked you. "I've been waiting for you to come back."

"My lord," you acknowledged, with a slight bow of your head. "I was talking to people. Looking around."

"My father never fled," said Mawat. Not vehemently or angrily. Just matter-of-factly.

"No, my lord," you agreed. "He can't have gone out the gate. I can't imagine any bribe that would keep the gate guards silent all this time, with not even a whisper. And there are guards at the tower door besides."

"He couldn't have gone out of the tower," agreed Mawat. "Not without the tower servants knowing about it. And none of them would have helped him flee. The Raven's favor is granted in exchange for the Lease's life. To default on that debt..." Mawat turned, strode to the shuttered windows and back. "He never would." His voice was tight and vehement. "My father was no coward."

You looked at Mawat a moment, and then said, "My lord." And nothing more.

Mawat frowned. "I know that tone. Out with it."

"The lady Tikaz told me the sea side of the fortress is watched, but..."

"Tikaz told you!" Mawat laughed. "And when were you conversing with Tikaz?"

"I met her in the fortress yard, earlier, my lord."

"Well, this is something." Mawat was grinning. "So quiet and patient, but when you see what you want, you move, don't you." He waved away any potential protest or denial. "Well, you have as much of a chance with her as anyone. Better than I ever did with her, Raven knows. I wish you luck. I won't warn you to be careful of her, you'll already have seen that she can take care of herself. But you were saying?"

You took a deep breath, and then said, cautiously, "My don't know anything about tides."

"No, my lord," you agreed.

"*My father never fled.*" Mawat's voice was angry now.

"No, my lord," you repeated. "I'm just trying to find out how things stand. What's possible, what might have happened."

"And anyway," said Mawat, voice conversational again, though he was clearly still on edge, "where would he have gotten a boat? That no one saw, even though there are always ships and boats going back and forth in the strait?"

"My lord." Your voice was apologetic. "If I were charged with handling this situation, I would likely not want any foreign ships to realize what had happened. And given that, I would perhaps not be able to ask very many people directly what they might or might not have seen. Even posing the question indirectly hints at trouble in the fortress, and not every captain who sails through the strait is a friend of Iraden."

"I daresay most of them aren't," conceded Mawat. "And in any event, Hibal—I won't call him Lease, Raven take him." You winced to hear that. "He doesn't deserve that name. That's my father's place! And mine after!"

"Yes, my lord."

"Hibal must know what really happened. He's always been meddlesome. He wanted to be heir to the Lease, but my father was chosen instead. He's always 'consulting' with the Directions, urging them to counsel the Lease to change some policy or other he was sure *he* knew better about. Always saying sideways things to let everyone know when he thought matters would have gone better if only the Lease had done as he'd suggested. And now, so conveniently, he's on the bench. Oh, Hibal knows what's happened to my father, depend on it."

"My lord, might he have helped the Lease to flee? So that he could take his place?"

Mawat took a step toward you. *"My father never—"*

"Yes, my lord," you cut in. Somewhat to my surprise—I never knew Mawat to take that sort of thing well. "You yourself have told me that one doesn't win battles by planning for what one assumes or wishes to be true."

"I don't need you to tell me what I said!" Mawat snapped.

"No, my lord," you said shortly, and turned to go.

"Wait!" cried Mawat. You stopped but did not turn

back. "Apparently I do need you to tell me what I said. But, Eolo, *my father never fled.*"

"I'm sure not," you agreed, still not turning around.

"M...f..th...i...l...li...i...l...M...

...he had...," you began.

Mawat angrily cut your words short. "He must have had help, yes. Stalker surely helped him, it was worth her while to do it. Do you think it would be less worth the Raven's, to offer such opportunity to my father? Even with the god so distant, between Instruments, it's a small thing to provide a sharp edge, a weapon in reach, anything. And do you imagine that, offered that help, my father would have failed to *take it*? He was loyal to the Raven. He was the Lease, and he knew his duty." You said nothing, and after a moment Mawat continued, fierce and emphatic. "Will you tell me that some starved stripling managed to keep his word and sacrifice himself in the most unlikely circumstances, but my father, who had expected and prepared for this his whole life, would not? No, it's impossible. And Hibal could not sit on the bench if my father were still alive. My father is dead, and there is only one way the Raven's Lease can

die—he must sacrifice himself to the Raven. Anyone trying
to kill him—it's happened—anyone trying to kill him ends
up dead. It would take a god's power to kill the Lease before
his time, and even then, why do that, when his time was
mere days away? Which means no matter what Hibal did,
my father has died for the Raven, as he was meant to do. He
would never have let Hibal, of all people, stop him. No, this
isn't about my father. It's about the bench. Hibal has always
wanted my father's place. He has to be involved."

You frowned then, and turned around to face Mawat.
"But how did he manage it, whatever it was he did? And
why would your uncle be confirmed so quickly, when you
were nearly here?"

"It's risky between Instruments. Ordinarily anyone can
talk to the Raven, and he can speak to anyone he wishes,
but when he doesn't have a body to inhabit it's more complicated. Only a few people have the means to speak with
him at such times, and his replies or advice can be difficult
to decipher. He keeps commitments he's already made, of
course, but if there were some new crisis that required his
intervention, he might not help in time. And that's assuming we've kept our bargain with him and he was entirely
well disposed toward us. And what if..." Mawat stopped,
and took a breath. "What if the council could be convinced
that my father's supposed flight was planned somehow,
and I was involved? Or that I've inherited whatever weakness led my father to flee? Before long the fact of the Lease's

absence will be obvious to everyone, and now is not a time to appear weak. Hibal will have had some such argument ready for the Directions. Radihaw will have swallowed it

her assistance!"

"I don't understand," you said. "I don't understand why the Raven hasn't said anything. I know they said they asked…"

"*There will be a reckoning,*" Mawat quoted. "It's not exactly clear, is it? A reckoning for what?"

"That's what I don't understand. Why is it so difficult to talk to the Raven right now?"

"While the new Instrument is in the egg, he doesn't have a mouth to talk with, so getting an answer when you need it is a little complicated. Still, I would like to ask him myself."

"You said you had the right to do that."

"I do," Mawat agreed. "If I'm the heir. And Hibal said I was still the heir." He gave a bitter *ha*. "Still."

"Then ask him. The Raven surely knows what happened, and what's happening. He's got to give you more of an answer."

"No, he doesn't. Hibal sat on the bench and still lives. The Raven said long ago that only the Lease could do that, and what the Raven says is true, or his power makes it true."

"So Hibal is Lease," you said. "Let him be Lease. You're still heir. Let's go back and fight the Tel. Let Hibal die for the Raven."

"If anyone else had said that to me," said Mawat coldly, "he would be dead now. That place is *mine*. Hibal doesn't belong on that bench. What has he done to get there? And I'm to disgrace my father and prove myself useless, and watch as Hibal enjoys the privileges of the Lease?"

You said nothing. After a moment Mawat went over to the cushioned chair, sat heavily, and put his face in his hands. "I won't let him profit from this," he said after a while. "And Zezume!" He looked up, tears in his eyes. "She might as well have been my own mother." The woman who had given birth to Mawat had died doing it.

"I'm sorry, my lord," you said.

He wiped his eyes then. Shook his head. "But you. How have you been keeping? I threw you on your own resources, I'm sorry, but I couldn't trust myself even to speak these last two days. Has anyone in the hall given you trouble?" He waved you to sit on the bench, next to the trays with their empty dishes.

You sat. "Mother Zezume thought it unsuitable for me to stay in the hall. She gave me lodgings in the guesthouse right outside the gate."

"Where the Xulahns are staying?"

"Yes. They have a snake with them. It doesn't look like any snake I've ever seen."

the bench."

"Ha." Mawat, again bitterly amused. "They made friends with Hibal, and now he's on the bench, they were expecting him to give them whatever they wished, but they've been disappointed. It's the Council of the Directions preventing him, I suppose. You can have whatever you want, as Lease. Take nearly anything. But if it has to do with what the laws are, or trade, or war, the Directions will have their say. Well. I wonder what I can make out of that. Has anyone else sought you out?"

"My lord," you said, "the lord Direction Dera is staying in the same guesthouse."

Mawat frowned. "Did he recognize you? From Oenda, I mean?"

You hesitated. "I don't think so." And shook your head. "I don't think he'd have any reason to. He just said someone told him I sounded like I was from his district."

"Let me guess, he wanted to know if there was any

way he could be of service to me." You inclined your head, confirmation of his guess. "Dera and Radihaw have never liked each other. And neither Dera nor his home territory of Oenda is wealthy enough to outweigh Radihaw's authority. But of course, if he had the favor of the next Lease…" He shook his head. "Watch yourself with that one. They're feeding you, I suppose?"

You seemed unfazed by the sudden change of topic. "Yes, my lord."

"Then go have supper. If anyone asks, I'm still too upset to speak about this. But don't be surprised at anything I do in the next day or two. And whatever you do, don't tell anyone about these suspicions. Not even Tikaz!"

"You can rely on me, my lord."

"I know I can," he said. "Now go."

The Raven of Iraden is not from Iraden. That would be a strange thing to say in that first language I learned to understand. In Iradeni there are two words—one for belonging to or being a part of, and one for coming from somewhere.

It's not that the Kaluet and their cousins don't know the difference between those things. They assuredly do. But when they talk they slide back and forth between those meanings,

"belonging to" and "being a part of" aren't necessarily the same thing. Sometimes they are, certainly, but not always, and I wonder if I notice that only because this language is so different from my first, and I have had such a long, uninterrupted time to consider it.

In any event, it is as I've said. The Raven of Iraden is not, in fact, of Iraden. Where exactly he came from I don't know. Somewhere in the mountains to the south, I should imagine. He did not come from any part of the far north that I'm familiar with. But wherever he came from, I imagine it was someplace that did not offer the wealth or power his ambition demanded. Or perhaps something or someone made his former home less congenial to him. Drove him out, pushed him farther north.

Here is a story I have heard: The Raven, having decided to settle in what would become Vastai, sent his people there with orders to build a house, and a tower in which he might roost. And they, believing themselves protected by the powerful word of their god, arrived and set about building. The story says they began by taking axes to the largest trees in the nearby forest.

Can you hear me? At the very least I don't think you can understand me, or I'm certain you would have shivered when I said that, or even recoiled. The God of the Silent Forest has not spoken for decades. For at least a century. Indeed, that god may as well be dead, and some Iradeni have dared whisper the possibility, one to another, in secret. But never aloud. Almost no Iradeni quite dares to defy the God of the Silent, and those foolhardy enough to do so are silenced at the first opportunity. Such is that god's hold on your people, even now.

The influence of the God of the Silent stretched for miles down the coast of the Shoulder Sea, almost to the mountains, and well inland. At first it concerned itself only with what happened under and among its own trees. But the humans and smaller gods who eventually came to live in the forest's shadow could not afford to ignore the forest. First of all, as I'm sure you are already aware, humans use wood: for cooking and heat, for buildings, for record keeping, for storage, for boats, and more. And second, the boundary between inside the forest and outside it was— and is—always changing. What was safely outside might, in future years, be swallowed up. And people's attempts to prevent this, to define and maintain a boundary beyond which the forest would not grow, could and did elicit the wrath of the God of the Silent.

It was not a simple thing to come to an agreement and the god itself did very little that cost it much power, and so that god was strong with offerings without ever having to give much in return. The forest had no real reason to even respond to human petitions, let alone enter into a long conversation that might lead to future obligations on its part. But at long last a Mother of the Silent convinced the god that, powerful as it was with so little effort on its part, it might be yet more powerful, and hold its trees even more securely, if it would only make a single, small agreement.

As a result of that first agreement—that the forest might occasionally give permission for wood to be gathered and, occasionally, trees to be cut, at times and quantities the forest would dictate, in exchange for certain offerings and observances—the God of the Silent became stronger and more powerful, still at very little expense to itself, and the people living near the forest were safer and wealthier. Which of course led to more offerings and prayers, and, as the god realized just how much its power had increased, more agreements with the House of the Silent, and by extension the people of Iraden. The forest would protect the people of Iraden from stinging and biting insects—to a point, and only in exchange for regular offerings of blood. It also agreed to protect the people of Iraden from plagues, and various contagious diseases. It allowed a road to cut across it, with the understanding that anyone who strayed off the road without the god's permission was at the forest's mercy. It tolerated the construction of a town—what would become Vastai—on the shore of the Shoulder Sea, and let wood be cut for its first buildings. But it only ever spoke to the Mother of the Silent, and it was she who conveyed the god's wishes and requirements to the people of Iraden. And as the years went by, the people of Iraden were generous with grateful prayers and gifts, though they never lost their respectful fear of the forest. And the forest grew more and more powerful.

The newly arrived followers of the Raven had no regard for such things. They went into the trees with axes and saws and the presumed protection of their own god, and did not come out.

I imagine the Raven had thought the forest complacent. Perhaps he had tested its borders before this and gotten no very alarming response. And if you were to visit this land in those days, you might have thought it was a region of small-to-middling gods, each with their territory or specialty, each receiving a fair supply of offerings, but

none of them particularly notable. And then the forest—
an object of superstitious fear, certainly, but unless you
already knew to the contrary, you might not suspect the

sacrifices to that god were and are largely made in secret,
silence, and darkness.

Perhaps a more cautious, canny newcomer would have
thought twice before starting a war with a forest that all
the surrounding peoples held in superstitious dread. But
while the Raven can certainly be canny, I would say that
he is cautious only where he is compelled to be. And having clearly offended what was very likely the most powerful god for hundreds of miles around, he did not retreat, or
respond with anything but the brashest aggression: with a
word, he set fire to the trees.

The people of Vastai and the surrounding area had not
thought too much about new arrivals before this, either
humans or gods. They lived by the sea, near an adequate,
if small, harbor and in sight of another, busier one. Travel-
ers came and went all the time. Sometimes those travel-
ers stayed. New people were generally welcomed, along
with the goods they often brought, or the connections to

faraway places that fed the trade that helped make both Vastai and Ard Vusktia good places to live. And what was one more god, in the scheme of things? Ambitious gods were naturally attracted to places like Ard Vusktia and Vastai, and if those gods could provide the sorts of favors that would earn them steady offerings, well, so much the better for everyone. So the inhabitants of that older Vastai had likely wasted little thought on the arrival of the Raven and his followers. And they likely had not troubled themselves when those followers went into the forest with their axes, beyond warning them not to do it. The God of the Silent could take care of itself.

As indeed it did. Whole trees uprooted themselves and walked into the sea. That same sea rushed, roaring, up onto the shore and into the trees. Rivers large and small broke their banks and washed over the trees, and where that water did not reach, the fires simply ceased to burn. And when all that fire was contained and extinguished, the trees that had doused themselves in the sea walked again to their places, and sent their roots back down into the earth. These actions were, I am sure, more than just self-defense; they were a show of power. The Raven had presumed that he was stronger than the forest, that he could disregard it. The forest now showed the Raven his mistake.

And the next morning, the remaining inhabitants of the

Raven's house woke to find dozens of people sitting outside their gate, naked and smeared with ash. This might
not seem strange to you. You are, after all, Iradeni, and so

would be taken as a serious threat. But in Iraden, as in the
lands farther to the southwest, people in authority—kings,
lords, wealthy landowners—will sometimes go to impres-
sive lengths to appease complainants willing to do this, in
order to prevent damage to their reputation and standing.
It is, if not a common sight, a well-known and effective way
to shame someone who has dealt unjustly with another.
And so accordingly the Raven was shamed by this, or so
the story goes. I have my doubts. I suspect that the Raven
and the God of the Silent had each made their own cal-
culations. The forest's display of power, in extinguish-
ing the Raven's flames, would likely have left the Raven
finally aware of just how powerful the forest was. And
he no doubt recognized that he had no way of knowing
if the God of the Silent had spent all or most of its power
in this one spectacular display of it, or if there was far, far
more the forest could do to threaten the Raven. I am quite

certain the Raven now realized that he had gotten himself into a situation from which he might not be able to extricate himself with dignity.

The God of the Silent, for its part, had doused the fire, and might or might not have been able to do so a second time. Were I in the place of the God of the Silent I might have wanted to end the argument as quickly and with as little further damage to myself as possible. Were I in the place of the God of the Silent, I would have said to the Raven, *I can outlast you.*

Whatever communications passed between the Raven and the God of the Silent, in the end they came to an agreement. Even then, as you no doubt already know, the Tel pressed at the southern boundaries of Iraden; so they agreed the Raven would assist in the defense of those boundaries. The Raven would also assist the Silent Forest in its existing commitments to the people of Iraden. As part of this agreement the Raven—now the Raven of Iraden—would be due a periodic human sacrifice. That sacrifice would come from among the descendants of the Raven's followers.

I speak of course of the Lease. In exchange for the Lease's voluntary sacrifice, he would share authority over Iraden with the Council of the Directions. And to be sure that authority was indeed shared, and no doubt because the God of the Silent (or at any rate its representative) was no fool, the Mother of Vastai's Silent must approve the appointment of any new Lease, and she must have the right to speak to the Lease for the God of the Silent—and to speak to the Raven of Iraden directly.

the bench. And in the meantime, Iraden would benefit from the Raven's power. He had, after all, dared to attack the forest and still lived, which suggested that the forest either dared not or could not retaliate by merely striking him dead.

And the Raven did not plan to sit secure in Vastai. He had ambitions. Ambitions that centered on the strait between Vastai and Ard Vusktia.

By this time Ard Vusktia was a thriving town. Ships and boats passed daily through the strait, from the Shoulder Sea into the wider ocean and back, bringing goods and people. Ard Vusktia was home to quite a few powerful gods, and even more who were less powerful but who for the most part lived well, granting a steady flow of small favors in return for similarly small prayers and offerings. I daresay the gods of Ard Vusktia had found long ago that things were better for everyone when gods cooperated and when humans followed suit. There was no single god of

Ard Vusktia, no one supreme power. Why would there need to be?

But the Raven did not, when he looked at the strait, see a bounty in which he might take a share. No, the Raven looked at the strait and saw that all of its riches might be taken for himself.

The Strait of Ard Vusktia is one of the very few navigable outlets to the ocean from the Shoulder Sea. Nearly every ship that wants to make that voyage must pass through that strait. And if you can control the strait, you can control that traffic, and even take a cut of that trade all for yourself. I am sure the Raven of Iraden had settled in Vastai with precisely that aim in mind.

I don't know how much work he had to do to convince the God of the Silent to assist him in that project, but assist him that god assuredly did. And according to the story I have heard, it began very simply: once two or three Leases had been paid, the Raven simply stated that henceforth no ship or boat would safely traverse the strait without the approval of the Raven of Iraden.

So simple, for a god! Speak what one wishes to be true and your power will make it so! But so many simple statements stand before a reality that is not simple at all. Only the most powerful gods may rely on stating their wishes so sweepingly. The insufficiently powerful, and insufficiently wise, run great risks in speaking this way.

I think the Raven knew this. I am given to understand

that he made sure to obtain the assistance of not only the forest, but most of the other, smaller gods in Iraden before he spoke. And I am sure he also appraised the com-

So far as I could tell, you slept soundly in your room on the upper floor of the guesthouse outside the gates of the fortress in Vastai, until you were awakened by a furious pounding on your door. The moment the first knock sounded you were on your feet, reaching for your knife, cloak cast aside. You stared wide-eyed at the door, and then shouted, "Who is it? What do you want?"

The pounding stopped. "Eolo!" Did you recognize the voice? Or had you heard it too few times yet to know who it was? "Eolo! Wake up, child! I need to speak to you!"

You hesitated a moment, sheathed your knife, pulled your cloak around you, and opened the door, to find Mother Zezume. "I'm awake, Mother," you said.

"You need to talk to Mawat."

"Excuse me, Mother," you replied. "I don't understand."

"He listens to you, doesn't he? You said that he doesn't sulk in the field, and he brought you here with him and no one else. You must know how to talk to him."

"I still don't understand, Mother," you said, polite but clearly confused. Your heart must still have been pounding from the sudden noise moments before. "Why is it suddenly urgent that he come out of his room?"

"Oh, he's come out of his room!" exclaimed Zezume. "That's not the problem. He was always going to come out sometime, he always does. The problem is"—she lowered her voice—"what he's doing now he's come out."

"I still don't understand you, Mother," you admitted. "Surely the lord Mawat will send for me if he needs me."

"*I* am sending for you," Zezume snapped. "Go down into the square and talk to Mawat. Tell him he's being ridiculous and the Lease won't put up with his foolishness for long. Tell him whatever it is you usually tell him to stop him sulking like this!"

You appeared to think about this for a few moments. "Where is the lord Mawat?"

Zezume closed her eyes and took a long, frustrated breath. "I've just told you where he is. He's in the square outside, in front of the fortress gate." And then, sardonically, "You can't miss him."

You said, with a small bow, "I'll be downstairs in a moment."

Zezume looked at first as though that was not soon

snake—and you pushed your way through to find that people had gathered all around the edges of the square, to stare at Mawat, sitting naked on the ground.

Although Zezume had told you that Mawat was sitting in front of the fortress gate, this wasn't precisely true. He was in actual fact sitting in the middle of the square. The object of this sort of action, as I understand it, being not to block or otherwise hinder traffic in and out of a place, but rather to be sure everyone who goes through that gate sees one, and knows what one's presence means.

You walked up to him. "My lord," you said. "Good morning. Mother Zezume asked me to speak to you."

"What did Mother Zezume wish you to say?" Mawat asked, not looking at you but staring blankly ahead. The morning air was chill, and his skin was pricked with goose bumps.

"She said to tell you that you're being ridiculous, and

that—forgive me, my lord, I only report her words—that the Lease won't put up with your foolishness for long. And she bade me say whatever I generally say to you to stop you sulking in the field."

"You are a faithful messenger," Mawat said, with a trace of bitterness.

"I do my best, my lord."

"I know you do." Mawat's voice was gentler now, though there was no change in the expression on his face.

"My lord, Mother Zezume is right. Your uncle can't tolerate this for long."

"How generous of her to warn me." The bitterness was back in his voice. "You'd better go back in and have your breakfast. I'm sure you'll be extra popular today."

"My lord," you said, and went back to the lodging house.

You made your morning prayers, and took your morning's bread and beer and went to sit at one of the polished wooden tables, pulled out again now it was day and everyone awake. As you had the day before, you chose a seat from which you could easily see the door to the outside, the kitchen entrance, and the stairs, and you sat with your back to the wall. You ate in silence. A few people came back in from the square outside and sat down to their own meals, casting sidelong glances at you, speaking quietly to each other.

One of the Xulahns came in then, the one who had

spoken to you yesterday. "Good morning," the Xulahn said, walking up to where you sat. Everyone else in the room tried hard not to look as though they were staring at

You chewed, deliberately. Swallowed. Took a swig of beer. "Eolo," you said finally.

"Eolo," Dupesu said with a smile. "Eolo, assistance to the Prince Mawat."

"That's not a word in Iradeni," you said. "*Prince* is a Tel thing."

"Ah, you are still help practice Iradeni, thank you, Eolo!"

"Don't mention it." You took another bite of bread.

"The... What is the good name, then?"

"The Lease's Heir."

Dupesu leaned his elbows on the dark wood of the table. "The Lease's Heir Mawat. He does a strange thing. Our guide tells that this is force the king—excuse, I beg, *king* is also a Tel thing?"

"Yes," you said, shortly.

"The Lease? This is force the Lease to do a public thing? Is this yes? What is the Lease's Heir wish?"

"You'd have to ask him."

"But I am not known him," explained Dupesu in apparent dismay. "I am talk to you. And you are talk to the... the Lease's Heir soon past. Tell me, friend Eolo, why is the Lease's Heir sit naked in the square? It is a complaining, yes, but complain what?"

"As I said. You'd have to ask him."

"I am hear, friend Eolo, that something is wrong. That the king—no, you say the Lease, yes—that the old Lease is not have a, what do you say when someone dies..."

"A funeral," you supplied.

"A funeral. The old Lease is not have a funeral. There is a new Lease—I know it is so. I am in Vastai for days and days and the Lease is not see us. Now the Lease is see us—once—and this man who is the Lease is not the Lease before."

"You know this," you suggested, "because you had met with the lord Hibal before, and he was not the Lease at that time."

"Just so!" Dupesu agreed. "I am met the lord Hibal, the brother of the Lease. I am hope he can tell the Lease, *You should see these Xulahns!* And I am think it work and we are go in to see the Lease and... the Lease is Hibal!"

You did not reply to this.

"The lord Mawat is the Lease's Heir at that time. But he is not Lease now. Still he is Lease's Heir. Is that, friend Eolo, why the lord Mawat is sit on the ground outside? What is he expect happen from this?"

"Were you surprised that Hibal was Lease, then?" you

Lease is die soon, but already is a new Lease! And there is no funeral for the old Lease, and I am think everyone is not want to talk about that."

You finished the last of your bread, washed it down with the last swallows of your beer. "I don't want to talk about it either."

"Your lord is *make* everyone talk about it," Dupesu pointed out. "I am think even you he wish to talk about it. A thing is strange about this new Lease. Is there not a promise with the Raven of Iraden? The Lease may do as he likes until the god's bird dies, and then the Lease must die. We are hear of it, it is not a thing that happens in a secret. The tower of Vastai wears black, all of Iraden is at a funeral. Our guide says you carry the king's body in the street when he is dead and the heir walks along. And everyone makes offerings, and a feast. But there is no funeral, no body in the street, no feast, and still there is a new Lease, and it is not Mawat. I am think something is happen that is strange, but why is the Raven of Iraden do nothing?"

"Ask the Raven of Iraden," you said.

"Ah, we are try! The Raven of Iraden will not speak to us. But I am think the Lease's Heir Mawat is treated badly in this, and I am think he agrees and is wish to change this. He is naked outside and everyone must see what is happen. Everyone must ask why is this. And the Lease Hibal must answer or seem wrong, yes?"

"Tell me," you said, "is there one of you missing?"

"What?" Dupesu seemed puzzled by your question.

"Where is the man who interpreted for you the other day?"

"He is gone away," acknowledged Dupesu. "He is afraid here, we are wait so long, and he will not stay. He is say he is safer away." He took his elbows off the table and leaned back. "We are try pray to the Raven and offer gifts direct but the Raven is not answer. And this is a question for Prince Mawat as well. Why does the Raven nothing? Why is the heir must sit naked before the fortress gates to complain of this wrong, to tell the people, to make Lease Hibal to deal with his complain? Why is he not complain to the Raven himself? Where is the god of Iraden?"

"Wherever he wishes to be, I suppose," you said.

"Is it not strange," observed Dupesu, "that he is not here now and I am think he might be needed?" From under his collar, the snake's tongue flickered out and then back, no other sign of the snake itself but a bulge under the fabric of his tunic.

"Excuse me," you said, rising. "I have business to

Mawat still sat in the middle of the square. People still stood around the edges, but fewer than before. Others walked through, apparently on ordinary business, some staring at Mawat as they passed, some affecting to ignore him.

He still stared ahead. And Tikaz stood beside him.

"I'm impressed," she was saying as you came up. "You're going to be the only person I know who dies of cold and gets sunburned in very delicate areas at the same time." Mawat didn't answer her. "Whatever do you think you're doing?"

"What does it look like I'm doing?" Though he spoke to her he still did not look at her. "Why are you here?"

"My father told me to tell you I'd sleep with you if you'd stop this nonsense."

"I see no nonsense," Mawat said. "If this were nonsense,

my uncle would not have sent his chief counselor to stop me. Nor, for that matter, would the Mother of the Silent have tried to send Eolo to dissuade me."

Tikaz turned to look at you. "It's you again, then, is it?"

"Good morning, lady," you said.

Without answering you, she turned back to Mawat. Said, in an even quieter voice than she had been using, "I know what you're doing. Everyone knows what you're doing. But it won't do any good. Hibal is seated on the bench and there's no changing that."

"My father never fled," said Mawat. The hint of a shiver in his voice, likely the cold. "My father never fled and his brother sits on the bench as though he belongs there. And no one says or does anything about it. Well, I will do something about it."

"No one wants to think about it," Tikaz replied, angrily. "No one wants to think about what the Raven will do if the Lease isn't paid as promised. Everyone just wants things to go forward as they always have. There isn't anyone in Vastai who will thank you for making it impossible not to ask those questions."

"We've known each other since we were small," replied Mawat. "I'd think you'd understand me by now."

"Oh, I understand you!" Tikaz was clearly angry, but still keeping her voice hushed. "Everything's fine until *you* get angry, and then it's all about you being angry. Don't you know, sometimes you need to stop and wait? Sometimes you need to think before you jump into something. You expected to take the bench. Hibal took it instead. With the support of the Directions and the Silent, so you can't just

~~1~~ ~~~~ "

The Lease is paid!" insisted Mawat. "My father never fled, and he'll have found a way to pay what he owes, no matter what Hibal did to stop him. And if Hibal truly believes the Lease is unpaid, he should pay it now, himself." Loudly enough for a bystander to hear, and put a hand to her mouth and hurry away. If the guards at the fortress gate heard, they did not show any sign of it.

"Maybe he means to," you suggested. "Maybe he's only stepped up so he can make the payment in the next few weeks, in place of his brother."

Tikaz rolled her eyes. "Who, him?"

"If he meant to, he would have said so," Mawat pointed out. "If he meant to pay this time, the flags would be flying from the tower and preparations would be underway. Instead he's trying to pretend like nothing has happened. And the Directions and the Silent are going along with it! Why?"

"Why, indeed." Tikaz folded her arms. "You might

want to ask that question before you do anything drastic. More drastic than what you already have done, and honestly I'm not sure what that would be."

"I will make everyone ask the question," replied Mawat. "I will make Hibal answer it."

"If you don't die of cold overnight," said Tikaz.

Mawat shrugged. The sun had risen further over the rooftops and warmed the stones around him, and Mawat himself, just a bit. "Eolo will bring me a blanket when the sun goes down."

"Yes, my lord," you said.

Vastai is full of people. And so, of course, it is also full of drama and interest. If, that is, you are interested in humans. I have been interested in humans since I learned to speak with them—though I did not realize that until somewhat recently. But since I realized it, I have wondered why that might be. Was it because they had fed me? Was it because, now that I was able to speak to them, they seemed extra worthy of my attention, as though I had finally found another being in some way like myself and was no longer

so alone? Or was it perhaps that their speaking to me—
taking so much time to teach me to understand and speak
in my own turn—made them so unusual in my experi-
~~...~~ ~~...~~ ~~...~~ ~~to speak~~, ~~the Kaluet~~

to me, I still find them interesting. ~~The tower of the~~
fortress, the town surrounding it, provide a surfeit of activ-
ity and conversation, of triumphs and defeats. I watch,
and listen, and learn. And of course I have good reason
to pay close attention to certain people: the Raven's Lease,
for instance, whoever that may be. And his heir. People
whose small dramas will affect nearly everyone in Vastai,
if not Iraden, and will potentially affect me quite directly.
And so I do not wonder why I pay such close attention to
them.

But you. I cannot explain why I find myself so fascinated by you, why I feel the need to tell you these things,
even though I strongly suspect you cannot understand
me, perhaps cannot even hear me. You came riding out
of the forest, stiff and uneasy in the saddle beside Mawat,
who sat his horse as though he had been riding since he
could walk, as indeed was the case, and at first I noticed
only Mawat. Of course I did—I knew that a messenger had

been sent for him, and I knew what awaited him in the fortress. Knew that even if Mawat had been the sort of person to take this situation with patience and quiet equanimity, the next few hours would be full of distress and anger. And Mawat had never been the sort of person to take any situation with patience or quiet equanimity. You—I did not recognize you. Perhaps you were a servant. But when I looked closer, heard you and Mawat speak, I realized you could not be merely a servant. For one thing, though you sat your horse like a farmer, and sounded like one, your bearing, your weapons, and even your small bit of gold suggested that you were in fact a soldier. And for another, Mawat clearly trusted you. Had wanted, I suspect, to ride alone, knowing he rode toward his father's death and the promise of his own, defined, fixed, and unignorable. But he did not ride alone. He rode with you. And furthermore spoke to you as though he did not resent your presence. As though you were his friend—or as close a thing to a friend as someone like Mawat can have.

And why you? To judge by your manner and accent, you are the child of a reasonably prosperous farmer, and no doubt many such run away hoping to find glory (or wealth) in battle, or else they find themselves on the battlefield through chance, or conscription. They do not, as a rule, find themselves the confidant of the heir to the bench in Vastai.

These days, the people closest to me are the ones I know

the best. I have long understood in a vague and general way how human bodies are put together, how they work—when they work—and some of the most obvious ways

tle and sudden stillness of death. I have heard anguished cries alternately begging and cursing a god who seems not to hear, the chafe of bound wrists turning bloody and blistered. I have seen these things, and thought about them, what they imply. What they mean.

I don't know your thoughts or your feelings, but I can guess. I can guess what it means that you stop and stare at Tikaz the way you do. What might be happening when Mawat speaks and why you follow him.

I might understand more if I were one of those gods who took another form. There were—and are—gods who find it useful or pleasant to inhabit animal bodies. This, the Myriad informed me, can be done well and deftly, or it can be rough and careless, ultimately injuring or killing the subject. The more one understands about one's chosen vessel, the more successful such a possession will be. I suspect that, in addition to individual taste and inclination, this is why so many gods in my experience seem to choose the same sort of form over and over; the Myriad and her swarm of mosquitoes, for instance. Or the Raven of Iraden.

The safest way to do it, or so I'm told, is also the most laborious—to lay claim to a creature in embryo and so be present as it grows. It is entirely possible to enter a more or less full-grown body, but I am told this requires more power, and skill and practice.

This had never interested me. I was content to be a stone on a hillside. To watch and listen.

I watch and listen still. I hear every word uttered in the fortress of Vastai, and nearly all in the town. I can tell you, if you should wish to know, the number of rats in the fortress and even how many fleas are carried by those rats. I knew when Mawat was born, and his father before him. I have seen and heard the private moments of all who have lived within these walls, and I have had time to think about what I see and what I hear. I have learned a great deal.

I can guess that at some point relatively recently your shoulder was injured—you don't raise your left arm as often as I might expect you to, and when you do you move only in particular ways. I can also see that you are, for the most part, good at concealing the most obvious of your reactions, though traces can still be seen—a catch of breath when something jars your shoulder; a tight, displeased quirk of your mouth when someone has angered you. The flash of fear across your face. I can see all of these things, can guess what they mean. I have very little else to do, and I have always watched and listened and pondered, and besides, the Raven Tower of Vastai is made of stone.

When the Raven of Iraden spoke his authority over the strait, the effect on the gods of Ard Vusktia was immediate and dramatic, or so I am told. But it took months for anyone in the north to become concerned. After all, it did not matter to the Kaluet—or their neighbors—who it was who bought their narwhal tusks, jadeite, or carefully hunted white fox furs. There were more important concerns for all of us—for the various peoples of the far north there was the urgent business of preparing for winter, lest it be the last they saw, and gods and humans both had their own relationships with each other to manage, their own claims to food and territory to sort out, their own feuds to prosecute.

But over the centuries that I had sat alone in the ice, waiting for humans to return, those furs and tusks and stone had been steadily flowing southward in exchange for metal knife blades and swords, bronze cooking vessels, and fine painted pottery. And even I, who did not yet fully understand the new-to-me language of the Kaluet, sitting alone on my hillside, thinking my slow thoughts—even I could see that people dressed differently from those I had known formerly, and carried different tools. Coats were embroidered with glass beads—brilliant blues and greens and oranges—or bright-colored thread. These had come through Ard Vusktia. An indication, in fact, of how very freely goods and people flowed from there to the north. And while the beads and the dyed threads were largely vanities—take them away and there would be new ways to decorate clothes, new styles—the knives and the cooking pots had made life a good deal easier, and would be difficult to give up, if the supply ever ceased.

But why should that supply cease? Even when news of the dispute over the strait reached us, very few imagined that we would be affected. Whoever occupied the strait would doubtless want high-quality white fox fur, and whale teeth, and there was no reason they would not continue to trade bright bits of glass and thread, and knives and metal pans to get them. Why should Ard Vusktia's local affairs matter, so far away?

For months this seemed entirely reasonable. Every now and then I would hear news from Ard Vusktia, attenuated almost to incomprehensibility by time and distance: The gods of Ard Vusktia had struck back at the Raven with a speech of their own, contradicting his. This the Raven had survived, despite the unlikelihood of his having enough power on his own to stand up to the gods assembled against him. Clearly he had allies who were helping him,

harbors, not for the open ocean but back to the Shoulder Sea, to wait until the matter was resolved and travel safer. Some of those ships carried goods that now would not find their way into the hands of the northern peoples.

Many of my fellow northern gods were concerned by this news. The gods who had been drawn into the struggle against Vastai had, themselves, relationships and agreements with gods farther away, who had agreements with other gods, and those with still others, in a web that reached all the way to my own hillside, and yet farther, to the ice-rimmed arctic sea. Many southern associates of the Myriad sent word asking for her assistance, expressing their anxieties about the ultimate aim of the Raven's ambitions, worried by the thought that he had far more power than anyone on the Ard Vusktia side of the strait had ever suspected.

But they were closer to Vastai than we were. In the end, we were sure, no matter who ruled Ard Vusktia or Vastai, the traders would return to Ard Vusktia, and would want those furs and stones again.

The winter came, and I was alone again on my hillside, watching the sky, the pleasant and satisfying rounds of the sun and the stars. At length warmer weather brought the Kaluet back. Distraught. The conflict between Vastai and Ard Vusktia showed no signs of resolution. And spring had come with barely any usable wood washing ashore in the places it should have. There were, it was true, a few stunted willows growing near my hillside, but not enough to support the needs of the Kaluet, and they had become used to trading for driftwood with the people who lived on the shore of the sea. But there would be none this year, or, likely, the next.

You are, I think, an experienced soldier. If you have understood my story, you will doubtless have anticipated this turn of events. As the gods' stalemate over the strait stretched out, each side sent boats and soldiers against the other. Boats were nearly always built at least partially of wood, and the soldiers required bows, arrows, spears, swords, and knives, all of which either had some wooden parts or were made and shaped with fire. Agreement or not, there was no wood to spare. Of course, the sooner the fight was over, the sooner the north could have its supply of wood again. And thus many of the gods and the humans of the far north began to seriously consider going to war.

But not all, not even every god concerned in the

agreements that had brought wood so unfailingly and abundantly to northern shores. I myself had no pressing reason to go. At the worst, most of the humans who traveled

if no people came at all, well, I would (I had to admit) miss them, but I had been fine without humans for so very, very long that I did not fear being without them again.

I told the Myriad so. She gave a distressed buzzing whine, and said, "Do you think you stand apart? Do you think that because this place is so remote and rarely visited that what happens elsewhere will not affect you?"

"I did not say so," I replied. "Only that I expected that if these humans ceased to visit me, my life would be affected only in inconsequential ways."

"You may expect that," the Myriad said. "And you may be wrong."

"I am used to being alone." I had thought the Myriad was as well, but it may be I was mistaken.

"You may never be truly alone again," retorted the Myriad. "Perhaps you never were. This world we inhabit may seem large, full of unimaginably wide spaces, but from above one sees that it is a tiny island in the vastness of the wider universe. From where we are now, it may seem that Ard Vusktia is too far away for its affairs to trouble us, and indeed were we to set out now for the shore of the Shoulder Sea—you in a wagon, let us say, and myself riding and flying along—it would take us weeks or even months to reach it."

"So I have heard," I agreed.

"But," continued the Myriad, "were I to send a message— not go myself, you understand, but tell the right person that I wished my words or some news to be passed to a god in Ard Vusktia—my words might travel from here to there in a matter of days."

"You yourself had a hand in making it so," I pointed out. "This business with the wood and the metal is, I suspect, largely of your own making. I believe that if not for that, events in Ard Vusktia would have a good deal less effect on people here.

"And what do I care if wood or metal becomes scarce again? If the people who visit me find they cannot live here without those things, well, I am sure they must do whatever they think best, but I do not think it will trouble me. Things change. People come and go. I have always been sufficient for myself." Though, I had to admit, learning that there were others somewhat like me, with whom I could communicate, had added something pleasant and secure to my solitude. "I like offerings," I admitted. "And prayers. But I have no great need of them that I can see. Let the people go where they think best. I believe I will be fine regardless.

"Perhaps you would," agreed the Myriad. "Other gods,

again. The war between Ard Vusktia and Vastai will end one way or another. The Raven of Iraden will be defeated or he will be victorious. I have no doubt the specific outcome is of great concern to any number of people. I do not doubt that it matters to you, though I am convinced that its importance to you is entirely a matter of your having made it so yourself. But I am a stone on a hillside. I have been one since before Ard Vusktia existed. Before *humans* existed. Why should that change because one god rather than another lays claim to some water?"

The Myriad was silent. Then at length she said, "I also was alone for a very long time. My first remembered sight of this world was of a distant, water-covered rock, and this did not change for so many of my long circuits. I did not even imagine the possibility that anyone—god or otherwise—might be found here. I did not wonder whether there was anyone else in the universe like me. I circuited merely, around and around the sun, and never sought to question, or wonder, or change my circumstances. But let me tell you what I saw before I fell to earth! I saw two rocks collide, so far away from this world that it might seem no more than a bright speck, and one of those rocks might have passed silently by this world on yet another long trip around the sun, and yet because of that collision thousands of years ago and so very far away, it tumbled to earth instead. And I thought to myself that if I knew enough, if I had enough pieces of that puzzle, I could see what will happen and when, across those unspeakable distances, across those many thousands of years. Things change—you and I are both old enough to know it. But not all changes are inconsequential to us."

"Perhaps not," I agreed. "But consequential for us is not the same as bad for us. And even if it were, even bad conditions pass eventually."

"We gods are usually long-lived enough to see that happen," the Myriad agreed.

While we had been talking the sun had gone down, and the tents of the people flashed now and then as the flaps were raised and lowered, people coming and going. Occasionally a reindeer grunted into the quiet darkness, or took one or two clicking steps. The Myriad landed atop me and sat silent a moment. The stars stood bright now in the dark sky. I have heard them compared to jewels, but they do not seem like jewels to me. Gemstones may come in many colors, bright or subtle, and can flash prettily enough, but a star's fire is its own. Excepting, of course, those few that are not stars but balls of rock like the one on which we live, and that were they closer or larger would appear to us as

moments a ...

coming slowly up the hillside path toward me.

"The question is not," said the Myriad, "whether distant events will affect us. This is not truly a question—they can, and have and will. Nor is the question how we will be affected. One can make any number of careful and informed guesses, but until events occur any predictions are subject to error, to the extent that one's information, or one's understanding, may be incomplete."

"I daresay one's information and even understanding are bound to be incomplete," I remarked. "The universe being so wide, and containing so much."

"Yes," agreed the Myriad. "The relevant question here, it seems to me, is not any of those things. It is, rather, *Do you care?*"

The priest came before us, then. Set down the tiny lamp she carried, and prostrated herself. "O Strength and Patience!" she said. "Stable and solid! On whom can we rely but you?"

"She has not come to chat," I remarked to the Myriad.

"Do priests generally come up here to chat with you?" she asked.

"This one does." This priest had been born below my hillside, and since she was small she had liked to come up to where I sat and talk to me. At first she had babbled, nonsense syllables imitating the rise and fall of speech, or held up some leaf or rock she had found, as if to show it to me. As she grew older, and her speech clear, she would sit down next to me and say whatever came into her head as we looked down at the camp—what she had had for breakfast, what her mother had said the night before, what the clouds looked like that day. Or she would sit companionably silent. No one in the camp was surprised when she showed signs of becoming a priest, though the person to whom she went for instruction was, I am told, astonished to find that she could already read the tokens—she had taught herself, just watching and listening. And even after her training, she approached me as she always had, walking up the hill to sit and lean against me and talk, sometimes about the needs or requests of those in the camp, sometimes about inconsequential things. "In a hopeless moment," continued the priest, who had not heard the Myriad, or me, "it is you we turn to. When all other gods fail us, you do not."

"Flattery," I said to the Myriad. "And she's following all the forms. She does not, generally, not with me. She wants something delicate or difficult, I suppose."

The priest rose and bowed three times, saying again, "O Strength and Patience!" Then she knelt, and with her steel striker—that had come from the south, almost cer-

she said, still kneeling, and she took a handful of polished tokens from out of the bag. Sorted through them until she found the several she searched for, and as she lay them down on the ground before her, said aloud, "Strength and Patience! Foundation of the Earth! Surely you know that gods are quarreling in the south. And what gods do among themselves is their own business, but this quarrel has deprived us of metal and glass. There is furthermore a shortage of wood. Even sticks cannot be found, for the trees they might have fallen from were cut down last year." As she spoke she lay down the corresponding tokens, that would convey her meaning in that first language of mine—or some approximation of it, since she did not speak that language herself. Could only roughly convey by their means what she more eloquently spoke aloud. "But what little we now have, the Tsokch of the coast would take from us! They raided a camp on the river, northeast of here. You know the people who stayed there, many of them visit us regularly every summer. The Tsokch took everything, every scrap of wood, every fire striker, everything down to the last steel needle. They killed everyone in the camp; only some girls out gathering eggs escaped, and came to us this morning.

"It seems to me," the priest continued, "that this has been caused by the same shortages I have just mentioned. They needed those same things we do, and because of the quarrel in the south there were none to trade for, or gift. And so they took them."

She took a few moments to clear the tokens before her and re-sort them in her hands. "It seems to me," she continued then, laying tokens down in a fresh arrangement, "that this will continue so long as matters in the south remain as they are."

"They might do as their forebears did," I suggested to the Myriad, "and make needles of bone, and knives and spearheads of obsidian, and cooking vessels and hearths of soapstone." The priest hesitated—she might or might not have heard me. I was not trying to be heard by human ears.

"Bone needles break more easily," replied the Myriad. "And moreover take time to make, time that might be more profitably spent otherwise. The same for knives and spearheads. As for hearths and cooking vessels—an iron firebox does not crack under a flame's heat, nor an iron kettle. Which is, moreover, a good deal lighter and easier to travel with. I never knew a dog or a bear to chew through a metal storage box, and metal fishhooks, like metal needles, break far less often than their bone counterparts. Small wonder

heard something but had not understood it. "O Strength and Patience! O Foundation of the Earth! This is my question." Again she swept away the tokens before her, again began once more to lay them out, slowly, each one carefully chosen. "When will this dispute in the south end and trade be restored?"

"Why do they ask me questions like that?" I wondered, to the Myriad. "I don't necessarily know the future any more than they do. How can I answer such questions at all usefully?"

"They believe you already have," replied the Myriad. "I have heard several times of people calling on you and receiving accurate and helpful answers, even though you were so distant, though no one had visited you for a hundred years or more. Watch, and perhaps we shall see how it happens."

The priest swept all the tokens into the bag, and shook it, then let one tumble out of the bag's mouth onto the ground. Then another, and another, until a haphazard row of them lay before her, gleaming faintly in the small lamplight.

"Bear," she read. "Toward a bear? Under twice. A question regarding grass that is above at some time between underneath a white... thing?" She sat back on her heels. "What does it mean?" she muttered.

"Has she not learned better than this?" I asked. I confess I was surprised. Always when I had spoken to her before I had given clear answers that she had understood more or less easily. It seemed quite obvious to me that the assortment of tokens on the ground was no answer at all.

"I think she has been accustomed to such results many times in her life," said the Myriad. "Among the people who know how to use these tokens you are reputed to answer infallibly, if nearly always somewhat cryptically. The skill, they say, lies not only in reading the tokens but understanding what you mean by them."

"But I have always to my knowledge spoken quite plainly to this person," I argued. Somewhat foolishly, I admit, since the Myriad was certainly telling the truth. "And the same with the priest before her."

The Myriad said, "And when you choose not to speak, or when you cannot reply because you have not even heard the question, some arrangement of tokens is dealt out anyway. If the petitioner is in your presence they may question you further and thus learn that an answer that is clearly nonsense is no answer at all. But people have been speaking to you this way for hundreds of years, speaking where you almost certainly would not have heard them,

them all this time, then?" I asked. "Even when they are nowhere near me and cannot reasonably expect me to have heard them, let alone understood them?"

"Some of them."

"No!" The priest looked up from her study of the tokens, frowning. "No, this is not an answer."

"Ah!" I said, to the Myriad. "I was sure that after dealing with me for so long she must know better." I felt obscurely vindicated, and relieved. "Look!"

The priest swept the tokens again into the bag. "Was that an answer?" Tipped new ones out of the bag and read them. *It was not.* She looked up at me, astonished. "But why?"

I don't answer that sort of question, I told her, by means of the tokens. *I thought you understood that. I don't foretell the future, except in the way that anyone does.*

"But you do!" insisted the priest. In her consternation forgetting to lay out her words in the tokens. "I've seen it many times!"

No, I replied, the tokens tumbling out of the bag to lie before her. *You have not.*

She thought about that for a while, frowning. "But then," she said, at last, "have you heard anyone who speaks to you, who is not here before you?"

Some, I replied. *After a fashion. I can feel when someone makes an offering, and sometimes I can feel a petition.* I did not say so, but suspected that I heard only those petitions that were enclosed in a prayer, or explicitly connected to an offering.

"Other gods can hear when people address them from far away," the priest objected.

"Some other gods," said the Myriad, "make an effort to do so. I do. This one does not."

Still kneeling, the priest bowed low. "Kind and merciful one," she said. "I did not know you were here or I would have made an offering."

"I don't think I would know how to make such an effort," I said, to the Myriad.

To the priest, the Myriad said, "I am seen when I wish to be seen. Why are you here in the dark, devoted one?"

The priest hesitated. "Surely you know, merciful one. But I suppose you want me to say it. Since the girls from the River Camp arrived, there has been talk of revenge. I understand why, and even if I didn't I won't be able to stop people from going north to kill what Tsokch they find. But what can the results of such an expedition possibly be, except disastrous? Will the Tsokch not take revenge in their turn? And is it possible that gods will not involve themselves? We all have gods we favor, who favor us. Will

with your own theft and murder, do not ask for me to approve it."

"Some," agreed the priest. "But perhaps they would not, or perhaps as time went on they would be drawn in despite that."

"I don't imagine the Drowned One cares much about feuds on land," I said to the Myriad. And to the priest, by way of tokens, *I was under the impression that such matters as robbery and murder were brought to the annual assembly of the peoples.*

"I've suggested that," said the priest. "Most people don't want to wait that long—it's a year away. What if the Tsokch mean to rob and murder us as well, in the meantime? And if these people are desperate and cruel enough to kill all of the River Camp, perhaps they will simply disregard the rulings of the assembly. That would be very bad. The assembly works because we all agree that it should. What happens when whole camps, whole peoples, say otherwise?"

"It's happened before," remarked the Myriad. "It was not pleasant for anyone involved."

"Are the Tsokch involved part of the assembly?" I asked the Myriad.

"I believe so," she replied. "I don't think their withdrawal would necessarily break the assembly. But it would not be good. When the Tsokch joined, it was to the profit of nearly everyone involved—they gained a reliable source of metal and wood, and their neighbors gained a respite from their raids. For the most part."

The priest may or may not have heard the Myriad speak. "And if things continue as they are in Ard Vusktia, where will we get metal or wood or glass, except from each other? If the assembly declares the raiders in the wrong, with what will they pay the fine? How will anyone pay a fine if we none of us have anything but what we need to live? And if that is how things are, if we all of us will have barely enough for ourselves, what then? The elders in the camp below are canny enough to ask these questions, and have answered them by resolving to lay claim to what they can, and defend it with blood if necessary. Best, they say, to let all comers know that trifling with us is a dangerous act. But I don't see how this can lead to anything but disaster.

"If I can go back down to the camp and say, *I have spoken to the Strength and Patience of the Hill! This is a temporary thing, this shortage of goods that drove these Tsokch to robbery. We have only to get through this year—perhaps we can move our camp south and west of here, where another raid could not reach us quite so conveniently, and then bring our case to the winter assembly. If there are no southern traders there this year, there*

times," she said. "They seem to mean one thing, or nothing, until afterward when you see what was truly meant." She knelt silent a moment. "And if you were going to say there was no end to this in the near future, then my attempts to prevent bloodshed would be undermined."

The night breeze blew chill over the hillside, and an owl screeched. *I don't know the answers to your questions*, I said with tokens. *I don't know when or how the dispute in Ard Vusktia might be resolved, nor do I know when or if trade with the south might resume, nor do I know the fate of the assembly of the peoples.*

"So very clearly said." There was despair and also puzzlement in the priest's voice.

"There are gods who speak routinely in questions, or vague generalities that might mean anything," said the Myriad. "I imagine it might be safest to do so. But the Strength and Patience of the Hill has never, to my knowledge, made a habit of doing so."

"But what about the times the Foundation of the Hills said things that seemed to be nonsense but turned out to be true?" asked the priest. "I've seen it myself, on many occasions."

The Myriad said, "It's easy enough once events are clear to you, if you already believe some prediction must have been made true, to twist and turn the words until you find some way to make them so, however labored, however tortuous. I've seen it myself, on many occasions."

"I'll have to think about this," said the priest.

When she had gone, I said, "Friend of mine, the lives of humans are brief in comparison to ours. Live as long as they might, they are here and then gone, as it were in a flash. They all must die of some cause or another. And this assembly of peoples may have lasted several human lifetimes, and might or might not last several more, but there have been many such arrangements in the time I've known humans, and those all ended eventually and were replaced by others—or by nothing. Why ought I care about this time, these humans in particular? When I know all are doomed to end no matter what, and shortly, from my point of view?"

"Because I do not. And nor do they."

I thought about that for several weeks.

I knew that things changed. I had seen that change happen over hundreds, thousands, millions of years. I knew—or, I should say, I believed—that as this was just the nature of things there was no point in attempting to prevent this change from happening, no point in becoming upset or unhappy about it. No change, I thought, had ever been enough to trouble me very much.

But then, there were those times when I ought to have been covered in drifting sediment, in leaves or soil or ice, but I was not. If I had in truth merely accepted whatever change came to me, I would have been far, far under my hill rather than on it. I had done that, had for millennia continually prevented my own burial. The fact that I had not been conscious of doing it did not change the fact that I had done it.

In all the long years I had been aware of things around

me, aware of myself, I had learned that likely nothing was permanent. Had it ever occurred to me that *I* might not be permanent? It seemed to me that I had thought such a thing once or twice but quickly turned to other subjects. Thinking of it now, I found the idea unappealing. Unpleasant. I did not want to end. But it would seem to follow, from what I had observed of the world so far, that I would. I was, and am, cautious of how I might say such a thing, because I do not want to speak my own death. So I say only that it seems probable.

At any rate, that being the case, why should I care if I lay under layers of rock the whole time? Why, as long as I'd been in this world already, should I care if my end came in another millennia, or a hundred of them? What sort of urgent business did I have in the world that I did not want to leave it? When I had spent my long time listening to fish, or staring at the stars? What was the point, what had ever been the point, in my constant, unconscious effort to keep that view of the stars?

None except that I had wanted it. It had made things pleasant for me.

What was the point, when short-lived humans would die anyway, and others take their place?

And humans, who by my reasoning had less ground than I to think anything they did might matter in any real way, did far more. They traveled. They changed the landscape in large and small ways. They put plans in motion that they knew they would not see completed—plans that would benefit not them but their children and their grandchildren. When I—I had kept myself clear of dirt and

of that change might be something one could manipulate. Perhaps one could not prevent change entirely, but one could try to guide events so that things would be better, if not for you, then for some future being or beings whose welfare mattered to you.

Certainly most humans cared about the welfare of other humans. Or specific other humans. Children, parents, friends. Fellow camp members. Even theoretical children and grandchildren—people not yet born or even conceived. Even, sometimes often, strangers. I had watched them do it—dig and build to leave behind stores and shelters for whoever came next season, though they knew they themselves might not. Skin and tan and sew for some child not born, or some future spouse of a child too young yet to marry, or even think of it. And I had thought it just a peculiar thing that humans did, as so many animals have their particular habits and behaviors.

I had not thought it was something I might do myself.

Had I ever been asked to keep the camp safe from disaster? Oh, many times. Had I ever said that I would do so? Never in such general terms. But it seemed I had done it anyway. Why?

How different was I from the humans camped below me?

Well, quite different in many ways. So much is obvious. But perhaps, in some other ways, not so very different at all.

While I was thinking about these things, the Myriad did not visit me. She had gone elsewhere, I think. But one morning as I watched the people go to and fro in the camp below me, fetching water, mending tent walls, gathering berries from along the stream bank, chatting or singing or just silent, as the mood struck them, I heard the Myriad's whine above me. "The Tsokch are coming," she said.

The more I think about it, the odder it seems to me that the Iradeni have clashed so often with the Tel. It's not unusual for there to be difficulties between groups living near each other, of course, but in this case I might have thought the Tel and the Iradeni would have had all the forest between them. I might have thought that, given the difficulty of traversing the forest before the God of the Silent allowed a road through the trees, contact between people from oppo-

selves Iradeni, and not the same as the Tel. It is enough to suggest to me that the stories I've heard about the history and origins of Vastai, of Iraden and the Iradeni, are false in some way, or at least incomplete.

As I believe I have already mentioned, when the Raven took Iraden to war against the gods of Ard Vusktia, the Tel were mostly no more than a nuisance. Granted, they were clearly a large enough nuisance that the Iradeni had asked the forest to help them with it. But the threat the Tel posed was mostly a matter of the occasional raid on some outlying farmstead. It was not, as it became some decades later, a question of massed and more or less organized forces. (Usually less organized—the Tel, though they consider themselves a single, related people, and though most of them profess loyalty to a king, have often done as each clan—or even each individual—sees fit.)

No doubt if the Tel had been much more trouble than they were, the Raven would not have had the luxury of dedicating so much of his attention to taking control of the strait. But something has changed between then and now. Something that has made it desirable, or even urgent, for the Tel—and the Ona, and others—to move toward the Shoulder Sea. Somehow the occasional raid became a sustained attempt to push the amorphous, ambiguous border of Iraden back toward the forest. I sometimes wonder if this had anything to do with the beginnings of Xulahn expansion, with their conquering and holding other nearby cities, pushing their influence outward, to lay claim to the fields, vineyards, and orchards that fed Xulah, to protect and control the routes that brought them luxuries and necessities. Xulah is very far away, it's true, but not so far away that nothing from Xulah can reach Iraden. And I can't help but notice that both the Tel and the Iradeni seem to have had more and easier access to Xulahn goods in the past few decades. Can't help but notice that Dupesu speaks Tel well enough that he likely learned it some time ago, and when he and the other Xulahns needed someone to translate Iradeni for them, they found someone among the Tel who could speak both Xulahn and Iradeni.

The Tel attempt to gain the assistance of Stalker against Iraden had come during the latter part of summer, bare weeks before the weather turned. Once winter sets in there's very little serious fighting until spring. Quite a few soldiers go home—to plant crops that need ...

... ...age against the Tel. That he had delayed and had only a small victory, when he might have acted immediately and gained a large one. That the Lease's Heir was timid and indecisive. That if only he, Lord Airu, had been in full command that day, he would have fallen on the assembled Tel forces without delay, ravaged the territory beyond the hills, and made sure that the Tel would never trouble Iraden again. That when the day came for Mawat to take the bench in the Raven Tower, Airu, in command of the border forces at long last, would not make the same mistakes. Mawat's father would not receive Airu, but Hibal did, and several of the Directions. Though, as I'm sure you're already aware, some of those Directions did not have as high an opinion of Lord Airu as he doubtless would have wished.

But he found Hibal a friendly listener—after all, Airu's father is one of the Directions, and Hibal at that time was courting any Direction who might support him in the future. And perhaps Hibal, with an eye toward moving the bench across the strait, was glad to hear from someone who promised to rid him of a distraction that would surely make that move seem unwise, or dangerous for Iraden.

On the other side of the forest, Mawat ordered the regular patrols kept up, even though the Tel had not shown themselves since the attack on the camp. Not even so much as the smallest raid—the farms and villages south of the forest sat safe under the snow, all winter, and the riders and messengers Mawat sent out saw nothing. Except, I heard, for one boy who'd taken a message to the next camp, alone under the gray sky, in the snow-covered quiet, and seen what he thought was a lynx atop one of those hills that marked the southern edge of Iraden. It didn't move as he rode by, and he had the uncomfortable impression that it was staring at him. The lynx, of course, is the preferred shape of the god the Tel call Stalker.

The boy reported what he'd seen, but everyone he told laughed at him for being unsettled by such a small thing— lynxes were hardly uncommon, after all. And so when he returned—the hilltop had been empty this time—he went to you, knowing that you would take him seriously. Knowing, no doubt, that you had Mawat's ear.

You reported this to Mawat, who said, "Maybe it was her. And I don't think the Tel will be able to make that bargain with her again, but who knows? They very nearly succeeded this time. They would have, if Airu had been in command. Who knows what might have happened then? The Raven would have protected Iraden, no question, but I imagine we'd have lost a good deal of our forces if not

ıııus.

After the sun went down on Vastai, after your supper of bean porridge and flatbread with salt and thick sour milk, you went up to your room, rolled up the thin woolen blanket, and took it down the stairs and out into the square for Mawat.

"Thank the Raven," he said, voice trembling with cold. "I thought you'd never come and I was going to freeze to death." You handed him the blanket, and he threw it around his shoulders. "I swear these stones are made of ice."

"I'm sure you don't have to sit here all night, my lord," you said. "I'm not sure people who do this generally do. Or even if they do, there's no one here now. You could come inside for the night and come out again in the morning."

"I'm sure I could," replied Mawat. "And then my uncle—or the good lord Radihaw, whatever difference there may be between the two of them—will doubtless be happy to tell anyone who'll listen that obviously I'm not serious about this, and can be safely ignored."

"Very possibly, my lord," you conceded.

"There's no *possibly* about it," he snapped. And then, after a pause to collect himself, "Who sought you out today?"

"The Xulahns," you told him.

"There's something odd there," Mawat observed. "The only worthwhile thing across the strait is Ard Vusktia's harbor. Without that, Ard Vusktia is nothing. It's what comes through there that matters. What else could there be, that they would want so badly?"

Your glance flickered over to where two guards stood before the closed fortress gate, though neither seemed to be looking at you, or at Mawat, and both your voices had been too low to carry so far, even across bare, echoing stone.

"What comes through Ard Vusktia?" you asked. Still standing, looking down at blanket-wrapped Mawat.

"Everything!" Mawat gave a small laugh. "Silk, jewels,

furs. Dried fish. Salt. Spices and wine. Tin and copper and iron and glass. Slaves."

"The Xulahn I talked to said he had heard there might be gold in the far north."

Mawat made a skeptical noise. "Th

. . . . cross the strait freely, to get it back home as safely and quickly as possible."

"And gold or no gold, control of the strait is a prize worth having. Worth the risk of whispering sedition into your ear."

"But, my lord, Xulah is so very far away, to be so concerned with us."

"Maybe. Keep listening, will you? Learn what you can."

"Yes, my lord."

"In the meantime, I fully expect my uncle to bring pressure to bear once he's decided I'm serious. I'll be in danger then. You'll be in danger too. Possibly more danger—my uncle can't afford to remove me in any obvious way, while I'm here. I'm not sure even sitting on the bench could protect my uncle from the people of Vastai—let alone the Directions and the Silent—if he openly interfered with me while I sit here. But you—watch your back."

"Yes, my lord."

"But for the moment," Mawat asked, with a shiver, "do you think you could bring me some mulled beer?"

The next morning you left the guesthouse early, ignoring the Xulahns as they sat at breakfast, and set off across town. You seemed not to have any particular goal in mind, but strolled one way and then another. Had you ever been to a town as large as Vastai? Small as it is in comparison with Ard Vusktia across the strait, I think few towns in Iraden can come close to Vastai. Did you think about what it was you saw, heard, smelled as you walked? As you came through the far corner of the town where the tanners worked, did you wonder how it was that the stench of piss and rotting flesh you wrinkled your nose at didn't escape into adjacent neighborhoods? Did you consider what must have been the source of the fuel the blacksmiths used to heat metal to glowing again and again, as you walked by the workshop and heard hammers ringing? Did you wonder as you passed a well how, with all the people living in Vastai, all the waste they must produce, that water stayed clean and safely drinkable? Did you wonder, walking through a stone-paved square, stopping to look at stalls with goods laid out for sale—bread, some of it studded with dried fruit or spiced with cinnamon, cardamom, or saffron: field herbs

You stopped in front of Vastai's House of the Silent. This is one of the few buildings in the city made almost entirely of wood, and before the Raven came it was well outside what was then a largish village. The fence fluttered with strips and strings of blood-spotted wool, offerings tied to the pales: teeth, animal or human; eggs or feathers (never ravens'); hair. The ground inside this fence is dirt and grass, a gravel path leading to its darkened door, a tall wooden stake beside it, bulge eyed and gape mouthed. The path is surrounded by a flock of smaller stakes, each one with a strip of cloth tied to it, or a tuft of hair, each stake's upper end smeared with blood. There is no gate barring the entrance to that yard—for the most part no Iradeni would dare enter who was not eligible to do so.

The stakes are petitions to a god who has not granted one in decades, but still the Iradeni bring them, and if the

God of the Silent has recovered any power at all, even the slightest bit, it is my hope that these constant requests drain it away before it can do the god any good. I wish I could say that the God of the Silent is dead, but I dare not, because I do not know whether or not that's true.

The street you stood on led straight to the square in front of the fortress gate—you and Mawat had ridden past here the day you arrived, but had paid little or no attention to this building. At first I thought perhaps you intended to make an offering, but you only watched as three young women went up to a relatively empty stretch of fence and each pricked a fingertip, to bleed on narrow strips of cloth they then used to tie lengths of their hair to a wooden slat, muttering prayers the while. (In Vastai this is usually part of a petition for the God of the Silent to send one a good husband and a happy marriage. These three, however, were asking for the forest to preserve their friendship so long as they lived, and keep undesirable complications like husbands far from their doors.) No one else approached the house, but nearly everyone who passed it muttered some prayer, or made a quick gesture of reverence.

Well, but it wasn't the time for anything more than small, passing devotions. More would happen in the proper season, in the dark of the night, where no one would see but those respectable matrons who had achieved initiation into the secrets of the Silent. That god was still worshipped, though to someone unfamiliar with Iraden, or the forest itself, it might seem that this place was strangely abandoned.

You turned and walked to the guesthouse, to find a
tower servant in a black

presence.

The servant led you past Mawat, who affected to ignore you. Into the fortress, where everyone passing also affected to ignore you, into the tower and up the stairs to the room where Mawat had taken you when you'd first arrived. Today there were no Xulahns, no counselors or courtiers. Only Hibal, white clad, sitting on the carved bench on the dais, and not far from him a round, three-legged iron brazier, lit, to drive some of the chill from the bare stone room. "Eolo," he said. "It is Eolo, isn't it?"

You dropped your gaze to the stone floor. "Raven's Lease," you said, stiff and formal.

"I hear you've served with my nephew in the field. You must be capable or he wouldn't have wasted his time on you. And you must know by now what he's like."

Still you kept your gaze fastened on your feet. Did you hear, did you feel, that low vibration, that ever-present grinding? "Raven's Lease. I'm sure I don't know what you mean."

"Come now, Eolo." You shivered, just slightly, whether from the chill of the room or from the unnerving similarity of Hibal's voice to Mawat's. "You have not served any amount of time with Mawat without learning that he has a temper. He controls it better these days than when he was a child, certainly. And still he locked himself into his room for nearly two days—and left you outside, unprovided for, with no orders! I'm glad Mother Zezume took care of you, but if she hadn't, what would you have done?" He paused, perhaps waiting for you to answer, but you stared fixedly at the floor, silent. "But this—" He gestured outward, indicating no doubt that square in front of the fortress gate where Mawat still sat. "This is not a mere fit of temper. This is sedition. A direct challenge to my authority. It's a dangerous game my nephew is playing. I thought perhaps the cold and discomfort would drive him indoors, but he is apparently determined to do this, to rouse the people of Vastai against me, and perhaps even of Iraden." Hibal shook his head sadly, although you could not see it. "This from the man who wants so badly to sit on the bench. He is willing enough to undermine the legitimacy of the very office he so badly wishes to hold—no matter what damage he may do to Iraden in the process. ...

...better of it.

"Please!" Hibal entreated. "Please do speak plainly!"

"The lord Mawat has been sorely tried these past few days," you said.

"The lord Mawat is not alone in that!" retorted Hibal. "Though he often forgets that he is not the only person whose feelings matter. His father was much the same, I am sorry to say. Even to the point of sometimes forgetting his duty to Iraden, in his pursuit of his personal desires." You did not reply to this, and you did a fair job of hiding your trembling. Fear, I think, and consternation, and I cannot blame you for that. "I understand that my nephew is upset. I understand that he doesn't want to believe the worst of his own father. I would have wanted to break the news to him more gently, but he rushed in here as soon as he arrived." Your head jerked, just a bit, as though you were about to look up, about to protest that it had been Hibal who had summoned Mawat here, Hibal who had chosen that time. "Listen, Eolo. I have done this not just for Iraden's sake, but for Mawat's. The Lease is unpaid. And when we asked the Raven for guidance, the reply was, *This is unacceptable. There will be a reckoning.* Now, that might be a reckoning Mawat's father will face. But it could mean something else. What if the new Instrument hatches and the Raven, now able to speak clearly and publicly, demands an immediate payment of the Lease from whoever has been confirmed to the bench? I'm taking a risk here." Did you think to yourself that this was an odd way to put that, when late or soon, payment would be demanded of any Lease? Maybe. You closed your eyes, swayed a little, and took a deep, calming breath. Hibal continued. "If Mawat were to have taken the bench, and the Instrument hatch and demand immediate payment, it would be a tragedy. He's so young, and he has no heir. By taking the bench, I thought to prevent this. If so needed, I can pay, and leave Mawat to take the bench as he always would have, and moreover if I'm fortunate enough to live more than a few weeks he will have time to temper his spirits, to learn patience, before he is given a Lease's power. Perhaps you can help him do that. I think you can. But you must persuade him to leave off this dangerous course."

You took another deep breath. Spent a moment clearing the expression from your face as best you could, and then looked up.

"Do you think," Hibal continued, "that Mother Zezume

would have confirmed me as Lease if this were to Mawat's disadvantage?"

"Raven's Lease," you said then, "I am just the son of a farmer. I don't know about these things. How does the

to the Raven instead of locking himself in his room and then making a spectacle of himself in front of all Vastai by attacking me, he'd have had an answer by now." I think you tried to hide it, but your doubt showed on your face. You remembered, surely, that Mawat had demanded just that, and Hibal had put him off. "But your loyalty to Mawat speaks well of you. He trusts you, and I can see why. I need—*Iraden* needs you to use that trust for all our good. For Mawat's good. Come, I will summon the lord Radihaw, and you may ask what questions you like of the Raven, in Mawat's stead. Perhaps the answers you bring him will help him to remember his duty."

When Hibal had explained to Radihaw what he wanted, Radihaw frankly stared at you standing there before the bench. "Young man," he said, apparently having reached some conclusion, or solved some puzzle. "You are going to have an experience few of your station have had. I would advise you to remain sensible of this."

"My lord," you said, bowing your head. Perhaps in deference, perhaps to hide the expression on your face.

"Assuredly," Radihaw continued, "this would not even enter the realm of serious possibility if not for the sake of the Lease's Heir. Had he not chosen to behave so outrageously toward the Raven's Lease, he might be standing here himself. But as you see, the Lease still wishes to do what is right concerning his heir."

"I am only here on account of the lord Mawat," you said, head still bowed so that your grimace—of fear? Of irritation? Of anger?—was not visible to him.

"It is indeed a privilege," agreed Hibal. "We grant it, as the lord Radihaw has said, because of Mawat. Hopefully answers from the Raven—which he might have sought himself before taking the drastic step of attempting to stir up the people of Vastai—hopefully what answers the Raven might give will settle all doubts about this matter."

You smoothed over your expression and looked up. "Raven's Lease, did you not say the Raven's last reply on this matter, when questioned, was equivocal?"

Radihaw said, "The Raven's replies at such times—

between Instruments, I mean—are always equivocal. One must have the skill and the wisdom to understand, is all. You are young and impetuous yet, and such a thought does not come naturally to you, no doubt, but you will learn as

those stone steps that lead above and below. Radihaw followed, and you followed Radihaw, up those stairs, past the next level, its entrance covered with blue and yellow hangings, past two black-liveried servants who stepped aside at Hibal's approach, and farther up, onto the roof of the Tower of Vastai.

You blinked and braced yourself as the wind hit you. The spring sky was blue and near cloudless and the low wall that circled the tower's top did lessen the strength of the breeze there, but it was still enough to blow away much of the sunshine's warmth. If you looked north you could see the gray-blue water, wrinkled and rippled with waves, and the white sails of the boats passing. You would have had to step up to the northern wall to see the ones in Vastai's own harbor, but you would have seen, merely by lifting your gaze, the white quays of Ard Vusktia across the strait, the mass of spars and sails, and past those the blocky huddle of warehouses, the rest of the city spreading out beyond. To the southeast lay the Shoulder Sea. To the northwest the open ocean stretched away to the horizon. If you had turned around you would have seen Vastai town, meadows, and the apparently endless forest beyond.

"It's quite a view," said Hibal. "Not many have seen it."

"A signal honor, young man," agreed Radihaw. "Be sensible of it."

"My lord," you said.

The roof was, like the audience room, mostly empty. A few stone seats were placed at intervals along the wall, and in the very center of the roof a platform some four feet high, on which sat a tangled mass of twigs and sticks.

"That's it," Hibal said to you. "That is the Raven's nest." He gestured you closer. "Keep a few feet away, only the Lease or the heir can go any closer, but as you're already up here you may as well look. Look, and report every particular to Mawat, so he knows I've dealt honestly with you."

You stepped cautiously forward. Gazed unblinking at the brown-speckled green egg in the center of the nest, cushioned with fur and feathers and here and there strips and shreds of woven wool. Slowly you circled the nest on its platform, staring, as though you needed to see it from all angles before you could believe what you had seen. Or as though you were trying to make some sort of sense out of what you saw.

Halfway around you stopped, your attention drawn by

a wide, shallow bowl of water, and a few feet away from
that the dismembered carcass of a rabbit. And beyond that,
the dark emptiness of another entrance to the roof, another
set of stairs entirely from the one you had just ascended.

part, the actual offering of these things to the Raven, that
the Lease regularly does.

"Of course, Raven's Lease," you murmured, ducking
your head again briefly. Tearing your gaze away from that
second entrance that you'd seen no sign of anywhere but
here—wondering, I imagine, where it led—and finishing
your circuit of the Raven's nest.

Radihaw nodded approvingly. "Yes, yes. I see that you
feel it, that reverence any Iradeni must have for the god
who has given us so much."

"And the trees in the forest," you said, I'm sure without thinking, making a small, quick gesture with your left
hand.

This seemed to amuse Hibal. "Very reverent. I'm glad
to see it."

"Indeed," agreed Radihaw, though he seemed somewhat taken aback by your words. "The point is, the

important thing to remember, that one should wish to impress upon you...young man." He stopped, seemingly at a loss for a moment. And then found his way forward again. "Is that not just anyone can be Raven's Lease. One is not only born to it, but brought up to it. There are few, very few, who might be able to even be considered for the bench."

"So the Raven's Lease explained, my lord," you said. Your voice solemn. If I am not mistaken, you had resolved on some course of action or other, some stratagem suggested or confirmed by something you had just seen or heard. "How does it work, my lord, what do I need to do?"

Hibal nodded at Radihaw, who drew from his robe a black silk bag embroidered with gold. "Being still in the egg," said Radihaw, "the Instrument has no mouth with which to speak. Or," he added, "it may, depending, you understand, how far along the egg is. But even so, even if the new Instrument is old enough to have a mouth, to have a beak, to be able to make sound, it is not an easy thing to do, or beneficial for the Instrument itself, to speak in that way from inside the unhatched egg." He looked at you as if awaiting some response.

"No, my lord, now you explain it, I can see just what you mean," you said, to all appearances still sincerely respectful.

"And so," Radihaw continued with an approving nod, "one asks the question in the proper form..." He looked over at Hibal. "Your pardon, Raven's Lease, what is the question we will be asking?"

Hibal looked at you. "Well, Eolo? What three or maybe four questions do you think it would set Mawat's mind at

might have been standing here himself if not for his current open defiance. But do not waste our time, or try the Raven's patience. You would not be here if I thought that likely, but I give you the warning in any event."

You looked at the nest, frowning. Seemed to ponder for a bit, though I'm fairly sure you had been considering what questions to ask as you came up the stairs, and had moreover settled on one in particular when you'd seen that other set of steps.

"I am ready, Raven's Lease," you said at last. "This is my first question: Where was my lord Mawat's father when the last Instrument died?"

Your question startled Radihaw, and he dropped the black silk bag. It fell to the stone pavement and out of it tumbled a half dozen polished wood disks inlaid with copper.

"I didn't mean to offend, my lords," you said as Hibal

and Radihaw stared in alarm at the scatter of disks. "I was instructed to ask what my lord Mawat would ask, or what might settle his mind if answered. He is so unwilling to believe that his father has fled. But if the Raven himself says it, or if the Raven by his answers shows that as things were there can be no other conclusion to reach, then he will have to face the truth of the matter."

"I see," said Hibal, still staring at the tokens on the ground. "I understand you. Radihaw, pick up the tokens and we'll ask the question properly."

"I think, Raven's Lease," Radihaw replied, "that we must take the answer we have been given. Such accidents are rarely without significance in this place, at such a time."

"I suppose so," agreed Hibal. Could you see his reluctance? Could you read the answer?

Radihaw could read it, and he spoke what he read out loud for you. *"Can you hear me below?"*

"Forgive me, my lords," you protested. "That doesn't make any sense to me, and I fear it will make none to my lord Mawat."

"It is the answer we have been given," Radihaw told you, and bent to retrieve the bag and return the spilled tokens to it. "Before you ask the next, give me a moment to prepare." He straightened, gave the bag a shake or two and loosened its mouth, and then held it before him on the palms of his outstretched hands.

"Raven of Iraden! God of Vastai!" said Hibal. "When

you came to Vastai you promised to work for the profit and
good of Iraden. To that same end we are here to ask for assistance in matters of state. I am your Lease, confirmed by the
Silent, and your tokens are in the hand of Radihaw, Chief of
the Council of the Directions, as required by the old ----

out. Frowned, puzzling out the results. *A thing that's old.
The stars—no, negation of the stars. Tree. Bear. Water.*"

You and Radihaw were both looking at the tokens, not
at Hibal, who seemed to be visibly relieved at this answer.
"We have already asked this question, and received a similarly incomprehensible reply. This is the sort of answer the
Raven gives at this time, for whatever reason."

"It must mean, I think," said Radihaw, "that the lord
Mawat's father is in some cold place where there is no sight
of the stars. Some dark northern wilderness, perhaps."

"The lord Radihaw has a great deal of experience in
these matters," said Hibal. "The Chief of the Council of
the Directions is always present at these sessions, and he
has served through the tenures of two Leases—before
me, I mean—and moreover studied with the previous
Chief of the Directions before that. I would rely on his
interpretation."

"Raven's Lease," you agreed. "I know nothing about these matters. I'm sure it's as the lord Radihaw says."

"Do you have another question, young man?" asked Radihaw.

Oh, so many questions I imagine might have occurred to you then, so many answers you might have wanted or the answers to which might have helped you to understand what had happened, what was happening, how to turn events in what you believed to be the best direction. I don't doubt that in that moment many of those questions were there in your thoughts. But I am quite certain you were too shrewd to ask them with Hibal standing, listening, with Radihaw watching, judging, sure to alert Hibal to any implications of your questions that Hibal might have missed.

"Raven's Lease," you said, your voice innocently troubled. "You told me to ask questions that might set my lord Mawat's mind at rest. I am very sure that the lord Mawat's current extreme behavior is not only on account of his distress at his father's doubtful fate, but also the strangeness of recent events and his concern for the future of Iraden. The questions I have in mind are proper questions for my lord Mawat to ask, but in my mouth they might seem presumptuous or even disloyal."

"Your hesitation in this becomes you," said Radihaw. "But you are speaking for the lord Mawat. We understand that, do we not, Raven's Lease?"

"We do," agreed Hibal, genially. "This is not a time to be shy or too discreet," he admonished you, though still smiling. "This matter must be settled in Mawat's mind. He is my heir, after all, and it would be better for Iraden if he

"My third question, then, is, Will the lord Mawat be Raven's Lease in the future?" You turned your head toward the clattering tumble of tokens spilling from the bag in Radihaw's hands, but I thought your eyes looked, for at least a moment, at Hibal. Some expression crossed Hibal's face, quickly hidden by the resumption of his former pleasant concern.

"Can you hear me," read Radihaw. *"He will be will be when you bring him here bring him here I will say hear me can you hear me."*

"He will be," Hibal repeated. "That seems to be a quite emphatic yes. And I think the Raven doesn't generally make statements like that about the future, not unqualified ones. And look, the Raven says he will say so himself if Mawat comes himself to ask. Report that to your lord, Eolo. Report it faithfully."

"Raven's Lease," you acknowledged as Radihaw picked

the tokens up and yet again replaced them in the bag. "There is one more question that I believe my lord Mawat would ask, since it touches matters that trouble him."

"I am ready," said Radihaw, steadying the bag in the palms of his hands.

"What," you asked, "are the Xulahns doing here?"

Hibal frowned. "They are on their way to the north, and want permission to cross the strait, since that's the shortest and safest route to their goal. Surely you can spend a question on some more pressing issue."

"Raven's Lease," you demurred. "I was bidden to ask questions that might set my lord Mawat's anxieties to rest. What the Xulahns want may be one thing. My lord's misgivings are another."

"Indeed, indeed," put in Radihaw. "That is very true."

"So, my lords," you persisted. "With your permission, what are the Xulahns doing here, and did they have anything to do with the disappearance of my lord Mawat's father?"

You, Radihaw, and Hibal started and braced yourselves as a sudden gust blew across the tower roof. The bag tipped and fell out of Radihaw's hands, and the wind took it, upended it. *"Deception can you hear me can you hear me,"* Radihaw read out. "Oh, what a disordered heap this is, one token piled on another, or scattered here and there! *Theft to claim another's power bring him here this...*" He hesitated.

"I'm not sure what order to read these in. *Unacceptable this last words last chance do something bring him here pay debt...* Or is it *look at egg*? Or *egg debt theft*? What order should I read them in?"

Generally speaking," said Radihaw, still frowning in perplexity at the pile of tokens, "Generally speaking the Raven is impatient with repeated questioning. Generally speaking, an answer is an answer, no matter how confusing or difficult to understand. But perhaps this once it may be called for."

"I think so," said Hibal. And when Radihaw had gathered up the tokens and stood again with the bag in his hands, "God of Vastai, why are the Xulahns here?" You blinked, and bowed your head. Hoping perhaps to look humbly grateful at this second chance for an answer to your question, perhaps incidentally concealing any expression that might betray the fact that you'd noticed the question had been abbreviated.

Radihaw shook the bag and tipped it. "*Enter.*" Another shake. "*One.*" And, by a slow series, tokens falling one by one, "*Lamb. Offering. Cart. Ask. Nothing. Young. Over. Under. Happy. End. Apple. Return. Mend. Ever.*" He gave a vexed sigh. "It is entirely different. I don't know what to make of it."

"*Ask nothing young*—perhaps the Raven warns Eolo—or I should say Mawat—against asking this question," suggested Hibal. "But he has also said, *happy end.* Or, no, I see it. *Enter one*—that is, Mawat should come back inside. *Lamb offering cart*—the god asks for an offering of a lamb, easy enough to obey, I will order it so for tomorrow. *Ask nothing young*—as I have already said, perhaps the Raven considers Mawat's doubts to be presumptuous, but, for the rest of the tokens, all will end well and be well, if Mawat will only mend what he has broken."

"Yes," Radihaw muttered, frowning. And then, surer, "Ah, yes, it must be so. It makes sense."

"You will report all that has been said and done here," said Hibal, to you. "You will tell Mawat everything I have said."

"I will, Raven's Lease," you said. "Thank you for this generous honor."

"I accord it to you for my nephew's sake," replied Hibal. "And for the sake of Iraden. Remember that. Now go."

The Kaluet priest had convinced the camp not to take revenge for the slaughter at the River Camp, without my having spoken on the matter. No vengeful expedition went north. Neither had they struck camp—anywhere

put all their reliance on my aid—hunters made a point of scouting, and everyone watched the surrounding land with more than usual attention, and uneventful days had gone by.

So at the Myriad's declaration that the Tsokch had come, I looked around. The small stream below ran along a line of low hills, of which mine was one. On the other side of the stream lay gently undulating ground, grass covered, with here and there the occasional slouching stand of low shrubs, or an outcrop of lichened rock. It was not terrain that would hide attackers well. But the hills on the northwest of the camp might hide an enemy's approach. I looked, and did not see anything but grass, and more hills, but that might only mean the potential attackers were well hidden, or farther away than I saw. But it did not matter what I saw. The Myriad had surely spoken truly.

Without thinking I caused the priest's bag of tokens to

upend itself and spill a warning onto the ground. Within minutes she was out of her tent and into her neighbor's.

"They must arm themselves," I said to the Myriad. "The children looking for berries by the river must go indoors immediately. Why does the priest not sound a general alarm?" A child ran out of the tent the priest had gone into, straight to the next tent along the way.

"I think she has," said the Myriad. "It is wise for these people to conduct themselves in such a way that the raiders think they have the advantage of surprise, even though they no longer do."

"Surely, being warned, the people below might arm themselves immediately and go out to destroy the raiders."

"Tell me, friend of mine, why do you not just speak the raiders gone?" Below, a woman came out of the tent the child had run into. She carried a basket of mushrooms calmly and deliberately to another nearby tent.

"I do not know precisely where they are, or what resources they may have," I replied. "I might speak too generally and cause unforeseen difficulties, for myself or for the people of this camp, affecting either more than I intended, or less. I might unknowingly injure the people below, when I would prefer not to do that. I might cause some future harm I have not predicted."

"Just so," said the Myriad. "Or you might, unknowing, say something impossible and thereby injure or even kill yourself."

"Yes," I agreed.

"The humans must do more than speak, in this situation, but the principle is similar. They would know more, and think how best to use what advantage they have. Let

tent to tent, talking and laughing. The priest lay before the door of her own tent, a knife in her throat, blood pooling beneath her. Her hands twitching, as though making some effort to move, to take hold of the knife, and then she was still. Dead. The priest who had sought out my company since she could crawl, who spoke comfortably and confidently to me, even fondly sometimes. As though I was her friend.

"Oh!" cried the Myriad beside me, a keening whine. "Oh, someone will regret this, and I will take care that it is not I! What god agreed to help them in this fashion?" For it made sense that only a god could have clouded our awareness in such a way.

But I was not paying much attention to the Myriad, or her conclusions about how this had been accomplished. The fact that somehow my—and, it was easy to gather, the Myriad's—awareness had been occluded was of secondary importance, somehow, to the fact that the priest had some-how managed to call to me, and I had awakened—but too late to save her. The sense of wrongness, of per-sonal offense—She had been *my* priest! My friend!—overwhelmed me. "The god who did this...," I began.

The Myriad interrupted. "Wait! I advise you to think more carefully and learn more, before you say this!"

"...is dead," I continued.

The effect of my words struck me as though they were a lump of near-molten iron hurtling from the heavens. I was suddenly aware of little more than weakness and pain, and the stone surrounding me. Was I not that stone? I couldn't tell, nothing seemed right. I reeled. For how long I did not know.

After a while I was able to look outward from myself. I found only darkness and ice. I was covered and cased in ice and snow. Winter had come. There would be no one in the camp, not in this season. I did not try to remove the ice, but lay still beneath it, resistless. Exhausted. I knew that above me the moon and the stars still circled, that perhaps the sun peeked above the horizon for a few minutes or hours each day. That eventually the daylight would grow longer and warmer, the nighttime dark shorter. It would not be so very long. A single year was nothing to me. Perhaps if I lay quiet and thought of the stars, I would recover some strength. Perhaps people somewhere would make prayers or offerings to me, even a very small few such would help,

I was sure. But what had happened to the people in the camp? What had the Myriad done?

She had advised me not to speak so impetuously. She had been right. Speaking without thinking first had never

losing power in a failed, fruitless attempt to make my words true. So more than likely that god was dead. That pleased me. I would wait. And, waiting, I discovered that I had not been forgotten—offerings were still being made, quite a few, in fact. I could feel them. Spring would come, and I hoped the Kaluet and the Myriad would come shortly thereafter, and would answer my questions.

They did not come until the spring after that one. The people were fewer than I remembered, wary and more heavily armed, and they set regular lookouts on the hill-tops, and began digging a ditch around the camp, piling the soil into a rock-lined wall beside it.

"Who was the god?" I asked the Myriad, when she arrived.

"I could not discover that," she said. "I suspect it was someone small and insignificant, who was not party to any agreements or alliances, nor any entanglements that would make attacking your people an obviously dubious idea."

"*My people?*" I asked, indignant.

"I am not in a mood to be trifled with," she replied, with some asperity. "Had you but waited a few minutes, and followed my advice and instruction, we might have dealt with the Tsokch quickly enough, and possibly even delivered them prisoner to the assembly of the peoples. Instead you nearly killed yourself, and left me not only to deal with the raiders as best I could, but to give you what aid I could afford to prevent your dying. I was left weakened, and still had—still have!—obligations to fulfill. It has been a trying two years, and that almost entirely on your account."

"Why did you not just leave me to die?" I asked. Genuinely puzzled.

"Because if you had died, that other god would still have been a factor I would have been obliged to deal with," the Myriad explained. "And because you are my friend. Though, mind you, I am still somewhat out of temper with you."

I thought about that for a while.

Here is a story I have heard.

The attack on the River Camp—and the camp below my hillside—was not addressed by the assembly of the peoples until the next winter. This was not because no

after all, and there was a matter before the assembly even now in which a Kaluet was accused of a theft of foxes from Tsokch traps.

But most of all, most offensive to them, was the accusation that a god had assisted in the wholesale slaughter of an entire camp, and the attempted slaughter of another. It was a lie, declared the appointed speaker for the Tsokch, and it could be proved a lie. No god of the northern coast, or for that matter any of the areas inland, would take part in such a thing. No Tsokch would be so depraved. It must, they claimed, be some gang of Kaluet who had done it. If indeed it had actually happened.

The surviving girls of the River Camp cried aloud at this, tore their hair and called on the gods of the peoples to vindicate them. One man snatched up the knife that had been in the priest's throat, brought to the assembly as evidence, and rushed at the Tsokch delegation amid cries of horror and dismay from the spectators—offering violence in this place at this time was a serious offense, among the most serious possible within the assembly of the peoples.

"Stop!" cried the Myriad, her voice inaudible among the tumult, but a god's words do not always need to be heard to have effect. The attacker, knife in hand, halted and fell, overset, sprawling to the ground. "A minute's silence from you all!" cried the Myriad, and the assembled people fell suddenly quiet, and looked around, perplexed and angry. "Hear from me before you break the peace of this camp!" the Myriad said then, and now, with quiet at last, she could be heard. "I was there, not at the attack on the River Camp, but at the second. I was beside the Strength and Patience of the Hill when it happened. Some god spoke much of the camp into sleep, and myself and the Foundation of the Hills into unconscious stupor. We awoke, I know not how or why, to see people dressed in Tsokch furs despoiling the camp. I observed that some god must have spoken us into unaware-ness and in anger the Strength and Patience of the Hill spoke the death of that god. The Foundation of the Hills was a year or more recovering from these uncharacteristically hasty words. I say this plainly—the raiders that day were Tsokch, they were assisted by some god, and if that god is not dead, then it is sorely injured and very near death."

In the meantime, the man who had tried to attack the Tsokch delegate knelt, weeping and trembling on the grav-eled assembly ground, realizing too late that had it not been for the Myriad, his life would certainly have been forfeit. Indeed, a great many unfortunate events might have followed such impetuous violence, to the great detriment of many, but quite naturally the one foremost in his mind

his life. Then and there he vowed himself a changed man, the special devotee of the Myriad, and publicly resolved to deal more patiently and gently with others for the rest of his life. Five years later he died in an argument over the ownership of a reindeer calf.

I don't think there is any particular lesson to draw from this. But, like the account of the rest of these events, I had it from the Myriad herself. If I ponder it long enough—as, indeed, I have had plenty of opportunity to do—I can see several potential lessons or morals one might draw from such a tale, and no doubt many of them would be salutary, or at least salutary for someone.

Here is another story I have heard:

A young man of the Tsokch, out setting snares, felt something drop onto his head. Looking up he saw a gull bank and fly away. Looking down, he saw the skull of a shrew.

It was an odd event. He picked up the skull, meaning to put it in his bag to show later, but the skull spoke to him. He could not understand what it said, but that did not much matter to the young man—a skull stripped of flesh that speaks must, he concluded, be speaking for a god.

It so happens that in the very far north, on the icy shores of the northernmost sea, there are many very small gods who have attached themselves to a single family, or even a single person. Generally speaking such gods do small services. I do not say unimportant ones—on the ice such small matters can make the difference between life and death. These gods do such things as strengthening fishing nets, or preventing a harpoon line from snapping. They make sparks to start fires, or they turn storm-muddled wanderers toward home. And so the young man thought that this was a fortunate and valuable find.

He took it home and showed it to his mother, who advised him to make a bag for it and carry it with him. Moreover, he should speak to it daily. In the meantime the family would watch their luck, and if small things went well, then the young man should offer some seal fat or an egg to the god. But if things began to go badly for the young man, or for the family, he should take the skull and throw it into the sea.

Things began to go very well indeed for the young man—no fish slipped out of his net, his snares were always

another house in this camp there is another young man, a very handsome one. I think you would like to come to this young man's attention."

This was true, the young man admitted. But, he informed the skull, that handsome young man did not return our young man's feelings.

"Would he not be impressed," said the skull, "if you could lay wealth at his feet?"

"Possibly," replied the young man, but thought to himself that to pay such a price for the handsome one's affection would render it not only worthless but repellent.

"To the east and the south of here," said the skull, "is the territory of the Kaluet. They are laden with luxuries from the south—kettles, knives of metal, and so much wood. Do they have any more right to such luxuries than you? I do not think so."

"You may be right," said the young man.

"Listen, then," said the shrew skull. "Why not gather three or four of your bravest, most daring friends and let me advise you? I can lead you to riches. Riches you can show to that handsome young man! Indeed, with such riches you would be able to make me such an offering as would help me to secure that handsome young man's love for you."

For a moment, our young man was tempted. Who could blame him? The handsome young man in question was handsome indeed, and intelligent and charming into the bargain. But our young man was tempted only for that moment. In the next, he realized that he was in a great deal of danger. The same shrew skull god that had made things go well for our young man could easily make his life much, much worse.

"Your proposal is an attractive one," said the young man. "Can you really do this?"

"I can," replied the shrew skull.

"Then you are a more powerful god than I had realized," said the young man.

"That I am," said the skull. "Does it not please you, to have had such luck as to find me?"

"Indeed," said the young man, thinking to himself that now he would like to have such luck as would allow him to lose the skull. But he could think of no better way to be rid of it than to do as his mother had instructed, and so, having told the skull he would bring it to meet his friends, he instead took it out on the water and threw it, bag and all, into the sea. He added a prayer to the Drowned One, asking that god to keep the skull in the depths, safely away from any human who might discover it.

This account was conveyed to the assembly of the peoples, and the assembly concluded that the arrival of the skull god was an attempt by some foreign god to meddle in the affairs of the far north. Quite possibly to prevent the gods of the north from turning their attention south, to the dispute over the strait between Ard Vusktia and Vastai.

As I've said, you are used to an Iraden with only two gods—the God of the Silent and the Raven of Iraden. But there used to be more. Before you left home to become a soldier, did you ever pile stones at a crossroads? Did you name the Raven when you did it? Years ago, those were not meant for the Raven, no, nor for the Silent Forest. And when you became a soldier, did your comrades give you a prayer to say before your first battle, a verse dedicating the first blood you drew to the Raven, the god of Iraden? That was once a dedication to another god, the Defense of Iraden, the Mounder-Up of Skulls, who received the prayers and the blood of Iradeni warriors. I think the Mounder-Up of Skulls had been a small, quarrelsome god before the Raven came, but saw in the God of the Silent's agreement with the Raven an opportunity to grow larger than it might have under the shadow of the forest. Once a small god who delighted in small arguments, it now aspired to be the god of all Iraden's warriors. And look, now, it is as I told the Myriad. All things change. Now the proud Mounder-Up of Skulls has no more need for offerings, and that name is almost never heard, in Iraden or anywhere.

Here is another story I have heard:

One of the Council of the Directions, whose fields bordered on the Silent Forest, heard a baby cry as he inspected his herd. He knew he should ignore it, but he was, the story says, a soft-hearted man, and a curious one, so he looked over the fence that kept his cattle from wandering into the forest. And there, just under the trees, in among the bulge-eyed stakes that marked the boundary between the forest

concerned itself with—indeed, the forest rarely concerned itself with anything outside its trees that did not directly affect it.

It may be that the god had little or nothing to do with the matter. It was perhaps already a custom of the Iradeni for some reason, or it suited some Mother of the Silent to say the forest had issued such instructions. I don't doubt that if such was the case, the forest would not have seen any reason to protest. After all, the babies were left as offerings for it.

Whatever the reason for the practice, for long centuries in Iraden twins were left at the edge of the forest to die. It was popularly imagined that people wandering unwary into the forest without the god's permission, off the road, past those staked offerings, would be pursued and devoured by the ghosts of those thousands of long-dead twins.

But this had changed some years back. There were various accounts of why or how it had changed—a pair of twins had been instrumental in saving the forest or one of its favorites from some indignity, or someone the God of the Silent cared for or had made some promise to had borne a pair of twins and the god found itself in a quandary. The Raven of Iraden featured in quite a few of these stories, as it happens. Vastai was one of the few places in Iraden where one might actually meet twins (or at least twins openly acknowledged as such), though even there they were looked at with some dread. And still, anywhere in Iraden, a person who gave birth to twins would be looked at with some suspicion that they might have done something to bring such a misfortune on themselves. A member of the Silent discovered to have given birth to twins would be expelled.

The councillor of the Directions had of course been to Vastai quite a lot, so perhaps he was used to the idea of twins not being immediately banished to the forest, and felt bad for the babies. And perhaps he hoped to find whoever it was who had given birth, so that he could convey that information to the local Mother of the Silent to help prevent (or at least minimize) any potential sacrilege. Or, as some gossip at the time suggested, perhaps he was himself the twins' father or grandfather, and wished to preserve the lives of the twins without implicating his lover or his child.

Whatever his reasons, he retrieved the twins from the forest, sacrificed a heifer in their place (as had become expensively customary), and sent them to Vastai, where they were given the names Oskel and Okim, and they

While you were atop the Raven Tower, Oskel and Okim arrived in Vastai.

They had been sent for. They would not otherwise have left Ard Vusktia. There was no history of twin sacrifice in Ard Vusktia. Though it wasn't that the gods of Ard Vusktia (or the gods of the north for that matter) had never taken human lives as offerings. On the contrary. But human sacrifice there had never taken that particular form. So I suppose Ard Vusktia was more comfortable for them. But also, no boat would take them across the strait without a token from the Lease authorizing their crossing, despite the fact that any Iradeni might cross without such a token. This sort of thing may be why they grew up to be the sort of people that they were.

You passed them on the stairs as you came down from

your audience with Hibal and Radihaw. Do you remember them? Two men, their faces near identical, their beards trimmed close, their hair cut short, each with the same slightly sullen expression, each wearing a new cloak of undyed wool fastened with a bronze pin, one in the shape of a raven, one shaped like an oak leaf. No more gold on them than you wore—Oskel had a cuff of it around one wrist, Okim a heavy gold ring on a finger of his right hand. In fact they were reasonably wealthy—Oskel worked for the official tasked with collecting duties from ships traversing the strait, and it would take a naive man indeed—or a very honest one—to hold such a position without finding some way to enrich himself. His brother Okim had shares in several ships and their cargoes. You can imagine, I'm sure, what an advantage it would be to him to have Oskel as a brother.

They could have well afforded to dress better, on being summoned to Vastai. But I imagine they were both canny enough to see the dangers of looking too well off when appearing before the Raven's Lease.

As you passed them on the stairs, I think you noticed or at least suspected what they were, by the sudden small twitch of your eyebrow, the tightening of your already-tense shoulders. The almost imperceptible movement of your left hand as you stopped yourself from making that gesture you had made earlier, atop the tower. You hid it well. But Oskel and Okim had seen such looks, and that gesture, all their lives. I am sure they noted your reaction as they continued up the stairs.

You came out of the fortress gate, only glancing over

being overheard, and you walked by without speaking to him. He clearly noticed you as you passed, but did not call you over or make any sign that he wanted to speak to you, though there was curiosity in his expression. He had seen you brought to the fortress and doubtless wished to know what had happened.

You went into the guesthouse, up to your room. Sat at first on your bed, but not for long. Soon you stood and paced the small space, frowning, stopping occasionally to stare at one plain plastered wall, and then pacing again. After fifteen or twenty minutes of this you left your room again, strode down the stairs and out into the square. And halted, seeing Oskel and Okim standing beside Mawat, speaking to him, smiling and friendly. Mawat was not smiling—but he was speaking to them, apparently without excessive rancor. You watched this—what did you think about it? What did you feel? Were you frightened? Disconcerted? Angry? Worried? Perhaps all of those.

For a few moments you watched Mawat, still looking up as the twins spoke to him. Then you walked over to where they stood, where Mawat sat. "Eolo!" he cried, as you came up. "Meet my childhood friends, Oskel and Okim. They've been over in Ard Vusktia for several years now, but they've come back to Vastai out of concern for my well-being, they tell me."

Oskel and Okim had never been Mawat's friends, excepting that time they had all been too young to understand much at all, let alone have reasons to resent each other.

"Lords," you said, and inclined your head. Oskel stared at you. Okim smirked.

"Indeed, lord," said Oskel, looking away from you, toward Mawat again. "We had no other reason to come."

"None at all?" asked Mawat, seemingly sardonically amused. "I'm touched. You're both of you a credit to whoever bore you."

Your eyes widened to hear Mawat speak so. I knew you suspected Oskel and Okim to be twins, and had perhaps resolved to pretend you hadn't noticed, didn't realize it. And it would have been disconcerting enough if either Oskel or Okim had admitted it plainly, but here Mawat

was, throwing it in their faces that their birth had been a
disgraceful thing.

Okim scowled. Oskel's expression barely changed.
"Indeed, lord Mawat, we've missed you and your gracious-

we knew you'd know what was *really* going on."

"Did you, now."

"We did," asserted Okim.

"And we can just imagine," agreed Oskel earnestly,
"how galling it must be to know that your rightful inheritance has been denied you. And for what? No, we've come
entirely out of concern for you, and our desire to know the
truth behind these recent, very alarming rumors."

Without waiting to hear him say any more, you turned
and walked away from them, across the square and down
to the water, where you pulled your cloak around yourself
and sat down on the sand, watching the waves, and the
boats as they went in and out of the harbor across the strait.
You did not turn your head toward the tower, though I am
quite certain you were thinking of it, thinking of standing atop it, of Radihaw reading off the messages the tokens

formed. Of that second stairwell. Of passing Oskel and Okim on your way down the stairs, and then seeing them again, so soon after, talking to Mawat in the square.

When the water was dazzling with the light of the setting sun, too bright to look at any longer, you closed your eyes and muttered, "Surely they're gone by now." Still you sat, until the sun had set and the sky began to grow dark. Then you rose, and brushed the sand off your trousers and your cloak, and trudged across the beach, back up into the town.

Not three steps into the shadow of the fortress wall, someone grabbed your arm. You spun, bringing up your other arm, and your fist met your assailant's face, and your knee his stomach. He let go of you and doubled over, gasping, the knife he'd held fallen clattering to the stones of the street. You reached for your own knife and someone swore—your assailant was not alone—and dived at you, slamming you up against a nearby building. This second assailant gave a cry of pain as the blade of your knife glanced off his ribs, and your knee landed solidly in his crotch, but still he held you pinned to the wall. By now the first assailant had straightened, and he cried out, "Raven take you!" and swung his fist at your face.

Farther down the street a voice called out, "Hey, there! What are you doing?" and your first assailant's fist, weighted with a heavy gold ring, met your face; the back of your head met the wall; and you collapsed, unconscious.

be alive? What business did they have complaining about anything? Being angry or indignant about anything? Who around them would fail to remind them of this, at the least sign of resentment?

Who protected them, comforted them, spoke up for them? Oh, they were housed and fed and clothed. Taught reading and figuring, learned riding and arms alongside the Lease's Heir. But they were so often reminded, in large and small ways, that they did not deserve any of it.

And if (as was sometimes whispered) some resident of the fortress had gotten or borne them, that person did not ever own them in public, or speak up for them. They learned early not to rely on anyone but each other for anything beyond the bare necessities of life. And for this—for their exclusive reliance on each other, and for their obvious efforts to conceal their reactions to the many large and small insults they faced—they were often called (in private, or to their faces) scheming or conniving. It was proof, some said, that they didn't truly belong there, or anywhere, that they were indelibly marked by the cursed circumstances of their birth. Small wonder if they grew up angry and resentful. Small wonder if they could not entirely conceal it.

Perhaps two other children, some other pair of twins rescued from the forest, would have reacted differently to all this, grown up to be people not at all like Oskel and Okim. But they were not some other pair of twins, and I daresay they could be only who they were. And I think life was better for them after they left for Ard Vusktia. Ard Vusktians didn't much care how many others had grown in the womb with you, except perhaps as a curiosity. Transplants and visitors from Iraden generally did care, of course, but Oskel and Okim would have been far more able to make their own way in Ard Vusktia, to be accepted as just a couple of ordinary men. I doubt they would ever have become paragons of kindness and open honesty, but then, who is? It was, perhaps, not kind to summon them back to Vastai.

I think you may have had the experience of someone in authority telling you that you should be content with your lot, and not claim anything more or different from the place and privileges assigned you at birth. That so much had already been given you, and there could be no good

reason to wish for anything more, or anything else. I suspect that at least in this matter, if not in others, you might
have sympathized with the twins.

But the fact remains that they did try to kill you.

You opened your eyes—or tried; your left eye was swollen
near shut. Blinked, trying, I suppose, to clear your vision,
or to understand how you had come to be here, and then
you winced, with a sharp intake of breath. Your face was
bruised, your upper lip cut open. I don't doubt you had a
headache as well. Did you remember how that had happened? I'm told sometimes a person doesn't remember a
blow to the head, or the events immediately surrounding
it. But surely you remembered leaving the darkening shore
and walking into the even darker town.

The door opened, and Tikaz came in, carrying a basin
of water. "Well," she said. "You're awake. That's good. If
you'd slept much longer we'd have started to worry. Don't
talk," she admonished, seeing the beginnings of a frown,
your indrawn breath as though you were about to speak.

She pulled a stool up to the edge of your bed and sat, pulled a cloth out of the basin. "This is just cold spring water. It helps with the bruising." She wrung out the cloth and laid it across your left eye. "But you probably already know that."

"What happened?" you asked. Or tried to. Swallowed and tried again. "What happened? How did I get here?"

"You were set on in the street," Tikaz told you. "Don't you remember?"

Did you? Did you remember the gold ring on the hand that hit you? "I remember, yes. There were two of them. But I don't know how I came here."

"You were carried," Tikaz informed you. "Someone saw you and shouted, and the robbers ran away."

Cautiously, you licked your dried lips. "Was I robbed, then?"

"No, they didn't get the chance." She lifted the cloth, rinsed it again in the basin, wrung it, and replaced it on your face. "Do you think you could sit up? I'll help if you need." Brusque and businesslike.

You sat up mostly on your own, and leaned against a pile of cushions, more than had been in your room before. "My clothes," you said, then. "You said I wasn't robbed."

"And you weren't," agreed Tikaz. "But your shirt was all bloody and once we had it off you it seemed like a good idea to just wash all of it." You said nothing. "When I say *we,*" Tikaz continued into your silence, "I mean me, and the landlady's daughter."

Your expression did not change, but you closed your eyes and made a short, breathy *huh.*

"̄ ̄ ̄ ̄ ̄ ̄ ̄ ̄ ̄ ̄ ̄ question?" When you did not reply,

̄ ̄ ̄ ̄ enough." She put a fresh cloth over your ̄ ̄ ̄ said dryly, "There were robbers all over town last night. You weren't their only victim. Oskel and Okim were set upon last night too. Okim has a broken nose, and Oskel was slashed with a knife. It's a lucky thing the blade didn't end up between his ribs."

"It wasn't for want of trying," you said.

"Two against one," Tikaz observed. "And you still almost did for them. I guess they forgot you were a soldier. Or they might have discounted you because they thought you were a girl."

You opened your eyes then. "I'm not a girl. And most girls I grew up around knew how to look after themselves. Kind of had to."

"I was never more glad than the day they left for Ard Vusktia," said Tikaz, vehement. "They were always saying *my lady* this and *my lady* that and smirking the whole time, dropping hints about me and Mawat and staring at me as though I were someone's prize cow." You said nothing. "I suppose it's not their fault they were born the way they were," she said, voice grudging. "But they were always jealous of Mawat."

"Is my lord still in the square?" you asked.

"Oh, yes," said Tikaz. "He saw you carried in last night. I let him know you were all right." She gave a small, ironic smile. "Mostly all right. I'll let him know you're awake when I go."

"No one looked after him last night," you said.

"Oh, he was looked after, never fear," said Tikaz. "He has near a half dozen blankets now, and people were sneaking him broth and warmed beer until the sun came up."

"My lady," you acknowledged, and then, after considering a moment, "What's under the tower?"

She looked away, as though you had said something unbearably unseemly. And when the silence stretched out she asked, voice pointedly casual, "What do you mean?"

"I was on top of the tower yesterday, lady," you said. "There was a second stairwell there. But I saw only the one set of stairs on the entrance level, and only one in the room where the bench is. Where does that other stair go? What's under the tower?"

"You're not supposed to ask that question," said Tikaz, frowning.

"Your pardon, lady," you said, your voice very, very polite, and very tired. "I am asking it."

"Only certain people get to go up there," said Tikaz. "*I've* never been up there."

"The bones of all the previous Leases," she told you, still frowning. "The Lease goes down there every day to… do something. Anyone else who goes doesn't come back up. That's what they say."

"Bones," you repeated, disbelieving.

"I heard my father say," she said, quietly, almost a whisper, "that there are weapons down there, captured in Ard Vusktia, during the war."

"What sort of weapons?" you asked.

"I don't know," Tikaz admitted. "I suppose they're there to keep them from ever being used against Iraden."

You thought about that a moment. "Servants can go up on the top of the tower, can't they? I don't think the Lease carries everything up there every day, that he needs."

"Oh, well, servants, of course," said Tikaz. "But they don't go under the tower. I don't understand why you're asking this."

"I just..." You stopped. "When they searched for the lord Mawat's father, did they look under the tower?"

"It was part of why they were so quick to confirm Hibal as Lease," said Tikaz. "Actually. Because then he could search there. No one else could go down there, and Mawat was still days away."

"So we only have the lord Hibal's word for it, then, that Mawat's father wasn't there."

"Why would he be?" asked Tikaz. "Why would he have gone down under the tower and not come back up? Unless something happened to him, some sort of accident or..." She stopped. "No, the Lease doesn't die until he sacrifices himself for the Instrument. No accidents, no getting sick. Not sick enough to die. And anyone who tries to kill the Lease just...dies. It's happened before."

"So maybe the lord Hibal did...something." You almost shook your head in puzzlement, then thought better of it. "Took him captive and hid him somewhere. Under the tower maybe. My lord is certain that his father didn't flee. That he'll have found some way to die for the Raven no matter what. But what exactly happened? And why did the lord Hibal rush for the bench the way he did, before my lord could get here?"

Tikaz crossed her arms. "There's no question Hibal was far too eager to take Mawat's place, Hibal has always been jealous of his brother. I'm sure he had something to do with the Lease's disappearance. I just don't see *how*."

"Lady," you said. "Respectfully. What does your father think?"

Tikaz snorted. "He wouldn't tell *me*." I think you tried to give her a skeptical look, but it was difficult to be sure

but cross him and you'll regret it," continued Tikaz. "Oh, you've been careful never to cross him, I'm sure, or at least you know how far you can go with him. I have no doubt of it. Mawat's father was much the same. Only worse. As Lease, there were very few occasions on which he needed to hold his temper. As far as he was concerned he was the ruler of Vastai and it was treason to contradict him or deny him anything he wished."

"The Lease is supposed to have whatever he desires," you pointed out. "It's his right. He's sacrificing his life for Iraden."

"That's easy to say when you're safely far away from Vastai. And the Lease is supposed to govern Iraden along with the Council of the Directions. My father..." She frowned, more than she had already been frowning. "This is not for anyone's ears outside this room."

"My lady," you acknowledged.

"My father felt that the last Lease had abandoned all his responsibilities to Iraden and cared only for the gratification of his own desires. And so when Hibal came to my father—and yes, Hibal did come to him—promising to truly serve Iraden and the Raven if only *he* could take the bench instead of Mawat, my father listened."

"Because Mawat is so much like his father," you guessed. "And the lord Hibal had already shown an interest in actually governing Iraden."

Tikaz gave a bitter laugh. "And besides that, Hibal would support my father on some matters that the Directions have been debating."

"But was the lord Mawat's father already...already missing when the lord Hibal came to your father?" you asked.

"Yes," said Tikaz. "A servant from the tower came to my father in a panic because the Instrument had been found dead but no one knew where the Lease was. The servant had seen the Lease just a few hours before, atop the tower, alone. The Lease had been there all day and would not see anyone. He threatened the servant for coming up, and told him it would be worth his life to intrude on the Lease's privacy again. But the servant knew well enough that his life would be equally in danger if he did not tend to the Lease's needs. So after a few hours he returned, with some supper and a warmer cloak. When he came up the steps he saw the Instrument lying dead, and no one else.

The tower was searched, and all the servants and guards questioned, but the Lease was nowhere to be found.

"My father left with the servant to search the tower again. By the time he came back it was quite late. Our ser-

father's chamber and closed the door. But I heard enough. The Instrument was dead, the Lease was nowhere to be found, and my father was being urged to help put Hibal on the bench before Mawat could arrive to claim it, and prove too much like his father. They still will have had to convince Mother Zezume, of course, but I didn't hear how they planned to do that."

"So they searched the whole tower," you said. "Except the part underneath. Because only the Lease can go there. Or is it that only the Lease can go down there and come out alive?" Tikaz didn't say anything to that. "But Hibal— who we are agreed most likely had *something* to do with the Lease's disappearance, even if we can't figure out what it is—Hibal, once he was confirmed as Lease, could go down below and come up to report that his brother wasn't there. His brother who had disappeared mysteriously, whose position Hibal was known to have wanted, and whose heir he actively schemed to displace—Hibal looked and tells us there was nothing there, and we are to believe him."

"Oh, I don't *believe* him," said Tikaz. "He's as bad as his brother, only he's had to hide his temper. No, I don't believe anything he says. But I don't see how it makes a difference. Once he sat on the bench, everything else was irrelevant. He's the Raven's Lease now."

"I still don't...," you began. Tikaz watched you, silent. "If you're right..." You fell silent again. "If Hibal was sincere about preventing Mawat from taking the bench because he might be too much like his father, then he— and the lord Radihaw—must have no intention of allowing the lord Mawat to remain heir."

"I never heard my father say that," said Tikaz.

You scoffed, just the quietest huff of disbelief. "He would not need to say it, lady. So my questions are not irrelevant to everyone here."

"They are relevant to Mawat," Tikaz agreed. "But for everyone else—do you think it makes a difference to most of us, whether the Lease is Hibal or Mawat? It clearly doesn't matter to the Raven, or he'd have done something about it."

You shook your head, and then winced, clearly regretting it. "I don't understand it. And why should Hibal want it so badly, if it comes to that?" And then, after some more thought, "Could the Xulahns have helped Hibal do this? I think they expected him to let them cross the strait. Now he isn't letting them, and they're making noises about supporting a revolt to put Mawat on the bench."

"They're what?" Tikaz, surprised. Shocked. "That's not how it works. Only the Raven can put someone on the

There was a knock at the door. Tikaz hastened to pull your blankets up closer to your shoulders as she called out, "Who is it?"

"A messenger from the Lease," came the reply. Tikaz rose, and, after looking to you for assent, opened the door. A man stood there, in the black overshirt of a tower servant. He bowed and said to Tikaz, "Lady, the Raven's Lease has sent me to inquire about the good Eolo's health, having heard he was set upon last night."

Tikaz stood aside and waved her hand in your direction. "Here is the good Eolo." And, turning to you, "How is your health, sir?"

"As well as can be expected, I suppose," you said. "I am...flattered by the Lease's interest in my humble self. Please thank him for me."

"As to that," said the servant, looking nervously at Tikaz, and then at you again. He stopped and grimaced.

"As to that, my lord the Lease was concerned that his heir, who ought to be looking out for you, was currently distracted with other matters. Has there been a doctor to see you, sir? I see that you are conscious, which will hearten my lord the Lease considerably. Is there any difficulty of vision, or speech? Any paralysis? These are dangers that may come on suddenly, some time after a blow to the head."

"There was a doctor here last night, sir," said Tikaz, with a smile, her voice uncharacteristically sweet. "And he will be here again today, to check on just those things."

"Very good, lady, very good," said the servant, still awkward, looking around the room as though suspecting someone else might be there, or as though he feared to be overheard. "The Raven's Lease will be happy to provide any medicines or treatment you may require, sir. Seeing, as I said, that the lord Mawat would appear to be otherwise occupied."

"I understand you," you replied. "I've been knocked on the head before, and I know a dangerous injury when I see one. I think I'll be fine. Though I do have a headache."

"That's only to be expected," said Tikaz, still sweetly.

"The Lease did offer a tincture," said the servant. "One he uses himself when he has the headache, or really any other pain. It's very effective, and he would be happy to send you some."

"I don't think I'll need it, sir," you said. "But do thank the Lease for me."

"Of course," the servant said. And looked around again, from you to Tikaz and back. And then seemed to

"No, it's all right," you said. And after another scathing look, at you this time, she left the room and closed the door behind her.

"Good sir," said the servant, when the two of you were alone. "I hardly know if I can trust you. But sometimes... sometimes one has to do a thing because it is one's duty, whatever the result."

"It isn't always easy to know what your duty is," you suggested.

"It isn't!" the servant agreed, still standing, stiff and awkward, near the door. "But... something's wrong. Something's very wrong. And... you've served in the field with the lord Mawat for some time?"

"A few years," you agreed.

"Has that been... all right?"

"He's been kind to me," you said. "And generous."

The servant thought about this for a moment. And then said, "I don't know why I'm asking, it hardly matters. Listen. When I tell you this, my life will be in your hands. You understand me?"

"You want to say something that might be considered disloyal to the Lease," you guessed. "I won't tell. I won't even tell the lord Mawat."

"No!" protested the servant. "I need you to tell the heir!" He almost seemed near tears. Or on the edge of panic.

"All right," you agreed. "I'll tell my lord, if you want."

He clasped and unclasped his hands, and then said, "I'm the one who found the Raven's Instrument dead, that day. An old, dead bird stretched out on the ground, you'd hardly think it had been a god." He hesitated. "Its neck had been wrung. Its neck had been wrung, and the Lease was nowhere to be seen, though I'd left him there hours before, and he hadn't come down the stairs, no one had, I'm sure of that. I searched. There was no one there, and nowhere he could have gone."

"He could have gone under the tower," you suggested, and the servant's brown face paled a bit and took on just the slightest greenish tinge.

"Listen, sir. Listen, if I take too long at this errand he might suspect. Listen: I went and got the lord Radihaw, and he came and we searched again and found nothing. And it was decided—it was decided to confirm the lord Hibal as Lease, I hardly know how, but that's not my business. I serve in the tower. I serve the Lease. And he's been...He's easier to deal with than his brother, you understand me?"

ιοι the next. And I was standing near the top of the stairs. Those other stairs."

You tensed, then, but did not move. "And?"

"And I heard something." Nothing further. He just stood there, watching you, wringing his hands. Waiting for your reaction.

You took a moment, I think to compose yourself. "What did you hear?"

"Screaming," the servant said. "I heard screaming, and I swear to you, it was the Raven's Lease. It was his voice. The last one, I mean, the lord Mawat's father, somewhere at the bottom of those steps, screaming *Help me! Help me! Murder! Treason!*" He took a shaking breath, and swallowed. Unclasped his hands, and resolutely placed them at his sides. "There's something very wrong," he said. "And I think the lord Mawat needs to hear about it."

When the gods who had entered the trading agreements with the gods of Ard Vusktia decided to join the war against Iraden, I was not obliged to come along. I had never been a party to any such agreement, and had no obligations to fulfill, no promises to keep. Still, I went south to Ard Vusktia. A god of Iraden had attacked me, and harmed the people who had camped in my shadow, who had been under my protection. The fact that I had only belatedly realized that those people *were* under my protection changed nothing. The fact that I had apparently killed the Iradeni god who had incited the attack also meant little to me. Apparently the Raven had thought it worthwhile to undermine the assembly of the peoples, or perhaps merely to distract Ard Vusktia's potential allies with troubles closer to home. This stratagem had failed, but he might try another. My peaceful and quiet hillside might not remain so, and for once I found I was not indifferent to this fact.

And besides, the Myriad was going, and she was my friend.

Getting to Ard Vusktia was not easy for me. Many of the other northern gods could travel quite easily—by running, by flying, or even just wishing to be where they wanted to go, though as I've already mentioned, that's a risky method if conditions are not precisely as you require or expect. I did not have legs to walk or run with, and I could fly only with the expenditure of a great deal of power. I was still

body."

"It wouldn't need to be permanent," the Myriad said, unwilling to give up the argument. Below us, people laid out the huge rollers that would help move me south, thick, smoothed tree trunks that had reached my hillside only with great difficulty and at outrageous expense, wood still being scarce. All around me people were digging, loosening the hillside's hold on me. They worked with a will— they had not forgotten the attack, or the earlier slaughter at the River Camp. "We could find you something to travel in, and there is no shortage of large stones in Ard Vusktia, you would almost certainly have a variety to choose from. I'm sure you'd find something comfortable for you."

"I don't want another stone," I said. "Have you abandoned your own, that fell from the heavens?"

"I was about to mention that, in fact," said the

Myriad. "I am not always in that stone—or more properly, its fragments—but I find I am still connected to them. I can be within them quite easily when I wish. If you left this stone on this hillside, you would in all likelihood not be abandoning it but leaving it temporarily, and could be back within it at your desire."

"I am sure you're right, since you say it," I replied. "But I have been this stone for a very long time and I have no desire to be anything else. I believe traveling this way will be more convenient for me."

"But not more convenient for anyone else!" protested the Myriad. "It would be far more convenient for the rest of us—not to mention for the people building your transport and digging you out of the ground—if you took my advice."

"No doubt," I agreed, and did not argue further. But neither did I change my plans. The Myriad was a good friend, and a wise one. But I can be very stubborn.

The Myriad traveled with me, a whole cloud of her, flying alongside or resting atop me as I rolled along. It was difficult at first, but the nearer I came to Ard Vusktia, the wider and smoother the roads became, until I rolled easily along with only a bit of assistance from my own power. The air grew warmer, the plants grew taller and greener

why that might be.

We passed woods and meadows, quite a few villages, and, eventually, as we grew closer to Ard Vusktia, the occasional tumbledown building amid barren, weed-filled fields. But as we went on we saw fewer trees and plants, and no people at all, until the landscape alongside the road was bare dirt, with here and there a half-fallen building, or even a collection of them. "We are very near Ard Vusktia now," said the Myriad. "But when I was here last these were villages, and woods, and fields planted with barley, and other things humans eat. And there were people working in the fields."

"I don't see anything growing here," I said. "What has happened? Has the Raven of Iraden done this?"

"I don't think so," said the Myriad. "Or not directly, at any rate. But I suppose we'll find out what happened here when we reach the city."

And so we did. Or I suppose I should say we found out when we reached the walls of Ard Vusktia, because I was not certain I could fit comfortably through the gate, and so I rolled off the road and sat in the dirt beside the wall, while the Myriad went in to tell her friends and acquaintances that we had arrived. I sat for a while, watching the wispy clouds drifting across the blue sky, and examining the stones of the city walls—huge white stone blocks that seemed to be made entirely of millions of small, ridged cylinders and tiny, holed disks crammed together, along with the occasional small bivalve shell. It took me some time and thinking to realize that the cylinders and disks were fragments of crinoid stems, and I was looking at limestone that had once been a seabed. Ard Vusktia sat at the edge of the sea, I had been told, but I had seen no sign of any sea nearby. I had also been told that Ard Vusktia was full of people, fuller of people even than the camp of the assembly of the peoples, which I had never seen, but I saw no one while I sat beside the city's wall, near one of its gates. All was silence, except for the wind and, when I listened closely, the occasional cry of a gull. So there was water relatively nearby, at any rate. As I sat pondering this, I began to wonder if I had not made a mistake in coming here, or not coming here in a way that would have allowed me to easily return to my hillside. But there was no simple remedy for such a mistake, if mistake I had made, and so

I sat there atop my raft of timber rollers, in the dirt beside the wall.

Eventually a god came out of the city to meet me, a small, skinny brown dog of the sort, I learned later, bred

"So I am called," I replied.

"Welcome," he said, and began to speak to me of Ard Vusktia. Behind the wall, he told me, was a city of multi-story brick-and-stone buildings, hard up against each other, and flagstone streets and convoluted, gravel-paved alleys. What had been a small settlement had expanded past its walls, twice, leaving the foundations of those old ramparts to decay in favor of building the latest boundary, and swallowing three other nearby villages in the process. This expansion—and the need for defensive walls—was due to Ard Vusktia's broad, quay-lined harbor. The harbor is much the same now as when I first saw it, though at that time the Raven Tower of Vastai, along with most of the fortress, had not yet been built, so the view across the strait from one of Ard Vusktia's quays would have been somewhat different.

In any event, Oissen the small brown dog explained to me that a city like Ard Vusktia has a great many people who require food, but very little space in which to grow that food, no space for any significant herding, and very little opportunity for hunting. The surrounding farmland had once supplied some of that food, but as I would have already seen, nothing grew there now. "Because of the war," Oissen said, without specifying further. In any event, even so, not all of Ard Vusktia's food had come from the countryside—Ard Vusktia was also fed from the sea. But the war with Iraden had cut off a great deal of that supply as well. Ships no longer came through the strait in any great number, because it was no longer safe. Even fishing had grown chancy. Ard Vusktia, in short, was in dire need of food. And Oissen, an old and revered god of the city, who specialized in healing, had thought of a way to provide it.

"Food," Oissen said to me, "is, among other things, fuel for animals. From all I can discover, animal bodies... I suppose I should say they extract needed substances from suitable food, and use those substances, or reassemble them into other necessary substances. If we can find those substances, or make them, then we can make food directly, without waiting for it to grow. When first I tried it, making suitable food from things humans couldn't eat cost me a great deal of effort. It was hardly worth doing, really, except for the fact that it was so much faster than waiting for barley to grow. But over time I've learned more about how and why it works, and I've been able to make my statements more specific." He cocked his head to look at me. "The whole thing seemed very strange to me at first.

can do it myself for short periods of time, but I cannot do it alone, as constantly as it needs to be done. And lives depend on it. I would welcome assistance. The other gods here are either too busy with other urgent matters, or else fundamentally unsuited to the task. That is to say, they can say the necessary words, but they do not entirely understand them, and make mistakes that cost them strength, or that jeopardize the wholesomeness of the results. The Myriad suggested to me that you would do well with it."

"I have been thinking," I said, "about the power we use to make things happen. It seems to me that when I make something happen by speaking, the amount of power I use might well be the same as the amount of..." I was not sure what to call it. "The amount of effort or strength it would take to do it by other means. Lifting a heavy object, for instance." The means and costs of lifting heavy objects had of course been much on my mind in recent weeks. "But there are ways to make lifting things much easier—levers, for instance, or ramps and wheels—and it's correspondingly easier to speak such mechanisms into work."

"Yes, yes, yes!" barked Oissen. "I do believe the Myriad was right! Such a relief. The other gods here who understand this are all preoccupied with weapons."

"I think that everything that happens requires some sort of force or power to happen," I said. "And when it comes to lifting things I believe I can see what that power might be."

"You can see it in action, at least," remarked Oissen. "You can see muscles lift and strain. And the power that allows those muscles to move, the fuel of it, is in food."

"But what force made the food to grow?" I asked. "Do you know? If you must spend power to combine dirt and air and other things into that fuel, what is the power that does it without your help?"

"Such an interesting question!" barked Oissen. "I look forward to discussing it with you. But I have one doubt remaining. The Myriad tells me you were recently drained of a good deal of your power and are still recovering."

"Did she also tell you that I am annoyingly stubborn?"

"She did," acknowledged Oissen, tail thumping on the ground. "I think that will be helpful to you in this. But I warn you, there are not prayers enough to go around here, nor other offerings, nor do we have anyone we can spare for human sacrifice. Oh, the people of the city make near-constant prayers and offerings, but there are only so many of them, and most of those offerings are spoken for. Do you have the strength to undertake this as you are, in such conditions?"

and plants had seemed greener and larger.

I thought also of wheels, and the things the Myriad had said about the sun, and the stones that circled it, and the stars that moved across the sky. While I was thinking the sun set and rose again.

"I've been thinking," I said to Oissen, when he returned the next afternoon.

"Yes, the Myriad had warned me you might do that."

"I think I can do it," I said. "But I will need at least one person—three or four would be better, if so many are available—to make regular offerings. And to help spin me around. I think that as long as I'm turning, I'll be able to make food for you." And maybe not just food, but I wasn't certain about that part, and so I did not mention it.

Oissen considered this for a few moments. "I'll do my best to find some people for you," he said at last. "Though I may only be able to provide one or two at the most. I can probably find a larger crew on a very temporary basis, to set you up so you can be turned more easily—it wouldn't be practical to try it with you flat on the ground as you are."

"No," I agreed. "I didn't think so. I have some ideas about how to do that."

"I am not surprised," he said. "And while that is being made ready, you can tell me why you think spinning will do anything at all."

"I think it may be difficult to explain," I admitted. "I am not entirely certain it will do anything."

"I am very interested in your thoughts, nonetheless," said Oissen. "And I am very glad you've come to Ard Vusktia. But first, let me explain the process."

Have you ever thought about where food comes from? You grew up on a farm, so of course on one level you must have been aware that food comes from somewhere, from almost the beginning of your being aware of anything. But beyond that, beyond *Food comes from the right plants, and from animals who eat those plants*, I had never thought much about it. It had seemed merely an obvious fact of the world, like the sun and the sky, and the way things fell downward if nothing held them up. But even these supposedly simple and obvious facts are more complex than it might seem, and as I sat listening to Oissen I discovered that food was also. "Not every animal eats plants," Oissen told me. "But every animal eats either plants or things that eat plants. Different sorts of plants contain various substances, according to their nature, but there is one thing all plants have in common: somehow, given air and sunlight, they make a substance that is a basic fuel that animals need to live and move. There is at least one other substance also,

about soil? Most plants I know of must have soil to grow."

"Yes, and there are other things plants take from the soil, but I don't fully understand why, or what their role might be in food. If only I had the luxury of investigating this as I would like! I specialize in healing and in maintaining health, and so this topic has long been of interest to me, but ever since Vastai attacked us, I have from necessity focused on the problem of pure survival, of providing *enough* food—in addition to healing sickness and injury—and have not been able to investigate the details of how food works as completely as I'd like to!"

He went on to explain his ideas about air and water, and what the essential substances of food might be, and what plants might be doing to turn air and water into these substances so essential to human life; and he named for me the series of statements he thought the most efficient for producing them. "If you just say, *This air and water have become a quart of barley,"* Oissen cautioned me, "there is no predicting just how that will happen, and thus how much power it will cost you. I don't advise attempting it, the results might very well be fatal to you. But if you say, *This air and water will combine as they do in plants to make sugar and protein"*—these were the words that he was using for those first two substances he had determined to be essential to human food—"that is far more specific, the range of possible actions is limited, and one can predict the cost of saying so much more reliably. In fact, the actual statement I use is far more specific even than that. You should try it on a small scale first. I advise being very specific about the location and volume of the air and water concerned. And where and when the resulting food will appear."

While he was speaking, a person in a light woven tunic and trousers came out of the city gate with a bucket of water and an empty bowl of unfired, unpainted clay. She set them beside Oissen and stepped back, waiting. "Here is some water," said Oissen. "And here is a bowl for the resulting food. I don't think it matters what air you use, so long as it's nearby."

I thought for a while. Eventually Oissen wandered back into the city, and more humans in tunics and trousers came out and measured me, and then stood talking and pointing to the ground near me, sometimes sketching out shapes in the dirt with their feet or their fingers. Watching me speculatively as they worked, talking to each other as they eyed me. I did not understand what they said. The person who had brought the bucket and the bowl did not leave, but crouched down beside them, waiting.

In the depth of the night, moonless, the stars moving slowly in the sky overhead, I spoke, and suddenly

The Ard Vusktians built me a platform, right there outside the city wall, on top of which was an ingenious arrangement of rollers and wheels. Once I was placed atop this—with the help of ropes, rollers, and ramps—I could spin, slowly, with a relatively few people pushing. At first eight were assigned to me, but that dropped to four once I had suggested some changes to the mechanism on which I sat. They turned me, slowly, from morning till night, rain or shine, their muscles straining, their bare feet dusty, or sinking into mud. Every few hours a full vat of grainy powder would be wheeled away and a new, empty one put in its place. Sometimes the people pushing me were grim and silent, or they wept—especially when their hands blistered, which happened frequently at first, until they became more accustomed to the work, and I learned to prevent it. Sometimes they chattered and laughed, though nearly always with a bitter edge to their laughter. I began to learn a bit of the language they spoke. The Myriad came occasionally to check on me, and pass on news and gossip, and I learned more of the language with her assistance.

Gods in the north did not have attendants as such—anyone might approach a god directly at any time. Well, approaching the Drowned One could be difficult, but in principle there was no need for specially appointed or trained attendants to help direct one's interaction with the god. The people I have been calling priests were people who had more experience than usual dealing with gods, and perhaps detailed knowledge about one or more gods. They had acquired their knowledge and experience through specialized training, or perhaps just circumstance. People would come to a priest for assistance, or advice, if they felt they needed it. Or if the god in question required more care than usual—like the Drowned One—or was difficult to communicate with, as I was reputed to be. But the assistance of a priest was not required, and was not always sought.

But the gods of Ard Vusktia, the largest, most powerful ones, had whole staffs—assistants and agents, priests,
servants to obtain or care for sacrificial animals. If a person needed or wanted something from, say, the god who

I had no establishment—never did. But here, daily, constantly, these four people turned me, at my request. Their
steady movement around and around me was satisfying,
in a small way to be sure, but in a way that reminded me
of my satisfaction with the apparent motions of the moon
and the stars. And I began to be interested in the details of
human lives, in a way I mostly had not been before. Or, at
least, interested in these particular human lives.

One woman lacked part of her left arm, but pushed
with a will for all that. Another walked with a pronounced
limp, and had to take more frequent breaks than the others, which none of us begrudged her. The other two of my
attendants were quite young—two adolescent girls, insep-
arable companions, in fact. One joked and smiled quite a
lot, but the other spoke rarely, and quietly, and would not
look at the person she was talking to, but she sometimes
spoke with a wry, unexpected sense of humor. She also

had a fascination with rocks—had been visibly excited to see me, and on breaks would wander nearby, poking into the bare dirt or mud with her hands or feet, digging up what stones she found. She particularly liked ones with impressions of seashells, or bits of sparkling quartz. She was the sort of person who tends to become a priest in the north, and I began to think of her as a priest, even though no Ard Vusktian would have considered her one.

In fact, I discovered as I listened that all four of my attendants were slaves owned by Oissen's establishment. None of them offered me prayers—Oissen had led them to believe that I was not a god, but a godspoken stone, and they had been instructed to turn me as part of a rite to Oissen himself. They had been given a series of prayers to make to Oissen as they worked. What prayers I received came from elsewhere, from, I was sure, among Oissen's most trusted attendants, ones who could be relied on to conceal the fact that I was indeed a god. I found I resented this, resented Oissen's attempt at deception, and resented his co-opting my attendants for his own profit. But I did not say anything about it—I plainly was not meant to know.

During all this, the war was still going on. You know how wars are, I'm sure. There is so much waiting, while one prepares, while things happen beyond one's control or knowledge, and then, finally, an action to take, or an assault to

our best to prepare for. But in some respects he does not need to make such physical attacks."

"I am told," I said, "that the Raven of Iraden has spoken possession of the strait." The water was indeed very nearby, I had learned. Sitting, turning, outside the wall of the city, I thought that if I concentrated I might even feel the regular pull of the tide.

"He has," confirmed the Myriad. "And as well he has spoken the submission of the gods of Ard Vusktia. This is where the battle happens daily—the Raven attempts to make his speech true, and the gods of Ard Vusktia try to counter his speech with their own."

"You'd think," I said, "that the matter would have resolved itself one way or the other by now. The Raven's power would have come up short against the combined power of Ard Vusktia, or the reverse." In my experience, gods' statements were generally made true as soon as possible, sometimes almost instantaneously. But of course, a statement as simple as *I am ruler of Ard Vusktia* has, in practical reality, quite a large number of details that must be attended to to make that simpler statement true, and the matter becomes even more complicated if there is active, powerful resistance. Still, I was puzzled. "Surely none of the parties involved are possessed of inexhaustible power, to keep the question open so long."

"One would think," agreed the Myriad. "There is something odd in this, something I cannot explain. I would not have thought the Raven powerful enough to stand against the combined strength of the gods of Ard Vusktia, and yet this has continued for years. But Ard Vusktia..." She gave a small, troubled whine. "I am hearing things I do not like the implications of."

"What do you mean?" I asked.

"Do the people who turn you ever get dizzy?" she asked.

"Sometimes. Sometimes they just need a break, but sometimes they can't walk around and around that way without becoming sick. Does my turning make you dizzy?" Sometimes they seemed ill, or weaker than I thought they should be, for all they were allowed as much of the food I produced as they wanted, but that was something I was thinking about, and did not see the need of troubling the Myriad with.

"I don't think I can get dizzy in the same way humans

do," she told me. "But it *is* disconcerting, your spinning around and around, even slowly, when I'm used to you never moving at all. I mention it only because it occurs to me you might wish to watch these people who attend you

here before, there were dozens of them, here and there all through the city. Tiny things, most of them, but canny enough to stick to small favors, or particular things they did well, and there were enough prayers and small offerings to keep them well-enough fed. It made sense to me at the time—the large gods of Ard Vusktia are so very large, one doesn't generally trouble them for things like finding lost needles, say, or encouraging a single fish onto the hook. And there seemed to be enough people in Ard Vusktia to provide very well for such small gods."

"Have you asked?"

"I asked," the Myriad told me. "I have asked gods of Ard Vusktia and been told that it was because of the war. Which strikes me as an evasive answer. I have asked gods of the north who are here, nearly all of whom arrived here well before we did." A significant pause. "And learned that they have received the same answers to the same questions. Indeed, I am told that the Mother of Owls, on hearing this, and some other things that troubled her, returned to the north, saying she had not come so far to be fodder for the gods of the Shoulder Sea, whether of Ard Vusktia or Vastai."

"Fodder?" I asked. "What other things, then, troubled the Mother of Owls?"

"She was asked—as I have been asked—if she might agree to assign her power to another god."

"To what?" I was astonished. "Why would you do that? Is that even something you *could* do?"

"Apparently so. One might do such a thing if a particular project required a great deal of power wielded all at once, more than one god possessed. In such a case, it appears that one might lend one's power to the god who best knew how to wield it. It is, I was told, as simple as saying that my strength would be usable by some other god. Which would seem to me to be a rather foolhardy thing to do, even with a good deal of qualifying statements as a safeguard. Even if one trusted the god to whom one gave one's power. The statement that was asked of me did not, in my opinion, contain sufficient safeguards. I refused, and offered to assist in another way."

"Have any northern gods agreed to do this?"

"None that I know of," replied the Myriad. "Indeed, it wasn't only the Mother of Owls who took offense. The Fox with Red Eyes very nearly followed her. I myself considered leaving when the request was made of me." She made a buzzing whine. "But you would have been left here with few other friends, and perhaps not enough information to protect yourself. And you cannot leave here quickly

if it is possible to *take* it." Beneath me the wheels and rollers groaned as my attendants pushed me around and around. "I advise you to be wary. Be wary, even—perhaps especially— of the healer god. Do not say his name, unless you want him to hear you. But I have found that the gods here are close-mouthed, and jealous of their discoveries. There are things I have learned that I am enjoined not to speak of, and so I can say only so much to you. But keep in mind that the healer god will have told you only exactly as much as you need to do what he needs you to do. Do not, I advise you, tell that one, or any other god here, the whys and hows of what you can do."

"I have not," I assured her.

"I know," she said. "I have been asked several times, by several different gods, including the healer, how it is you can do this work so steadily on such a small allowance of prayers, and if the turning has anything to do with that, and if so how. I am sure they would not have asked me if you had answered such questions yourself. But let them continue to guess at your strength, I beg you. And be circumspect, even with me. I have made promises to conceal or reveal certain sorts of things, and I would not like to betray you, knowingly or not. For the moment we all wish to prevent the Raven from conquering, but beyond that, their interests are not our interests. Let us not forget that."

As the weeks went by, the people who pushed me, the ones who were with me day after day, became weaker and more tired. The conversations and the occasional laughter stopped, and they did not even exchange words when arriving or leaving for the day, or while they rested, where before they nearly always had. Now all of them stared dully ahead, gasping, as they slowly trudged, barely shifting me.

When Oissen came to check on me, he sniffed at one of the girls, who seemed to ignore his presence. "Yes, it's an illness that was quite common here several months ago, but I don't understand its cause."

"Should they not be resting?" I asked.

"I have not noticed rest to make much of a difference

Over those weeks, I also resolved to reach the sea. I briefly considered learning to inhabit one of the gulls I occasionally saw, or an insect. But for whatever reason, the idea did not appeal to me in the least, no matter how convenient it seemed for other gods. Instead, I thought about the stone wall of the city, and how Oissen had told me—and the Myriad had confirmed—that the largest of Ard Vusktia's streets were of stone. As were the quays of Ard Vusktia's harbor. I did not want to leave my stone—it felt like myself, after so long. Indeed, I couldn't quite imagine myself apart from it. But perhaps, if I considered carefully, I could extend myself into the limestone wall beside me, into the flagstoned streets, and perhaps all the way to the harbor, and feel again the wet, and the waves.

I moved slowly at first, feeling my way into the wall and then waiting, growing used to stone that was not made the way my own was, stone that was largely made up of the bones of once-living creatures accumulated over millennia. It was awkward and disconcerting at first, but the reminder of my old place on the seabed helped, and by the time I was ready to move to the stones of a road near the wall, I had grown more confident of my ability to extend myself this way. Still, I moved cautiously, and listened and learned as I went.

Ard Vusktia was indeed a city of multistory buildings of brick and stone, close packed, especially near the harbor. The bricks intrigued me—they were, I gathered, made from a particular sort of dirt and ground stone, shaped into blocks and then heated in a very hot fire. The buildings themselves were taller than nearly any building in Vastai today, except the Raven Tower, four, five, even six stories. Some of these housed the establishments of large gods, and some of them were warehouses, or the workplaces of the city's officials. But the rest were residences, either of single families, or of many families dividing the levels and rooms among themselves. Often there was a shop or workshop of some sort on the ground level, but many of these were shuttered now, there being no ships to bring silk or oranges to sell, no herds nearby to provide cheese or leather or wool. Before the war there had been room around some of the houses for keeping chickens, or small

and happier with more and better food to eat, I did not see anyone with the specific illness my attendants seemed to suffer from.

Eventually I reached the harbor. I did not go out into the water, but stayed there in the stones of the quay, feeling the waves wash against me, the tides rise and fall. When last I had been near so much water there had been no question of boats, but here there were many, or so it seemed to me, even though I knew there were far fewer than there might have been because of the war with the Raven. Fish swam beneath the waves, though not as many as I had expected, and clouds of small jellyfish, swallowing the tiny, shelled, multilegged things that swarmed the water. Garbage strewed the harbor floor, piles and scatters of it—broken clay jars, pieces of sunken boats, and bones— of pigs, of cattle, of humans—over which crawled shrimp and small green crabs. I was somewhat surprised those hadn't been eaten, but eating was not a thing I did, nor had I paid much attention to it until quite recently, so perhaps the inhabitants of Ard Vusktia did not know they could eat the jellyfish and the crabs, or did not care to eat them for some reason. The water itself was dirty with human waste, from the crews of the boats and from Ard Vusktia itself.

But it was the sea, and, I found, I had missed it. Not enough to stir myself, to move to keep myself under the water when it drained away from where I sat, no. Still, I had missed it, and was glad to touch the water again. For all the trash and waste, it felt familiar and comfortable, in a way nothing had since I had trundled away from my hill- side, the small cloud of the Myriad hovering over me.

That first day I reached the water, I only watched. Saw the gulls overhead, the sky and the clouds, and across the gray water, Vastai. There was no tower there, not then, just the town and its own smaller harbor. The quays themselves are not much different today, only of course nowadays there are far more people and ships, and there was no fortress in Ard Vusktia then, only a number of administrative buildings and gods' establishments. The Raven ordered the fortress built over the ruins of several of these after

"I have discovered what happened to the fields around the city," the Myriad said to me, on one of her visits. Careful to speak in that language we had first used with each other, that I was sure no one else near us could understand. "A few years ago, whether by the Raven's interference or not, there was a bad harvest—the barley crop was poor, much of it blighted. That winter people began to starve. The dog—along with some other gods, though I do not know precisely which ones—used some of what grew outside the walls as material for food. It was spoken into quarts and gallons of barley, on which the people here subsisted. But then when spring came there was not enough fodder for herds, nor edible plants near the city to forage, and the dog had to speak more barley into existence, at, I imagine, great cost to himself, so that there would be enough to plant. But again the harvest was not sufficient to feed the city through the winter, and again the dog was compelled to use his power to provide food, despoiling the land even further, and making the next year's harvest even less adequate for the city's needs. And so the dog was compelled to continue as he had begun, until the land surrounding the city was as you see it. Now the city lives mostly on the food that you are producing here, and fish and seaweed, and birds and eggs when people can get them."

Oissen's closest, most trusted attendants sometimes spoke to each other in places where I could hear them, and by now I had learned enough of the language they spoke to know what they said. When Oissen had told me that he did not understand the cause of my attendants' illness, he had spoken the strict, literal truth, but he had spoken dishonestly. He did not understand its cause, but he did in fact know, at least in a general way, what had caused it. Several of Oissen's establishment's other slaves were also ill, though not in precisely the same way as those who attended me, and the differences in their illnesses were of great interest to the healer god. None of the affected slaves were worth much, in the opinion of the people I heard discussing the matter, but the knowledge being obtained was beyond price, and would be useful.

"Is it the case," I asked, "that the people who have access to fish and seaweed—or who eat the food I provide only after it has been brought into the city and perhaps other things added to it—is it the case that they have for the most part not fallen ill in the same way as my attendants here?"

"Ah, you've noticed that, have you?" asked the Myriad. I had not had to notice it, I had only to stretch my aware-

I did, but did not admit knowing that. Or resenting it. "They are my attendants," I said. "They do their jobs well and faithfully when they are not ill."

"Well," whined the Myriad thoughtfully, "I am curious why Ard Vusktians used to regularly fall ill this way, but now it seems only your attendants do. And I do not think the dog is sufficiently powerful to strip so many miles of land of all plants and animals, on such a scale, and continue his healing of wounds and illnesses uninterrupted."

"From what I know now," I said, "the methods he will have used to do such a thing will have been cruder than what I am using"—this even before some refinements I had made over the weeks, but I did not say that—"and thus likely cost him more power. I am doing the work now, work that he told me he could not do unassisted for long."

"There is something strange here. If he needed you for this work now, what god helped him before?"

"That I don't know," I said. "What is it that you are doing for the defense of Ard Vusktia?"

"Some of it I am obliged to keep secret," she said. "But for the most part, I am asked to make small statements to bolster the city's main defense, and I prepare for an assault that we are sure must happen soon, but do not know the details of." She drifted a bit, with the breeze, and returned to where she'd hovered over me. "Your attendants seem better today, now I look at them closely."

"They do seem better, a bit," I agreed. I had come to my own conclusions about the cause of the illness. Had looked as closely as I could at the bodies pushing me around and around—ah, teeth and bones felt almost familiar to me, after the mineralized shell and bone of the city wall! I'd looked and—I will say I'd tasted, for want of a better word. And I'd listened to the hurried, whispered conversations of Oissen's close assistants, as I stretched slowly through the stones of the city, and thought about what I'd heard and seen. And then I'd changed the things I was putting in the food, just a bit. It was no longer only the sugar and protein that Oissen had judged necessary for human food. I had not said so to Oissen, partly because I did not have words for the things I had done, and partly because I thought he would be angry when he learned I had done it. But I was not willing to let my attendants continue to suffer and even die so that he could see the specific differences between different sorts of malnutrition. "I think they will improve even more as time goes on. Have you learned what happened to the small gods here?"

"Besides *It was the war*? No."

"Did any very small ones come south with us? Are they

they have refused, and have been doing what small things they could find around the city."

"I suppose we will learn more when the expected assault comes," I said.

A few days later, Oissen visited me. He lay down in the sun and watched for a while as I turned, as my attendants pushed me around and around, silently. Slowly. "Strength and Patience of the Hill," he said finally, "did you alter the makeup of the food you have been providing?"

"I did," I replied. "It seems to be more nourishing now."

"Why did you not tell me?" asked Oissen.

"Did I need to?" I asked. "You are very busy. It seemed to me that there was more in nourishing food than just what I was putting into it, and you yourself had said you did not have as much time as you would like to research the matter. I, on the other hand, have had plenty of time to think. I was quite sure my additions would not be dangerous, and my attendants had become quite ill. I did not like to think that everyone in Ard Vusktia who eats the food I provide might become ill. And you had told me there were few people to spare. I am grateful to have these, and I do not wish to lose them."

The dog was silent for a moment, panting. Then he said, "Do me the favor, Strength and Patience of the Hill, of telling me when you propose to make such changes again."

"I will do so when it seems to me that I can," I replied. "Will you also do me the favor of not starving my attendants to death?"

"Does the turning do anything at all?" he asked. I noted, of course, that he had not made any promise to do as I asked regarding my attendants.

"I am not sure," I replied. "It might." I did not mention the fact that he had done his best to find some way to gain power from it himself. I feared that if I did, it would reveal the fact that I understood a great deal of what my attendants said, and I thought it likely they would thereafter be ordered to silence, or replaced with attendants who would or could not betray him. And I certainly did not want any of the gods of Ard Vusktia to know that I had reached the sea.

"Ah," I said, "you wish me to lend you my power directly, so that you may wield it for yourself."

"It would be more efficient," agreed Oissen. "I can tell you the way to say it that will be most effective."

"Most effective for whom?" I asked. "Where are the small gods of Ard Vusktia?"

"You are not a small god," Oissen pointed out.

"Would it matter if I were?" I asked. "Am I an ally, or a resource for you to exploit?"

"I do not see a meaningful difference between the two," Oissen said. "My city is at war. Some will die. Many have already died. But Ard Vusktia continues. This is my priority. Did you come here with some other aim?"

"I came here because the Myriad is my friend," I said. "And because a god of Iraden threatened the people who camped below me."

"I have heard. You spoke that god dead. A small god could not have done that. Indeed, few gods I know could have done it and lived. You are feeding the city, with only the help of a few meager prayers, and you do not seem fatigued or injured. I think you could well spare us some of your power."

"Tell me the words you would have me say," I replied, "and I will consider them."

"Do not consider too long," replied Oissen, rising. "You might be famous for your patience, but I fear Ard Vusktia's time is running out."

In the guesthouse in Vastai, you had pushed the blankets aside and put on your freshly laundered clothes, and now you sat on the edge of the bed, one boot in your hands.

"He said," you told Tikaz, "that he could get me into the tower and up to the top without anyone seeing me."

Tikaz stood by the closed door, her arms folded, glaring at you. "And then what?" she asked.

"Then I'll go down the other stairs and see what I find

there." You put your foot into your boot, tugged it on. Winced, at your headache maybe.

"Only the Lease can come back up from under the tower," she told you, angrily. "Either you won't be able to

wasn't searched. Or wasn't searched by anyone but Hibal."

"After he took the bench," Tikaz pointed out.

"So he said. But the Lease disappeared *before* Hibal took the bench. So it seems to me Hibal managed to go down there and come back up without harm. I suspect the Xulahns were involved. At the very least I think they thought Hibal would give them permission to cross the strait, and they appear to think they might be able to help Mawat to the bench."

"How could they possibly have been involved?" Tikaz asked, arms still crossed. "Even if they were, how could that help Hibal go under the tower before he was Lease?"

"I said before that I think they've brought a god with them," you told her. "The Raven is very powerful, but sometimes even a small god can do more than you'd think." You pulled your second boot on. Set both feet squarely, maybe experimentally, on the floor. "The Tel bring gods into battle sometimes. Very small ones, nothing like the Raven. But they can still be dangerous. You have to be careful what you say, what information the Tel might have, because even a small god can take a tiny thing and turn it against you. A weakness in your armor, a resentment against the person fighting beside you—the more they know about how you do things, where you're going and when you'll be there and where you're vulnerable, the easier it is for them to damage you." You stood up. Sat down again. "Just a little dizzy," you said. "I should have taken that more slowly." You closed your eyes. "The lord Hibal, he knows things—about his brother, about how things are done in the fortress, and the tower. It might have been a very small thing the Xulahn god did, that helped Hibal do whatever he did to the Lease. And if that's the case—" You opened your eyes again and looked at Tikaz. "If that's the case then the Raven was unable to stop them for some reason, and needs our help."

"So maybe he won't kill you when you go below the tower, you mean," she said, angrily. "Because he'll be grateful."

You shrugged. "If I can't come back up, I'll call up what I find."

"And will anyone but Hibal be there to listen to you?"

"Possibly not," you conceded. "That's why I'm telling you what I'm doing. If I don't come back, you'll know what to tell my lord."

"Do you love him?" Tikaz asked, angrily. You stared at her, frowning, either from your continuing headache or from bewilderment at her question. "Do you love Mawat so much you'll go down and die like this?"

badly enough that the doctor found me out. I'd been fighting next to Mawat, so he came to see me and the doctor told him that... Well. The doctor wanted to have me beaten and send me home. Mawat said I deserved better, I'd fought well, and that I would be one of his aides and the doctor would keep his mouth shut if he knew what was good for him. And... he has lost his temper with me sometimes. But never enough to outweigh the times he's been willing to risk himself to save my life, or any other of the people he fights alongside."

Tikaz unfolded her arms and sat down on the bed beside you. "I had an aunt. My mother's aunt. Everyone thought she was pretending to be a woman for some reason, but she wasn't. There was a big scandal when she wanted to join the Silent. But she was admitted, and eventually people stopped being so worried about it. That was before I was born. She was an old lady when I knew her, when I used to go with my mother to visit her family. My father always said she should have gone to Ard Vusktia, where they think such things are normal."

"Do they?" you asked, with interest. "I've heard it said, but is it true?"

Tikaz shrugged. "People say they do. I've heard that way up north, where it's cold and icy all the time, the gods' favorite priests are all…" She made a vague gesture, searching for a word. "Like my aunt. Or like you. I don't know if that's true, or just a thing people say."

"So why didn't your aunt go to Ard Vusktia?" you asked.

"Why should she have to leave her home?" Tikaz retorted. She folded her arms and glared at you again.

"She shouldn't," you said, looking suddenly much younger than I was sure you were. "She was lucky in her family."

"Yes," agreed Tikaz, her apparent anger gone.

"Where's your mother?" you asked. "Is she here in Vastai?"

"She went back to her family," said Tikaz. "West of here. There was only so much of my father she could take. She told me when she left that no matter what my father said, I didn't have to marry anyone I didn't want, and if he tried to make me I should leave Vastai and come to her."

"Ah," you said, "and your father wants you to marry my lord Mawat."

"Or get pregnant by him anyway," Tikaz agreed. "I don't think Mawat would be a very good husband, what with one thing and another. Not even my father thinks so, really, but he would so like to have a grandchild in

You said, "I can see how he might turn out like his father. If I imagine him taking the bench and having nothing but flattery, and everything he wished for. But he's not like that." Tikaz made a skeptical noise. "He's a little like that," you admitted. "But I don't think he means it."

"Does it matter if he means it?" Tikaz asked. "He knows how much you owe him. You owe him more with every day that goes by."

"I'm not his type," you said. "He's never even hinted at wanting that sort of thing from me."

Tikaz snorted. "I can *see* you're not his type. But that hasn't stopped him in the past. Is he *your* type?" No hesitation, no looking coyly away from you as she asked.

"No," you admitted. "And anyway, I like men all right, but I generally prefer women."

"Do you now," remarked Tikaz, and unfolded her arms and rose.

"I do," you replied. "What's *your* type, lady?"

She laughed outright. "Never you mind that right now. There'll be time enough to talk about it if you're still alive come tomorrow." She turned and left the room, closing the door behind her, and you sat there on the bed with an odd expression on your face, as though you couldn't decide whether or not it was safe to smile.

The tower servant met you inside the fortress after dark with an old black overshirt, and, once you had put that on over your clothes, bade you say nothing if you were stopped and questioned, and keep your eyes down. And then it was as simple a thing as to walk, the two of you, unchallenged into the tower and up the stairs to the top. The sky had clouded, the breeze was chill and brisk, and only a few small lanterns burned at the top of the stairs where you came up from below. He picked up one of the lanterns, and you both walked over to the top of those other steps.

"Stand here," the servant said to you, "and maybe we'll

hear what I heard, and you can tell the heir that I've spoken the truth."

"It's ordinary for you to be up here, is it?" you asked.

"Yes. No one else will come up here for hours. The...

"How should I know what it is? All I know is, I heard it."

"Give me the lantern," you said.

"Why?" he asked, handing it to you.

"Because it's dark down there." And before he could protest, you stepped down and into that other stairwell, leaving the servant behind in astonished silence.

At first, as you descended, there were only the stairs, and the same yellowish limestone walls as anywhere in the tower. No doors. No landings. Like that other set of stairs that you had already climbed, these spiraled around the circumference of the tower, though the ceiling was close over your head, a good deal closer than on those other stairs. Close enough that someone as tall as Mawat—or Hibal—might have to duck, just a bit, all the way down.

Surely as you descended you could hear that ever-present grinding sound, louder as you went. Or perhaps it was such a constant background to the usual noises in the tower that you didn't even notice it. And did you hear the sound of water splashing? You frowned, just slightly, and continued slowly forward, downward.

You slowed when your lantern shone on damp stone walls and steps, and then halted where the steps continued down into water. Raised your lantern again. Some ten or twelve feet farther, steps rose out of the water.

You stood there for a few minutes. Looking at the water, looking at the walls. "How deep?" you asked yourself, quietly. "How deep does it get?" You turned and looked back the way you had come, the place where wet stone turned to dry. Then you shrugged, and stepped slowly down into the water. Two steps down, the water knee-deep, you nearly stumbled and fell when your foot found not a third step, but a landing. Cautiously you waded forward until your now-sodden boots met the edge of those upward stairs.

At the top of those stairs, a doorway. You stepped through it, lantern raised, into a room maybe ten feet square. The grinding noise was much louder here, unavoidable, unignorable. Directly before you was a massive oak door. To your right, a smaller doorway led to a sort of alcove in which sat stacks of long bones, and a pile of skulls, sixteen of them, though I don't know if you counted. On your left... You grimaced as the smell hit you. And when you recognized who it was lying on the stone floor of that other alcove opposite the bones, his white clothes disheveled and stained, his feet pulled back and bound to his hands behind him, you stared with an expression of horror. Even in this extremity his face was so like his brother's, so like his son's, as for there to be little doubt that this was Mawat's

was dead as the one thing in all of this that he could trust. And maybe for Mawat the stakes were too personal—what would it say about him, if his own father had failed in his duty?

But of course, the Lease's failure concerned more than Mawat. What could it mean for Iraden?

I believe I have already said that I take you for a thoughtful person. You had more or less openly doubted Mawat's assertion that his father must be dead, and I do not think it was mere idle speculation on your part. And you had heard the tower servant speak of hearing the voice of the previous Lease. Surely you were prepared to discover that he was still alive. But considering one disaster among several possibilities is not the same as being confronted with the reality of it.

Alive the whole time.

You let out a rough, angry breath and turned away.

Fear? Contempt for a coward? Was it the fact that it was not, after all, only Mawat whose world depended on the assumption that the Lease would do his duty when the time came? Or was it the realization that freeing Mawat's father now would be pointless? You had no reason to think you could return above. You might be certain that Mawat's father could—but he had lain bound here for days. Could he even walk a few steps, let alone climb those long, turning stairs? And even then, in the unlikely event he could manage it, what would happen once he was atop the tower? And once Hibal realized you'd been here...

How long had it been, since you'd come down here? How long did you have before Hibal came down those stairs and found you?

You turned, looked for a moment at the huge wooden door, but instead went to look at the alcove of bones. The bones of the Raven's Leases, as Tikaz had said you would find here, disarticulated, once the birds had picked them clean, and brought here to be neatly stacked in the center of this small room. You must have realized what they were— you turned your head to look again at Mawat's father, still bound and unconscious, and then quickly looked away from him.

And then, almost reluctantly, you turned again to face that massive wooden door. Your skin prickled, and the hairs on the back of your neck stood up. Surely you knew that whatever was making that unceasing sound, that ever-present grinding, was behind that door. You turned and went back to the stairs and listened a moment, came back. I think you must have heard me, all this time, must have felt that someone, something, was speaking to you, if

moan those hinges might have made. Slowly you pulled the door a few feet open, stepped around it, and raised your lantern.

And saw me.

That is to say, you saw a massive black stone with feathery white veins. The stone was some four feet high and twelve feet in diameter, set in a circular depression cut into the floor of the wide room. Turning. The floor, the walls, the air, your very bones vibrating with the sound of it. You've seen millstones before, I'm sure, but never one as large as I am. I am, in truth, too large to make a good millstone, and I grind nothing but myself, and the stone floor. You stared, for what must have been a long time to you.

And now I could see you closely, see the quick tightness of your breath, feel the fast, alarmed beating of your heart. You had, yes, been afraid from the moment you'd started down the stairs, and that fear had only grown as you'd descended, intensified when you'd seen the Raven's Lease bound and unconscious, alive against all expectation. As you realized that whatever secret was hidden down here, it must be behind that huge door, and it must be whatever had been calling to you, subtly, nearly imperceptibly, since you'd first set foot in the tower. The lantern shook in your hand, the flame wavering. You made yourself breathe more slowly, more deeply. "What is this?" you asked, but you could not even hear your own voice for the grinding.

Then you shook your head, took yourself in hand, and walked around me, stopping to look at another door, much, much smaller than the one you'd come through, though you never entirely took your eyes off me. You finished the circuit of the room—there is nothing else there, just me and those doors, the larger and the smaller—and then tried that smaller door. After some hesitation you took the narrow steps behind it, down, to the mechanism that turns me, which extends up through the floor where I sit and into a hole drilled in my center. This is another difference between me and any millstones you may have seen before. Like as not, you've seen one flat stone atop another, with a bar affixed by which people, or horses, or oxen can turn it. I was turned by a thick wooden shaft that led down from where I spun to a large, toothed wooden wheel. That wheel met another wheel, matched tooth by tooth to the first one, with its own huge shaft. Turning, that shaft turned its wheel, which turned the second wheel, which turned my shaft, which turned me. It was powered at least partially by water. It's quite an ingenious arrangement, I'll give the Raven that. That said, I've thought of a number of improvements over the years that

around me I said, "Now, Eolo, can you hear me?"

You nearly dropped the lantern you held in your still-shaking hand. I don't have a mouth. When I speak aloud it takes effort, and the result does not sound like a human voice. "Wh—?" you began. And tried again: "What?" But the sound of your voice was lost in the grinding, and I did not say anything further.

At length you went, trembling, out into the anteroom, and swung that huge wooden door closed. The Lease still lay quiet, apparently unconscious. You went past him, out onto the stairs. That once-flooded landing was merely wet, now, and you walked down to it, and then started up the stairs that led to the top of the tower, but after no more than a dozen steps you sat down, set the lantern on the stone beside you, and put your head in your hands and made yourself breathe slowly, counting with each inhalation and exhalation.

"This is too much," you said at length, quietly, into your hands. "I don't know what's going on. I don't understand." It had all been bearable, if frightening, until I had spoken to you. That one small thing had tipped your fear over into uncanny terror, the sort one feels when something utterly wrong and utterly inexplicable has happened. But you were a soldier. You had faced death before, and maybe even things you feared more than that. "My lord needs to know," you said, and looked up. Made yourself pick up the lantern and stand, though I could see that what you really wanted was to run as far away from me as you could, somewhere quiet where you could hide. But you did not run. You went resolutely on up the stairs.

Footsteps sounded, somewhere above you. You spun, came quickly and quietly as you could back down to that landing and up to the antechamber, looked around you, and went into the alcove of bones, lay down behind the skulls and a pile of femurs and tibias, and doused the light in your lantern. Rested your head on the floor, but there was a lump there, under your cheek. It hurt, one end of it poking into your face, and quickly, before Hibal could come through the door—for who could be coming down those stairs but Hibal?—you raised your head just a bit and scrabbled for whatever had jabbed you so painfully, coming away with something oblong and round, strung on a cord. You wrapped your hand around it and lay your head back down.

Hibal came into the room, lantern in hand. Walked over to where his brother lay and prodded him with one booted foot. "Hey! You! Are you still alive, then?"

The Lease opened his eyes.

"Then kill me. You have what you want, you've finally taken my place, and you've made damn sure I know it. Well, now I know it. What use am I after that?"

"Oh, no use at all, Brother," said Hibal. "Except so long as the Raven is alive—not his Instrument, but the god himself—you can't die except by sacrificing yourself to him. So when you die, I'll know the god is dead too."

You bit your lip to keep yourself from making a noise. *I'll know the god is dead too.* Hibal didn't just want to sit on the bench. He wanted to kill the Raven of Iraden.

He wanted to kill a god.

"It won't matter much for anyone but you and the Raven, really," Hibal continued. "All the prayers and offerings of every person in Iraden are not enough to keep him alive. He needs the death of the Lease to do that. I imagine he wishes he hadn't agreed to take only that one, occasional human sacrifice."

278 • *Ann Leckie*

"You're wrong," said Mawat's father. "The Raven is a powerful god. He'll destroy you for this."

"The Raven hasn't had the strength to do anything at all for Iraden for nearly a hundred years. That"—Hibal gestured toward the massive wooden door, behind which I sat, turning—"has been sustaining Iraden for decades now."

"No," groaned the Lease.

"Oh, yes, Brother. The Raven has overstretched himself somehow, and you know it. If you didn't know before you took the bench, it was because you never paid any attention to the ships that pass through the strait except as far as they brought you money and luxuries, and you never traveled anywhere except the other side of the forest to crack Tel heads. And then, once you did know it—you had to know it when you first came down here and saw that"—he gestured again toward me—"once you did know it, what did you do? Nothing. When you could have solved the whole problem the way I have—wringing the miserable bird's neck and waiting for the god to die. You could have done it as soon as you became Lease, just broken the egg and put another in its place."

"And then what?" asked the Lease. "Without the Raven there is no Lease. Who will protect Iraden then?"

Hibal made a *pfft* sound, inaudible over the background noise of me, in the next room, turning. "As far as the Lease goes, nobody wants to rebuild the government, nobody wants to give up the power they already have. The Council

of the Directions is more concerned with their own petty
squabbles than with the Raven, and the House of the Silent
isn't any better. Indeed, they're an example to me! The forest hasn't said or done anything in ages, not anything that

been doing—the Raven's job is what it's been doing
this time—by the time whatever god powers it dies, we'll
have already invited another god in, or a few gods, who'll
be grateful for the worshippers. Do you know how many
eager, hungry gods there are out in the world, beyond
Iraden's borders? Doubtless some have seen how things
stood and have been looking for decades for a way into
power here. If I'd left things to you, they'd have swept
down on us as soon as the Raven's power failed, as soon as
that thing there failed. But now I'm Lease, we can prepare
for it."

"You're not Lease," said the Lease.

"I am in the only way that matters," said Hibal.

When Mawat's father didn't answer, Hibal shrugged,
and went into my room to watch me turn. After a few minutes, he went away, up the stairs to the top of the tower
again.

You waited where you were for a while longer, and then, the thing you had found on the floor still clutched in your hand, you crept around the pile of bones, feeling your way out onto the stairs. All this time the Lease made no sound you could hear. Your reaching hands found the first step down, and carefully, cautiously, you descended. And stopped when you touched water. Perhaps sooner than you'd expected. Water had begun to fill the landing again.

For whatever reason—I can think of a few, but I don't doubt there are others—when the Raven Tower was built, the Raven wanted to be certain that what was under the tower stayed safely secret. But he also wanted his Lease—and himself—to be able to easily reach what he'd put there. It's true that the Raven did indeed say that only himself and the Lease could go under the tower and come back up again. And then he made certain that as many people as possible in the fortress knew that. In some ways, that knowledge alone is safeguard enough. But of course, there are also guards to be sure no one enters the tower or climbs the stairs to the top who is not supposed to be there.

And then there's the water. That landing fills and empties with the tide, the idea being, I gather, that the unwary might be easily trapped so, and the more cautious—well, even for a god it's easier to kill someone when one has something to kill them with.

You had been under the tower for some time, and

when you stood and walked. And stopped entirely when you saw sunlight on the stone, stopped short of that bar of sunlight and listened.

"Well, you've always told us it was important to take initiative." Oskel's voice. Petulant. "You said yourself that if he wouldn't be convinced, he was going to have to be dealt with somehow."

Okim's voice, now. "And he wasn't going to be convinced. Insolent, self-important..."

"It just made sense to get him out of the way." Oskel cut him off.

"Not that you've done a very good job of that." Hibal.

"Well, I'd think you'd thank us." Okim again. "He hasn't come out of his room since they carried him into it. He must be more badly off than he seemed at first. Sometimes a blow to the head will do that." He sounded satisfied at the thought. "He deserves whatever he gets. He broke my nose!"

"And stabbed me," put in Oskel. "But he's not important. It's Mawat who's the problem. And we can't just knife Mawat in an alley."

"Much as we'd like to sometimes," put in Okim.

"Well, apparently you couldn't knife Eolo in an alley either," said Hibal.

"We didn't know he'd be so quick," said Oskel.

"It doesn't matter," said Hibal. "As you say, it's Mawat who's the problem, and Mawat we have to deal with. And I *will* deal with him, but it's going to take subtlety. If he'd just stayed sulking in his room it would have been easy enough to be rid of him. I have to be careful now he's publicly attacked me and drawn the attention of all of Vastai." He made a frustrated noise. "Going to such extremes so quickly you'd think he risked looking like a spoiled, petulant child, who everyone can see is unworthy of the bench. But he doesn't seem to care about that so long as he gets his way."

"He never does," said Okim. "So long as he gets his way."

"And even if he's successful," Hibal continued, "he risks the wrong sort of success—the people of Vastai in open revolt against the Lease. And no easy way to resolve that, since the Raven isn't the power he once was. But Raven or no Raven, Vastai in open revolt would likely be as bad for him as for me, and he doesn't seem to realize that, or care. He's certainly his father's son! And the longer he sits there, the more likely it is people will be convinced he's in the right, or at least question my presence on the bench, before I can establish myself as firmly as I'd like. The sooner I deal with him the better, but panic and rashness won't serve

us in Ard Vusktia, and it's you who've called us over here to endure all that again. We've *been* patient."

"You've done very well for yourselves in Ard Vusktia," Hibal said. "With my help. And you'll do even better there in the future, if things go as I wish. The servant who helps keep Mawat's temper in check is bedridden, and unable to attend him. Sooner or later he'll lose that temper, publicly, in a way that will lose the sympathy of the people, and I'll be forced to..." Hibal's voice faded as they moved away from the stairs.

You waited, still, but there was nothing else to hear besides the crying of gulls, and that faint grinding noise that I was sure now that you heard. And finally, you came up out of the stairwell.

No one was there. You took a deep breath and walked confidently to the other stairs, and down them, as though you were just another black-shirted servant who belonged there, on those stairs, in the tower. Walked out into the fortress yard. No one looked at you, no one spoke to you. In a shadow behind the kitchens you pulled the black shirt off, one-handed, still walking, dropped it and continued on, out the fortress gate, into the square.

You walked up to Mawat, still sitting naked on a pile of blankets. "My lord," you said. He did not reply, did not even give the slightest impression that he had heard you or seen you, though you stood right in front of him, and spoke in an ordinary voice. "My lord." Still nothing.

For the first time since I'd seen you, I thought you might be near tears. And no wonder, after such a night and day as you'd had. "My lord," you said again. No response. You turned then, and walked into the guesthouse. The Xulahns weren't there. The few people sitting at the tables didn't look at you as you passed. The landlady's daughter walked right by you with a pitcher of beer, without even a glance.

You closed your eyes. Took a deep breath. Opened your eyes. "Am I invisible?" you asked. No one seemed to hear you. You looked down at your hands, and I suppose that it was only then that you realized that your fist was still closed around whatever you'd found in the chamber of bones. You opened your hand.

The landlady's daughter, on her way back to the kitchen, gave a little shriek. "Oh! Sir! You startled me. Wherever did you come from? I almost ran into you!"

You stared at her, blinking. "I'm...I'm sorry."

"It's all right, sir," she said. "I should be more careful where I'm going. And you with your sore head!"

"No, it was my fault," you said. And looked at what

head, letting the cylinder fall under your shirt, and went back out to speak to Mawat.

"Eolo!" he cried, on seeing you—seeing you, this time. "Are you well?"

"Well enough," you said. "My lord, I need to speak to you. Urgently." You looked around. It was late afternoon by now, and the square was nearly empty, only a few people passing through. "Wait. I think I need to start further back than I thought. I didn't...I was going to come speak to you after the...after your uncle summoned me, but at first you weren't alone, and then...I was on my way to talk to you about it when..."

"When you were set on by a robber," Mawat finished for you. "I can only hope you left him worse off than he left you."

"Them, my lord," you corrected. "It was your friends Oskel and Okim."

"Was it now." Mawat didn't seem surprised. "And what was it they didn't want you to tell me?" And when you didn't reply right away, "Are you all right? Should you be out of your bed? At least sit down!"

"I need to tell you now, my lord," you said. "And if I sit down now I might collapse entirely." And you told him about your audience with Hibal, about going to the top of the tower with Radihaw and questioning the Raven.

"Are you sure?" Mawat demanded when you'd told him of the replies. "You asked where my father was when the Instrument died, and the reply was *Can you hear me below*?"

"Very sure, my lord."

"And *Bring him here*, more than once, you asked if I would be Lease and the reply was *Bring him here*? Are you certain?"

"Very certain, my lord."

Mawat rose. "Then I must go to the top of the tower. Let Hibal try to stop me."

You swayed, just a bit, unsteady on your feet. "But there's more, and I need to tell you now, before you do anything else." You took a long breath, and then another. "My lord, after I was set on, while I was in bed, a... someone came to see me and said they'd heard screaming from underneath the tower. They wanted me to tell you about

"You're lying," said Mawat, his face suddenly expressionless, his voice deadly calm. "You're lying to me and I never thought that *you* would lie to me."

"I'm telling you the truth, my lord."

"No one but the Lease himself can come back up from under the tower," Mawat told you, now visibly angry.

"I know that, my lord, but I did it. I went down the stairs. And I found the bones of the Leases, all stacked up, and a room with a..." You had to take another breath before you could say it in an ordinary-seeming voice. "A black-and-white stone turning around and around. And I found...I found your father. My lord, your father the Raven's Lease is still alive and..."

Mawat did not wait to hear more, but grabbed you by the throat. "You're *lying to me*." He shook you.

You choked, trying to speak, trying to breathe, clutching at his hands on your throat. The cylinder on its cord swung, sliding sideways under your shirt, beside the fortress tokens.

"I thought I could trust you!" Mawat snarled.

You let go of his hands and scrabbled for that leather cylinder on its cord, wrapped your fingers around it and gasped as Mawat let you go, and he stood there blinking and confused. You dropped to your knees. "Eolo!" cried Mawat, and then looked around. "Eolo!"

"He was there!" said a guard at the fortress gate, who had come away from his post in his own astonishment. "He was there and then he wasn't!" You still knelt on the stones of the square, still gasping. Tears in your eyes. One or two passersby stopped and stared, having seen at least some of what had happened. Having seen you disappear.

Mawat knelt beside you, felt the stones all around you. "He's just *gone*! Eolo!" That last right by your ear. You didn't react, didn't startle, though it must have been painfully loud. After a few moments you pushed yourself to your feet and walked, unsteadily, through the small gathering crowd—they parted for you, without seeming to realize they'd done it—into the guesthouse and up the stairs, to your room, closed the door, and collapsed onto the bed.

I could not speak aloud to my attendants without making it clear to everyone that I did, indeed, understand at least one language commonly spoken there. There were tokens available—the idea of communicating with a god by

tans and frauds; I don't think any of the major gods in Ard Vusktia communicated by their means. But in order to use them myself, one of my attendants would have to obtain a set, and then we both would have to learn to read them, and my attendant would have to learn to use them. There was no way I could see to even begin that process without alerting everyone that I was in fact not a godspoken stone, a tool used by Oissen, but a god myself. And additionally alerting Oissen to the fact that I was able to speak with the people around me, and ask them questions.

I could, however, watch the girl I had begun to think of as a priest as she played with her rocks. She liked to line them up according to size, or color, or some other criterion that had just occurred to her. And watching her, it seemed to me that rocks might be used as tokens. The only problem was to work out some method of interpreting them, and convey that to her.

I thought of how that first priest had taught me, when she had first found me, how very simple those first exchanges had been, and how much had been built on them. And so I chose a very simple pattern, one I hoped would elicit a very clear and simple response—whenever my priest would line up three seashell fossils in a row, those three rocks would jump, just a bit. Just enough to tell her that something had happened, not enough to draw much attention from anyone else.

She caught on almost immediately. Tried three chips of gray granite—nothing. Three chunks of layered gray-and-white chert—nothing. Three rocks with fossilized shells— jump. She moved to another spot of ground, and tried again. And then—oh, I knew she would have been a priest in the north!—then she looked at me, and frowned. Three more seashell rocks tumbled out of her hand, into a neat row on the ground before her. When she looked at them, they jumped.

After several anxious, intense whispered conversations with the other young girl—Could she trust whatever god seemed to be trying to speak with her? Was it me? How could it be me, when I wasn't a god but a godspoken stone? What if it was an enemy? Everyone knew dealing directly with gods could be dangerous, and they didn't even have a name for this one!—they decided that they would question me (tokens were apparently common enough for the basic process to be familiar to them); three seashell rocks would mean yes and three granite bits would mean no. Of course

I answered them. No, I did not mean them any harm. Yes, I was the Millstone—that was what they called me. Yes, I was here to help Ard Vusktia. No, I was not an ally of the Raven.

"We're playing a game!" my priest's companion said,

about their foolishness.

"Leave them alone," said one of the older women who attended me. "They do their work, and if they've found some way to amuse themselves, why should you care? They're not hurting anyone, least of all you."

"You're right," he said. "I apologize." The girls both smiled—even Siat, who almost never smiled for people she wasn't entirely comfortable with—and said that was all right, and he didn't mention it again in my hearing.

In this way, with whispered questions to which I could, for a long time, only answer yes or no, I conversed with my priest, I hoped without Oissen knowing.

I had been careful in my stretching out through the city—had moved slowly, watching and listening, not touching anything I thought might call some god's notice, not even another northern god. I listened a bit to the people of the city in their homes, only enough to begin to have some idea of how people here lived, so very differently from those in the camp I was used to. And, though I never entered the establishments of Ard Vusktia's gods, I listened carefully to their attendants when they went about the city. I learned what I could from the things those attendants said in public, particularly the ones who worked in Oissen's establishment. Though I never did learn all Oissen knew on the topic of human bodies, and healing still does not come easily or comfortably to me. And the Myriad was right, the gods of Ard Vusktia were close with their knowledge, even more now they were at war, and their adversary was obviously, famously comfortable in a bird's body, and for all anyone knew any of the gulls circling over the harbor might be watching and listening.

I watched the harbor. Under cover of darkness, the Ard Vusktians were building boats and rafts, in some cases tearing down buildings for their wood, since there were no longer any trees near the city and few ships came at all any more, let alone ships carrying timber. These boats were for the most part flimsy and hastily built—the aim was to cross the strait in sheer numbers, forcing the Raven to use his power to prevent them, while the gods of Ard

Vusktia attacked by some other means, the specifics of which I did not know, but could guess. Across the water in Vastai, the same few boats were anchored as always, and nothing seemed to be happening. I considered trying to

had a simple, safe way to my own hillside, I would have used it then, and happily left Ard Vusktia and its gods to battle the Raven without me.

The more I thought about Oissen's supposedly safe way to channel my power directly to him, the less I liked it, and the less I liked the absence of the small gods that, according to the Myriad, ought to have been numerous here. As I listened to the city, as I turned outside the wall, I thought of ways that I might seem to agree to the plan but still protect myself. And the next time Oissen visited me, I said to him, "Here is what I will agree to: While I am turning, I will grant the petition of whoever is causing me to be turned, so long as that petition is not an absolute impossibility or a paradox. The petition must be clearly stated while the entity is causing me to be turned, and it must be within my power."

"This is not the proposal I made to you," said Oissen. He had not bothered to sit or lie down on this visit, and now his ears went back. "The words I gave you were carefully crafted so that they might be as safe and efficacious as possible."

"I did not like them," I replied. "I offer these instead."

His ears went up again, though I suspect it was a matter of conscious effort. "Have you thought these all the way through? The way you've phrased it, even these poor people"—he meant my attendants—"might compel you to grant their wish, any number of wishes, so long as it was a possible thing."

"Is that the case?" I replied, though of course I had thought of that. "I am more concerned with the fact that if I were to agree to your proposal, you could take as much of my power as you liked—as much as I have—and use it in ways I know nothing about. This way, at least, I can in some degree control how I fulfill requests." And, though I did not point this out, nowhere had I promised to give up all control over who would be able to turn me, and when. "My offer gives you a great deal of potential help. Nearly as much as your own proposal would, and I do not like the fact that there seem to be fewer gods here than there ought to be. It makes me wonder if you have not convinced or compelled gods to agree to this in the past, to their fatal disadvantage."

Oissen said nothing, only stood, panting. Watching Siat and her companions pushing me, all of them silent, subdued compared to their usual demeanor.

"Your silence is eloquent," I said, at length.

"It is as I said before," protested Oissen. "We are at war. There will be losses."

"I will not be one of them, if I can prevent it," I replied.

"Has the Myriad been sharing secrets with you?" he asked, at length.

"She visits me," I acknowledged. "She sometimes shares gossip. I know there are things she cannot tell me, because she has promised not to, or because it would compromise some project. Are you aware your question implies that you think she might have told me something that would, if I knew it, suggest that you have some design against me?" Oissen did not reply immediately. "I came all this way to assist you in your war against Vastai. I did not come here to sacrifice myself at your whim."

"Very well," said Oissen. "I accept your offer." And then he ordered my attendants to stand aside. "I have a request to make of you. How do I turn you?"

"That is your own affair," I replied.

With a word he caused me to move slowly around, and demanded that I lend power, not to him, but to one of the other gods of the city, who had contradicted the Raven's claim to the strait. I felt the power leave me—it was a considerable drain, but when I ceased to move, it stopped. "Are you making it more difficult for me to move you?" he asked. "You seem to turn quite freely when these people push you."

"I am a large and heavy stone," I replied. "My attendants have become used to this work. And I did not promise to turn myself for you."

"Strength and Patience of the Hill," he said to me then, "tell me, where are you from?"

"A hillside in the north," I said.

"And before that?"

"I hardly know what you mean," I replied.

He stood there, perhaps considering the possible implications of my answer. My attendants stood in a tiny knot, off to the side, the woman with the limp leaning on the fossil-filled wall of the city—it had been time for her to rest anyway. All of them eyed Oissen warily.

"Tell me, Strength and Patience of the Hill, that you will return to your northern hillside and not trouble us further, once this war is over."

"Oh, I will if I possibly can," I told him.

After that, Oissen instructed my attendants what to ask for when they worked. Not coincidentally, it marked the end of their turning me as a rite for the benefit of Oissen. And when the Myriad next visited me, she said, "The dog is angry with

potential dangers for you in that. What if someone besides the gods of Ard Vusktia turns you? Or what if one of your own attendants makes some disastrous request?"

"For the most part," I replied, "I suspect my attendants would wish for rest, or better-tasting food." And an end to the war, but nearly everyone here was wishing for that, and I was already working toward that end. Well, the woman with part of one arm missing had wished for a certain kind of cheese with honey, a wish that it had taken me some days to fulfill without raising the suspicions of the gods of the city. Still, fulfilling it had been costly, and I'd warned Siat to tell my other attendants that such wishes must be used carefully, and sparingly. But tricky to fulfill as it had been, I didn't begrudge it—the woman had divided the treat into four portions and shared it with the other attendants, and I was surprised at how gratified I was by their enjoyment of it.

"But are you certain you haven't spoken yourself into a trap, with this granting-wishes-for-turning-you business?" the Myriad asked.

"How could I be?" I did not tell her—mostly because I was sure that she already knew or suspected—that Oissen had already made use of my promise, and was steadily draining my power for his own ends, and those of the other gods of Ard Vusktia. So far the loss was not debilitating, but I knew that if it went on long enough it might be. The longer the Raven waited to attack directly, the weaker I would be when that attack finally came, and, I suspected, the weaker the Ard Vusktian gods would be.

But as it happened, we did not have to wait long after that for the Raven's assault.

At length you slept. And woke to find Mawat, dressed, sitting on a stool beside your bed, a lamp on another stool beside him. "Tikaz found you," he said, when he saw that you were awake. "And then she gave me an earful about attacking the one person I could actually trust." You didn't answer, just closed your eyes again. "I think she likes you." And then, after a few moments of silence, "Are you going to say anything?"

"It hurts to talk," you whispered. "Is there water?"

"I knew you'd be angry," you said, your voice gaining a little strength. "It would have been safer for me to lie. I wasn't lying."

Tikaz came in then, with a cup and a pitcher of water. Mawat reached out for them, but she held them out of his reach and sat on the bed herself. "Can you sit up?" she asked you.

You sat up. She poured a cup of water, gave it to you, and then took it away again when your hands shook so much the water spilled. "When did you eat last?" she asked. "I'll have some broth up for you."

"Tikaz," Mawat began.

"You be quiet," she snapped. "You and your temper, and your *I'm sorry* after. Look at him." She held the cup of water to your mouth, and you drank.

"He *lied* to me," said Mawat. "He said he went under

the tower, and found my father there. Still...still alive. It's impossible."

Tikaz glared at him. "Go away." She gave you another sip of water. "Your Xulahn friend, Dupesu, was very interested in the story of your disappearing in the middle of the square today. The landlady has thrown them out. But they haven't left Vastai. They're sleeping somewhere outside of town, and they were at the tower asking for an audience again today, like always."

"How did you do it?" asked Mawat. "You were there, and then suddenly you weren't."

"My lord, I'll tell you," you said. "I'll tell you the truth even if you kill me for it." Mawat said nothing. "Your father's still alive, my lord," you said. Nearly croaked. "The lord Hibal has him tied up, right outside the room with the stone. I was hiding behind the bones." I suspect you realized, then, that it had not been a very good hiding place. That it was not the bones that had prevented Hibal from seeing you. "I heard him talking. He said that the Raven was dying, that since the Raven promised that your father can only die by sacrificing himself, he—Hibal, I mean—has only to prevent that, and then wait for your father to die, and then he'll know the god is dead. The god has been weakening all these years, he said, it's the stone that's been keeping Iraden safe. Hibal spoke of deliberately killing the Instrument, of denying the Raven the sacrifice of your father's life. My lord, he means to kill the god."

"Lies," said Mawat, though he did not move from the stool.

whole day later. The tower is full of guards and servants, there's no way he could have come and gone without anyone seeing him."

"I'll show you," you said. And you held up that roll of leather wrapped with snakeskin on its cord. "I found this behind the bones. Watch." And you closed your hand around the cylinder.

Mawat stood so suddenly the stool tipped over and crashed into the one next to it, with the lamp. Tikaz grabbed the lamp before it could tumble over. "Eolo," she said.

Mawat reached forward, patted and smoothed the bed all around you. "He's gone." You let go of the cylinder, and he blinked. Asked, "Where did you go?"

"Nowhere," you told him. "I was sitting here the whole time."

"No," he protested. "I felt the whole bed, you weren't there."

"You may have thought you did," you said, "but you didn't. This is how I left the tower. I was holding this, and I just walked out and no one saw me. I tried to speak to you, my lord, but you just looked straight at me. I didn't even remember I was holding it until I came back here, to the house. In the square, before, when you were... You just... When I put my hand around this you just let go of me. And you were looking for me but you kept just walking around me."

"What is it?" Tikaz asked.

"It's godspoken," said Mawat. "It must be."

Tikaz seemed too surprised to stay angry at Mawat. "What, you mean like in stories? But I thought the gods stupid enough to make something godspoken had all destroyed themselves by now. Or near enough."

"Sometimes one of the Tel will carry a godspoken weapon," said Mawat. "If we capture it, we try to find some way to break it. Most Tel gods try to be very cautious about their speech when they make a thing godspoken. They usually include lots of qualifiers, or some condition that cancels whatever promise they've made, with little or no penalty to them. And that usually means the weapon can only do so much, or do it so often. Even so, not many gods try it."

"Maybe this one is from Ard Vusktia," Tikaz suggested.

"I heard there are weapons from that war, under the tower."

"It was on the floor behind a pile of skulls," you said. "And there's nothing else down there besides those bones.

move about the tower unseen and do whatever he liked. And then, when everyone was looking for your father, he could have hidden it. All he'd have had to do was drop it down that stairwell, or maybe he kept it on him until he took the bench, and then left it below, where he knew he could find it again if he ever needed it."

"The Xulahn god, whoever it is, won't have given this to Hibal without limits," Mawat pointed out.

"No," you agreed. "There'll be something."

"Can more than one person use it?" asked Mawat. "Can we both put our hands over it?"

You took the cord from around your neck and held your hand out flat, that small snakeskin-wrapped cylinder in your palm, and Mawat laid his hand over yours.

"Oh, the trees in the forest," swore Tikaz. "You're both gone. Let go, Mawat, this isn't right and I don't like it."

Mawat let go of your hand, and Tikaz drew an unsteady breath. "Don't do that again. Either of you."

"Nothing was different," said Mawat. "But you were gone before, Eolo. I've seen things that turned people invisible, the Tel have tried to use them, but if it rains, or if you bump into them... And I could still see us. But you were gone, before."

"I wasn't gone," you told him. "People moved aside for me and didn't realize they were doing it. Just now you ran your hand over the edge of the bed, but you thought you'd felt all of it."

"It doesn't exactly make you invisible, then," said Tikaz. "It makes people not realize you're there."

Mawat thought about that for a few moments, frowning. "I'm glad none of the Tel gods have thought of doing it that way."

You frowned down at your hand. And, probably guessing where Mawat's next thoughts would lead him, "My lord, I left your father under the tower."

"None of that," Mawat warned.

"I'm not lying, my lord," you insisted.

"What you're telling me," Mawat said, slowly and clearly, his words precise, "is not possible. If you had gone under the tower you would never have been able to come up again."

Tikaz stepped between the two of you and crossed her arms. "Mawat, don't be stupid. There's no one in Iraden less likely to be lying to you than Eolo." Mawat stared at her, and she glared back at him.

"I can prove it, my lord," you said. And gestured to the cylinder he still held. "I'll go under the tower and come

It was night by the time you left the guesthouse, you and Mawat, your hands pressed together. The guards at the fortress gate did not even glance at either of you as you entered, nor did the guards at the tower door. You walked silently up the tower steps, passing a pair of servants who did not seem to see you, though they stepped aside for you as they passed. Mawat said nothing, had said nothing at all since he had held out his hand to you in your room in the guesthouse.

A single lantern burned on a stand where the stairs came out onto the top of the tower. Mawat took it in his free hand. The sky was clouded, and the breeze had turned, blowing out over the strait. Here and there a ship's lantern glimmered over the water.

"How far down do I need to go?" you asked, when you were both at the top of those other stairs.

"You may as well go all the way down," said Mawat. "If you're so committed to the lie." He held out the lantern.

"I'm not lying, my lord," you told him, and took it. "I'll go all the way down, and I'll come up again." Without a word, Mawat let go of your hand, and you descended, your heart beating faster and harder as you went lower and the grinding sound grew louder.

The landing at the bottom was submerged again, the water about ankle deep. You trudged through it, stood and looked at the next flight, that led to the Lease, and to me. "No," you said. And turned around, and went back up to the top of the tower. Partway up you doused your light, and went slowly the rest of the way, feeling for each step, your hand touching the wall beside you. When you felt the open air on your face you stopped and listened. No sound except me, grinding away, and the faint sound of the waves below. Slowly, cautiously, you came all the way up the steps. A lantern burned not far from where you stood, but you didn't see anyone. You said, quietly, "My lord."

Nothing, for a full five seconds, and then Mawat opened his hand, and you saw him on his knees before the Raven's nest, Radihaw's bag of tokens in his other hand, a single, copper-inlaid token on the stone in front of him. You stood there, not speaking.

"I took Radihaw's tokens," he said, at length. "I opened

the door and walked right in, and the fool didn't even know I was there." And when you said nothing, "I asked the god why you lied to me."

"What does it say?" you asked.

The Lease still lay in the anteroom, facing the bones of his predecessors. Eyes closed, still breathing. Mawat held the lantern up so the light shone on him. "Father," said Mawat, his voice flat.

The Lease opened his eyes. "Mawat!" he said. "Cut me free! Quickly, before that shit-eating brother of mine finds us. Or have you killed him already? Is he dead?"

"No," said Mawat, still flat and toneless.

"You'll do for him," said the Lease. "But first cut me loose and give me your knife."

"No," said Mawat again.

"This is no time for one of your moods, boy," rasped the Lease. "Do you think I wanted this? Do you think *I* put Hibal in your place? It's Hibal who's done this, him and that bitch Zezume. Cut me loose so I can die for the Raven, and then you can do whatever you like with your uncle."

"You *failed*," said Mawat. "All you had to do was die. That's all!" The lantern shook in his hand, and disgust and fury filled his voice. Up to this moment he had held fast to the certainty that his father had kept his word, but now the truth was before him, unignorable. "Offer yourself to the Raven and die! Why are you still alive?"

"Look at me!" the Lease retorted weakly, and twitched against his bonds.

"My lord," you said. Though you said nothing further, and I wasn't sure what it was you had intended in speaking.

"Raven help me," said the Lease, weakly. "The only son I know of, and Zezume leading you around by the ear all your life. This is her doing, you never had the guts to do anything on your own. And now you're traitor to the Raven, just like your fucking uncle."

"Ten days," said Mawat, coldly. "*Ten days.* And still alive. Do you remember that Tel boy, last year? He kept his promise with a barely sharpened bit of metal he hadn't had when we'd bound him. Stalker gave it to him somehow, and he needed only his own determination for the rest. Am I to believe the Raven wouldn't have assisted you, if you'd asked?"

"I did ask. With no reply or result. Am I supposed to ~~kill myself~~ through sheer willpower? By wishing hard

~~father's~~

the floor and out onto that landing and wait for ~~the tide to~~ come in."

The breath went suddenly out of the Lease, and it seemed he could not find a reply.

"It's clear to me now," said Mawat. "You failed in your promise. You're no longer the Lease. You haven't been, from the moment Hibal left you down here and you did *nothing*." He made a disgusted noise and turned away, toward the door that led to where I was.

"You, there, boy," said the Lease, seeming to notice you for the first time. "Cut me loose!"

You stared at him, horrified. His betrayal had perhaps struck Mawat more personally—how could it not have?—but it was no less a betrayal of you. Of all of Iraden.

Mawat swung open that oaken door, and the sound of grinding drowned out anything further the Lease might have said. For a few moments Mawat stared at me, turning, and then he swung the door shut, and turned and went out onto the stairs, not even looking at his father.

You followed him. He stood two steps down, still holding the lantern out stiffly before him. There were tears in his eyes. "My lord," you said.

"All my life." Not to you, but to the air. As though you weren't even there. "All my life," he said again, and finally he looked at you.

You frowned, puzzled, not understanding, I'm sure, what Mawat meant by that. "My lord..." You seemed to change your mind about what you were going to say. "What is that thing in there? That stone?"

"I don't know," said Mawat. "I always knew there was something down here, something the Lease took care of. That must be it, there's nothing else here." He sat down on the step, set the lantern beside him, and closed his eyes. "What does Hibal want? What is he doing? What exactly did you hear him say?"

"My lord, if your uncle comes down here..."

Mawat made a dismissive gesture. "He won't. The tide is coming in. Look."

I doubt the water on the landing before you looked any deeper, but you seemed to accept this, sat down on the step beside him, and reported Hibal's words as well as you remembered them. "Hibal seems to think that that...that thing in there is a godspoken object. Before I came down here the first time, I heard that there were rumors of weapons down here, from the war with Ard Vusktia."

"It's Ard Vusktian, I'm sure of that," said Mawat.
~~~~d ~~~~ners *it,* you said he said. You're right, it
~~~~ ~~~~+? What

Mawat ~~~~~~~
one way to make sure not just anybody will use y~~~~~ g
spoken object," he said finally. "Make it too big to easily move it, and make moving it the way it works. It must be powerful enough that when the war was over the Raven thought it worthwhile to bring it here, and set it up so that it would always move."

"My lord," you said, and grimaced. From apprehension, fear of how Mawat would respond to what you were about to say. "When I was down here the first time, that thing...it spoke to me."

Mawat turned to stare at you. "*Spoke* to you? How? What did it say?"

"I don't know how it spoke," you confessed. "It sounded...I don't know, it was a horrible sound, it was..." You shook your head, distressed all over again at the memory of it. "It was awful."

"*What did it say?*" insisted Mawat.

"My lord, it said, *Now, Eolo, can you hear me?* And I said…I couldn't move at first, but then I said, *What?* But I couldn't even hear my own voice, and it didn't say anything else. And then I ran. I ran out here. My lord, didn't the Ard Vusktians, during the war, didn't they imprison gods so that their own gods could drain them of power?"

"They did," Mawat said. "Or so I've heard. But it hardly matters. What matters is, Hibal is determined to deny the Raven his sacrifice. Which means he has no intention of paying as Lease himself. He means to betray the Raven." He frowned in silence for a few minutes as you sat beside him, tense and tired and miserable. You closed your eyes, leaned forward, and rested your arms on your knees and your head on your arms. "What if Hibal is at least partly right?" asked Mawat. "The Raven is always vulnerable between Instruments. What if Hibal is right that the god needs the payment in order to inhabit the new Instruments? So he denies the Raven his payment. And he thinks that thing in there"—he gestured toward the doorway that led to the chamber where I turned—"will keep things running long enough for him to find some other god to serve Iraden. You told me he said as much."

"My lord," you said, and lifted your head from your arms. "How is your uncle sitting on the bench? How is he still alive?"

Mawat brushed that aside with a gesture. "He'll have

managed that on some technicality. Zezume…He couldn't have done this without Mother Zezume's approval." His voice wavered.

think   Where is the God of the Silent

"I…," you said.

Mawat waved away your barely formed protest. If the God of the Silent isn't dead, it's dying, or at least too weak to do anything anymore. No, it's not the forest helping Hibal. But the Xulahns." He looked down at the snakeskin-wrapped cylinder hanging from its cord around his neck. "No doubt the god my uncle wants to bring in is a Xulahn one. He gets to be Lease with all its privileges and no need to ever pay, and Xulah gets preferential treatment going through the strait, or crossing it." He gave a short, sardonic laugh. "If he thinks he can keep any sort of independence once he's made that deal, he's a fool."

"That's why he won't give them what he promised, now he has what he was after," you suggested.

"He's doubly a fool if he thinks he can get away with that, if Xulah has made up its mind otherwise. No, we have to stop him. He's determined that the Lease not be paid. So we make sure to pay it. By my preference, we make sure

Hibal himself pays it. And he's relying on that thing in there to do…something needful while he does whatever it is he's doing. So we stop it doing whatever it's doing. So how do we do that?" He rose. "Show me this room full of wheels."

"My lord," you said, "I don't…Are you sure? Can you ask the Raven?"

"I've just been telling you…" And he stopped. And then smiled grimly. "No, wait." He pulled out the black, gold-embroidered bag of tokens. "Let's ask." He loosened the bag's mouth and went to stand on the landing outside the doorway. "God of Vastai!" he said. "I am ashamed to say that my father has failed in his duty to you, and my uncle plots against you. What do I need to do, to help you?" He tilted the bag and shook it, gently. A half dozen tokens tumbled out, to lie in a perfectly straight line on the landing at Mawat's feet. *"Stop the wheels,"* he read aloud.

The hairs on the back of your neck stood up. "Mawat," you said, "are you sure that's the Raven answering?"

"Who else would it be? God of Vastai, what is that thing, that stone turning in the other room?"

A godspoken thing from the war with Ard Vusktia, came the reply.

"My lord," you insisted, "it *spoke* to me!"

"Did it speak to Eolo?" Mawat asked.

I spoke to Eolo, was the reply that Mawat read off. *I am the god of Vastai, who sustains Iraden. There is no other god in this tower. Help me. Stop the wheels.*

"There isn't a token with my name, surely," you protested.

"No, some of the tokens are whole words, and some-
‸ " Mawat said. "And rhyming." He

tower. Wait here, I won't ⌐⌐ ⌐⌐⌐ ⌐

He left you to sit on the stairs as he waded across the landing and went up. You sat for a while, and then, having
reached some sort of conclusion, you drew your knife and
went back up the steps to the room that led to where I was,
went over to Mawat's father and knelt—to cut his bonds,
I think—but you stopped and put your knife away when
you saw he was already dead.

You knelt there a few moments next to the corpse, your
skin prickling, perhaps with cold, perhaps fear. Then you
stood, and went back to sit on the yellow stone steps and

stare at the tokens that still lay on the landing. "You spoke to me," you said.

Two tokens rose, set themselves next to your hand, inlaid sides up. You tensed, frightened. "I can't read those," you said. The tokens turned themselves over. You frowned. "Was the first one *yes*?"

Yes.

"And the other one was no."

Yes.

"How can we come up and down these stairs? Isn't it supposed to be that only the Lease can do that and live?"

Yes.

"So is it you who did that? Who made it all right for us to come down here, me and my lord Mawat?"

Yes.

"And what about Hibal? How did he do it? Or did he?"

One token sat inlaid side up, one flipped inlaid side down. "What is that supposed to mean, *It's complicated*?"

Yes.

"My lord's father is dead." You shivered again.

Yes.

"Did you do that?"

Yes.

"Didn't my lord say that the Lease could only die by sacrificing himself to the Raven?"

Yes.

"Then how ... Wait, is it true, was he not the Lease any-more because he'd failed to pay?"

It's complicated.

~~~~~ asked.

It's complicated.

"Is Hibal right, is the Raven dying?"

No.

"Will stopping the wheels help the Raven?"

It's complicated.

"Am I right to mistrust you?"

Yes.

"Are there any other gods here in the tower right now, besides you?"

No.

You frowned. Thought for a few moments. "Are you the stone?"

"What sort of question is that?" Mawat, coming across the flooded landing below where you sat. He came splash-ing up the steps, a large, heavy, iron-headed hammer in his hands. He looked down at where you sat, saw the rows and rows of inlaid tokens so neatly laid out beside you. "I didn't think you could read these."

"I can't. What do they say?"

"I have been thinking about this question," read Mawat. "What is a name? Where do names come from? What if the sounds that make the word *the Raven* in Iradeni make some other meaning in another language, and that meaning is not what I am? What if sometimes I am called the Raven but sometimes something else? Is there one essential name for anything? How can I truthfully answer such a question with merely yes or no?" He looked at you. "Eolo, have you been interrogating the god?"

Those two tokens nearest you jumped, spun, landed both inlaid side up. *Yes.* "That means *yes*," you said.

Mawat shook his head. Then he hefted the hammer in his hands. "Show me these wheels."

At first Mawat was unsure what to do—the wheels and shafts were too large and sturdy for hammering on them to have much effect, even with so large a hammer as the one he had brought. But after watching things spin for a few minutes, Mawat said, "Ah, I see," and swung the hammer into a place where one wheel met another. Wood cracked,

and splintered, and the hammer caught and stuck between
the teeth of the wheels, and they both came to a straining
stop

                              but the sound of wood creak-

for someone to notice the sudden

must surely follow.

The wood of the wheels creaked and groaned, louder,
and then, somewhere below, something snapped, startling
you into a gasp, and then the whole arrangement of wheels
and shafts subsided into silence.

"Right, then," said Mawat, and strode back out to the
steps. You followed, stopped a moment, and stared at me,
finally motionless and quiet. It was difficult for me to say
whether you were relieved or frightened by my stillness.
Perhaps you were both. Then you caught up with Mawat,
went out into the antechamber, past the body of his
father—Mawat did not even glance in that direction—and
out onto the stairs, where Mawat swept up the scattered
tokens and put them in the bag.

"I've stopped the wheels," he said. "If I can make Hibal
pay his life, as he owes, will I be Lease then?"

Talk to Zezume, was the reply.

A sharp, angry hiss from Mawat. "Oh, I have every intention of doing that." He looked up. "Let's go."

"Where, my lord?" you asked, though from your obvious trepidation you already knew the answer.

Mawat held out his hand. The leather cylinder on its cord lay in his palm. "To talk to Mother Zezume."

There was a servant at the top of the tower, the one who had brought you to the stairs the day before. He was laying a new fire in the brazier. Without knowing that he did so, he moved aside so that you both could pass, the cylinder held between you. The eastern sky was beginning to lighten through the clouds. Mawat held your hand firmly in his and walked without hesitation to the other stairs, and all the way down, past the unseeing guard, out across the dark court of the fortress. Lights shone near the kitchen, the cooks and other servants there beginning their day. You followed him into the building where his own rooms were, but down a different corridor, to a different door. Unbarred, because Mawat opened it and walked in.

Benches and chairs. Dark, heavy hangings covered the windows. A banked fire in the fireplace, a servant dozing in a seat by the door. Mawat walked straight on through to ⸺ ᵗ⁻ Zezume's bedchamber, you fol-

Mother Zezume isn't there, ⸺

"Obviously." Neither of you spoke aloud the obvious conclusion—if Zezume was not in her own bed at this hour, then she was almost certainly in the House of the Silent. Your hand still tightly in his grasp, Mawat turned and strode out of the room, through the corridor, out into the fortress yard.

"My lord, what are we going to do?" you asked, your voice still hushed.

"Talk to Zezume," he replied. "As the god told me to."

His answer distressed you, although you'd already known that was his intention. You frowned and made a small noise as though you had been thinking of saying something but had, at the last moment, changed your mind.

You walked through the fortress gate, through the empty square, down the main street of Vastai. Here and there you passed someone walking in the slowly lightening street, but for the most part you might as well have walked openly—most of Vastai was still abed, or indoors laying fires, warming water, or going about any number of other tasks. By the time you reached the House of the Silent the sun had nearly risen. Still grasping your hand, Mawat strode unhesitating toward that stake-guarded gate.

"My lord!" you protested, and when he didn't slow you stopped, braced yourself so that in the moment it took for Mawat to realize you had stopped you wouldn't fall over.

He turned. "What?"

"My lord, I can't go in there."

"I've already told you," he said. "The forest isn't going to do anything to you."

"I'm not going in there," you insisted.

"Why are you being stupid about this?" Mawat demanded. "Zezume is in there, and the god told me to talk to Zezume."

"Only women can go in there. I'm not a woman."

"I never said you were," said Mawat. "*I'm* going in there. I'm going in there now." He turned away.

"Let go of me!" you cried. "I'm not going in there!"

Mawat made an impatient noise and let go of your hand, leaving the cylinder in your palm. You closed your fingers over it and stood, shaking with distress and anger, breathing hard, by the gate to the House of the Silent.

You cried out in dismay as Mawat came back into the street, dragging Zezume, stumbling, by her arm. "Since you insist," he said, and threw her to the ground. "We'll have this conversation out here."

"My lord," you said, "what are you doing?" But of

Raven and my father. ꞮꞮꞯ p⸱⸱

bad enough! Why, with my father gone and the Instrument dead, with me on my way, why did you rush to put my uncle in my place? *My uncle!*" His voice broke, and he took in a sobbing breath. "He doesn't belong on the bench any more than *you* do!"

"This is not the time or the place to talk about this," said Zezume, in a quieter though still angry voice. The sun had risen, the street was growing lighter, and people gathered around the commotion in the street. A wagon, pulled by a pair of oxen, pulled up short, and the driver sat, staring.

"You're the one who didn't want to keep this indoors," Mawat retorted. "Answer now! Let all of Iraden hear." He gestured to the watching people.

"Fool!" spat Zezume. "You grew up in the fortress, you were trained for the bench, how can you be so bereft of understanding?" She shook her head, but did not try to get to her feet. "Where is Eolo? Still bedridden, I presume, or he'd have talked some sense into you."

You gasped at the injustice of this. "How am I supposed to..." But she couldn't see you or hear you, and you subsided, frustrated.

"Or he'd have tried to, anyway," Zezume continued. "You don't listen to him nearly as often as you should."

"Eolo has nothing to do with this," Mawat said, coldly.

"More's the pity," replied Zezume. "Have your way, you always do. When your father disappeared, your uncle came to me, very eager, very urgent. It was clear he'd do anything it took to get himself seated. There were only two people who could have succeeded your father—you or your uncle. Hibal was determined it would be himself. And you—yes, you were riding here, you were on your way, and anything could happen, between here and there. Anything could happen once you'd arrived. If I'd denied Hibal, all he had to do was find some way to dispose of you before you could be seated, and there would be no one else to take the bench. All you had to do was be *patient*." She laughed, short and bitter.

"Patient, Mother of the Silent?" demanded Mawat. "Patient! My uncle never intended for me to succeed him. He never intends to pay the Raven! He has betrayed the god of Vastai, betrayed the agreement, betrayed all of Iraden, and you have *helped him do it*!"

"I saved your *life*!" Zezume insisted. "I did it for Iraden, and I did it for you, miserable boy! Because I might as well have been your mother." Her voice at those last words was choked with tears, and she put her face in her hands, weeping.

⸱ ⸱ ⸱ dozen fortress guards pushed through the

He's lost ...

A servant ran out of the House of the Silent to Zezume's side. The motion distracted you, and you turned.

And saw Dupesu, not far off. Looking directly at you.

"Friend Eolo," he said, unsmiling. "You have a thing that is belong to us." From under his short cloak, the snake's tongue flickered.

"Now, my lord Mawat, be calm," said Radihaw, and you turned again to see him pushing his way into the press. You hesitated a moment, torn: try to help Mawat, or deal with Dupesu?

You ran toward Mawat. Toward Radihaw. People moving unaware out of your way, and you arrived at Mawat's side in time to see Okim furtively pull Mawat's knife from his belt and thrust it toward Mawat's midsection.

At that moment Radihaw forced himself between the two, and the knife sank into his side. Okim quickly let go of the knife, and Oskel stared, frowning a moment, and then cried, "Murder! Hold Mawat fast! He's stabbed the lord Radihaw!"

You reached Mawat then, and the guards cried out in amazement at his disappearance as you took his hand and ran. Ran, and turned down an empty alley, where you pressed the cylinder into Mawat's hand and let go, and said, "Go!" And remembered Dupesu, then. Said, though you could no longer see that Mawat was still there beside you, "Dupesu saw me back there, my lord. The Xulahns can still see you. Be careful."

"I will," he said, still breathless from the struggle, and your flight. "I'm going back to the tower, to watch and listen, and decide what to do next."

But you neither saw nor heard him. You leaned forward, put your hands on your knees a moment to let your breathing settle, and then straightened and made your way by means of backstreets to the guesthouse.

A few days after the Myriad had warned me that Oissen was angry, a storm came through the strait. It was fierce enough that my attendants couldn't work, but huddled in

my lee as it swept over us. It blew all afternoon, and into the evening, but eventually it passed. In the morning the sky was still full of clouds, and a mist hung over the har-
~~~~ ~~~ ~~~~~ hevond. Out in the strait the waves rode

~~~~~ ~~~~ ~~~~~~ ~

then, anyone crossing the strait today might well be taking their life into their hands. Still, the watchers on the water-front were vigilant.

It was about noon when the ships loomed out of the mist, six of them, long, low, single-sailed things. When they reached the harbor mouth I felt the sudden pull of strength as the gods of Ard Vusktia called on my resources to bol-ster theirs, and a black, whining cloud shot past the quays and out over the water, sped along by a gust of wind. A whale, fifty feet long, mottled gray and white, crusted here and there with barnacles, rose out of the water and crashed down onto the foremost boat. Beyond, dozens of long, needle-toothed gar and brown-and-blue weevers, spines extended, leaped onto the other boats, biting and flipping. The whale slid into the water, the foremost boat righted itself, people floating or thrashing helplessly in the water beside it. More gar, more weevers jumped out of the water and onto the boats, and I felt another drain of power as a wave swept across their decks, leaving masses of stinging jellyfish behind.

The dark cloud reached the boats, hundreds of thousands of mosquitoes. They landed on the crew and passengers, biting and biting every inch of exposed skin, crawling into the smallest openings in armor, under collars and sleeves, and biting the skin beneath. People clinging desperately to ropes, to the gunwales, so as not to be washed overboard, let go and dived into the water, desperate to escape the Myriad's forces. The ships now were drifting, battered by the waves, by the whale, and by each other, and those remaining on the ships bitten and stung, hard-pressed to reach an oar, a tiller, or a sail, let alone bring their ships under control.

By now Ard Vusktia's own boats were launched, aimed straight for the Raven's beleaguered ships—the Ard Vusktian sailors hoped to capture some or all of those. The Myriad's cloud of mosquitoes was much diminished now, but the gar and the weevers continued to jump onto the boats, the waves continued to deposit jellyfish, and every few minutes that barnacle-crusted whale breached and smashed into whatever lay beneath its fall. The gust that had blown the mosquitoes out to the boats returned as a steady, powerful wind that blew out from the harbor toward the open water, pushing the half dozen boats around and back. That wind continued to blow steadily, but the mist did not blow away. I didn't know enough of the situation, didn't know enough about the Raven and his forces, to come up with a better plan, and so at the moment it was best to wait, to see what more the gods of Ard

But Vastai's boats were in disarray, drifting, uncontrolled, while their crew and passengers scurried here and there in panic. They would doubtless be easily captured when the Ard Vusktian boats reached them. Unless the Raven had something more planned, it seemed the battle was won. Was this all the Raven had sent against us?

It was not.

The mist rolled aside, and over the water came thousands of armed and armored soldiers, marching on the air above the waves as though over a bridge that lay across the strait. The boats, the jumping fish, parted before them.

Power drained out of me, and a wave washed over the marchers. They did not waver even a fraction of an inch, but marched steadily forward. Some of the column split off, to head for the Ard Vusktian boats, to step out of the air onto the decks and slaughter the sailors. No weapon seemed to harm them, they slashed and hacked, some of them with swords or arrows lodged in their bodies, oblivious to what ought to have killed them. As the main column came closer, a sudden drain of my own power nearly knocked me out of the stones of the quay, and the wind blew with deadly force and pushed the first several ranks of marchers out of the air and into the water, and I finally understood: the soldiers that had fallen floated in the water, now just rough-hewn logs of wood. The marchers were things of the God of the Silent Forest.

This was surely costing the Iradeni gods a great deal. One log of wood, made to look like a person, to move, to swing a sword—that might not be much, for a large, powerful god. But thousands of them? Moving and fighting continuously? Marching over air as though it were solid ground? Maintaining that movement, and the illusion of humanity, despite the combined opposition of all the gods of Ard Vusktia? That was surely the forest, and surely the result of a great effort. And how could the Raven be sure that this, finally, would break the gods of Ard Vusktia? He could not. I was sure this was not all that was coming.

Another sharp drain of my power drove me out of the quay, and I contracted back to only myself, turning, my attendants grim and silent as they shoved me around, tired, aching, the two girls weeping—they had been working without a break since the Raven's ships had come out of the mist, were now working through pain and exhaustion, but they did not waver. The Myriad landed atop me. "This is not good," she said.

"I don't entirely understand the purpose of the wooden marchers." I admitted. "It seems wasteful and showy."

pened in the harbor, because I momentarily found myself sightless, soundless, inside my stone self. "...keeping them off the quays!" The Myriad, still speaking to me. "The defenses are barely holding, but they hold. Perhaps this is all that Vastai can muster against us. Perhaps the Raven will exhaust himself with this attack." Surely the Raven of Iraden was nearly as worn as the gods of Ard Vusktia after all this time. And if he failed now, if he drained his own strength too far, the untruth of his claim to the strait would rebound on him. He would be finished. "Perhaps he is near the end of his own resources and has thrown everything into this final attack. If we can only hold out..."

And suddenly the drain, the steady sapping of my power, stopped. "Which god was drawing power from me?" I asked.

"Was?"

"Which god?" I insisted.

"Adim-Chak." Adim-Chak had specialized in weather—had no doubt been behind that profoundly unlikely wind from the land out to sea. "Have they..."

"They aren't taking power from me anymore. If they've died, can Ard Vusktia still outlast the Raven?"

"I wouldn't have thought so," said the Myriad. "But I believe the defenses still hold."

The Raven had hoped, no doubt, to prevail by now. "Is it near enough," I asked, "for the Raven to speak his victory?" The Myriad did not answer, preoccupied, I suspect, with events elsewhere.

My attendants still turned me. If those wooden soldiers made their way past the quays they would no doubt march through the city, killing mercilessly. What would they do once they reached this gate, and my few tired, unarmed people?

"Stop!" I cried aloud.

It took a few moments for my attendants to realize that I had spoken. "What?" asked Siat, my priest. Still pushing. "What is it?"

"Stop!" I cried again, and they all four stopped, half-unwilling—they knew their efforts were contributing to the city's defense. "Flee north! You will go unseen by enemies, flee! You are under my protection!" And to the Myriad I said, "You should go back to your stones in the north, without delay."

"But what about you?" asked the Myriad.

"But the battle!" protested one of the women.

And then the Myriad cried, "The Raven has..."

And suddenly I felt as though I had been struck a

Here is a story I have heard:

Long centuries ago, the gods of Ard Vusktia promised the Raven a share in the sacrifices and offerings they received, because of his help in building the harbor. But nearly the moment the last stone was in place, they reneged on their deal, having found (or laid) a technicality in the words they had used. What was Vastai, and what were the gods of Vastai, and Iraden, that the wealthy and mighty gods of Ard Vusktia would ever require their help or owe them anything?

And so the Raven declared war on the gods of Ard Vusktia. For years the Raven and the forest were sore pressed by the attacks of the many powerful Ard Vusktian gods—made more powerful by their detestable practice of imprisoning smaller gods and forcibly draining them of their power. The Raven's allies, of course, were all willing, even enthusiastic volunteers. Though the God of the Silent helped, at first, only in the most desultory way, when it finally realized the importance of the struggle to itself, the forest threw all it had into the war.

Finally the time came when Iraden's forces made their last, desperate venture, one that had to win the war for good and all. Every Iradeni boat on the Shoulder Sea set out that day for Ard Vusktia—every ferry, every fishing boat, every simple raft, filled with all the able fighters of Iraden. A terrible storm blew up to prevent them, but the Raven calmed it and the boats sailed on.

Then a swarm of bird-size insect horrors swarmed out of the skies, six-legged monsters that drank sailors dry with a single bite, leaving them desiccated husks. A dozen gape-mawed whales surged to the surface, swallowing whole boats. Horrible poison-spined, dagger-toothed fish leaped out of the water to gnaw the living flesh off the Iradeni soldiers' bones. Soon there were fewer than a half dozen boats left, and dismembered corpses bobbed in the strait, tugged and chewed by horrors under the water, as the Ard Vusktian boats bore down on the few survivors.

And then the God of the Silent came marching to the rescue.

At first the arrogant gods of Ard Vusktia thought it would be a simple thing to destroy the apparently human soldiers, even directly assisted by a god as they obviously were. But despite all the Ard Vusktian efforts to stop them, the marchers—the forest itself—came inexorably over the waves, dispatching the monsters, stepping into

overcome. The gods of Ard Vusktia exhausted themselves against the God of the Silent, and the Raven had but to speak them all dead: every god of Ard Vusktia, and every god aiding the gods of Ard Vusktia.

The Raven and the forest between them destroyed all the weapons, godspoken or not, that Ard Vusktia had used against Vastai, and then—still, after everything, as strong as ever—the forest returned to the silent contemplation of its trees, having promised to continue to protect and defend the people of Iraden at need.

One hundred and twenty-seven people were hung on the Ard Vusktian quay, as sacrifices to the gods of Iraden and a warning to any Ard Vusktians who might be thinking of rebellion. The Raven ordered a fortress built there, and a tower in Vastai, from which he could watch over the strait. Ever since, the two cities have been at peace, and health and prosperity have visited both Vastai and Ard Vusktia. The Raven, after all, has only ever been concerned with the well-being of his people.

Only a story, though if you have been listening to me, and have understood me so far, you know that it is a story built around a particular selection of facts, twisted to particular ends. This version of events is widely repeated and believed all through Iraden, but it is rarely told in Ard Vusktia, and then only by Iradeni. People who pass on a different account of the events of that day generally don't do so within earshot of their Iradeni conquerors.

All things pass. Human life is brief. Even if the people in Ard Vusktia on that day had been allowed to live long and peaceful lives, they would all of them be dead by now. What is the difference? Why should I care if one or another human dies sooner rather than later? Or violently rather than peacefully? I don't know.

What I do know is that none of my four attendants were among those killed the day that Ard Vusktia fell to the Raven. For various reasons, I am fairly certain that while I lay outside the city wall, insensible, they escaped the wooden marchers and the human solders and did as I had bidden them, and fled to safety in the north.

Tikaz came into your room in the guesthouse in Vastai and said, "Tell me Mawat didn't do this." Dry-eyed and blank-faced. Her voice was flat and calm. "Tell me he didn't kill my father."

"He didn't." You were sitting on the edge of your bed. "He didn't do it. I was there. I had the thing, that cylinder in my hand, and I was watching the whole time. Some guards had his arms and I was coming to give the cylinder to Mawat so he could get away. One of the...one of *those two* grabbed Mawat's knife, and he was going to stab him with it, and your father stepped between them. I don't think he realized. Everyone was pressed close. I don't know if anyone else saw it."

"You'd lie for him," said Tikaz. Not as an accusation, but as a mere statement of fact.

"My lady," you said, "I'm not lying. That's what happened." She said nothing, just stared at you, now frowning slightly. You said, "The lord Hibal has been looking for some excuse to be rid of my lord Mawat. Those two are working for him, I heard them talking the first time I came up from under the tower. I don't think they meant to hurt your father, but it happened so fast."

"Where's Mawat?" Tikaz asked, her voice still chilly and even.

"I don't know," you said. "I gave him the thing, and I don't know where he is now." Tikaz didn't say anything for a few moments, and you added, "I'm sorry. I'm sorry about your father."

"He was an ass," she said, and she sat down beside you then, and put her face in her hands and wept.

"I'm sorry," you said again, helplessly.

After a while, Tikaz said, her face still in her hands, "Which one was it?"

"I don't know. I can't tell them apart."

"I'll have to kill them both, then," she said, her voice slightly exasperated, as though she had just been presented with a minor, unexpected chore. You didn't seem to know what to say to that, and sat there, looking at her. "Where is Mawat?" she asked again. "Really?"

"I really don't know. He's probably trying to figure out some way to make Hibal pay the Lease."

Tikaz looked up. Tears streaked her face, and her eyes were red. "He could be right here and we wouldn't know it."

"He could," you agreed. "But I imagine he's in the

Not long after that, the tower servant came to find you. "Your pardon, sir," he said, as though he had not brought you secretly to the top of the Raven Tower just days before. "The Raven's Lease requests your presence."

"Mine?" You feigned unworried surprise.

"Yours, sir," the servant confirmed. "As soon as you may be able to attend him."

"Which is to say, immediately," you guessed. "If you'll give me just a moment, I'll come right with you." For all the world as though the summons did not worry you in the least. But you went, then, to find the landlady's daughter, and asked her if she knew where you might find the lord Direction Dera.

"He's gone to the tower these few minutes past," she told you, "to attend the Lease." You thanked her and followed the servant, out of the guesthouse, across the square, and into the fortress.

In the tower yard you met Dupesu, standing, frowning at the tower entrance. There was no sign of the snake. "Ah, the friend Eolo!" he said, as you passed. "You are not have that thing that is belong to us anymore."

"I don't know what you mean," you replied, not stopping.

"Tell the lord Mawat," Dupesu called to your back as you walked on, "that we are want to help, if he is want to help us."

Inside the tower, the ground floor was empty, as you had always seen it. On the next floor, the various members of the Council of the Directions stood in small groups around the dais with its carved bench, talking. Waiting for Hibal to arrive so the day's suddenly urgent business could be attended to. The lord Dera among them.

"A moment, please," you said to the servant, and went over to Dera. All the Directions fell silent, watching you. "My lord Direction," you said to Dera. "Can I beg a favor of you? I'm summoned to the presence of the Lease, and...I would prefer not to go unaccompanied."

Dera stared at you a moment, and then said, "Yes, of course." He nodded to the other Directions and followed you out onto the stairs. "Were you there?" he asked, quietly, as you ascended behind the servant.

You looked at him, calculating, perhaps, and then said, "No."

to not even glance toward that second set of stairs, or the Raven's nest behind you, with its egg. "You wanted me?" You did not acknowledge the twins at all, or say anything about Dera standing beside you.

"Ah, the good Eolo," said Hibal. Oskel and Okim smirked. "And the lord Direction Dera, I see." Hibal frowned—he had surely not expected you to bring anyone, let alone a member of the Council of the Directions. "Is there some reason you feel you need the assistance of the lord Direction? Is there some petition you would make, or some case you need to bring?"

"I'm only a farmer's son from Oenda, Raven's Lease," you said.

"It's my business to assist the people of my district," Dera agreed, mildly.

Hibal considered this, still frowning, and then asked, "Where is Mawat?"

"I don't know, Raven's Lease," you said. "I wish I did."

"He seems to have lost his mind!" He shook his head. "Poor Radihaw. I'm sure he was only trying to help Mawat."

"I heard what people are saying," you said. "I can hardly believe any of it." You looked at Oskel, and then Okim, who still smirked.

"If you heard what happened," said Hibal, "then you know that by all accounts Mawat just suddenly..." He waved a hand. "Disappeared. He was just gone! Half a dozen guards had been holding on to him the moment before."

"That does make me wonder, Raven's Lease, how my lord Mawat managed to stab anyone, if he was so tightly held. Who else was near, I wonder?" You did not look at Oskel or Okim this time.

"The interesting thing to me is," continued Hibal, as though he had not heard you, "that a similar story was told to me of you, recently. That you had come out to speak to my nephew, and he in a sudden, inexplicable rage grabbed you and choked you and you suddenly just...weren't there anymore."

You shook your head. "No, Raven's Lease. It may have looked that way, but that's not what happened. I pulled loose from my lord and ran off, back into the guesthouse."

"Witnesses insisted that you were there, and then

suddenly you weren't. That Mawat himself was shocked and astonished at your disappearance."

"Raven's Lease, that's a sign of how unlike himself my lord has been lately. He was only in a temper, not intent

things."

"Raven's Lease," protested Dera. "Surely..."

You cut him off. "Search me, lord, if that will put your mind at rest." You held your arms out.

"Do," said Oskel. "Strip him naked, right here. Take the conceited dog down a peg or two. I'd like to see that!"

"As for you, sir," you said, "give me my knife and a fair and open fight, my one against you two, and I'll give you a lesson in taking down pegs."

Okim stepped forward and put his hand on his own knife. "I'd like to see you try!"

"I already have once," you said. "I'll be happy to repeat the lesson, since you need it."

"Gentlemen!" interjected Dera. And then, to Hibal, "Raven's Lease, this is unseemly in the extreme. You've summoned the good Eolo here to answer your questions, and it seems to me he's done his best to oblige you. And these two…" He hesitated and then continued. "In return for his obedience, Eolo has been met with insults and threats."

"Silence, you two!" demanded Hibal of the twins. And then, to you, "I'd thought you had more sense than this, Eolo. I brought you here because you're the person in all of Iraden most likely to know where Mawat is."

"I don't know, Raven's Lease." Your voice was tight and tense. "I wish I did know."

Hibal was silent a moment. "I know how loyal you are to Mawat, and it speaks well of you. But you yourself said he's not acting like himself. To attack you—you! Who are so devoted to him! To assault Mother Zezume—he walked into the House of the Silent and dragged her out into the street! And then to murder the lord Radihaw. No, he's not acting like himself at all, and he's become a danger to Vastai. I need to know where he is before he does any more harm, or even harms himself! It would be a great service to Vastai, and to Iraden. One I would be distinctly grateful for. You understand me, I hope."

"I understand you, Raven's Lease," you said, managing with great effort to make your voice even and sincere-sounding. "And I wish I knew where he was, but I don't."

"You'll tell me, if you learn where he is, won't you?" asked Hibal.

"Raven's Lease," you said, "if I learn where Mawat is, you will be the first person to know it."

"I can't ask better than that," said Hibal. "Now go. See what you can find out for me. Lord Direction Dera, I will

"It's no more than my duty, Eolo," he replied. "And that was a very interesting conversation. Call on me again if you need me." And he left you on the stairs and went to join the rest of the council in their wait for the Lease.

Outside the walls of the fortress, the air was still and close. And just faintly smoky. Of course, there was plenty of smoke in Vastai, but it seemed always to blow away. Today the smoke hung low over the roofs of the town, billows of

it rising somewhere away to the southeast. People in the square had turned to stare in that direction.

But you did not look where they looked. Instead you stared at Tikaz, kneeling on the stones of the square, her hands fists, the red and green silk of her dress slashed and torn.

She saw you and made a shrieking wail, leaped to her feet, ran over and grabbed you by your cloak, and pulled you toward her. "You!" she cried. "You! Where is he? Where is the murdering dog?"

"Lady," you said, "I don't know."

She grabbed hold of your shirt and pulled you closer. "Give me your knife," she whispered urgently, her face a mask of snarling anger. "They took mine from me, they said they were afraid I'd hurt myself. *Hurt myself!*" She shook you roughly, and threw her head back and wailed.

"Lady, be calm," you said in a loud voice, and made as if to pull away, shifting your cloak to fall around your body. "Take it," you whispered. And then, louder, "You shouldn't be out here, lady. You should go home and let your friends look after you."

She slid your knife from your belt and tucked it away behind the torn silk of her skirts. "I have no home!" she cried. "He's dead! Dead! And your master murdered him!" She shook you again, pulled your face close to hers, and whispered, "I'm telling you what I'm going to do with Mawat when I find him." And indeed her face and her voice were filled with distressed fury. "I've packed some things, not much, and hidden them. As soon as I've done for those two I'm going back to my mother. Come with me or don't."

tempt. And then wailed again, and cried out, "I will, do you hear me? I'll slice him open and have his guts out on the ground! I'll hack his limbs from his body and his head from his neck and leave him in pieces to rot in the street!" She shoved you away, and you stumbled back from her, nearly falling. "Tell him! Tell him I will!" and she collapsed to her knees again, her face in her hands, sobbing.

You were the center of attention now, everyone in the square staring at you both. You started to walk toward the guesthouse, saw the smoke still rising over the southeast of the town, and went that way instead.

A small house was on fire at the edge of the town, its thatched roof burning, smoke pouring out of its door and single window. The house's residents—two women and a half dozen children of various ages—stood in the street, away from the heat of the flames. The roof of the building next door had already begun to smoke and catch. Two lines were forming for passing buckets of water from the neighborhood well, not for the burning house—that was beyond hope by then—but to wet all the surrounding ones in the hope the fire wouldn't spread farther. You joined them, spent hours in a futile battle with the fire that, in the end, claimed three more buildings before it was finally put out, leaving you and everyone else exhausted and coughing and smelling of smoke, standing stunned in the street before the charred stone walls. Five minutes later the wind blew hard, one gust after another, clearing the last of the smoke from the air, and then rain swept across Vastai from the sea.

By the time you made it back to the guesthouse the rain had filled the street ankle deep with water. The water that ran off you in streams when you stepped into the guesthouse only added to the pool that had slipped under the door, that had grown even in the brief time it had been opened to admit you. The landlady's daughter ran to wad more blankets at the base of the door. "You were at the fire, then," she said, shoving one blanket into place with her foot. "It could have rained like this a bit sooner."

You gave a small, exhausted laugh. "That would have been nice. Is the lady Tikaz still outside?" There had been no way to see anything more than a few feet ahead of you.

"She's upstairs. I went out to fetch her as soon as it got

stone. And many of them are roofed with tile. But quite a few are thatched with straw, and nearly all of them have at least some wood in their construction—roof and support beams, stairs, doors. Not to mention all the various flammable contents of those houses. Open fires burned every day in nearly all of them, but there hadn't been a building burned in Vastai for three hundred years. This is the sort of service a god can do for people—a small one, when it comes to camps and villages, larger and more difficult for towns and cities. It's made easier by people taking care to keep flammable things away from the hearth, and to bank fires at night. But even a banked fire can flame to life if the wrong thing falls into it. And if there's been no accidental fire for centuries, likely people aren't taking quite as much care as they might to prevent them. "I heard they were going about their business, and suddenly saw the cloth on the loom burning—they'd set it near the fire, for light. The roof caught before they could put it out." You wiped rain-water out of your eyes. "I think everyone got out all right. And the other houses too." You took a deep, jagged breath, and coughed. "I need something to drink."

The rain lessened an hour after you had that drink, and something to eat, but still fell steadily all night. The water in the common room rose slowly, and the guests climbed onto the tables to sit, and sleep. The landlady and her daughter and the various servants did what they could to keep supplies in the kitchen from getting soaked, to keep the kitchen fire alight.

By morning the rain had stopped, and the sky was blue and cloudless. Tikaz resumed her vigil in the square, her red and green silk more tattered than ever, her hair ragged and wild. An inch or so of water still stood in the street, here and there the sodden corpse of a bird or a squirrel, and by afternoon it began to stink. Not just because of the dead animals, but also because nearly all the latrines in Vastai had flooded.

"Well," said one woman to another, eying Tikaz, her voice just slightly louder than it needed to be, "if some other man had gone into the House of the Silent, and thrown the Mother of the Silent into the street, his body would be in the forest by now. And murdered one of the Directions, to boot! The Lease can do anything he wants, but he can't just up and kill the Directions!"

"Apparently the Lease's Heir can," said her companion,

also just a bit louder than necessary. Carefully not looking toward the fortress gate to be sure any of the guards there had heard her. "If *I* were one of the Council of the Directions I'd be wondering about all this. First there's suddenly

into the fortress, where you found Dupesu and another Xulahn walking away from the tower. "Ah, friend Eolo," Dupesu said, coming near, the other Xulahn trailing him. "We are try to speak with the Raven's Lease but he is not see us again today. Are you speak to the Lease's Heir Mawat?"

"I told you, I don't know where he is."

"Do you not," replied Dupesu, not making a question of it. "We are want a thing, friend Eolo, and we are help a person who is help us get that thing."

"No doubt," you said shortly, and turned to go.

"We are not help a person who promise us a thing and then is not give it," said Dupesu, putting his hand on your elbow. "I am think the Raven's Lease Hibal is have problems."

"Remove your hand," you said. "Or I will remove it for you."

Dupesu raised both his hands, palms toward you, a placatory gesture. "I am not mean offend, friend Eolo."

"I'm not your friend."

"The heir is murder a councillor, yes? And…" Dupesu frowned. "I am seen such flood as was yesterday, and if there is not proper care there will be sickness."

"The forest protects us from sickness," you said. "It's not a problem here."

"Ah, but the Lease's Heir is…" Dupesu frowned, looking for a word. "He is do a bad thing to the god from the forest. He is do this thing, and then the storm. Such a storm! It is the sort of thing gods protect us from, is it not? It is just the sort of thing with illness following, and this god protects from illness." He shook his head. "It is maybe a problem here. The Raven's Lease is maybe need our help, but he is not see us. Maybe the Lease's Heir is see us, maybe we are help him instead."

"It's the Directions," you said. "Before he was on the bench, Hibal could see you whenever he wanted, he could meet people in the town, wherever. He could pay bribes, or receive them, discreetly. But now he's on the bench, now he goes nowhere but the tower, and on the few occasions he leaves the tower he goes surrounded by servants and councillors. It's much more difficult to meet with you privately. Hibal knew this when he made his promises to you, he surely understood that becoming Lease would remove him from your reach. If you yourselves did not understand this, that is no concern of mine, or my lord's. My lord will not sell Iraden to you for his own advantage."

"But we are only wish to cross the strait!" insisted

head. "Even for gold, you would not go to so much trouble. Not *just* for gold. But for gold and control of the strait? For that, I think you would go to great lengths."

"Friend Eolo," reproved Dupesu. "Xulah is very far away."

"Nearer all the time, I think."

"The mountains are between," Dupesu pointed out. "And the Tel."

"You found a way over the mountains," you said. "Or a god made you one. And you speak Tel very well. Much better than you speak Iradeni. You've spent a lot of time with them. You've spent a long time, or someone has, making a path that Xulahns can safely and conveniently follow."

"I am not call it safe or convenient, friend Eolo."

"No, not yet. But you're working on it."

"I am suggest you to think," Dupesu said, as you turned and walked away from him. "Hibal is Lease or Mawat is Lease. Maybe some other is Lease. We are not care." You did not answer him, only kept walking.

You had come to the fortress to visit Zezume, and when her maid ushered you in, the Mother of the Silent was sitting in a chair by the fire. "Well, child, it's good of you to come see me. I assume you heard what happened."

"I was there, Mother. I saw everything."

She frowned. "I don't remember seeing you there. Your lord could have used your good sense that morning."

"That's not fair, Mother," you protested. "Why do you expect me to be able to make my lord Mawat do anything, or keep him from doing whatever he takes it into his head to do?"

Zezume did not reply to that.

"Were you injured, Mother?" you asked. "My lord was very rough with you."

"My hip and my knee," Zezume said with a wry half

smile. "They were neither of them what they once were, and I can still walk, with help, but I won't be running or dancing anytime soon. If ever."

"I'm sorry," you said.

the rest of my family," she waved a hand. "I have outlived two husbands, several lovers, and all of my siblings. And their children have their own families to look after. They're none of them in Vastai."

"My lord didn't stab the lord Radihaw," you said.

"No, of course he didn't," agreed Zezume. "How could he have? Half a dozen guards were holding on to him, and the knife went in on the wrong side. It'll have been one of those two." Her voice gave only the slightest hint of disgust at the reference to Oskel and Okim. "And between them and the guards, Hibal surely knows it." She clenched one hand into a fist. "Oh, how long has Hibal been planning this? How long has he been sneaking and flattering and bribing? And how could Mawat not understand that now of all times he needed to hold his temper?"

"Mother," you began, and then hesitated. "My lord was

recently presented with undeniable proof that his father....
that his father failed to honor his obligation to the god of
Vastai."

"As if proof were needed!" exclaimed Zezume, before
you could elaborate. "Of course he failed to honor his obligation. So much is obvious. And he was never shy about
claiming all the privileges of the bench, on account of having pledged his life to the Raven. And now..." She was
silent a moment. "I have never been sure if Mawat did not
see his father's selfishness, or if he saw it and ignored it.
After all, what was he to do? What was any of us to do?
We have endured worse from the bench and doubtless will
again."

"I think, Mother, that you had some say in the matter."

Zezume laughed bitterly. "Do I look as old as all that?
No, I wasn't Mother of the Silent when Mawat's father
took the bench. For Hibal, though, I must take responsibility. Understand, I knew he was scheming. I knew he must
have had something to do with the Lease's disappearance.
If Mawat's father defaulted, it will have been Hibal who
put him in the way of it. But what I said to Mawat was
true—I did what I did to protect Mawat's life."

"Mother," you said then, "the aim was not only to take
the bench in my lord's place. Hibal is trying to kill the god
of Vastai. He is convinced that without the Lease's sacrifice,
the Raven will die." And at her incredulous look, "Please
believe me, Mother, when I say I heard Hibal say as much.

He didn't know I was there to hear him." Zezume stared at you, aghast. "My lord Mawat doesn't believe that's possible. But he suggested to me that...that the forest is...that the forest is no longer able to intervene in affairs."

"Mother," you said, "I have never been in the House of the Silent. I couldn't."

She nodded approval. "Of course not. The Silent doesn't speak by means of tokens, as the Raven does while in the egg, but it has its own ways of communicating. And... Well, I won't say more. A long silence from the forest means nothing."

"And have you heard news from the town lately?" you asked. "Mother, a house burned down the other day. Everyone is saying they don't understand how it could have happened, because the forest protects us from accidental fires. And that rain, it came just after we put the fire out, and the town was flooded."

"I heard," said Zezume. "The fortress was flooded as well."

"There's a man who came over from Ard Vusktia staying in the guesthouse. He's from far away, but he's visited Ard

Vusktia frequently. He warned us not to drink from any well in Vastai without pouring the water through finely woven cloth, folded many times. He also warned the landlady that she must boil the same water if she could, to prevent her guests from falling ill. There's a sickness he's seen…"

"Yes," Zezume broke in. "It's a sickness they've had in Ard Vusktia. There's always a danger of it when wastewater mixes with drinking water. But we've never had it here. The forest protects us from all such sickness."

"Mother," you said, "some children near the guesthouse have fallen ill. The visitor has been walking the streets, knocking on doors and warning people and telling them what to do so as not to fall ill. He brought us news of the sick children. I spent this morning carrying boiled water to them from the guesthouse, as the visitor advises they must drink a large amount of clean water if they are to have any chance of surviving."

"Well, you see?" said Zezume. "You doubted the forest's protection, but here is this person with the knowledge to help, at the right time."

"I would have thought the right time was before the children were so near death," you pointed out. "And quite a few people have refused to listen to him, saying that they never heard of such a thing, and besides the God of the Silent will protect them."

"The God of the Silent is a powerful god," said Zezume.

"But it has always done what it wished, when it wished, in the way that it wished. And it is not called *silent* for nothing." And, after a moment, "Are the children so very badly off?"

"I think some friends and servants are watching over her, as much as they can."

"Her sitting in the square is an embarrassment for Hibal so long as neither the Lease nor the Directions can produce Mawat, to face what he's done." Zezume shook her head. "Indeed, the Directions themselves are shamed by her, and they know it. There will be trouble between the council and the Lease on account of this. Still, what does she think she's doing? Haven't you told her that Mawat didn't kill her father?"

"She won't listen to me," you lied. "I tried to talk to her, but she only told me to carry her message to Mawat, what she would do to him when she found him. She's...she's not behaving sensibly. And after all, her father is dead."

"If she pushes too far," Zezume warned, "Hibal will have her forcibly removed. Not openly, no, that would be even more embarrassing to him than her presence in the square. He won't send guards in broad daylight to carry her off."

"Might he send...those two?" you asked. "I've noticed he's kept them close lately."

"Of course he has." Zezume's voice was scornful. "Foundlings, sent to the fortress, to be reared with the Lease's Heir? Someone knows who birthed those two, and who got them, and the rest of us have our suspicions." She sighed. "I tried to treat all the children just alike. I know that in Ard Vusktia no one cares about such births. I know there are other twins in Vastai, and the forest has never punished us for it. But..." She shivered, a small, barely noticeable movement. "When I look at them, it just seems wrong. I suppose they knew. How could they not?"

"So they're Hibal's children," you guessed.

"I always thought so," she agreed. "They'd be fools if they thought either of them could take the bench after Hibal, though. No Mother of the Silent would accept them. No Iradeni would."

"But if the bench were moved to Ard Vusktia?" you asked. "I hear rumors that Hibal is looking to do that. He could ignore the forest, ignore the House of the Silent. He could ignore the Council of the Directions. After all, the council only really rules in Iraden."

"Here or in Ard Vusktia, he can't ignore any of those," said Zezume. "Not without the Raven breaking his agreement with the forest. And anyway *those two* wouldn't need to think they could step up to the bench, to know that they would profit from being the Lease's sons. It matters, I suppose, how much he trusts them. But then, I heard have happened to me."

"Well," said Zezume. "Well. I'll have to think about all of this."

Recognizing that for a dismissal, you took your leave of her and went out, into the fortress yard and through the gate to the square, where Tikaz still sat. Two young women who were clearly friends or at least allies of hers stood in one corner of the square talking, trying to look as though they were merely loitering and gossiping when in fact they were keeping an eye on Tikaz. You made sure to keep your distance from her as you walked through the square and into the guesthouse.

I woke in the dark, turning, grinding. Alone. Too weak at first to do anything more than that. But I was used to long darkness, used to waiting, and I had plenty of time to think. As the weeks and months and years went by, I stretched, slowly, inch by inch, into the stones around me. I discovered the arrangement of wheels and shafts that turned me, that would never cease turning unless the mechanism broke somehow, but, I realized, whoever had caused me to be turned had required me to use my own power to keep the machinery in working order.

Over more weeks and months I stretched farther, through the outer wall of the building that held me, and found the water. The day was cloudy, and the sun was low. There was no quay here, barely any harbor worth the name, a few small boats bringing passengers to and fro across the strait. One ship was anchored off the shore, near some pilings that stuck up out of the water. Farther out were scattered silhouettes of ships with here and there a lantern shining. And farther yet, the quays and buildings of Ard Vusktia. As the sky darkened, more lanterns flared to life, tiny sparks along the quays.

Well, I had already suspected that I was in Vastai. So it seemed certain now that I had been captured by the Raven. Moreover, I had trapped myself. I had made my promise to Oissen—to all the gods of Ard Vusktia—assuming that if I did not wish someone to turn me, I could prevent it. And ordinarily that would have been the case. But the defeat of Ard Vusktia had driven me into unconsciousness, and during that time I could not prevent anyone doing with me whatever their desires prompted and their abilities allowed. I had not been able to prevent the Raven from

sibly end badly for me. And if it did not? I would still be trapped inside those thick stone walls, with no allies near that I knew of, with no easy way to escape. Well, I might leave my stone behind, inhabit some other body, but I didn't think I could ever entirely leave behind what I had been for so long, and besides that would leave the problem of the Raven's steady use of me unresolved.

That steady use left me badly drained. I had recovered consciousness, and I had just enough power to expand into the stones around me, but much more was, I thought, beyond me. I could feel a small but steady trickle of offerings from the far north, but those mostly drained away as soon as they reached me, put into service for the Raven's demands. If I was to truly escape, I needed something more. Something large. But I had never been interested in the largest, most dramatically powerful of offerings. My worshippers gave me water, or seashells, or milk, and pleasant but insubstantial prayers. It had always been enough, before, but it would not serve me now.

No, I would have to watch, and learn, and think.

Over the next months and years I stretched landward, into the fortress yard, saw the people going here and there, the ravens that lived in the fortress—at first I was wary of them, but I realized soon enough that the Raven himself rarely inhabited any but the one Instrument. I thought about what that might mean, and about what it might mean that the Raven seemed still attached to this tower here in Vastai. That this small harbor seemed to be much as it had been years ago, when one might suppose that the residents of Vastai, and the Raven himself, might find even a small quay convenient, at the very least.

I understand, now, that the Raven, having won his victory over Ard Vusktia, began building—a fortress in Ard Vusktia, and the Raven Tower in Vastai. He had intended to improve Vastai's own small harbor and build a quay there. But this ambitious program was curtailed when the Tel turned from a minor annoyance to a real threat to Iraden south of the forest. Not so much for a powerful god to deal with, one might think, but the Raven had spent a catastrophic amount of his own power for his victory over Ard Vusktia. Even without fresh trouble from the Tel, he would surely be a long time recovering. But at the time I knew nothing of these matters.

Well, I was still near the water. That was good. And now I had extended myself I could see the stars, and the sun. I watched the people come and go, listened to them. And after about fifteen years of this, of my watching and

in his face, in the way he stood. He was quite young—in his midtwenties. He had taken the bench only months earlier. "This," croaked the fledgling Raven, close into the Lease's ear, "I discovered in Ard Vusktia. The people we...*questioned* called it the Millstone, because, they said, it ground out food for the city. Rumor suggested that so long as the gods of Ard Vusktia caused it to be turned it gave them what was demanded of it. Rumor only, but at least some of that rumor proved true. I do not doubt that the gods of Ard Vusktia would have used it against me, against Iraden. But I have brought it here, and I have arranged things so that it turns constantly, for the benefit of Iraden."

"That was more than forty years ago," said that long-ago Lease. "Surely it draws its power from a god. Has that god done nothing, all this time? Will it not try to stop this?"

"It has not so far," said the Raven. "I think it likely that

the gods of Ard Vusktia trapped some god in some way—
we know they fatally stole the power of the small gods of
their city, and the countryside, willing or not."

The Lease made an appalled noise. "Cruel and vicious
gods, those of Ard Vusktia." The Raven did not comment.
"You did well to destroy them. So they trapped some very
powerful god and set it up to be drained of its power, for
their own purposes. But surely that god's power will eventually be exhausted."

"One would think," agreed the Raven of Iraden. "So far it
has shown no sign of it. I am curious as to how it was accomplished. Perhaps it was one of the Ancient Ones who spoke
concerning this stone, long ago, and the Ard Vusktians discovered it and put it to use. The words of those oldest gods
sometimes seem to linger even now, so long after the gods
themselves have died. But no matter. I spoke the deaths of
all the gods who fought for Ard Vusktia, and now what our
enemies would have turned against us has been turned to
our own use. Now what they would have used against Vastai, against Iraden, belongs to Vastai, and to Iraden."

The Lease swung the door shut, and I was left again to
darkness, and my own thoughts.

Outside the tower, the stars and the moon and the sun,
indeed the world itself, moved in their accustomed paths,
around and around, so satisfyingly. As they had ever since
I could look upon them, and even before. I thought of how
pleasant that motion was to me. How if I sat quiet and

attentive I could imagine I almost felt it, even under the tower, the motion and the rightness of it.

No doubt the Raven would have been more wary if he'd known I was both a godspoken stone *and* a god. And

largest and most powerful gods of Ard Vusktia, the ~~~ and the God of the Silent drained away all the power of the small gods of Iraden, willing or unwilling. And I suspect— though I cannot be certain—that in the end, the Raven did the same to the forest. That god has been oddly, entirely silent since I woke under the tower.

Here is what I think happened: The Raven was indeed badly injured in his effort to defeat the gods of Ard Vusktia. Badly enough that he took power from the forest, in the same way that he and the forest had taken power from the smaller gods of Iraden. The forest, weakened by the long struggle with Ard Vusktia and by that last assault, did not have the strength to defend itself, and then the Raven took all that it had. But it wasn't enough. The Raven owed continuing debts to Iraden, and to Vastai. He could not pay those debts, and so he set me to turning, constantly, and ordered me to pay them.

And judging by what was being demanded of me as I turned, the Raven did try to play fair with the forest after all, at least in some respects—for among my other tasks I was set to meet some of the obligations of the God of the Silent, obligations that I imagine it could no longer fulfill after that assault on Ard Vusktia.

I imagine the Raven was greatly relieved to find me in the mud outside Ard Vusktia's wall, and to discover how much I could do. Even after taking all the forest's power, even after those many human sacrifices on the quay, even with the continuing daily prayers and offerings of the people of Iraden, the Raven was still dangerously weak.

But those regular Iradeni offerings would continue. The inhabitants of Ard Vusktia might be compelled to add to them. And in the natural course of things another Lease would be paid. No doubt the Raven believed that he had only to wait, believed that I could fulfill the most immediately pressing of his continuing debts to Iraden while he recovered his strength. I was difficult to move—of course he could not safely leave me where he'd found me—and a trifle inconvenient to operate, but I otherwise seemed to be exactly what the Raven needed at that moment. Or so he must have thought.

It likely took him some decades—or at least until the Tel began to attack regularly, in force—to realize that somewhere he had made a mistake. To understand that those prayers and offerings, even with Ard Vusktia added

(and the Raven never could compel all of Ard Vusktia to pray to him quite as much as he wanted, though I
gather that he tried), were not enough. Even with the
payments of the Leases, even with my unwilling assis-

The illness that had struck Vastai is one that I had not seen
before, myself, but I knew of it from listening to Oissen's
attendants. They spoke of it with much dread—the illness might begin with horribly painful cramps, with the
afflicted spewing watery vomit and excrement, and then,
sometimes within hours of showing signs of the illness,
the sick person, untreated, might subside into unconsciousness and then death. Or they might live as long as
a day, or two. As that knowledgeable traveler told you, it
is spread through water that has come into contact with
human waste, and if much care is not taken to prevent
the effluvium of the sick and dying from contaminating
nearby drinking water, it will spread.

You returned from your conference with Zezume to find three people huddled around at the end of one of the tables, arguing. About what should be done, if anything, about what had caused all this, and how it could be happening. "And where is the forest?" one of the two men asked. "Has that god abandoned us?"

"Ask the Lease's Heir!" replied the one, older woman. "He's the one who desecrated the House of the Silent! And where is he?"

"And where's the Raven, come to that?" asked the other man. "If the Raven isn't helping with this, is he still holding back the Tel?"

"Our own men are holding back the Tel," said the first. "But we all knew it would be trouble, with the Lease unpaid, and now look. Maybe this won't stop until the Raven gets his due."

A moment of silence, as the implications of that suggestion penetrated. As, perhaps, they each considered how willing they might be to attempt to compel payment of the Lease.

"What's this?" you asked.

"Foolishness," said the landlady's daughter, coming from the kitchen with an empty bucket. "People are dying, and they're sitting here listening to rumors. And spreading them."

"We can't all of us walk far, or carry things," the older woman said.

"Plenty of people who can't walk far or carry things are helping other ways," said the landlady's daughter sharply.

"There are houses nearby with no one in them alive," said the second man. "Everybody's running around with

~~············~~ doing any good

"We need messengers, then," you said, "and someone to collect messages and tell people where they're needed. You." You pointed to the older woman. "Messengers will report to you, and you'll send them back out to where their news is needed."

"Who do you think you are?" she demanded.

"He's the Lease's Heir Mawat's right-hand man in the field against the Tel," said lord Direction Dera, who had come in from the square while you were talking. "Has anyone here fallen ill?"

"No, lord," said the landlady's daughter.

"The water does make a difference, then. We need to be sure everyone in Vastai knows what to do. Messengers aren't a bad idea."

"Lord Direction," you acknowledged. "We could spread word about keeping the water clean, and where we find people who aren't sick, we can ask them to help with those who are."

"If they aren't doing that already," Dera put in.

"Just so," you agreed. "And we could use people to help fill bottles and flasks for others to carry to those who need it. In the meantime I'll send people here as I find them, for this good woman"—you nodded at the older woman you'd first addressed—"to send wherever they seem most useful." You didn't wait for a reply, only bowed to Dera and strode out, into the square.

You worked all night, carrying water and corpses, sending messengers—a fleet of children, the core of which was three young girls you'd found weeping in the street. You gave them their charge with such seriousness that they immediately took up their duties to deliver news and recruit more of their fellows with sober, single-minded determination. In the depths of the night one of them came across you and told you, entirely seriously, that she had marched up to the guard at the fortress gate and, claiming your authority—she had heard someone mention your connection to Mawat—demanded to know why the Lease hadn't sent more help into the city. "After all," she said, exhaustedly indignant, "even the lady Tikaz is helping draw water. And she's not right in her head." The guard had only stared at her and then told her to go home to bed, there were enough troubles within the fortress.

You came back to the guesthouse just before the sun

rose. You smelled of smoke—there had been two more fires in the night. The square was empty except for Tikaz, slumped disheveled on the cold stones with a rough-woven blanket around her shoulders, apparently asleep, and a

Tikaz seemed to have awakened—now she sat in the middle of the square, doubled over, her arms crossed on her stomach. And Oskel and Okim stood over her. Oskel, speaking to Tikaz, leaned over and laid his hand on her shoulder. You started forward, knife drawn, walking at first, and then breaking into a run as Tikaz unfolded her arms and drove the knife she held into Oskel, just below his ribs, angled upward. Oskel gasped, looked down at her hand as she yanked hard on the knife and surged to her feet. She grabbed Okim's shirt, pulled him toward her and brought the knife up to his throat. He caught her wrist, pushed her arm back, and she cried out in frustrated rage and then bit his hand.

Oskel dropped to his knees, his hands over his breast.

Okim cried out and loosened his grip on Tikaz just enough for her to wrench her wrist free and stab at him, but the knife caught in his cloak. You reached them, then, and Tikaz dropped the knife and fled.

374 • Ann Leckie

Oskel fell over, to lie on the ground, unmoving. By now the guard stationed at the fortress gate had reached you, and another was coming into the square. "Stop her!" Okim cried. "She's murdered my brother!"

"Which of you killed her father?" you asked.

At that moment a horse came staggering into the square, covered in mud and scratches, bleeding, gasping. The boy on its back slid down, staggered himself, and then the horse gave two lurching steps and collapsed onto the stones of the square. I'm sure you recognized the boy, because suddenly all your attention was on him, as though you had forgotten Okim entirely.

"The Lease!" said the boy, choked and breathy. "The Lease! The lord Mawat!" He caught sight of you, swayed. "It's you! Tell the lord Mawat. They're all dead. The Tel attacked this...No, it was yesterday. I don't know how many...There's nothing between them and Vastai but the forest." He dropped to his knees beside the dead horse and put his head in his hands, and began to weep.

Everyone in the square was frozen, staring at him, you with increasing horror as you understood what he had just said. "Can you walk?" you asked him. And turned to the guard. "The Lease needs to see him. The Directions need to see him! Right now!"

"And who are you to be giving me orders?" asked the guard.

"I fell," said the boy. "I don't know if I can walk." He raised his head to look at you. "*You'll* listen!" Tears streaked his face. "You can tell the lord Mawat. Tell him now! You have to."

"Well, they can't get past the forest," said the guard after a moment. "The god won't let them." You managed not to reply to that, and instead put your arm around the boy's shoulders and walked with him into the fortress.

The fortress yard was all but deserted, the only sound the occasional churr of a raven and the clank and thunk of a bucket as a servant drew water. At the sound, the boy broke away from you and went limping toward the well. You reached him in a step, caught his arm. "Stop," you said. "Don't drink from there. I'll get you some beer from the kitchen."

"I don't want beer," the boy whispered. "I need water."

"Not that water." You hesitated. Looked over toward the tower, back at the boy. And then made up your mind and pulled him toward the kitchens. Fortunately he was too weak to do anything but go where you led him.

Giset greeted you at the kitchen door with, "It's you then, is it? Still on your feet, I see." Though you hadn't spoken to her since she'd given you meal and lodging tokens, days and days ago.

"Auntie," you said, greatly presuming. "This boy rode all night from the border, and he has an urgent message for the Lease and the Directions, but he desperately needs something to eat and drink. He doesn't have a token but he's one of our messengers. He's known to me, and to the lord Mawat."

She looked at the boy, gave you an appraising look, and then shouted over her shoulder, and turned back to you. Stood aside as the maidservant came from the well with a full bucket, slumping and exhausted. "You didn't drink from the well, then?" Giset asked.

"What's wrong with the well?" asked the boy, hoarsely.

"It's…," you began, but perhaps were unsure of how to explain.

"The water has sickness in it," said Giset. "Don't go in the hall. Any of them still alive is lying there doubled over with pain and shitting themselves. The ones who wouldn't listen to me, anyway."

"Mother Zezume spoke to you, then," you said. "About the water."

A .... behind Cisot with a leather bot-

than that. I started boiling water as soon as I saw the yard flooded. It's why Mother Zezume isn't sick herself." And then, addressing herself to the boy again, "When you've delivered your message, come back and I'll give you more."

"Thank you," said the boy.

"Thank you, Auntie," you said, and turned, taking the boy's arm.

"Sir," he said as you pulled him along, "how can there be sickness in the water? The forest protects us from sickness." He did not add, *There's only the forest between us and the Tel.*

"I don't know," you said.

And then, when you were nearly to the door of the tower, he asked, "How do you keep from crying?" He'd begun weeping again.

"I don't always," you admitted. "Sometimes you can't."

"Oh," said the boy.

The guard didn't want to let you in. He'd had no word of your coming, he could not leave his post, and there was no one to send to ask—anyone who might have run the message for him was sick. He had seen you in the tower before, though, and so in the end he waved you up the stairs.

The audience room was damp and chill, the brazier unlit. Okim was there, away from the entrance, his back to the wall, staring balefully at Hibal, who sat, white clad, on the bench. Around the dais stood a half dozen of the Council of the Directions, in gray and red and black embroidered robes. The lord Direction Dera was among them. He was addressing Hibal as you came into the room. "...forest has always been difficult to deal with, and that is a concern for Mother Zezume. But you, Raven's Lease, must acknowledge that there are serious concerns about the Raven's failure to protect us. Is this happening because..." He fell silent when he saw you and the boy. Over by the wall, Okim stared stonily at you.

"We don't have time for foolishness," Hibal observed. "Why are you here, Eolo?"

You nudged the boy forward. "Lord councillors," he

began. "Raven's Lease." He looked around. "Where is the lord Mawat?"

"That," said Hibal dryly, "is a question we would all like the answer to."

the hills, where we could surround them and take them by surprise while they slept, if we were quick and careful." You closed your eyes and made a small noise—I think you couldn't help yourself. The boy continued, "So we did that, the lord Airu gathered all of our forces that he could and we surrounded them and waited and..." His voice failed him. He swallowed. "They were just shirts stuffed with grass, but I swear we saw people moving in the camp, and heard them! And horses! But there was no one there. And by the time we realized..."

"They attacked you," Hibal guessed. His voice was even and steady, his face expressionless. "How many escaped?"

"I don't know, Raven's Lease." The boy was weeping again. "I got away and I rode here as fast as I could. The stupid horse kept..."

The lord Direction Dera said, sharply, "There are

fortified encampments all along the southern edge of Iradeni territory, and men riding between them, regular patrols. If one post has been overwhelmed, the others near it can surely come to assist. And as for Vastai being threatened, there is a walled camp full of soldiers guarding the road where it enters the forest. The lord Airu is hardly a brilliant tactician, but surely he wasn't stupid enough to empty that camp, let alone pull every nearby border patrol for a single opportunity to ambush the Tel."

You made a rough exhalation that might, in other circumstances, have been a bitter laugh. Dera looked at you, frowning.

"My lords," said the boy, "the lord Airu had learned that the Tel had heard about the Instrument being near death, that on this account they thought Iraden would be weak. They believed they had something that would let them pass through the forest. They, along with the Ona, had decided to put all their resources into an attack on the forest road camp, to be certain of overwhelming it, and then move as quickly as they could through the forest to Vastai. The lord Airu said that... that it was a good thing the lord Mawat wasn't there, because the Lease's Heir would spend all his time thinking about what to do next, and then would do something small and cautious, where here we had the opportunity to hurt the Tel so badly they never troubled us again, if only we would act boldly, as we should have done all along. He ordered all the camps and patrols in reach to come ambush the Tel and be ready to press forward into Tel territory."

After a silent moment, the lord Dera said, "They knew the Instrument was near death, so they knew the lord

"May I remind the Lease," said one Direction, angrily, "that fully a third of Iraden is on the other side of the forest."

"And this messenger," put in Dera, "has said that they do, indeed, aim at Vastai."

"He also said, lord Direction," replied Hibal, "that the Tel were all camped together, when they were not." He turned his attention to the boy. "Are the Tel actually on their way here at this moment?" asked Hibal.

"I don't know," the boy confessed.

"The forest is between us and them," said one of the other Directions. "How can they be?"

"The forest should have been between us and sickness," said another. "And yet."

There was a long silence. "Could the Tel have found some way to attack the forest itself?" asked Dera. "Have they found some god powerful enough to help them in this? Did they tempt Stalker into another bargain? Is she strong enough to do this? And could that be the reason half of Vastai is incapacitated right now?"

On the bench, Hibal closed his eyes. "Surely not," he said.

"And why has the Raven done nothing?" asked Dera. "Raven's Lease, I think we might need to consult with the Raven directly. I think we might need to reconsider the question of the payment due to that god."

"That matter is settled," said Hibal, opening his eyes again. "And the Raven has always told us that by dealing with matters ourselves, we give him more and better opportunities to assist us. Even if the Tel are on their way to Vastai, they surely won't kill their horses to get here. We have a few days at least. The matter of this sickness that has struck down so many, and the fires, is more pressing at this moment. We should make some provision for—"

"Raven's Lease," you said, "as to illness, a few people are already beginning to recover. All of Vastai has been dealing with that, and with the fires, with no help from the fortress."

"That was you, then, was it, sent that urchin to importune the gate guard?" asked Hibal.

"She did that on her own initiative, lord," you replied. "And she was right to do it. I am only ashamed I didn't do it myself. But it seems to me the Directions and the bench might be best advised to turn their attention to the Tel."

"Between his actions last night and his words today," said Dera, "I see why the lord Mawat relies on the good Eolo's counsel in the field."

"Surely if we consult the Raven of Iraden directly, he

was in the

meet with me."

"But, Raven's Lease," said one of the Directions, "as we were saying before the good Eolo and this brave messenger arrived, the senior member of this council was not in attendance, and neither was the Mother of the Silent. And you won't have consulted the god about this business with the Tel, since we all of us have only just now heard of it."

"The lord Radihaw is dead," replied Hibal, voice tense but even. "And his replacement is gravely ill. Mother Zezume is injured and cannot attend. The situation is serious enough that I would not delay seeking aid."

At that point Zezume entered the room, walking slowly, leaning on her servant. All the Directions present bowed. "Mother of the Silent," they murmured.

"Mother Zezume," Hibal greeted her, alarm evident in his tone. "Are you well enough to be exerting yourself like this?"

"I appreciate your concern, Hibal," said Zezume. "But I'm not so badly injured that I can't attend to urgent matters. Which these clearly are. I heard a messenger had come from the south with dire news." And then, to her servant, "Take this boy to Giset." She gestured toward the messenger beside you, who swayed. You put your hand on his shoulder. "Tell her he's to stay in the same guesthouse as the good Eolo, on the same terms. If there's no room available, I'm sure Eolo can share." She gave you a sharp look. "Can't you."

"Yes, Mother," you agreed.

"Now, come over here, child, and let me lean on you." You did as you were bidden, taking the servant's place as she led the messenger away. "Now. What's to do?"

"Mother Zezume," said Hibal. "As you know there has been sickness sweeping through Vastai, and fires..."

"Contrary to our agreements with the God of the Silent, and with the Raven," put in lord Direction Dera.

"And now we hear that the Tel have used trickery to defeat our entire force south of the forest."

Zezume closed her eyes. "Airu," she murmured.

"Airu," Dera agreed.

"The Tel may or may not be on their way here to attack Vastai," continued Hibal, as though neither of them had spoken.

"Indeed," said Zezume, opening her eyes. "You must have thought I was quite unwell indeed, to have had such news and not sent for me. I heard, as I came into the room, a suggestion that the Raven be consulted, for information and advice. I thought I heard that you, Raven's Lease, had consulted the god on a matter concerning the governance

here. Though I never expected to be in this position and I cannot read the tokens well."

"I can read the tokens," said Hibal, in a reassuring voice.

"Yes, of course you can." Zezume spoke sharply, almost impatiently. "So can I. The question is, can any of the Directions read them, who are well enough to be here?" No one answered. "Both the Lease and the Chief of the Directions must be present at any such consultation with the god, when it concerns a matter of state."

"Now, then, Mother Zezume," said Hibal, smoothly reproving. "It has been a very long time since the tower and the Directions were so mistrustful of each other."

"Trust doesn't enter into it, Raven's Lease," said Dera. "Mother Zezume is right. But we can't wait, and I am willing to rely on Mother Zezume's reading of the tokens. I know she's more expert than I am."

"We can't wait," agreed another Direction. "The Tel are very possibly on their way here, and most of what defenders we may have are too sick to fight. Yesterday I would have said that the forest would keep them away from Vastai, but today…" He gestured helplessly. "It would be helpful if the God of the Silent were less silent, Mother Zezume. Not that I blame you for that." He looked toward Hibal. "It was your heir, Raven's Lease, who desecrated the House of the Silent and laid violent hands on the Mother of that house."

Hibal gave a mournful sigh. "I don't know why the lord Mawat did such a terrible thing. I can only say he hasn't seemed to be in his right mind lately, and…" He shook his head. "Obviously recent events have been more than he could deal with. I only thank the Raven that we've discovered this weakness of his now, rather than after he was put on the bench." Silence, from the Directions, from Zezume. You had to force yourself not to make a protesting noise.

Hibal continued, "Since you all seem not to trust my word about the god's advice, we should perhaps be extra cautious, given that this is indeed an emergency and anything the Raven tells us will be of extreme importance. We must be sure that we all trust that the message, as conveyed, is accurate. It may be that we must delay asking our questions for just a bit, until we can solve this problem."

"It's hardly a problem, Raven's Lease," protested Dera. "I've already said that…"

"Raven's Lease," you interrupted, "you can ask yes

or no." Hibal stared at you. "Anyone can read that," you continued. "Two tokens faceup for *yes*, two facedown for *no*. One and one for questions that cannot be sufficiently answered with yes or no."

"But, Raven's Lease," insisted Dera. "Eolo's idea is a good one. There are any number of very useful questions that could be answered that way. Such as, *Are the Tel indeed on their way here?* If we knew the answer to that, we would know better what actions to take next. I really don't see what reason there is to delay even a moment more."

"We need more than just *yes* or *no*," insisted Hibal. "And I won't have it said that there was any reason at all to mistrust the words of the god." The Directions present frowned, and cast uncomfortable, disbelieving glances at each other.

"Please excuse me, lords," you said before anyone could say anything else. "But if the Lease were to read the tokens, and then we were to ask if that reading had been accurate and faithful, yes or no, that would be something everyone could read and understand."

There was a moment's silence. Then Dera said, "Good Eolo. I imagine if you had been the lord Airu's aide instead of the lord Mawat's, a good deal of our troubles today might have been prevented."

"Lord," you replied, "the lord Airu would never have listened to me."

"Let us not make the same mistake," said Zezume. "Let us question the Raven of Iraden, immediately, on the terms that the good Eolo has so happily suggested."

All this time Okim had watched and listened in silence. Now he said, vehemently, "The *good Eolo* stood by while the lady Tikaz murdered my brother."

"It's a serious accusation," said Dera. "And we will be sure to consider it, just as soon as the threat to all of Iraden is dealt with."

"Can you blame him, lord Direction Dera?" asked Hibal, before Okim could make his bitter reply. "If your brother were dead, would you have much attention for anything else?"

"My brother may well be dead," retorted Dera. "Or will be soon enough, and the rest of my family with him, as well as quite a few others' brothers. I have sympathy for Okim's grief, I'm sure we all do, but we must deal with the threat to Iraden first."

"Yes, yes, of course we must," said Hibal. "Good Okim…"

"You…," began Okim, stepping toward lord Direction Dera.

"Okim!" Hibal, sharply. "We will deal with your

complaint, I give you my word, but now is the time for patience. We must carefully consider our questions for the Raven, but you can speed things if you go above and make things ready for us. So many servants are ill. No one

For a moment, everyone stood tense and silent. Then Hibal said, "Now, let us consider our questions. And someone must fetch the tokens from Radihaw's chamber."

"You have the tokens right there," said Zezume, pointing to where the gold-and-black bag sat on a corner of the bench. You shivered—you knew that bag had not been there the moment before. Hibal knew as well as you did where it must have come from, what its sudden presence meant. He stared at it with barely concealed horror.

"We know what we need to ask," objected Dera, before Hibal had a chance to say anything, or even change his expression. "Are the Tel on their way, if so when will they be here and what should we do? Anything more we can only decide on once we have those answers."

"Exactly right," agreed Zezume. "There's no reason for delay, and every argument against it. Come, child." This to you. "Help me up the stairs."

There was no guard at the top of the tower. You and Dera, carrying Zezume between you, found only Okim, standing by the newly lit fire in the brazier. The day was well advanced by now, the sun high, the blue sky streaked with light, feathery clouds.

Hibal, coming out of the stairs behind you, said, "Here we are, Lord Dera, Mother Zezume." He hefted the bag of tokens. "I will ask and cast. But this yes-or-no business—how do we put this proposition to the god?"

"Lords," you said, stepping forward, leaving Zezume on Dera's arm. "Like so." You pulled your two tokens from under your shirt, the one for meals and the other to allow you into the fortress. Laid them both inlaid side down. "Raven," you said, "god of Vastai, the Acting Chief of the Council of the Directions can't read the tokens well, and the law requires that both the tower and the council have accurate knowledge of your answers. By means of these tokens the lord Dera can ask you if your messages are being accurately reported to us, and you can confirm or deny this. Two tokens faceup for yes, two facedown for no—as they are now—and one and one for questions that cannot be sufficiently unambiguously answered by such means. Do you understand?"

The two tokens rose, flipped, and settled again, inlaid side up. Hibal stared at them in horror.

you, and it was as though some thought had struck him, and his expression changed to one of slightly puzzled relief, which he tried to conceal with a thoughtful frown. "Let us begin then, I suppose."

Yes, said the tokens.

Hibal held out both his hands, the black-and-gold bag on his palms. "God of Vastai! We have learned this morning that we have suffered a catastrophic defeat by the Tel, and that they may be on their way to Vastai. Is this true? Are the Tel coming here in force?" He tilted his hands, shook the bag, and three tokens spilled out. "*It is, and they are,*" Hibal read.

"God of Vastai, is this what you said?" asked Dera. Your two tokens rose, spun, landed both inlaid side up. *Yes.*

"Will the forest not prevent them?" asked Zezume.

This time the bag fell out of Hibal's hands and tokens

spilled out. *"It will not. They will be here by this time tomorrow,"* read Hibal. Before Dera could ask, your two tokens rose and spun again. *Yes.*

"Then what are we to do?" asked Dera.

"Trust in the god of Vastai," said Hibal, with growing assurance.

You frowned at him, thinking, I'm sure, of the events of the past few days, of things you'd heard Hibal himself say. He had intended to kill the Raven, had killed that god's Instrument and then prevented the god's Lease from sacrificing himself. Surely you doubted his sincerity when he spoke of trusting the god of Vastai. Doubted that he would be calm in the face of any demonstration of the Raven's survival and continued power.

"Why does the forest not protect us?" asked Zezume.

"What god is talking to us?" you asked. Zezume seemed not to have heard you, but Dera stared, astonished at your question.

Hibal smiled. "What god can it be but the god of Vastai?"

"Where are the Xulahns?" you asked him. "Where is their snake?"

"Where is the forest?" demanded Zezume. "Answer me! Why does it not protect us?"

The tokens rose, rearranged themselves. *"The forest has done nothing for many years now,"* Hibal read, with some satisfaction. Perhaps he was glad to be diverted from your questions. *"Perhaps that god is dead."*

Yes, confirmed your two tokens.

"I don't believe it!" Zezume protested. "It's not true. The forest has done many things. It's spoken to me often!" But there it was before her on the sunlit, yellow stone—the

is secure we can ask questions about the God of the Silent."

"Where is Dupesu and his snake?" you insisted.

"What can the Xulahns have to do with any of this?" asked Hibal. "I fear, Eolo, that you've been taken ill and are raving. Okim, fetch a guard and..."

And suddenly Mawat was behind Hibal. Everyone—Hibal, Okim, Dera, Mother Zezume, even you (though you surely had suspected Mawat was there) stood paralyzed with surprise, speechless as Mawat grabbed Hibal's hair and pulled his head back, laid a knife against his throat.

Mawat said, into your shocked silence, "As usual, Eolo cuts to the core of things. I have been in the tower these last two days, and I heard everything I needed to hear. My uncle"—he pushed the blade of his knife just a bit harder into Hibal's throat—"killed the dying Instrument, and bound my father and dragged him below so that he would be unable to pay the Lease. To my father's shame, Hibal succeeded in preventing him. Or I should say, my father failed in his duty. I found him still alive below, just days ago, the coward. Isn't that so, god of Vastai?"

Yes, said the pair of tokens. Dera stood frozen in horror.

"Oh, you treacherous worm!" cried Zezume. It was unclear if she meant Hibal or Mawat's father or both.

"My uncle," Mawat continued, "thought that the Raven was weak, and near death. He thought that a godspoken stone below the tower was in fact fulfilling the Raven's obligations to Iraden."

"There is such a stone," you confirmed. "I've seen it." Dera looked at you, now, aghast. "But, my lord—"

"I never would have known about it if not for you," Mawat said to you. "I was sure you were lying. I should have known better. I've known your worth since I met you, and if I hadn't been... If I had been able to admit to myself that my father might have failed in his duty, I'd have listened to you sooner. I've treated you very badly in all this, Eolo, and you've been unceasingly loyal. I won't forget that. I won't forget that ever again."

"But the forest...," began Zezume.

"The God of the Silent is long dead," said Mawat. "My uncle hoped to kill the Raven as well by denying him his Lease. He thought the stone would continue to protect Iraden while he looked for some new god to serve in the Raven's stead. He led the Xulahns to believe that their snake god might have the office, if only they would help him to the bench. Do I speak the truth, god of Vastai?"

Yes, confirmed the pair of tokens. Silence, except for ⸱⸱ ⸱⸱⸱⸱⸱ ⸱⸱⸱ the gulls, and the faint sound of the waves

⸱⸱⸱ ⸱⸱⸱⸱⸱⸱ ⸱

through the city, and the fortress. And the Directions—the ones left standing, anyway—began to question whether Hibal needed to pay the Lease himself. My uncle couldn't have that! So he invited Dupesu here, late last night, and he and his snake have been all this time in the Lease's chamber, negotiating the terms by which Iraden will be surrendered to the control of a Xulahn god. Dupesu is there still."

"Lies!" Hibal croaked.

"Lies!" agreed Okim.

Mawat gave a bitter laugh. "God of Vastai, am I telling the truth?"

It's complicated, replied the tokens.

And then the reason for Hibal's odd confidence—before Mawat had revealed himself—became plain to you all, as Dupesu came up out of the stairwell that led beneath the tower, the snake he carried curled around his neck, its brown head held up over his shoulder as it stared unblinking at you all, its tongue sampling the air.

"I am find this interesting," said Dupesu. "Raven's Lease, I am wait in your room for you to return, but you are not return. There is a guard but he is become sick. I am think I would like to see the top of the tower, and so I am find this." He gestured to that second stairwell behind him. "I am go down and see things. And I am come up and hear things."

"That's impossible," said Zezume, but without conviction. After all, she had just seen Dupesu come up out of that stairwell. "This is all impossible."

Dupesu spread his hands, seemingly helpless to explain. "I am here, Mother Zezume. The Lease's Heir is say the truth. But I am not want this. I am come here only to go over the water and go north. We are hear there may be gold away north." The brown snake at his neck still stared, head still raised, tongue flickering out and back. "Are you not tell me before, Raven's Lease Hibal, that no one is go down these stairs and come back up alive, who is not Raven's Lease?" He paused, as though waiting for Hibal to answer, but Hibal stood silent in Mawat's grip, knife at his throat. "And yet I am go down and I am come back up and I am here alive. It is that your god is not harm me, or it is that your god is too weak to do as he is say. I am think your Raven is dead, or almost nearly dead."

"You're wrong," said Mawat. "The Raven is not dead."

"Then why is your Raven not do the things he is to do?'
asked Dupesu. "The Tel are come through the forest, which
I am hear is impossible, both your gods of Iraden forbid it,
and yet they come. So many of your soldiers are dead, this is

much time, and I am think the Raven's Lease Hibal will
die soon." He waved toward the knife at Hibal's throat and
smiled. "It may be we can help you, Lease's Heir Mawat."

"No," said Mawat. "The Raven will help us, as he
always has. None of this is happening because the Raven
is dead. How could he be? No, this is happening because of
my father's cowardice and my uncle's greed."

Dupesu shrugged again, and then walked over to sit on
one of the seats along the parapet. "I am wait."

"Wait then," scoffed Mawat, his knife still held across
Hibal's throat, and Hibal made a small, distressed noise.

"My lord," you said. Since the messenger's arrival you'd
been filled with dread and dismay, which had only grown
until now you were nearly overcome with it. "My lord, listen to me! If the Raven is alive, then how can the Tel be riding here? They shouldn't be! But if the Raven is dead, who
is speaking to us now?"

Everyone except Mawat and Hibal turned to look at Dupesu, sitting on the stone seat, leaning, apparently relaxed, against the wall, the brown snake curled around his neck. The snake opened its mouth and said, "Is not I."

You frowned, and then said, "No. No, you can't read the tokens, can you, or even speak Iradeni well enough to do it."

"This is a thing that is often happen," said Dupesu, with a wave of agreement. "This is a way of speaking to gods that is always give an answer even when no answer is. You are lay down these pieces and you are make some message from them, not from any god. It is a thing to have care about. You are easily see what is please you best."

Mawat gave a short, sharp laugh. "No, Dupesu, that's not what's happening here."

You could no longer restrain yourself. "God who's speaking to us, are you the Raven of Iraden?"

The black-and-gold bag at Hibal's feet twitched, and tokens flew out of it, arranged themselves in a neat line on the stones before him. Beside you, Zezume gasped.

"Ah," said Dupesu, still apparently at ease, "so your Raven is have just enough strength to move these pieces of wood. I am think he has little more than this."

"What does it say?" you asked, urgently.

"*You've asked me this question before, Eolo,*" Zezume read, and gave you a look full of accusing dread. "*Were you not satisfied with the answer?*"

"No," you said. "I was not."

"*I am the god of Vastai, the Sustainer of Iraden,*" Zezume read as the tokens rearranged themselves again, her voice shaking. "*There is no other god in this tower but the Xulahn*

Mawat frowned. Looked at you as he still held firmly to Hibal. "How can it not be?"

The tokens rearranged themselves again. "*I will settle all Eolo's doubts soon enough,*" Zezume read. "*This much is true: My enemies have drained me of power, and if I am to deal with the problems besetting Iraden I must have your help. Hibal is no longer Lease. Give me his death, Mawat. I will take it as payment and you will succeed him.*" And the confirmation, *Yes.*

"No!" you insisted. "My lord, please listen to me. Don't do this. This isn't the Raven, I'm sure it's not, but I can't say how! We should ask more questions, we should think more about what the best course might be. Deal with your uncle after we've made some plan to deal with the Tel. Maybe we can make a temporary bargain with the Xulahn snake. At least we'd know what we were dealing with."

"It is a good idea, friend Eolo," said Dupesu. "We are do this favor for you if only we are go safely north after, and are come back through Iraden with no trouble. We are want nothing more."

"I notice your god didn't say that itself," said Dera.

"You always ask questions and look into things," said Mawat to you, tightening his grip on Hibal's hair. "And that's why you nearly always give good advice. But I've been here in this tower, watching and listening. All of this is because of Hibal. He wanted the privileges of the bench without having to pay for them. And for this he condemns his brother, steals my inheritance, and schemes to sell Iraden to whatever god will solve his immediate problems—so long as the cost is not too high to himself."

"My lord," you began.

But Mawat went on. "He tried to kill the Raven! He thought he had, but"—with a nod toward the tokens scattered on the stones—"he failed. Don't tell me to think more about this. I've *been* thinking. And the first thing we need to do is what my father failed to do. What my *uncle*"—the word came out nearly a snarl—"had no intention of doing. The first thing we do is pay the Raven. Then we'll deal with the rest of it."

"My lord, wait!" you cried.

Mawat slashed the knife across Hibal's throat. "For you, god of Vastai!" Blood spurted, spilled crimson on Hibal's white shirt, as he gasped and choked and fell to the stones, clutching his neck.

"*I'm* Lease now," said Mawat. "Or near enough."

Yes, said the tokens.

He turned to Dupesu. "Now, let's deal with the other matters. All of this was because of my uncle, but it was also because of *you*." He stepped over Hibal's bloodstained

that right, god of Vastai?"

On the stones, your two tokens said, *Yes*.

Dupesu smiled, grimly. "Raven's Lease Mawat. It is not simple to kill a god, and your Raven is not so strong as you are think."

"My lord!" you cried. "Don't! This isn't the Raven! It's the stone!" Ah, I knew that you would recognize me at last. Had you realized what it might mean that Mawat had just given me the life of Hibal, once Raven's Lease of Iraden? It is a stronger offering—oh, far stronger!—than milk or water. And though I have indeed sustained Iraden until quite recently, I have made no promises binding me to Iraden's welfare. I am certain that in this moment you understood all this.

And in that same moment, Okim plunged toward Mawat, knife raised. You moved to stop him, managed to grab his wrist.

"Let him!" said Mawat with a laugh, not even turning toward you, still facing Dupesu and his snake. "My life belongs to the god of Vastai."

Okim wrenched free of your grasp, surged forward. Stumbled over Hibal's body. His knife grazed Mawat's arm as he fell dead at Mawat's feet.

Mawat did not even glance at him. Did not even seem to notice his sliced sleeve, or his own blood welling, dripping to his wrist. He looked only at Dupesu, and Dupesu's god. "You see?" he said, to Dupesu.

"That is a simple thing," said Dupesu. "A small thing, to stop a heart, if you are know how this works. Truly, it is nothing." The snake's tongue licked the air. "But I am ask, can your Raven do more than this? While I am in Vastai I am see proof of his weakness. Is this"—he gestured toward Hibal's body—"a thing that happens if that god is strong? Ask yourself, Raven's Lease Mawat. You are have other matters in your attention, and we are only pass through."

"I do indeed have other matters requiring my attention," replied Mawat, coldly. Bloody knife still in hand. Seemingly relaxed, but he had not even glanced at Hibal's body when Dupesu had gestured at it, only kept his gaze fixed on Dupesu and the snake, intent. "You are traveling to discover things to your own advantage—to yours, to your snake god's. To Xulah's. Hibal proposed to sell Iraden to you, and you entertained his proposal. That tells me what you are, and what you will do in the future. If I allow you to cross the strait, you will eventually be back to cause trouble again. And you are too well known among the Tel for me to leave you alive on this side of the water."

"Listen to your adviser, Raven's Lease," said Dera. "I don't understand what he means about the stone, but I know him for a thoughtful, practical man, and so do you, lord. Send these Xulahns away from here. Now."

"Eolo *is* thoughtful and practical," acknowledged Mawat, still staring at Dupesu. "But he is not infallible." He raised his knife, and the snake hissed. "Whatever the snake promises, it has only to send some other Xulahn god against us, one who has given us no assurances at all."

"Mawat, you stupid boy!" cried Zezume. She was weeping now, whether from the realization, finally, that the God of the Silent was no longer any sort of power, or from her fears for Iraden, or for Mawat.

"Try to kill me," Mawat said to the snake, "You've seen what happened to Okim. That's what will happen to you if you try to kill me now."

"You will die, Raven's Lease Mawat," said Dupesu.

"I was born for nothing else," replied Mawat, voice even and edged. "And if I do, the god of Vastai will be that much more powerful. And Iraden will be rid of you."

"I am not want this," hissed the snake on Dupesu's shoulder. "But I am do it, if it comes to it."

"Last chance, Raven's Lease Mawat," said Dupesu. "We are go away in peace, or we are go away fighting and leave destruction behind."

"The god of Vastai will not allow it," said Mawat. Knife in one hand, he raised the other with a beckoning gesture. "Do your worst."

"I am accept your invitation," hissed the snake, and said something more that you could not understand.

Mawat smiled. And then his eyes widened, and he swayed, and fell to his knees. Put his hand to his chest, gasping. You ran to him and knelt beside him. "My lord!" you cried as he pitched forward onto the stones, beside Hibal and Okim. You grabbed his shoulder, tried to roll him over, but he was slack and still, unbreathing. Dead.

"It is a simple thing," said the snake. "If you are know how it is done."

"Councillor," said Dupesu. Dera looked away from Mawat's body, stared at Dupesu, speechless. Appalled. "Mother Zezume." Zezume looked only at Mawat, her hands over her mouth, as though holding back some sound she could not stop herself from making. Dupesu made a small bow toward you, where you knelt, weeping, beside Mawat's lifeless body. "And the friend Eolo. We are live yet. Raven or stone, this god of Vastai is not harm us. But we are go now. And you are not stop us, or try to hurt us."

be the first god I have killed. No, nor even the second.

You kneel beside Mawat's lifeless body, momentarily immobilized with terror. But you alone of everyone atop this tower have heard my voice before. And surely you knew that, late or soon, it would come to this.

Stand up, Eolo! Wipe the tears from your eyes, and look out over the water! I know you mourn for Mawat, and fear for yourself. For Iraden. But while Mother Zezume and the lord Direction Dera still stare, still unable to move from shock, while Dupesu and his snake stand astonished, not yet understanding that both their lives are unavoidably forfeit, rise, Eolo, and look!

Do you see those wisps of white in the northeast? They are not clouds but sails. Can you count them? Is your vision so acute? Perhaps not.

I won't commit yet to a definite number, but I don't think they would have come except in strength. If my surmise is correct, there are many ships, and in the prow of one of them sits part of a stone that fell from the sky more than ten thousand years ago, iron and chunks of peridot. If my surmise is correct, it houses a god. My friend, the Myriad. One of the Ancient Ones.

As am I.

The Raven said he had spoken the deaths of all the gods who fought for Ard Vusktia, but even with the power of every small god of Iraden, even having taken all the God of the Silent Forest had, he could not make those words true. I still lived, and the Myriad as well. The ancient gods are, I have been told, difficult to kill.

Perhaps the Raven thought that if he could just hold on long enough his words would prevail, and he would be able to regain his strength. In the meantime he could draw power from me to make up his lack, to keep himself alive from hour to hour, to meet his obligations to Iraden. And to conceal the fact that he was steadily weakening. Even after so long, if certain interests in Ard Vusktia had ever realized how easy it would be to break away from

Vastai—well, that would have been the end of the Raven. He was well aware of this.

Given a bit more time he might have realized that what ~~....~~ the same god whose continued exis-

is hiding, waiting for ~~....~~ hand and leave Vastai together. Go west with all speed and take refuge with her mother's family. You will go safely, unseen by your enemies. You are under my protection.

As for the rest of Vastai—as for Iraden—well. That is another matter. They will all have to take their chances, with Stalker and the Tel, or with the Myriad.

I have waited for this moment. Patiently. Watching. Planning. Making what small moves I might. It's nothing personal, it's just that the Raven and the God of the Silent tried to kill me. Perhaps you can understand that. I hope you can.

Go, Eolo! Leave this place!

It's time for me to throw this tower down.

CAST
OF
CHARACTERS

GODS

Ancient Ones
The Strength and Patience of the Hill
The Myriad

Gods of Iraden
The Raven
The God of the Silent Forest
The Mounder-up of Skulls

Gods of Ard Vusktia
Oissen
Adim-Chak

Gods of the Tel
Stalker

Gods of Xulah
The Snake

Other Gods of the North
The Drowned One
The Mother of Owls
The Fox with Red Eyes

HUMANS

Lord Hibal—Mawat's ~~uncle~~, ~~~~

Lord Radihaw—Chief of the Council of Directions

Zezume—Mother of the Silent

Lord Dera of Oenda—member of the Council of Directions

Tikaz—Lord Radihaw's daughter

Oskel and Okim—twin brothers from Iraden; Hibal's sons

Dupesu—Xulahn traveler in Vastai

Airu—soldier of Iraden, son of a councilman

Giset—housekeeper of the Tower

Siat—Strength and Patience's priest in Ard Vusktia

ACKNOWLEDGMENTS

Many thanks to Judith Tarr for her invaluable horses—much of which didn't make it directly onto the page, but was incredibly helpful to me. Thanks also to Aidan Leckie-Harre and Erin Barbeau for help with plant biology and bugs, respectively. Thanks to Quentin Bourne, Rowan G. Bullock, Charlix, Felix, E. K. Green, Meriwether Grey, Margo-Lea Hurwicz, Cory Moore, Mugsie Palmer-Pike, Ray, Anna Schwind, James Shelstad, Rachel Swirsky, and Teddy for invaluable assistance and advice during the writing and revision of this book. All of their advice was fabulous, and any missteps or failures are my own.

As always, thanks to my wonderful editors, Will Hinton and Priyanka Krishnan in the US and Jenni Hill in the UK, for helping to make this book far better than I could have done on my own. Thanks are also due to Ellen Brady Wright, my publicist at Orbit, who is far more organized than I am. And a huge, huge thanks to my fabulous agent, Seth Fishman.

I will always, always thank my local libraries: the St. Louis County Library, the Municipal Library Consortium of St. Louis County, the St. Louis Public Library, the Webster University Library, and the University of Missouri–St. Louis Thomas Jefferson Library. And all you interlibrary loan librarians out there—thanks for what you do! Libraries are a public good. Please support yours in whatever way you can.

Last but certainly not least, thanks to my family, my husband, David, and my children, Aidan and Gawain. They've been incredibly patient with my writing, and I couldn't do it without their help and support.

extras

orbit

meet the author

Mission

ANN LECKIE is the first author to ever win the Hugo, Nebula, and Arthur C. Clarke awards all at once, with her record-breaking debut novel, *Ancillary Justice*. She lives in Saint Louis, Missouri.

if you enjoyed

FIVE WINDS

Hostage of Empire: Book One

by

S. C. Emmett

The imperial palace—full of ambitious royals, sly gossip, and unforeseen perils—is perhaps the most dangerous place in the empire of Zhaon. Komor Yala, lady-in-waiting to the princess of the vanquished kingdom of Khir, has only her wits and her hidden blade to protect herself and her charge, who was sacrificed in marriage to the enemy as a hostage for her conquered people's good behavior, to secure a tenuous peace.

421

But the Emperor is aging, and the Khir princess and her lady-in-waiting soon find themselves to be pawns in the six princes' deadly schemes for the throne—and a single spark could ignite fresh rebellion in Khir.

The Throne of the Five Winds *is the first installment of the* Hostage of Empire *series, an intricate and ruthless East Asia–inspired epic fantasy trilogy by S. C. Emmett.*

LITTLE LIGHT

Above the Great Keep of Khir and the smoky bowl of its accreted city, tombs rose upon mountainside terraces. Only the royal and Second Families had the right to cut their names into stone here, and this small stone pailai[1] was one of the very oldest. Hard, small pinpoints about to become white or pink blossoms starred the branches of ancient, twisted yeoyans;[2] a young woman in blue, her black hair dressed simply but carefully with a single white-shell comb, stood before the newest marker. Incense smoked as she folded her hands for decorous prayer, a well-bred daughter performing a rare, unchaperoned duty.

Below, the melt had begun and thin droplets scattered from tiled roofs both scarlet and slate, from almost-budding branches. Here snow still lingered in corners and upon sheltered stones; winter-blasted grass slept underneath. No drip disturbed the silence of the ancestors.

A booted foot scraped stone. The girl's head, bowed, did not move. There was only one person who would approach while

---

1. A single family's tombs.
2. A tree similar to a cherry.

she propitiated her ancestors, and she greeted him politely. "Your Highness." But she did not raise her head.

"None of that, Yala." The young man, his topknot caged and pierced with gold, wore ceremonial armor before the dead. His narrow-nosed face had paled, perhaps from the cold, and ⋯⋯ winter sky, grey as any noble blood-pure ⋯⋯ ⋯⋯ with

"Others." A contempt⋯⋯ no shortage."

Yala's cloud-grey eyes opened. She said nothing, watching the gravestone as if she expected a shade to rise. Her offerings were made at her mother's tomb already, but here was where she lingered. A simple stone marked the latest addition to the shades of her House—fine carving, but not ostentatious. The newly rich might display like fan-tailed baryo,[3] but not those who had ridden to war with the Three Kings of the First Dynasty. Or so her father thought, though he did not say it.

A single tone, or glance, was enough to teach a lesson.

Ashani Daoyan, Crown Prince of Khir newly legitimized and battlefield-blooded, made a restless movement. Lean but broad-shouldered, with a slight roundness to his cheeks bespeaking his Narikh motherblood, he wore the imperial colors easily; a bastard son, like an unmarried aunt, learned to dress as the weather dictated. Leather creaked slightly, and his breath plumed in the chill. "If your brother were alive—"

---

3. Carrion-eating birds with bright plumage, often kept as garbage-eating pets.

"—I would be married to one of his friends, and perhaps widowed as well." *Now* Komor Yala, the only surviving child of General Hai Komori Dasho, moved too, a slight swaying as if she wished to turn and halted just in time. "Please, Daoyan." The habit of long friendship made it not only possible but necessary to address him so informally. "Not before my Elder Brother."

"Yala..." Perhaps Dao's half-armor, black chased with yellow, was not adequate for this particular encounter. The boy she had known, full of sparkstick[4] pride and fierce silence when that pride was balked, had ridden to war; this young man returned in his place.

Did he regret being dragged from the field to preserve a dynasty while so many others stood and died honorably? She could not ask, merely suspect, so Yala shook her head. Her own words were white clouds, chosen carefully and given to the frigid morning. "Who will care for my princess, if I do not?"

"You cannot waste your life that way." A slight sound— gauntlets creaking. Daoyan still clenched his fists. She should warn him against so open a display of emotion, but perhaps in a man it did not matter so much.

"And yet." *There is no other option*, her tone replied, plainly. *Not one I am willing to entertain.* "I will take great care with your royal sister, Your Highness."

Of course he could not leave the battlefield thus, a draw achieved but no victory in sight. "I will offer for you."

"You already would have, if you thought your honored father would allow it." She bowed, a graceful supple bending with her skirts brushing fresh-swept stone. "Please, Daoyan." Her palms met, and her head dropped even further when she straightened, the attitude of a filial daughter from a scroll's illustrations.

---

4. A handheld firework.

Even a prince dared not interrupt prayers begun before a relative's tomb. Daoyan turned, finally, boots ringing through thin snow to pavers she had not attended to with her small broom, and left the pailai with long, swinging strides.

Yala slipped her hands deeper inside her sleeves and regarded ... of course, would have sniffed at the ... ... weight, and Yala could have bowed ... ... of insisting upon her duty as a noble daughter must before a distinguished parent.

Perhaps that would have been best. Was the cringing, creeping relief she would have felt cowardice? The other noble families were scurrying to keep their daughters from Mahara's retinue, marriages contracted or health problems discovered with unseemly haste. The Great Rider, weakened as he was by the defeat at Three Rivers and the slow strangling of Khir's southron trade, could not force noble daughters to accompany his own, he could only...request.

Other clans and families could treat it as a request, but Komori held to the ancient codes. It was a high honor to attend the princess of Khir, and Yala had done so since childhood. To cease in adversity was unworthy of a Komor daughter.

Burning incense sent lazy curls of scented smoke heavenward. If her brother was watching, he would have been fuming like the sticks themselves. A slow smolder and a hidden fire, that was Hai Komori Baiyan. She could only hope she was the same, and the conquering Zhaon would not smother her *and* her princess.

425

First things first. You are to pay your respects here, and then to comfort your father.

As if there could be any comfort to a Khir nobleman whose only son was dead. Hai Komori Dasho would be gladdened to be rid of a daughter and the need to find a dowry, that much was certain. Even if he was not, he would act as if he were, because that was the correct way to regard this situation.

The Komori, especially the clan heads, were known for their probity.

Her fingertips worried at her knuckles, and she sighed. "Oh, damoi,[5] my much-blessed Bai," she whispered. It was not quite meet to pronounce the name of the dead, but she could be forgiven a single use of such a precious item. "How I wish you were here."

She bent before her brother's grave one last time, and her fingers found a sharp-edged, triangular pebble among the flat pavers, blasted grass, and iron-cold dirt. They could not plow quite yet, but the monjok[6] and yeoyan blossoms were out. Spring would come early this year, but she would not see the swallows returning. The care of the pailai would fall to more distant kin from a junior branch of the clan.

Yala tucked the pebble in a sleeve-pocket, carefully. She could wrap it with red silken thread, decorate a hairstick with falling beads, and wear a part of both Bai and her homeland daily. A small piece of grit in the conqueror's court, hopefully accreting nacre instead of dishonor.

There were none left to care for her father in his aging. Perhaps he would marry again. If Bai were still alive...

"Stop," she murmured, and since there were none to see her,

---

5. *Khir. Affectionate.* Elder brother.
6. A small, slightly acrid fruit.

Yala's face could contort under a lash of pain, a horse shying at the whip. "He is not."

Khir had ridden to face Zhaon's great general at Three Rivers, and the eldest son of a proud Second Family would not be left ╵ ╵ ╵ᵈ The battle had made Daoyan a hero and Bai a corpse, ⌐⌐⌐⌐⌐ꞏꞏꞏ⌐querors had dictated their

be reꞏꞏꞏꞏꞏꞏ ꞏ
fort in the observation, even if it was ꞏꞏꞏꞏꞏꞏ
the defeated.

For the last time, Yala bowed before her brother's stone. If she walked slowly upon her return, the evidence of tears would be erased by the time she reached the foot of the pailai's smooth-worn stairs and the single maidservant waiting, holding her mistress's horse and bundled against the cold as Yala disdained to be.

A noblewoman suffered ice without a murmur. Inside, and out.

Hai Komori's blackened bulk rested within the walls of the Old City. It frowned in the old style, stone walls and sharply pitched slate-tiled roof; its great hall was high and gloomy. The longtable, crowded with retainers at dinners twice every ten-day, was a blackened piece of old wood; it stood empty now, with the lord's low chair upon the dais watching its oiled, gleaming surface. Mirrorlight drifted, brought through holes in the roof and bounced between polished discs, crisscrossing the high space.

Dusty cloth rustled overhead, standards and pennons taken

in battle. There were many, and their sibilance was the song of a Second Family. The men rode to war, the women to hunt, and between them the whole world was ordered. Or so the classics, both the canonical Hundreds and supplements, said. Strong hunters made strong sons, and Yala had sometimes wondered why her mother, who could whisper a hawk out of the sky, had not given her father more than two. Bai the eldest was ash upon the wind and a name upon a tablet; the second son had not even reached his naming-day.

And Komor Madwha, a daughter of the Jehng family and high in the regard of the Great Rider and her husband as well, died shortly after her only daughter's birth.

Komori Dasho was here instead of in his study. Straight-backed, only a few thin threads of frost woven into his top-knot, a vigorous man almost into the status of elder sat upon the dais steps, gazing at the table and the great hearth. When a side door opened and blue silk made its subtle sweet sound, he closed his eyes.

Yala, as ever, bowed properly to her father though he was not looking. "Your daughter greets you, *pai*."

He acknowledged with a nod. She waited, her hands folded in her sleeves again, faintly uneasy. Her father was a tall man, his shoulders still hard from daily practice with saber and spear; his face was pure Khir. Piercing grey eyes, straight black hair topknotted as a Second Dynasty lord's, a narrow high prow of a nose, a thin mouth, and bladed cheekbones harsh as the sword-mountains themselves. Age settled more firmly upon him with each passing winter, drawing skin tighter and bone-angles sharper. His house robe was spare and dark, subtly pat-terned but free of excessive ornamentation.

He was, in short, the very picture of a Khir noble—except he was not, as usual, straight as an iron reed upon his low backless chair with the standard of their house—the setting sun and the komor flower[7]—hung behind it.

Finally, he patted the stone step with his left hand. "Come, sit." His intonation was informal, and that was another surprise.

With her dress arranged and

barely touching winter's lingering chill.

scrubbed even when winter meant the buckets formed ice which needed frequent breaking, stared blankly at the ceiling, polished by many feet. Yala stilled, a habit born of long practice in her father's presence.

The mouse that moves is taken. Another proverb. The classics were stuffed to bursting with them.

As a child she had fidgeted and fluttered, Dowager Eun despairing of ever teaching her discretion. In Yala's twelfth spring the weight of decorum had begun to tell, and she had decided it was easier to flow with that pressure than stagger under it. Even Mahara had been surprised, and she, of all the world, perhaps knew Yala best.

After Bai, that was.

"Yala," her father said, as if reminding himself who she was. *That* was hardly unusual. The sons stayed, the daughters left. An advantageous marriage was her duty to Komori. It was a

---

7. A native, very hardy Khir plant with seven petals on its small highly fragrant flowers; the root is used for blue dye.

pity there had been no offers. *I wonder what is wrong with me*, she had murmured to Mahara once.

I do not wish to share you with a husband, Mahara answered, when she could speak for laughing.

"Yes." Simple, and soft, as a noblewoman should speak. She wished she were at her needlework, the satisfaction of a stitch pulled neatly and expertly making up for pricked fingers. Or in the mews, hawk-singing. Writing out one of the many classics once again, her brush held steady. Reading, or deciding once more what to pack and what to leave behind.

She wished, in fact, to be anywhere but here. After a visit to the ancestors, though, her presence at her father's wrist was expected. Brought back to endure scrutiny like a hawk itself, a feather passed over her plumage, so as not to disturb the subtle oils thereupon.

"I have often thought you should have been born male." Komori Dasho sighed, his shoulders dropping. The sudden change was startling, and disturbing. "You would have made a fine son." Even if it was high praise, it still stung. A formulaic reply rose inside her, but he did not give her the chance to utter as much. "But if you were, you would have died upon that blood-field as well, and I would have opened my veins at the news."

Startled, Yala turned her head to gaze upon his profile. The room was not the only thing that looked different from this angle. The thunder-god of her childhood, straight and proud, sat beside her, staring at the table. And, terrifyingly, hot water had come to Komori Dasho's eyes. It swelled, glittering, and anything she might have said vanished.

"My little light," he continued. "Did you know? I named you thus, after your mother died. Not aloud, but here." His thin, strong right fist, the greenstone seal-ring of a proud and ancient house glinting upon his index finger, struck his chest.

430

"I knew not to say such things, for the gods would be angry and steal you as they took *her*."

Yala's chest tightened. A Lord Komori severe in displeasure or stern with approval she could answer. Who was *this*?

Her father did not give her a chance to reply. "In the end it does not matter. The Great Rider has requested and we must ⸺ in Zhaon."

⸺ ⸺ she had been to her father since…she could not ⸺ last time. She could not remember when he last spoke to her with the informal inflection *or* case, either. Yala searched for something else to say. "I will not shame our family, especially among *them*."

"You—" He paused, straightened. "You have your *yue*?"

Of course I do. "It is the honor of a Khir woman," she replied, as custom demanded. Was this a test? If so, would she pass? Familiar anxiety sharpened inside her ribs. "Does my father wish to examine its edge?" The blade was freshly honed; no speck of rust or whisper of disuse would be found upon its slim greenmetal length.

"Ah. No, of course not." His hands dangled at his knees, lax as they never had been in her memory. "Will you write to your father?"

"Of course." As if she would dare *not* to. The stone under her was a cold, uncomfortable saddle, but she did not dare shift. "Every month."

"Every week." The swelling water in his eyes did not overflow.

431

Yala looked away. It was uncomfortably akin to seeing a man outside the clan drunk, or at his dressing. "Will you?"

"Yes." *If you require it of me.*

"I have kept you close all this time." His fingers curled slightly, as if they wished for a hilt. "There were many marriage offers made for you, Yala. Since your naming-day, you have been sought. I refused them all." He sighed, heavily. "I could not let you go. Now, I am punished for it."

She sat, stunned and silent, until her father, for the first and last time, put a lean-muscled, awkward arm about her shoulders. The embrace was brief and excruciating, and when it ended he rose and left the hall, iron-backed as ever, with his accustomed quiet step.

He is proud of you, she had often told Bai. *He simply does not show it.*

Perhaps it had not been a lie told to soothe her brother's heart. And perhaps, just perhaps, she could believe it for herself.

if you enjoyed

THE RAVEN TOWER

COLD SILVER

The Crimson Empire: Book One

by

Alex Marshall

FIVE VILLAINS. ONE LEGENDARY GENERAL.
A FINAL QUEST FOR VENGEANCE.

Twenty years ago, feared general Cobalt Zosia led her five
villainous captains and mercenary army into battle,
wrestling monsters and toppling an empire. When there
were no more titles to win and no more worlds to conquer,
she retired and gave up her legend to history.

*Now the peace she carved for herself has been shattered by the
unprovoked slaughter of her village. Seeking bloody vengeance,
Zosia heads for battle once more, but to find justice she must
confront grudge-bearing enemies, once-loyal allies, and an
unknown army that marches under a familiar banner.*

CHAPTER 1

It was all going so nicely, right up until the massacre.

Sir Hjortt's cavalry of two hundred spears fanned out
through the small village, taking up positions between half-
timbered houses in the uneven lanes that only the most charita-
ble of surveyors would refer to as "roads." The warhorses slowed
and then stopped in a decent approximation of unison, their
riders sitting as stiff and straight in their saddles as the lances
they braced against their stirrups. It was an unseasonably warm
afternoon in the autumn, and after their long approach up the
steep valley, soldier and steed alike dripped sweat, yet not a one
of them removed their brass skullcap. Weapons, armor, and
tack glowing in the fierce alpine sunlight, the faded crimson
of their cloaks covering up the inevitable stains, the cavalry
appeared to have ridden straight out of a tale, or galloped down
off one of the tapestries in the mayor's house.

So they must have seemed to the villagers who peeked
through their shutters, anyway. To their colonel, Sir Hjortt,
they looked like hired killers on horseback barely possessed of
sense to do as they were told most of the time. Had the knight
been able to train wardogs to ride he should have preferred
them to the Fifteenth Cavalry, given the amount of faith he
placed in this lot. Not much, in other words, not very much at
all.

He didn't care for dogs, either, but a dog you could trust, even if it was only to lick his balls.

The hamlet sprawled across the last stretch of grassy meadow before the collision of two steep, bald-peaked mountains. Murky forest edged in on all sides, like a snare the wilderness had set for the unwary traveler. A typical mountain town here in the _____ reinforced stone wall to

and a half stories tall, its windowless redbrick face ___ into a grid by the black timbers that supported it. The mossy thatched roof rose up into a witch's hat, and set squarely in the center like a mouth were a great pair of doors tall and wide enough for two riders to pass through abreast without removing their helmets. As he reached the break in the hedge at the front of the house, Sir Hjortt saw that one of these oaken doors was ajar, but just as he noticed this detail the door eased shut.

Sir Hjortt smiled to himself, and, reining his horse in front of the rosebushes, called out in his deepest baritone, "I am Sir Efrain Hjortt of Azgaroth, Fifteenth Colonel of the Crimson Empire, come to counsel with the mayor's wife. I have met your lord mayor upon the road, and while he reposes at my camp—"

Someone behind him snickered at that, but when Sir Hjortt turned in his saddle he could not locate which of his troops was the culprit. It might have even come from one of his two personal Chainite guards, who had stopped their horses at the border of the thorny hedge. He gave both his guards and the riders nearest them the sort of withering scowl his father was overly fond of doling out. This was no laughing matter, as should have been perfectly obvious from the way Sir Hjortt had dealt with the hillbilly mayor of this shitburg.

"Ahem." Sir Hjortt turned back to the building and tried again. "Whilst your lord mayor reposes at my camp, I bring tidings of great import. I must speak with the mayor's wife at once."

Anything? Nothing. The whole town was silently, fearfully watching him from hiding, he could feel it in his aching thighs, but not a one braved the daylight either to confront or assist him. Peasants—what a sorry lot they were.

"I say again!" Sir Hjortt called, goading his stallion into the mayor's yard and advancing on the double doors. "As a colonel of the Crimson Empire and a knight of Azgaroth, I shall be welcomed by the family of your mayor, or—"

Both sets of doors burst open, and a wave of hulking, shaggy beasts flooded out into the sunlight—they were on top of the Azgarothian before he could wheel away or draw his sword. He heard muted bells, obviously to signal that the ambush was under way, and the hungry grunting of the pack, and—

The cattle milled about him, snuffling his horse with their broad, slimy noses, but now that they had escaped the confines of the building they betrayed no intention toward further excitement.

"Very sorry, sir," came a hillfolk-accented voice from somewhere nearby, and then a small, pale hand appeared amid the cattle, rising from between the bovine waves like the last, desperate attempt of a drowning man to catch a piece of driftwood. Then the hand seized a black coat and a blond boy of perhaps ten or twelve vaulted himself nimbly into sight, landing on the wide back of a mountain cow and twisting the creature around to face Sir Hjortt as effortlessly as the Azgarothian controlled his warhorse. Despite this manifest skill and agility at play before him, the knight remained unimpressed.

"The mayor's wife," said Sir Hjortt. "I am to meet with her. Now. Is she in?"

"I expect so," said the boy, glancing over his shoulder— checking the position of the sun against the lee of the moun- ... ill ... doubt. "Sorry again 'bout

"Mayoress is probably up in her house, sir, but ... ... allowed 'round there anymore, on account of my wretched behavior," said the boy with obvious pride.

"This isn't her home?" Hjortt eyed the building warily.

"No, sir. This is the barn."

Another chuckle from one of his faithless troops, but Sir Hjortt didn't give whoever it was the satisfaction of turning in his saddle a second time. He'd find the culprit after the day's business was done, and then they'd see what came of having a laugh at their commander's expense. Like the rest of the Fifteenth Regiment, the cavalry apparently thought their new colonel was green because he wasn't yet twenty, but he would soon show them that being young and being green weren't the same thing at all.

Now that their cowherd champion had engaged the invaders, gaily painted doors began to open and the braver citizenry slunk out onto their stoops, clearly awestruck at the Imperial soldiers in their midst. Sir Hjortt grunted in satisfaction—it had been so quiet in the hamlet that he had begun to wonder if the villagers had somehow been tipped off to his approach and scampered away into the mountains.

"Where's the mayor's house, then?" he said, reins squeaking in his gauntlets as he glared at the boy.

"See the trail there?" said the boy, pointing to the east. Following the lad's finger down a lane beside a longhouse, Sir Hjortt saw a small gate set in the village wall, and beyond that a faint trail leading up the grassy foot of the steepest peak in the valley.

"My glass, Portolés," said Sir Hjortt, and his bodyguard walked her horse over beside his. Sir Hjortt knew that if he carried the priceless item in his own saddlebag one of his thuggish soldiers would likely find a way of stealing it, but not a one of them would dare try that shit with the burly war nun. She handed it over and Sir Hjortt withdrew the heavy brass hawkglass from its sheath; it was the only gift his father had ever given him that wasn't a weapon of some sort, and he relished any excuse to use it. Finding the magnified trail through the instrument, he tracked it up the meadow to where the path entered the surrounding forest. A copse of yellowing aspen interrupted the pines and fir, and, scanning the hawkglass upward, he saw that this vein of gold continued up the otherwise evergreen-covered mountain.

"See it?" the cowherd said. "They live back up in there. Not far."

———

Sir Hjortt gained a false summit and leaned against one of the trees. The thin trunk bowed under his weight, its copper leaves hissing at his touch, its white bark leaving dust on his cape. The series of switchbacks carved into the increasingly sheer mountainside had become too treacherous for the horses, and so Sir Hjortt and his two guards, Brother Iqbal and Sister Portolés, had proceeded up the scarps of exposed granite on foot. The possibility of a trap had not left the knight, but nothing more hostile than a hummingbird had showed itself on the hike, and now that his eyes had adjusted to the strangely diffuse light of this latest grove, he saw a modest, freshly whitewashed house perched on the lip of the next rock shelf.

from his town?"

"I can think of a reason or three," said Portolés, setting the head of her weighty maul in the path and resting against its long shaft. "Take a look behind us."

Sir Hjortt paused, amenable to a break himself—even with only his comparatively light riding armor on, it was a real asshole of a hike. Turning, he let out an appreciative whistle. They had climbed quickly, and spread out below them was the painting-perfect hamlet nestled at the base of the mountains. Beyond the thin line of its walls, the lush valley fell away into the distance, a meandering brook dividing east ridge from west. Sir Hjortt was hardly a single-minded, bloodthirsty brute, and he could certainly appreciate the allure of living high above one's vassals, surrounded by the breathtaking beauty of creation. Perhaps when this unfortunate errand was over he would convert the mayor's house into a hunting lodge, wiling away his summers with sport and relaxation in the clean highland air.

"Best vantage in the valley," said Portolés. "Gives the head-person plenty of time to decide how to greet any guests."

"Do you think she's put on a kettle for us?" said Iqbal hopefully. "I could do with a spot of hunter's tea."

"About this mission, Colonel..." Portolés was looking at Sir Hjortt but not meeting his eyes. She'd been poorly covering up her discomfort with phony bravado ever since he'd informed her what needed to be done here, and the knight could well imagine what would come next. "I wonder if the order—"

"And I wonder if your church superiors gave me the use of you two anathemas so that you might hem and haw and question me at every pass, instead of respecting my command as an Imperial colonel," said Sir Hjortt, which brought bruise-hued blushes to the big woman's cheeks. "Azgaroth has been a proud and faithful servant of the Kings and Queens of Samoth for near on a century, whereas your popes seem to revolt every other feast day, so remind me again, what use have I for your counsel?"

Portolés muttered an apology, and Iqbal fidgeted with the damp sack he carried.

"Do you think I relish what we have to do? Do you think I would put my soldiers through it, if I had a choice? Why would I give such a command, if it was at all avoidable? Why—" Sir Hjortt was just warming to his lecture when a fissure of pain opened up his skull. Intense and unpleasant as the sensation was, it fled in moments, leaving him to nervously consider the witchborn pair. Had one of them somehow brought on the headache with their devilish ways? Probably not; he'd had a touch of a headache for much of the ride up, come to think of it, and he hadn't even mentioned the plan to them then.

"Come on," he said, deciding it would be best to drop the matter without further pontification. Even if his bodyguards did have reservations, this mission would prove an object lesson that it is always better to rush through any necessary unpleasantness, rather than drag your feet and overanalyze every ugly detail. "Let's be done with this. I want to be down the valley by dark, bad as that road is."

They edged around a hairpin bend in the steep trail, and then the track's crudely hewn stair delivered them to another plateau, and the mayor's house. It was similar in design to those ~~in the lands her but with a porch~~ overhanging the edge of the

~~mentioned such a beast being spied in the area, Sir Hjortt had~~ assumed the boy full of what his cows deposited, but maybe a few still prowled these lonely mountains. What a thrill it would be, to mount a hunting party for such rare game! Then the door beneath the skull creaked, and a figure stood framed in the doorway.

"Well met, friends, you've come a long way," the woman greeted them. She was brawny, though not so big as Portolés, with features as hard as the trek up to her house. She might have been fit enough once, in a country sort of way, when her long, silvery hair was blond or black or red and tied back in pigtails the way Hjortt liked . . . but now she was just an old woman, same as any other, fifty winters young at a minimum. Judging from the tangled bone fetishes hanging from the limbs of the sole tree that grew inside the fence's perimeter—a tall, black-barked aspen with leaves as hoary as her locks—she might be a sorceress, to boot.

Iqbal returned her welcome, calling, "Well met, Mum, well met indeed. I present to you Sir Hjortt of Azgaroth, Fifteenth

Colonel of the Crimson Empire." The anathema glanced to his superior, but when Sir Hjortt didn't fall all over himself to charge ahead and meet a potential witch, Iqbal murmured, "She's just an old bird, sir, nothing to fret about."

"Old bird or fledgling, I wouldn't blindly stick my hand in an owlbat's nest," Portolés said, stepping past Sir Hjortt and Iqbal to address the old woman in the Crimson tongue. "In the names of the Pontiff of the West and the Queen of the Rest, I order you out here into the light, woman."

"Queen of the Rest?" The woman obliged Portolés, stepping down the creaking steps of her porch and approaching the fence. For a mayor's wife, her checked dirndl was as plain as any village girl's. "And Pontiff of the West, is it? Last peddler we had through here brought tidings that Pope Shanatu's war wasn't going so well, but I gather much has changed. Is this sovereign of the Rest, blessed whoever she be, still Queen Indsorith? And does this mean peace has once again been brokered?"

"This bird hears a lot from her tree," muttered Sir Hjortt, then asked the woman, "Are you indeed the mayor's wife?"

"I am Mayoress Vivi, wife of Leib," said she. "And I ask again, respectfully, to whom shall I direct my prayers when next I—"

"The righteous reign of Queen Indsorith continues, blessed be her name," said Sir Hjortt. "Pope Shanatu, blessed be *his* name, received word from on high that his time as Shepherd of Samoth has come to an end, and so the war is over. His niece Jirella, blessed be *her* name, has ascended to her rightful place behind the Onyx Pulpit, and taken on the title of Pope Y'Homa III, Mother of Midnight, Shepherdess of the Lost."

"I see," said the mayoress. "And in addition to accepting a rebel pope's resignation and the promotion of his kin to the same lofty post, our beloved Indsorith, long may her glory persist, has also swapped out her noble title? 'Queen of Samoth, Heart of the Star, Jewel of Diadem, Keeper of the Crimson Empire' for, ah, 'Queen of the Rest'?" The woman's faintly lined face wrinkled further as she smiled, and Portolés slyly returned it.

"~~D~~ ~~~~ ~~mistake~~ ~~my~~ ~~subordinate's~~ peculiar sense of

carry out his command, ~~so he'd have an excuse to get rid of~~ altogether. In High Azgarothian, he said, "Portolés, return to the village and give the order. In the time it will take you to make it down I'll have made myself clear enough."

Portolés stiffened and gave Sir Hjortt a pathetic frown that told him she'd been holding out hope that he would change his mind. Not bloody likely. Also in Azgarothian, the war nun said, "I'm...I'm just going to have a look inside before I do. Make sure it's safe, Colonel Hjortt."

"By all means, Sister Portolés, welcome, welcome," said the older woman, also in that ancient and honorable tongue of Sir Hjortt's ancestors. Unexpected, that, but then the Star had been a different place when this biddy was in her prime, and perhaps she had seen more of it than just her remote mountain. Now that she was closer he saw that her cheeks were more scarred than wrinkled, a rather gnarly one on her chin, and for the first time since their arrival, a shadow of worry played across the weathered landscape of her face. Good. "I have an old hound sleeping in the kitchen whom I should prefer you left to his dreams, but am otherwise alone. But, good Colonel, Leib was to have been at the crossroads this morning…"

Sir Hjortt ignored the mayor's wife, following Portolés through the gate onto the walkway of flat, colorful stones that crossed the yard. They were artlessly arranged; the first order of business would be to hire the mason who had done the bathrooms at his family estate in Cockspar, or maybe the woman's apprentice, if the hoity-toity artisan wasn't willing to journey a hundred leagues into the wilds to retile a walk. A mosaic of miniature animals would be nice, or maybe indigo shingles could be used to make it resemble a creek. But then they had forded a rill on their way up from the village, so why not have somebody trace it to its source and divert it this way, have an actual stream flow through the yard? It couldn't be that hard to have it come down through the trees there and then run over the cliff beside the deck, creating a miniature waterfall that—

"Empty," said Portolés, coming back outside. Sir Hjortt had lost track of himself—it had been a steep march up, and a long ride before that. Portolés silently moved behind the older woman, who stood on the walk between Sir Hjortt and her house. The matron looked nervous now, all right.

"My husband Leib, Colonel Hjortt. Did you meet him at the crossroads?" Her voice was weaker now, barely louder than the quaking aspens. That must be something to hear as one lay in bed after a hard day's hunt, the rustling of those golden leaves just outside your window.

"New plan," said Sir Hjortt, not bothering with the more formal Azgarothian, since she spoke it anyway. "Well, it's the same as the original, mostly, but instead of riding down before dark we'll bivouac here for the night." Smiling at the old woman, he said, "Do not fret, Missus Mayor, do not fret, I won't be garrisoning my soldiers in your town, I assure you. Camp them outside the wall, when they're done. We'll ride out at first"—the thought of sleeping in on a proper bed occurred to him—"noon. We ride at noon tomorrow. Report back to me when it's done."

"Whatever you're planning, sir, let us parley before you commit yourself," said the old woman, seeming to awaken from the anxious spell their presence had cast upon her. She had a stern ~~l~~ ~~~~ ~~h~~ ~~~~~~'~ ~~~~ ~~ll~~ ~~~~~~~~ ~~h~~ ~~l~~~~~~ "Your officer can surely

keep his smug gaze on the old woman.

"Whether or not she is capable of doing so, Sister Portolés will *not* wait," said Sir Hjortt shortly. "You and I are talking, and directly, make no mistake, but I see no reason to delay my subordinate."

The old woman looked back past Portolés, frowning at the open door of her cabin, and then shrugged. As if she had any say at all in how this would transpire. Flashing a patently false smile at Sir Hjortt, she said, "As you will, fine sir. I merely thought you might have use for the sister as we spoke, for we may be talking for some time."

Fallen Mother have mercy, did every single person have a better idea of how Sir Hjortt should conduct himself than he did? This would not stand.

"My good woman," he said, "it seems that we have even more to parley than I previously suspected. Sister Portolés's business is pressing, however, and so she must away before we embark on this long conversation you so desire. Fear not, however, for the terms of supplication your husband laid out to us at the

445

crossroads shall be honored, reasonable as they undeniably are. Off with you, Portolés."

Portolés offered him one of her sardonic salutes from over the older woman's shoulder, and then stalked out of the yard, looking as petulant as he'd ever seen her. Iqbal whispered something to her as he moved out of her way by the gate, and wasn't fast enough in his retreat when she lashed out at him. The war nun flicked the malformed ear that emerged from Iqbal's pale tonsure like the outermost leaf of an overripe cabbage, rage rendering her face even less appealing, if such a thing was possible. Iqbal swung his heavy satchel at her in response, and although Portolés dodged the blow, the dark bottom of the sackcloth misted her with red droplets as it whizzed past her face. If the sister noticed the blood on her face, she didn't seem to care, dragging her feet down the precarious trail, her maul slung over one hunched shoulder.

"My husband," the matron whispered, and, turning back to her, Sir Hjortt saw that her wide eyes were fixed on Iqbal's dripping sack.

"Best if we talk inside," said Sir Hjortt, winking at Iqbal and ushering the woman toward her door. "Come, come, I have an absolutely brilliant idea about how you and your people might help with the war effort, and I'd rather discuss it over tea."

"You said the war was over," the woman said numbly, still staring at the satchel.

"So it is, so it is," said Sir Hjortt. "But the *effort* needs to be made to ensure it doesn't start up again, what? Now, what do you have to slake the thirst of servants of the Empire, home from the front?"

She balked, but there was nowhere to go, and so she led Sir Hjortt and Brother Iqbal inside. It was quiet in the yard, save for the trees and the clacking of the bone fetishes when the wind ran its palm down the mountain's stubbly cheek. The screaming didn't start until after Sister Portolés had returned to the village, and down there they were doing enough of their own to miss the echoes resonating from the mayor's house.

home in her familial castle at Hwabun she was one of three, and the middle one at that. And here, in the capital, with all the court gathered, there must be more princesses than there were stars in the sky, all crammed into a multiplicity of ballrooms. Even without being the sole princess in the palace, however, getting away had proven difficult, since Princess Ji-hyeon was here in part to formally meet her fiancé for the very first time. Prince Byeong-gu of Othean, fourth son of Empress Ryuki, Keeper of the Immaculate Isles, seemed every bit as stuck-up as his title had implied, and so Ji-hyeon set herself to escape at all costs, but she never would have managed it without the help of her three guards (especially her Spirit Guard, Brother Mikal, much as he had protested the plan initially). Now the fifteen-year-old woman traipsed through tangled vines under a moon as fat as the gourds at her feet, the hubbub inside the palace walls reduced to a drone much softer than the rasping of fuzzy leaves against silk skirts.

"Your Highness," Brother Mikal called from where he and Keun-ju, the princess's Virtue Guard, strolled along one of the straight paths that cut through the field. "I wonder if you might favor to walk with us here, between the rows rather than across them? Keun-ju is concerned for your gown."

"If Keun-ju would prefer to carry my dress for safeguarding, I have no objections to walking naked on such a pleasant eve," said Ji-hyeon, happy to hear the reserved boy splutter by way of response. He hardly minded such joking when they were alone in her chambers, but in front of Brother Mikal and Choi was another matter.

"In all seriousness, Princess, I wonder if he might have a point—" Mikal began, but Ji-hyeon cut him off.

"Wonder no longer, then, for I favor my own approach," she said, but the wit of her riposte was spoiled as she tripped over a pumpkin. She would have gone down if Choi hadn't been there to catch her arm; Ji-hyeon grinned at her Martial Guard, and Choi warmly flashed her shark teeth in response. Stitched up in her own slick black gown at the ceremony, Choi could have passed for human, a princess even, if not for her petite horns. She had also looked about as comfortable as a lobster sitting on the edge of a pot, and no more talkative. Ji-hyeon preferred her wildborn guard when the woman was relaxed enough to open her deceptively small, fang-filled mouth; apparently guests to her home at Hwabun sometimes assumed the woman was mute, so rarely was she at her ease.

"Do you think we'll find one?" Ji-hyeon asked eagerly.

"The moon's full and the equinox is near," said Choi in her gruff, quiet voice. "I'll be surprised if you don't, this near to a hungry mouth."

Ji-hyeon liked Choi's sharp teeth, and her ebony horns, and her sometimes frightening speed, and even her sword lessons, exhausting though they were, but most of all the princess liked the way Choi would use the wrong words for things. It was never an error in vocabulary, Ji-hyeon knew, but rather that the wildborn thought the Immaculate tongue was often mis-used even by native speakers—every cat was actually a trouble, every sword a tusk, every arrow a disgrace...and every Gate a hungry mouth. Looking at the tall pearl walls of the Temple of Pentacles shining ahead of them like a lighthouse across a vege-tal sea, Ji-hyeon shivered with delight. She liked being scared, a

swordplay as Choi, plus Keun-ju was better at dressmaking than either, which Ji-hyeon enjoyed just as much as fencing.

And once she was married to Prince Boring, she would have to leave them all behind and accept whatever new guards her husband provided for her. It made her heartsick, and she turned her mind from it, hard though it was to do when she had just met the man who would take her closest friends away from her. None of the others mentioned it, either, their numbered days the proverbial whale in the carp pond.

"Is there anything else we can do?" she asked. "Other than walk around, hoping we get lucky?"

"Luck is an excuse," said Choi. "If you kept a better vigil you would have already succeeded. I've seen three so far."

"Nuh-uh!" cried Ji-hyeon, imitating her younger sister's imitation of some yet younger cousin. "Choi! Why didn't you show me?"

Choi's eyes flashed like rubies even in the colorless pall of the moon, and she gestured to the plants at their feet. "Keep a better vigil."

"Mikal!" Ji-hyeon called a good deal louder than was necessary, knowing how much Choi despised an excess of volume... or an excess of anything, really. Other than vigilance. "Mikal, can you do something to make them appear?"

"Ji-hyeon, the brother's function is the very opposite of *that*, as you well know," said Keun-ju huffily. "Stop trying to get him in trouble."

"If my parents find out he bribed the palace guards to spirit me away from the festival, I think that will cause a lot more embarrassment than if he fulfills the dearest wish of a darling daughter," said Ji-hyeon. "Don't you think?"

"Princess, do you believe I am making sport with you when I profess my ignorance of the spirits of your land?" The path Mikal and Keun-ju followed was taking them away from Ji-hyeon and Choi, and so the pair began tramping over to their noble ward. "I would be reluctant to make any assumptions as to their character or, for that matter, their humor at being addressed by a foreigner. Why not return to the palace and ask one of your priestesses if—"

"If I wanted to talk to the nuns I would have stayed at the party," said Ji-hyeon, wishing every night could be this perfect, just she and her guards questing beneath a full moon. "I want to see a harvest devil."

"Then hush your mouth and be vigilant," said Choi.

"I am being vigilant, I just—oh!" Ji-hyeon froze, her heart plunging into ice water as if she had noticed a snake underfoot, her muddy silk shoe suspended in the air above a twisting coil of black vines. The round pumpkin at its center rolled backward in its nest, revealing the triangular eyes and jagged mouth of its face—a faint yellow glow emanated from within the gourd, pouring from maw and eyes to illuminate the gilt hem of Ji-hyeon's jet gown, shining off the silver buckle of her shoe and the abalone inlay of her dress sword's scabbard. Then, fast as she'd seen it, the saffron light faded, the eyes and mouth closed over, and it was just a pumpkin again.

Ji-hyeon squealed in delight, looked up to see if the others had seen... and then gasped, stumbled back, dumbstruck by what reared up in front of her, twenty feet tall, rasping, churn-